The Assassin's Tale

The Ottoman Cycle Book 3

Revised edition

by S.J.A. Turney

For Robin, Jane & Mia

I would like to thank everyone who has been instrumental in this book seeing the light of day in its final form, as well as all those people who have continually supported me during its creation: Robin, Alun, Barry, Nick, Miriam, Rosie, Prue and of course Jenny and Tracey and once again my little imps Marcus and Callie who interrupted me at the most opportune moments, driving me to wonderful distraction. Also, the fabulous members of the Historical Writers' Association, who are supportive and helpful as ever.

Cover image by J Caleb Designs.
Cover design by Dave Slaney.
Revised Ed. editing courtesy of Canelo.
Many thanks to all concerned.

Also by S. J. A. Turney:

The Marius' Mules Series

Marius' Mules I: The Invasion of Gaul (2009)
Marius' Mules II: The Belgae (2010)
Marius' Mules III: Gallia Invicta (2011)
Marius' Mules IV: Conspiracy of Eagles (2012)
Marius' Mules V: Hades' Gate (2013)
Marius' Mules VI: Caesar's Vow (2014)
Marius' Mules: Prelude to War (2014)
Marius' Mules VII: The Great Revolt (2014)
Marius' Mules VIII: Sons of Taranis (2015)
Marius' Mules IX: Pax Gallica (2016)
Marius' Mules X: Fields of Mars (2017)

The Praetorian Series

The Great Game (2015)
The Price of Treason (2015)
Eagles of Dacia (Autumn 2017)

The Ottoman Cycle

The Thief's Tale (2013)
The Priest's Tale (2013)
The Assassin's Tale (2014)
The Pasha's Tale (2015)

Tales of the Empire

Interregnum (2009)
Ironroot (2010)
Dark Empress (2011)
Insurgency (2016)
Invasion (2017)

Roman Adventures (Children's Roman fiction with Dave Slaney)

Crocodile Legion (2016)
Pirate Legion (Summer 2017)

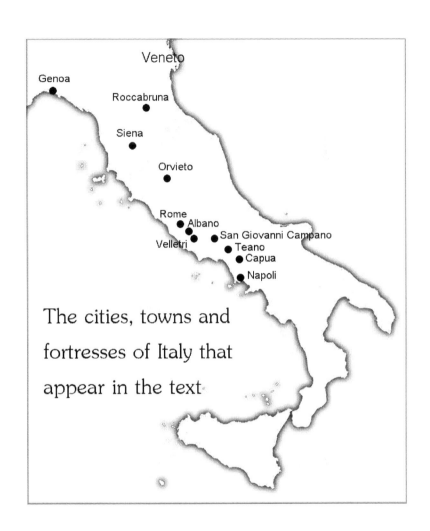

The cities, towns and fortresses of Italy that appear in the text

ROMA

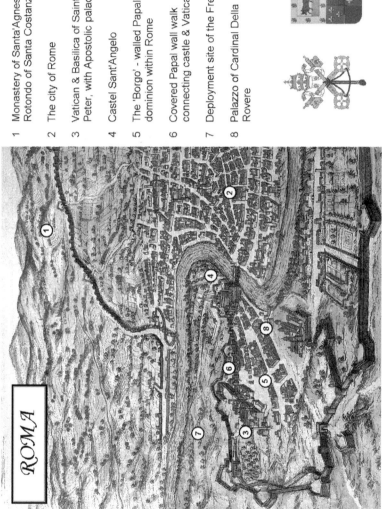

1 Monastery of Santa'Agnese & Rotondo of Santa Costanza

2 The city of Rome

3 Vatican & Basilica of Saint Peter, with Apostolic palace

4 Castel Sant'Angelo

5 The 'Borgo' - walled Papal dominion within Rome

6 Covered Papal wall walk connecting castle & Vatican

7 Deployment site of the French

8 Palazzo of Cardinal Della Rovere

*D*ragi leaned back against the top strake of the ship's side, listening to the water lap against the timbers as he threaded stray wisps of his hair into a braid. The silence of the moored vessel was broken only by the sounds of the night sea and the squeak of bats.

'My people have many tales,' he smiled.

'I know little of your people.'

'Have you heard the tale of the day of the cock? It is an old tale. Older than the empire of the Greeks. Older than the city of Constantine. But it is a tale that has yet to come to pass – whatever some gadjo say – and is one among several that mark you in some way. In fact, I have three tales for you this night, and each is significant.'

'I am not in the mood for stories, no matter how old or... significant.'

Dragi shuffled into a cross-legged position, his eyes glittering in the moonlight. He wagged a bony, narrow finger at his listeners. 'Our tales are not mere stories for amusement.'

'You have a captive audience, Dragi. Can you not sing instead? Your people are known for their lively music.'

'I sing at funerals,' Dragi replied in a flat tone. 'Tonight I tell tales, and you would be advised to heed them. Some tales are more than

1

entertainment, as I said. Some are warnings from God. Some are cautionary lessons. Some are prophecy.'

'Some are too long. Go on, then. Tell me of your cock.'

Ignoring the crude jest, Dragi took a swig from the flask that sat beside him on the deck, wetting his throat, and rolled his head, the bones of his neck issuing clicks as he did so.

'The Emperor took a dislike to our people,' Dragi said, chewing on his lip for a moment.

'What emperor?'

'As I said, this tale is older than Rome, but has yet to come to pass. Our ancestors thought it would be the Emperor of Byzantium, driven by his church to suppress our 'wicked' ways, but the Byzantine world is gone and I for one believe it is a Turkish emperor – a sultan.'

'Go on.'

'The Emperor took a dislike to our people, and decided that we should be no more. He sent an order to his soldiers to kill all the children of our people, so that there would be no more generations to disgust him.'

'This does not sound like Bayezid the Just.'

Dragi gave his audience a hard look. 'That day, the Emperor's army went out among the streets and found any door where our people had been foolish enough to settle, and they ripped open the doors, barging inside.'

'I suspect I have heard this tale told before, though about a little Jewish boy...'

'In each house, the soldiers searched thoroughly, and wherever they found a child, they put a sword through it. Thousands were murdered and with no warning, for the Emperor's soldiers were many and everywhere in the city all at once.'

'Why didn't he just kill them all? Why only the children? Evil he may be, but efficient he is not.'

'One woman, a woman called Sarah, saw the soldiers in the street, and she knew that she was next, for her son was a boy of three summers. She hurried to her house and pushed the frightened boy to the floor and told him to lie still and quiet. Then she went back into her kitchen, and she brought out a cock bird, squawking and kicking, and held it over the boy as she slaughtered it, the blood drenching the frightened child.'

'Smart woman.'

'*Yes. She returned the dead bird and the knife to the kitchen and, reminding the boy to be quiet and still, she threw her front door wide again and crouched by her son, clutching the blood-soaked shape and crying. The soldiers came along the street and looked inside, surprised that someone had got to this place ahead of them. But seeing the job done, they shrugged and moved on.*'

He took another pull from his flask.

'*And that is what my people have been doing ever since the story was first told: moving on. Some settle for a time, but the fear always returns, for the tale will one day be a true one, and so we move on, and we celebrate the day of the cock.*'

'*So your own Herod will one day kill your children. Not a joyful tale, Dragi.*'

'*No. But it informs everything at the heart of your future. And it is the first of my three tales because it is one of the reasons I must tell the other two.*'

His audience nodded their understanding and shuffled into more comfortable positions.

'*Go on, then.*'

'*Very well. Settle in for this one, for it is not brief. Let me tell you the tale of the vengeful priest...*'

PROLOGOS - A return

March, the year of our Lord fourteen hundred and ninety three.

The stranger stood in the rowing boat, his legs planted firmly apart to allow for better balance despite the rocking of the vessel in the swell. The man at the oars expertly guided the small craft up against the timbers of the jetty with a deep wooden 'clonk' and grabbed hold of one of the mooring rings. The rope remained coiled in the bottom of the boat. He would not be here that long, and the port officials in this bustling city were notoriously stringent. Roped or not, if the oarsman lingered overlong, his purse would lighten and the crown's vaults would tinkle that little bit more.

'You been here before?' he asked as the stranger picked up his kit bag and slung it over his shoulder, causing the boat to lurch and wobble further.

'No. Not here.'

'Be careful. It was a dangerous enough city under the Moors. Under that pair of mismatched lunatics everything's either a crime or a sin. Breathing's probably ungodly by now.'

The stranger smiled and something about the expression sent a shiver up the rower's spine. 'Rabid Catholics hold no fear for me.'

'Then you're an idiot.'

'I'll be fine. Enjoy your triumphant return, Alonso. I suspect you'll be heading west again in short order.'

As the stranger heaved his bag up to the jetty and vaulted nimbly up onto the slippery timbers, the oarsman shrugged. ''Tis a sailor's lot, mate. You go careful.'

The stranger straightened and stretched, shading his eyes with one hand to peer at the port before him. His dark grey doublet was worn and frayed, but clean and tidy for all its condition. His breeks and hose of matching grey showed signs of hard wear and his boots were almost beyond hope. Yet despite his dishevelled and impoverished appearance, there was about his manner something that warned of strength, resolve and a depth far beyond that which was visible. At his side, hanging from a sword belt of Spanish leather, he carried a long, curved Arab blade with an ivory hilt. His skin was a healthy, sea-beaten bronze and his hair, bleached by the sun, was naturally salt-curled and somewhere just short of shoulder length. His chin was covered with several weeks' growth, and a golden ring twinkled in his ear.

If anyone observing the stranger had a level of acuity they would notice other oddities about the man. The tip of colourful inked designs poked out of the neck of his doublet as though they climbed his arm and back, reaching for his face. And opposite the sword, at the far side of his belt, hung not the parrying blade or knife one might expect of a swordsman, but a wooden club an inch thick and almost three feet long from the ornately-carved handle to the polished, stone-hard tip.

'Malaga,' Skiouros said with a long exhale that seemed to contain half a world of anticipation, tension and resignation. Picking up the bag and slinging it over his shoulder once more, causing several heavy clunks within, he strode off down the jetty with the rolling gait of a man far more used to the buck and wallow of a ship.

This city had been staunchly Muslim only six years previously, and the architecture even from here was achingly familiar to Skiouros. He had seen so many variants in a few short years, from the delicate tracery and decorative brick of the Byzantine-influenced Ottoman cities, through to the Graeco-Turkish starkness of Crete, the ancient functionality of Tunisia and the brown, desert-tinted structures of the African Maghreb.

5

If he could weep, he might do so at the sight of the minarets standing proud of the mosques that were even now being demolished or just reassigned to 'good Christian purpose'.

One of the most important things the past year or two had taught him was that God lived in the heart and not in a building, no matter how elegant, and that God listened to the quality of a man's soul, not to the words he uttered by rote from a prayer of any set faith. Simply: God was greater than that. The Taino people had opened his eyes to the meaning of belief, and his confusion and conflicts had fallen into meaningful place.

His tread changed tone from the timbers of the jetty to the hard flags of the dock, and he realised he was standing on familiar land for the first time in over half a year. It had felt like a lifetime, of course, but in the real world of Europe it had only been seven months. Little would have changed here. Hopefully...

On the dock, teamsters and workmen sweated and cursed, heaving boxes, sacks and crates everywhere, piling goods together, shuffling carts and their snorting, stinking beasts out of the way, calling to their counterparts on the ships at berth. It was such a far cry from the almost-solitude of a ship journey into the unknown with a crew who spoke no language he could understand.

Of course, learning Spanish from a couple of the more helpful crewmates had been his first priority, though the fact that one of them had later turned out to be Portuguese and that he had been simultaneously learning two similar yet distinct tongues had been something of a setback.

Among the chaos of the port, he could see a small group of Catholic monks in their black cassocks, with tonsured heads boiled pink by the Iberian sun. Leading them through the bedlam was an old man with straggly white locks and a beard of which Moses would have been proud, holding aloft a gleaming silver cross. Their dirge-like chanting as they wound a snake-path between the goods was unpleasant to Skiouros, who had grown up with lively Greek music and more recently become attuned to the rough and often coarse sea-shanties of the Iberian sailors.

Remembering the ferryman's words and not wanting to get too close to them, Skiouros ducked around a pile of boxes, only to find himself face to face and only a few yards from a fat, sweating official in maroon and gold with a jaunty hat and an expression of fierce avarice, accompanied by two guards, both armed and alert. Torn between the twin discomforts of bureaucracy and religion, Skiouros

6

backtracked for a moment and then headed off towards the town in a dogleg.

A huge, sprawling brick fortress loomed on the mountain to the right, its rock and scree slopes dotted with cacti, juniper and pine trees. To the left the minarets and the new golden-stone towers of the Christian regime cast their shadow on the ancient roofs.

With a nod to the seething area in the middle, Skiouros aimed for there, where the streets were narrowest and the buildings poorest. That morass would be the best place for him… where the poor and disaffected lived and the lesser mercantile types traded. An area soldiers would ignore and the rich and bureaucratic would avoid; which the fanatical touch of Ferdinand and Isabella's new Spanish church would shun as a pit of filth and indolence. His kind of place.

In a matter of minutes he was away from the port and its bustle, noise and endless gulls in search of an easy meal, and in among the maze of streets that made up the ancient city. Here most of the houses were still the low, whitewashed buildings that had been built and lived in by many generations of Moors before their ejection from the country. Even here, in the underbelly of the place, the new Christian stamp was being slammed down on the city, white buildings half-demolished and grand stone residences with the new leaded windows and painted signs rising in their place.

Metalworkers, coopers, spice merchants and every other kind of shop lined the streets, interspersed with poor housing. There was a distinct lack of taverns, but then the place had only been Christian for six years, prior to which they had been absent by Shari'a law. He decided that he would settle for a good Muslim khave house, but it occurred to him that if the rabid Catholic conquerors had driven the Moors back across the sea, the chances of finding one of those was small, too. It was hard to know what to expect in a city in such flux. No taverns under the Moors and no coffee houses under the Christians and he in the middle, parched for a drink of some kind.

As he moved through the streets in the shade, the sun's blinding rays unable to penetrate these narrow alleys and streets, it struck him as an odd symmetry: perhaps the world turned in the most curious of ways? In his homeland in the east, the followers of Mohammed had driven north and conquered the mighty Christian strongholds, securing their grip on that world. Here in the west, the Christians with equal fervour had swept down from the north, driving the Muslims from the land and securing that region. Would they both keep going? Would the rulers of Spain soon be driving the Muslim world back across Africa towards Persia while the great Sultan Bayezid marched across the Carpathians and the Alps with his kapikulu, forcing the Christians back into France?

Who would be a priest or a theologist in these complex days?

His eyes played around the narrow street he found himself in and he spotted an old man with grey bristles and rheumy eyes supping from a jug that contained something he seemed to be enjoying. Skiouros' heart fluttered in anticipation.

'Ho fellow,' he smiled in an easy manner, his Spanish accent probably distressingly cacophonic for the man, given his half-Portuguese teaching by sailors with all their colloquialisms and peculiarities. The old man looked up from his drink without slowing his pace of consumption. One of his eyes remained pointing into the jug while the other settled on Skiouros.

'Whatcher want?'

'You seem to have found a tavern? Or at least a wine shop? I wondered if you could direct me?'

The old man shrugged. 'Tavern's round the corner to the right. Can't miss it. Sign outside for the neckings.'

Skiouros frowned at the unfamiliar phrase but the old man had already forgotten about him and moved on. With a sigh, he turned and was about to follow the directions when a figure stepped out from a tiny stairway that ran up between buildings. His intentions were immediately apparent, given the glinting, pitted sword-breaker in his dirty, shaking hand. Barely had Skiouros registered him before his eyes picked out the second man stepping slowly from a side alley on the far side of the road. The two men stalked forward to converge at the centre of the street.

'Evening, my pretty young sailor boy,' grinned the first man, a single metal tooth glinting among the blackened stumps of the others. He swished his short blade back and forth in preparation. His companion across the street drew a heavy dagger with a serrated blade.

'What's in the bag, friend?' added the second man with a leer.

'Trouble, woe and a few interesting leaves I picked up.'

The two men frowned in surprise at the reaction, but quickly recovered into evil grins. 'If'n you feel like breathing another day and walking with both legs, you might want to toss that bag over here and piss off?'

Skiouros sighed. Confrontation already? He'd barely set foot on the continent and already someone was seeking blood. They'd picked the wrong target today, though. The Skiouros of three years ago would have fled and hidden already, his mind fixed on safety and an easy penny. The Skiouros of a year ago was more than competent with a sword, but uncertain and floundering a little – not quite sure of whom he was. The Skiouros who stood in this Spanish backstreet was the man who had grown from those youths. Self-assured, skilled, and with a sense of purpose most men would never achieve in a lifetime.

'I'll give you but two warnings. Here's your first. I am not the easy prey you think, and what's in my kit bag is not worth the cost to you. Go find some other poor soul to rob before I decide to take a real dislike to you.'

The anger flared in the first man, his blackened and metal teeth clenched as his brow beetled and his free hand twitched. The second man, Skiouros noted, looked momentarily rather unsure, but then a calmness settled on him. That man knew something to his advantage, and with an ear cocked, Skiouros was reasonably confident he knew what it was.

The first man sneered and stepped forward. 'I don't care whether you can handle that darkie sickle at your side or not, you don't want to mess with us, laddie. Give us the bag and I might not cut off your balls and feed you them.'

Again, Skiouros sighed, though this time more for dramatic effect than genuine despair. With a deft flick of his hand, he gripped the carved hilt of the hardwood club at his side, ripping it from the leather loop in which it hung and spinning it once before jabbing backwards with it over his shoulder.

There was a cry of pained alarm behind him where the third man – who had been sneaking up – suddenly forgot all about the knife in his hand and reached up to his eye, which had taken the full force of the blow. The other two in front faltered for a moment as Skiouros swung the club once more, still facing forward with his eyes on them, and cracked the wooden tip with some force into the man's knee. As the unseen assailant yelped and wobbled, Skiouros hooked his foot behind him, around the man's ankle, and jabbed with his elbow, sending his would-be mugger to the ground with a thump.

'There's your second warning. Go home.'

With a snarl, old Black Teeth ran at him, brandishing the knife angrily. Skiouros watched him come and at the last moment stepped lithely aside, watching his attacker stumble over the fallen form of his comrade, the pair ending up in a heap on the ground. With an arched eyebrow, Skiouros beckoned to the man with the serrated knife, who suddenly found new value in his skin and backed away into the alley from whence he had come before turning and pounding away across the cobbles.

Skiouros looked down at the pair, who were struggling. Black Teeth was trying to rise, the knife still in his hand, but the other man was motionless. His chest heaved, so he was still breathing, but the small pool of red beneath his head, gathering around and between the cobbles, revealed that his skull had struck the ground hard when he fell.

With a single breath, Skiouros flicked out his club, rapping the end sharply on the metal-toothed man's wrist. There was a crack of bone and the sword-breaker fell from his agonised grasp. As the mugger gasped for air, Skiouros delivered a second, similar tap to the man's head, driving his wits from him and sending him into the deep black of unconsciousness.

'Idiots,' Skiouros hissed. 'If the Taino had been as stupid as you two I'd have been a king by now.'

He smiled lightly and, leaving the pair unresponsive on the cobbles, tried to recall the old man's instructions. A moment later he was turning the corner, his eyes wandering around until they fell upon a sign.

Neckings!

The building had probably been a Muslim khave house – it had all the hallmarks of one – but now it had become a tavern. The sign above the door did little to warm Skiouros and endear him to the city. On a well-painted board, a ringletted Jew swung by the neck from a Three-Legged Mare, the rope taut and a crowd of black-robed men watching in approval.

'Nice. Friendly.'

With more than an ounce of trepidation, Skiouros took a step inside. The place was dingy and smelled of the cured and salted meats that hung from the ceiling near the bar. Perhaps half a dozen men sat at tables, though none of them even looked up at him and despite his worries Skiouros relaxed, grateful for now for a place with few patrons and fewer questions.

In his best Portu-Spanish, Skiouros ordered a mug of beer and carried it across to the most secluded table he could find, in a dark rear corner next to an unlit fireplace. Sinking into the seat with gratitude, he thought on what had just happened. Perhaps it had been the Arab blade that had drawn the idiots? They couldn't have had a clue what was in his bag. Most sailors' kits would hardly be worth the effort of a mugging. He resolved to pack the blade away in his bag and attract fewer eyes from this point. His macana club would do nicely anyway, giving him the considered choice of lethal or non-lethal blows. He was grateful for the many happy hours he had spent at sea, learning its use from one of the natives they had brought back.

He wondered for a moment what would become of Caracoa and the other Taino who had crossed the sea with them. Colombo had taken them to display to the Spanish rulers and their court as a curiosity of his 'New World'. No good end awaited them there, Skiouros felt certain, and he offered up a private prayer to the universal God for their safety, his fingertips brushing the cold stone zemi figure of Maquetaurie Guayaba which hung on a thong around his neck beneath his doublet.

But it didn't do for Skiouros to brood on such sentimental matters. Sentiment had no place in Skiouros' life now, for the time of his revenge was at hand and he felt, for the first time since Lykaion's death in that church in Istanbul, ready to face it and control it. He was the very spirit of vengeance, coming to claim the soul of the pretender sultan, Cem.

With a quick glance to make sure no one was observing and manoeuvring his chair so that his body hid his actions from the room's occupants, he unlaced the top of his bag and brought out three items, laying them on the table before him. Yes... if the Taino had been as stupid as that pair in the street, he might have been a king, but thanks to their innocence and generosity, he might yet be nearly as rich as one. And what he had to do next would require money.

He smiled for a long moment at the three heavy, intricate gold idols he had brought back from that warm, green, sweat-ridden island. They would afford him all he needed to bring the usurper to a just end and allow the soul of Lykaion to rest in peace.

'I'm coming for you, Cem, son of Mehmet.'

11

CHAPTER ONE - Malaga, March 1493

'I presume it is hopelessly optimistic to wonder whether there would be a Jewish moneylender anywhere in the city?' Skiouros enquired of the bartender.

The man shook his head with a none-too-pleasant smile. 'Only Jews in this city have decided to kiss the cross and trim their hair. An' there's fewer of them by the month. The Dominicans keep uncovering their secret *ikey* temples and hangin' the Christ-killin' bastards. None of 'em's really converted, y'know.'

Skiouros restrained his arm which seemed to have taken on a life of its own and was already rising to grasp the ignorant pizzle by the throat. With some effort he forced his arm back down and smiled as though the barkeep spoke his own mind.

'So without them, and assuming I don't want to bother the good Dominicans with this, to whom would I turn in Malaga if I had a few saleable items and a need for ready cash?'

The barkeep scratched his head. Flakes of skin drifted down to the wooden counter and Skiouros leaned back out of the flurry.

'You could try Black Bob.'

'Black Bob?' Somehow, Skiouros already had the feeling that he wasn't going to like what he was about to hear.

'Aye, Black Bob. He's a Morisco, an' about the closest thing you'll find here to one o' your *ikey* moneymen.'

'Morisco?'

'A converted Moor who works from a shop out by the Granada Gate. Probably about as Christian as any o' them Jews they keep rootin' out, but he goes to church and does what he's told, an' the authorities have give him license to trade and bank in the city. But watch out. He's not one to trust or cross.'

'I am starting to get the feeling that such is a common trait in this city,' Skiouros sighed and straightened, dropping a coin on the bar and leaving the building before the barkeep's slow brain informed him that he'd probably just been insulted.

Outside, Skiouros stretched. He would have to get out of Malaga… Clearly the place ate away at a man's soul without him noticing. A few months here and he'd probably be kissing crosses and hanging Jews and Muslims with the rest of them. He could just book passage to Italy now, of course, but years of stumbling from one disaster into another had impressed upon the once-naïve young Greek the value of patience. What was coming had to be approached with care and restraint. Besides, for all his urge to leave this dangerous place, he had no desire to board a ship any time soon, given his record with sea travel thus far.

An urchin was watching him with interest from a doorway on the other side of the street as he emerged into the light, and Skiouros fished in his purse for a small, cheap coin, flashing it at the boy.

'Granada Gate?'

The boy sprang to his feet. With impressive energy, he gestured to the wall next to him, a rough, featureless brown stone one, and picked up a piece of broken pottery from the gutter. Quickly, he began to draw lines on the wall.

'We're here, see?'

Nod.

'This big thing is the Alcazaba – the big castle on the hill. Follow this route,' he tapped along three of his marked lines, 'til you find yourself facing a big curve. That's the old theatre beneath the castle. Turn left there and follow the main street past the foot of the hill and the gate you'll see at the end is the Puerta de Granada.'

'So this grand cartographic show was a long-winded way to say left, left, right and left, then?'

'Man pays for directions when they're so easy might want more for his money, else he might think to keep the coin,' grinned the boy and Skiouros couldn't help but smile. There was a distinct reflection of his own youthful self in there.

'Good lad. You'll go far, I'm sure.' With a chuckle, he tossed the coin to the boy, who caught it, bit it and scurried off, laughing. With a last glance at the wall – the map might prove valuable, after all – he followed the directions until he found himself at the base of the hill with the towering fortress above. What could have once been an ancient theatre occupied the lowest slopes, though it was more like a muddy upturned bowl full of cacti than anything grand. Sparing it only the interested glance of the first-time visitor, he walked on down the wide avenue towards the distant Puerta de Granada.

The tall towers of the gate stood proud of the heavy defensive walls and though the main thoroughfare marched straight to it, a number of side streets led off in the area into a veritable maze of smaller alleys. An initial scan of his surroundings gave no indication of the Morisco's place of business on the main street and, given the attitudes he had encountered so far in the city, he thought it impolitic to start asking around. Instead, he peered down a couple of the side streets until at the last one before the gate he noted where it widened out into a long, narrow plaza. One building in particular drew his attention, not for the architecture or any official sign, but for the fact that a couple of thugs sat on chairs beside the door, and both of them had the swarthy skin tone of the Moor, for all their western doublets. Neither was armed, but Skiouros was willing to bet they would be more than capable of dealing with most troublemakers. Just the sort of men a moneylender might have protecting his place of business.

With a deep breath and his most disarming smile, he strode purposefully across to them. Neither man moved, but they both watched his approach with suspicion.

'I've come to see the man in charge.'

The pair were silent and Skiouros frowned at their implacability. With a sly grin, he switched to Arabic: 'I've come to see the one the morons in town call Black Bob.' The comment had the desired effect. Surprised at the young man's easy and colloquial command of Arabic, they paused for a moment as broad white grins spread across their faces.

'In the back, young master. God be with you.'

'*As-salamu alaykum*,' Skiouros replied quietly with a smile. The grins swept from the two thugs' faces and they hustled him through the door.

'Get inside, idiot,' one of them grunted in Arabic.

Skiouros' eyes slowly adjusted to the dim interior and he spotted the man who could only be Black Bob seated behind the counter with a mug of frothing ale, jotting something in a ledger. The big, dark face looked up at him as he entered, appraised him in one glance, and then nodded to a chair opposite. Skiouros opened his mouth to speak, but the Morisco silenced him with a 'Tsch!' noise and finished working his figures. Skiouros took the offered seat and waited, dropping his kit bag by his side with a clank that drew the man's eyes momentarily.

When Black Bob finally looked up, Skiouros smiled. 'Your doorman seemed in a rush to invite me in when I wished peace upon him in the traditional manner.'

'And well they might. That kind of talk buys a man the dangling jig around here.' The Morisco looked him up and down again. 'What is a man like you doing talking my tongue?'

'I'm no Spaniard,' Skiouros smiled. 'I was brought up in the Ottoman Empire.'

'You don't look like a Turk.'

'And you don't look like a Christian, so let's agree that appearances can be deceptive and get down to business. They tell me that you are the man to look to around here for money.'

The Morisco leaned back and smiled. 'I *have* had a run of good fortune. My countrymen – and the children of Abraham – were urged to leave this place in a hurry. Many were forced to sell their lands and goods at a regrettably pitiful price. A steal, really. And as long as I continue to prove myself a good Christian and a friend of all Spaniards, the new citizens of the province seek to purchase those self-same lands and goods at a healthily inflated price. A few years ago I sold pots and pans. Now, for the price of a little lip service, I am a wealthy and influential man, and that means that I am in a position to dole out money to those who please me. Will you please me, do you think?'

Skiouros smiled. 'I am not selling favours or promises or land or titles. I am selling hard goods: treasure of the highest quality, for cash.'

Briefly, he rummaged in his bag and retrieved the three gold idols which he lay carefully down on the table between them. 'These are worth a great deal. They are – and I can vouch for this as I watched one being made – formed from solid gold. And gold of a deeper glow than the impure debased rubbish floating around here. Even as bullion they are worth a great deal. To a collector of curiosities, however: far more.'

'May I?' As Skiouros nodded, the Morisco picked one up, weighing it and then turning it over and over, examining it closely. He nodded appreciatively. 'They're certainly the correct weight. And yes, some folk would pay a pretty penny for them, but pagan art is not exactly at a premium in Spain these days. Where are they from? Somewhere in Africa?'

'If I told you, you wouldn't believe me. Suffice it to say they are the only examples to be found in Europe. Or Africa or the east for that matter. They are – in effect – unique.'

'In Spain they are basically pretty bullion,' the Morisco shrugged. 'Man could find himself on the wrong end of the nice men in black robes for toting such graven images around.' He sat back and blew a faint whistle through his teeth. 'I'll give you three hundred florins for the lot.'

Skiouros frowned as he performed a quick mental calculation. 'Each of these contains enough gold to make that, and purer than that crap in the coins. So even at a bullion level you're offering me considerably less than a third of their value. As artworks they are worth a great deal more.'

'Not around here. And I have to have them melted down into bars before I can do anything with them that might draw church attention. It's my offer. I'm hardly desperate for the things, so take it or leave it.'

'*Four* hundred?' prompted Skiouros, trying to put on his hard-bargaining face.

The Morisco leaned back further in his chair and drummed his fingers on his chest. 'No. I will give you three thirty and no more. And that extra is only because I haven't heard my native tongue in far too long and against all my better judgement I like you. I have other matters to attend to, so decide now.'

Skiouros narrowed his eyes, peering at the Morisco and then at the idols. It was clear from the man's expression and posture that he would not shift his offer any further upwards. The young Greek nodded. 'Three thirty it is, then. And enjoy your *very* healthy profit.'

'Oh I will, young man. I will. How do you want the money?'

'I am presuming that carrying it in bags through the streets might be a touch risky?'

The man simply shrugged.

'But I presume there's a Medici banking house in the city? Big port like this.'

'There is. A draft for the Medici is it, then?'

Skiouros nodded and stood quietly as the man filled out a monetary draft and signed and sealed it. Handing it over, the Morisco waited as the young man ran his gaze carefully over the details. 'All seems to be in order.'

'Come back any time,' the Morisco grinned as Skiouros collected his bag and turned, making his way out of the building.

'Not bloody likely,' the young man whispered under his breath in Greek. As he stepped into the street and nodded to the two 'converted Moor' heavies outside, it occurred to him that he'd not asked the location of the Medici house, and what to do next was therefore a matter of some haziness. Of course, he was far from pushed for time. Things needed to unfold at the natural pace and if he forced events forward, he might end up the prey of a heartless slaver once more, or launched into a voyage into the unknown with no turning back. Patience. It was all about patience and planning, as he continually reminded himself. After all, as he'd had his tattoos applied, Inamoca of the Taino had been adamant that three full cycles would occur before Skiouros' fate came to pass, and with some calculation, that placed it some time in fourteen ninety-five, still well over a year away.

His hand went involuntarily to the colourful image of Bayamanaco on his upper arm, hidden beneath a good grey doublet. Inamoca had warned him that the restlessness in the face of 'Old Man Fire' reflected his own feelings on his end-goal, and Skiouros had been trying hard not to think on that for months now, particularly when his arm seemed to burn for no reason.

Taking a cleansing breath of the warm, dry Spanish air, he tucked the valuable monetary draft into the hidden pouch on the second neck thong beneath his doublet and walked out of the side-street and into the main thoroughfare once more.

Today he would spend the rest of the afternoon and evening getting used to this place, since it would clearly take some getting used to. Although he knew he'd have to move on from Malaga soon enough, he couldn't do so dressed and equipped like an impoverished sailor. He would need new clothes. And possibly to sell the curved Arab blade. Or probably just discard it, since no Spaniard would likely buy such a weapon in this atmosphere of religious intolerance.

A horse, too. He would need a horse, and a good one. And before all that he would need to cash the draft in the Medici house and draw some coin, and then there was the need to catch up on all the news and gossip since he'd left the old world. Was the usurper Cem still in Rome, even? He sucked on dry lips. Despite that mug of frothy beer before he visited the Morisco, he was still hungry and thirsty, and for all his planning and the need to change his appearance, the sign of a tavern in one of the other side streets close to the Puerta de Granada caught his eye. It showed a pair of crossed swords – one straight, one curved. Pausing, wondering whether this place might be a better class of tavern than the dreadful 'hanged Jew' one in the old centre, Skiouros decided to risk it and strode across the threshold and into the interior, patting the hidden pouch and its contents for peace of mind as he did so.

His heart lurched as his eyes adjusted to the light and he realised that the tavern had a good level of custom already, even at this time of the day, and more importantly that each and every occupant wore the uniform of the guard he had seen wandering back and forth on the wall's parapet and standing by the Puerta de Granada. But then what had he expected of a tavern marked with swords so close to the city gate? Soldiers came off-duty at all times, and it was in their nature to make a bar their first port of call.

Conditioning was a curious thing. For years he had lived as a thief, relying on his wits for survival and keeping out of sight of the authorities, for they had been his enemy and would be his downfall. For almost three years now he had eschewed his thieving ways on a promise to his brother, yet even now, with no reason to fear legal reprisal, he still baulked at the presence of guards.

Foolish, really.

They turned to regard him as he entered, and he picked up a few curious glances, but nothing more than one would expect as a civilian stranger entering a soldier's bar. Once they took in the fact that he was clearly a recently arrived sailor and his only weapon in evidence was a wooden stick, they nodded a polite greeting to him and then went back to their conversations. Skiouros began to relax. He was quite clearly no Jew or Moor, and had no reason to feel uneasy here. Wandering over to the bar, he ordered a glass of the same cheap local wine that the soldiers appeared to be drinking and a plate of lamb and bacon (a confirmation of his Gentile nature, just in case) in a cider broth with bread.

Despite the busyness of the tavern, there were still a few tables free, and Skiouros took a seat at one near the bar with his back to the wall. Dropping his bag next to him, out of sight and secure, he took a swig of his wine.

Moments passed as the sharp-yet-sweet tang of the wine flowered on his tongue, and imperceptibly the activity in the bar seemed to fade into a dull, almost-muted background. He could hear the 'thump,

thump' of the blood rushing in his ears and felt the hairs stand up on the back of his neck.

He looked up, half expecting to see that familiar disapproving face, and felt a strange mixed rush of relief and disappointment as his eyes fell upon the empty chair opposite. No matter what his senses told him, he knew it wasn't *really* empty.

'Lykaion?' he whispered in disbelief.

The group of four soldiers standing at the end of the bar nearby turned to look at him in surprise, and Skiouros quickly delved in the visible purse at his belt and pulled out a folded piece of vellum – the names of a few people he could rely upon in Barcelona, Sevilla, Cadiz and Lisboa apparently. Flattening it on the table before him, he made as if to study it, running his finger up and down the list and tapping it repeatedly as if memorising. Best not to look like a lunatic if he could avoid it in a bar full of soldiers.

With the list as his focus he muttered again and the soldiers turned back to their conversation, ignoring him.

'Lykaion?' he breathed again. He had last spoken with the shade of his brother in a sickened fever deep in the unforgiving brown lands of North Africa. Not in all the months of sea voyage or that strange, lush, green land beyond had he felt the familiar eerie presence of the departed son of Nikos. He had begun to think that Lykaion's spirit finally rested, but then he would have no need to pursue his vengeance, and he could feel in the pit of his stomach that that was not the case – that his journey was far from over. Perhaps he had simply been too far away?

He could still sense his brother's presence somehow, though there was no sound from that lost soul. Shivering, Skiouros blinked in surprise. The world came back into aural focus suddenly and Lykaion's shade dissipated like mist as his brain replayed the word that had shattered the spell.

'Sorry,' he turned to the soldiers at the bar. 'Did you say *Teba?*'

The four guardsmen halted their discussion and turned as one to look at the foreigner at the table. 'What?' one of them asked.

'Apologies,' Skiouros held up a hand. 'I was not deliberately eavesdropping, but I thought I heard you mention Teba?'

He tried not to smile as the image of his former sword-teacher on Crete flitted into his mind, all elegant dress and graceful moves and haughty nobility, yet covered in white dust as he put a Greek youth through his paces.

'You know Teba?' one of the soldiers enquired – a man with a neat beard and a face that spoke of a veteran's wisdom.

'Actually no, but I used to know someone from there and I had often wondered where the place was.'

The guardsman shrugged. 'It's up in the mountains north of Malaga. Past the cracked rocks and the old bandit road. Shit-hole of a place, really. A small town and a run-down castle lying empty. Place is a hive of scum nowadays... bandits and murderers. We get sent up there every now and then to put things in order, but it's like trying to dam a stream with a fork.'

Skiouros nodded as he remembered Don Diego de Teba and his unwillingness to talk about his home and why he was so far from it and working for a living as a martial instructor.

'An empty castle? What happened to the lord?'

Another of the men, also a veteran and with bear-like shoulders, took a swig of his wine and scratched his chin. 'The Don's family have been gone more than a decade. They ruled there ever since we took it from the Moors, but they say there was more than a streak of Arab blood in the Don's family. This isn't a good time to be displaying such traits, so the family moved away, out of the reach of the damn priests.'

Skiouros nodded again. He could quite imagine how Crete would look good when faced with the 'new Spain' of Ferdinand and Isabella, especially for a man with Moorish ancestry. Someday soon, when this was all over, Skiouros would return to Crete to retrieve Lykaion's head. And when he did, he would seek out Don Diego, the exiled lord of Teba.

'And you, lad? You're new in Malaga, else you'd be in one of the sailor's bars near the port, and not out here with us. And you've a weird accent. Portuguese, yes?'

Skiouros tried a pleasant smile. 'Actually, I'm originally Greek.' No good would come of mentioning the Turk here, so he glossed over the events between his days on the farm and his time on the *Pinta*. 'Just returned from a half-year voyage and still to get used to a floor that doesn't move.'

One of the soldiers laughed. 'Couldn't do it myself. I hate boats more than I hate my wife!' The others laughed aloud.

'In truth, no one hates boats more than me,' grinned Skiouros. 'Never had a good journey in one yet.'

'So you're not hurrying back out to sea then?'

'No,' Skiouros took a sip of wine. 'Actually, I'm headed for Italy next, but I plan to go by land.'

'Good idea,' muttered Bear-Shoulders. 'That Turk pirate Kemal is at large between here and Italy, sinking and enslaving every Spaniard he can find.'

'You off to sign up with the new Pope?' sniggered the first veteran, and the other three chuckled.

'*New* Pope?' Skiouros asked in surprise.

'Of course,' the soldier said, slapping his hand on the bar. 'You've been away half a year, so you won't know. Old Innocent, the lunatic, passed on last year. They say he bled himself to death trying to cure whatever ailed him, the prick. Now they've put a Spaniard on the throne of Saint Peter. Well, a *Catalan*, anyway!' The four men laughed aloud and Skiouros waited politely for them to finish.

'He was archbishop of Valencia,' the man resumed, 'and they say he doesn't trust the old Pope's men, so he's got himself a Catalan guard. Men from the north are flocking to sign up with him, 'cause he pays better than the crown.' The older veteran's face took on a serious expression and his voice lowered. 'Not content with a united Spain, and still having a claim on the Kingdom of Napoli, now their majesties have got a son of Spain in the Vatican.'

'And that worries you?' Skiouros frowned.

'Only because the more power their majesties accrue, the more the French turn to look at us, and they've been itching for another good war since they kicked the Englishers' arses at Castillon. Forty years is a long time for a Frenchman to go without a battle.'

Skiouros could find nothing to say on that matter, having yet to meet a Frenchman, and simply smiled. After a moment the soldiers seemed to decide the conversation was over, nodded to Skiouros, and with a bawdy comment they returned to their own conversation and laughter. Skiouros waited for a long moment and then studied his list again.

'No, brother,' he whispered under his breath. 'No good will come of another voyage.'

There was a pause as he listened to the faint words in his head before he answered. 'Because I have no desire to meet Turkish pirates again, even if Etci Hassan is no more.'

'No, it is *not* because I am frightened of boats,' he hissed – a little too loudly, since the soldiers glanced at him again. In response to what appeared to be an increasing mania in this young foreigner, the four men moved away down the bar.

'I will buy a horse and go by land.' He leaned back and narrowed his eyes at the perceived reply from the shade of Lykaion. 'Whether the French are belligerent or not, they have nothing against the Greeks as far as I know. Spain should be safe, so long as I don't spout Arabic, and France should be easy enough.'

The dispute seemed to be settled, and Skiouros looked at the empty chair – truly empty once more – and heaved out a sigh. Lykaion was ever argumentative. In the absence of his brother, his mind turned to his other erstwhile companions. He dredged his memories of those endless days and nights in the African hills, seeking out a single conversation he'd had with his Italian friend. It had been as they left that land and were moving on to Spain, he recalled, that they'd spoken of the future. Orsini would return to Genoa, to the palace of his relatives. The Visconti. The Palazzo Visconti. If he was not still there, then the occupants might at least know of his friend's current location. And almost certainly, if he found Orsini, he would find Parmenio and Nicolo, too.

Genoa, then. First a good night's sleep, then the Medici house, re-equipping and purchasing a good steed, and then with care and ease, a couple of months' journey round the coasts of Spain and France and to Genoa, seeking out more information as he travelled.

By the time the barkeep arrived with his meal, Skiouros had decided on his plan of action and was already picturing the faces of his friends.

CHAPTER TWO - Genoa, Summer 1493

The one thing that was clear about the great metropolis of Genoa was that it was a city and a state that revolved entirely around its naval empire. It was not so much a city with a large port at its heart, but more a huge port with a city crammed around its edge and spreading up the hillsides beyond. The numerous harbours and docks and jetties that filled it played host to more docked ships than Skiouros could ever imagine seeing in the same place and time. So many different shapes and sizes, each with different colourings and flags, and surprisingly little of the water's surface to be seen between them.

The road from the northwest led down through sloping land dotted with farms and to a gate in the heavy, impressive walls, marked by two tall, elegant towers and the stream of carts and pedestrians passing beneath in both directions.

Despite his original plans, Skiouros found himself thinking more about the port than about the Palazzo Visconti, given its clear size and importance, and settled on the thriving naval hub as his first port of call. The horse he rode huffed in the warm morning air and shook her head.

Sigma, he had named her, and she had become less of a possession and more of a companion throughout the protracted journey from Malaga.

'I know, girl. It's been a long haul. But soon we'll rest. If Cesare is at the palace, he'll see us to good accommodation and fodder. If not, I'll find us the best inn in the city. Come on.'

Urging Sigma forward again, he walked her down the slope and soon joined the queue for the gate. A continual stream of vehicles, horses and pedestrians issued from the city and most of those carts were empty. The majority of the vehicles rolling down the gentle road to the twin towers were heavily laden with goods, mostly fruit or veg or livestock. Perhaps today was a market day and the local farmers were flocking to sell their produce? Slowly the line edged forward and Skiouros examined the powerful walls as he closed on them. Clearly Genoa felt exposed; the city demonstrated her need to protect herself. Such walls could vie with the great cities of the east and south for their strength. Genoa could withstand a siege for some time, he decided.

And then he was beneath the shadow of the gate, watching as the local farmer in front allowed the gate's guards to poke through the bags and bundles in his hand cart. With a nod they waved him into the city and then peered up at the man on the horse. Skiouros had shaved and trimmed back his facial hair before leaving Spain, adopting the current fashion of a neatly-tended goat-like beard. His travelling clothes were of plain, yet good quality and hardwearing browns and greys, and his horse was bedecked in good leather harness, saddle and bags, but nothing ostentatious.

'What's your business in Genoa?' the guard asked, holding up a hand and grasping Sigma's bridle.

'I have business at the port and at the Palazzo Visconti,' Skiouros said calmly. No point in dissembling now. The truth would do no harm, and might buy him quick passage.

'From where do you hail?'

This was, to Skiouros, such a complex question these days that he found it difficult to decide on an answer, but found himself saying 'From Spain,' before his brain had bothered to get ahead of his mouth.

The two guards looked at one another and shrugged. The first turned back to him. 'Two denari tax for foreign entrants, payable upon arrival.' He let go of Sigma's reins and held out his hand, palm up. Skiouros could see the falsity of the tax and the guard's apparent corruption in his expression, but such a small sum was simply not worth arguing over. Fishing in his purse and making sure to keep it positioned so that the man could not see the glint of gold from within, he produced two of the small coins he had been acquiring in change since he had crossed from France a few days ago. The guard looked down at the money produced with such a lack of argument, clearly wondering whether he could have got away with charging more, but nodded and stood back with his friend, allowing Skiouros to ride past and into the city.

'Perhaps you could tell me where to go to enquire about vessels in the port?' he asked as he walked Sigma slowly past. The second guard threw his arm out and pointed down one of the streets leading off towards the port.

'Go down there and when you get to the dock area, look for a long arcaded building with three stories between two sets of warehouses. That's the port authorities. They'll be able to tell you whatever you need to know. If you get lost, ask anyone down there. It's hard to miss.'

Skiouros nodded his thanks and crossed the busy area inside the gate, making for the road the guard had indicated. The street led between tall buildings housing shops and taverns and professional residences and more than one bawdy house, and he felt quite 'city-blind' by the time he reached the end of the road and it opened out into the wide space of the port, with its endless ranks of warehouses, official buildings and yet more and more taverns and brothels.

If he had thought the port of Malaga busy and chaotic, it seemed provincial beside this. The port of Genoa was like a seething anthill full of sailors, officials, dockers, teamsters, traders, guards, whores, drunkards, vagrants and the occasional religious zealot haranguing the passers-by from the top of a barrel.

Trying to ignore the chaos of it all, Skiouros made his way around the dock until he spotted his destination. Two sets of large, featureless, functional-looking buildings flanked an older, more palatial structure with delicate arcading and leaded windows. Smoke poured from four chimneys at its roof, and the port guards by the door had long since given up challenging the endless stream of officials and workers and merchants that poured through the entrance in both directions.

Skiouros rode closer and, spotting the tethering rail, slid from the saddle and walked Sigma over to the long hitching post, where he carefully affixed her reins. The attendant, wearing the same colours as the guards – denoting his official capacity – but devoid of weapons or armour, took two small coins from him in payment and gave him a chit marking how many bags the horse held. Their contents were not checked, and Skiouros had little choice but to trust him.

Inside, the place was no less busy and chaotic than the main harbour. Visitors and workers thronged every hall and corridor, shouting to each other, creating a din that made it extremely hard to think. Skiouros tried to shut out the noise and focused on using his eyes. Signs pointed down each corridor and marked each individual office, and Skiouros ignored the ones that were clearly dedicated to specific nationalities. Scouring the ground floor he found a number of potential rooms, marked by signs, but once he crested the stairs, his gaze picked out the sign 'Registered owners – Genovese' and he pushed through the throng towards that door.

Inside – and getting through the entrance had been a feat in itself – a desk sealed off most of the room. Three men stood at the counter, each with a large, leather tome. The rest of the room was filled with endless rows and racks of journals and books. With a breath of warm air, infused with distant wood-smoke and all-too-near body odour, Skiouros joined what could charitably be called a line and waited. Every minute or so, the queue shuffled slightly and the ranks of folk standing in it fought to be a little closer to their goal.

Skiouros' mind filled him with images of local thieves – there would undoubtedly be hundreds in a port like this – going through his saddle bags while the attendant's back was turned. Nothing he could do about it now, though he struggled forward with a little more force as a gap in the mob opened up.

After what felt like an age, he found himself at the desk, alongside a short man in a stupid green hat who had been behind him moments before. The official looked up from his journal, his eyes playing across the two men.

'Name?'

The short man opened his mouth to go first but the Greek dropped his boot heel on the bridge of the man's foot, and his jaw clamped shut in shock as Skiouros spoke. 'I'm looking for a captain named Parmenio. Not sure of his ship's name, but I believe he'll be based in this port.'

The official gave him a long-suffering look, weighted with boredom, and said 'Bear with me,' as he returned his ledger to a shelf and went in search of another. The short customer recovered quickly and gave Skiouros a hard look. 'There was no need for that!'

'I disagree. Where I come from, pushing past a citizen like that could get you a broken nose. Be content with a bruise.'

'Oaf!' sneered the small man, but he recoiled a little as Skiouros turned a fierce glare on him. Moments later the official returned with his book.

'I've checked. No Captain Parmenio registered here. Are you sure he's an owner, and not just an operator?'

Skiouros furrowed his brow as a thought struck him. 'Could be under Orsini. Cesare Orsini?'

The official cast him that same bored look, sighed and stumped off to the racks of ledgers again. Skiouros occupied himself glaring at the small man in the ridiculous hat who had now shuffled around just behind him, and muttered a few derogatory remarks about his parentage in Greek.

'Orsini,' said the official, returning. 'Cesare Orsini. Yes, he's registered.' The man tapped his lip with the first expression of remote interest Skiouros had seen from him. 'Didn't know the noble houses were bothering with such small concerns. Usually the big families deal through factors and circumvent the authorities.'

'He's not your average nobleman,' Skiouros smiled.

'Well you'll find his ships currently in port at berths fifty-seven and fifty-eight, opposite the church of San Marco by the Pier. There's the *Isabella II* and the *Dream of Carthage*. The latter's just been commissioned. The first is...' his tongue poked from the corner of his mouth, 'yes, the *Isabella II* is under a captain Parmenio. The *Carthage* is under one Nicolo di Siginella. That all?'

Skiouros grinned and tossed a coin onto the counter. 'Perfect. Many thanks.'

As he turned and left, the official looked down in distaste at the paltry coin on the desk and flicked it onto the floor with a fingernail before looking down at the short man with the green hat.

A quarter of an hour later Skiouros, somewhat relieved at still being fully burdened by his possessions, located the church, after some judicious enquiries, and found the twin berths either side of a jetty. The *Isabella II* wallowed heavy in the water, loaded with cargo ready for a voyage. She was clearly only a couple of years old, and still had a sheen of newness to her. Conversely, the *Dream of Carthage* opposite was so new she still smelled of carpentry and paint. Skiouros smiled as he looked at the pair of good caravels. It was hard to picture those days – not all that long ago – when the captains of these two ships had languished in a Tunisian slave cell alongside him and Cesare, having lost everything to pirates.

Dismounting again, he led Sigma along the jetty, pleased that the roan seemed not the least perturbed by the wooden walkway, the two huge, hulking ships and the water swirling around and churning beneath them. Neither vessel had a ramp down, and the lack of goods on the jetty made it clear that neither was currently busy loading or unloading.

Catching sight of a man coiling a rope as he walked along the side rail of the *Isabella II*, Skiouros cleared his throat and gestured to the man.

'Ho there, fellow. I'm looking for Captain Parmenio.'

The man stopped and looked over the side but before he could speak, a voice from behind Skiouros said, 'Then you're looking on the wrong ship.'

The young Greek turned and looked up at the deck of the *Dream of Carthage*. Parmenio leaned on the rail. His clothing was little better than Skiouros remembered, still worn and business-like, but there was about the captain an energy and a presence that he'd not seen since they first met.

'Parmenio.'

'I'm a busy man. What's your business?'

Skiouros experienced a crestfallen moment, but recalled how different he must look even after so short a time. 'Am I that unrecognisable?'

Parmenio narrowed his eyes as he peered down and a moment later the familiar face of Nicolo appeared at the rail beside him. 'Rub your eyes you old fart, it's Skiouros!'

Parmenio burst into a broad grin. 'By the saints, I do believe you're right. You've been gone a time, lad. And in bright sunshine by the look of it. You've changed colour almost entirely.'

Nicolo disappeared and a moment later a small group of sailors appeared further along and slid out a wide boarding ramp. 'Best bring your horse aboard. Can't leave animals alone around here,' Nicolo grinned. 'It'd be braised and eaten in an hour.'

As Parmenio wandered along the rail to join him, Skiouros led Sigma up the ramp, noting again how calm she seemed in the strange circumstances. Whatever she'd done before he bought her in Malaga, she had clearly been aboard a ship more than once. 'Have you somewhere to stable her?'

Nicolo gave him a sour look. 'And here was I telling Parmenio that I'd be doing no livestock runs and my ship would stay cleaner than his. If that beast drops a steamer in my hold, you'll be shifting it and scrubbing the boards.' He sighed. 'But yes, we've got a berth for her.' He turned and waved to a man tightening ropes at the ship's side. 'Giani, can you take my friend's horse down below and make sure she's secure and comfortable? And see if you can find her an apple.'

The sailor nodded and wandered over, grasping the reins and leading the horse away. Nicolo gestured for Skiouros to follow and the two men joined Parmenio, who had shuffled along to the rear rail. They were alone at the ship's stern, surrounded by the background noises of the port and its avian life.

'Some voyage you went on by all accounts,' grinned Nicolo.

'You've heard?'

'*Anyone* in the maritime world has heard, my young friend. The news has been racing around the ports of Europe for a month and more now, and Captain Colombo is from Genoa you know? Out towards the edge of the world, eh. A whole new land, they say?'

'And a green, lush one at that,' Skiouros replied. 'Although given that there were people already living there when we arrived, I'm not sure that 'new' is the right term. Colombo and the Pinzon captains congratulated each other at their discovery and slapped backs and all that, but a sailor got beaten for pointing out that the people we met there had obviously discovered it first. Apparently, if they don't follow the 'good book' they don't really count as people. Makes me sick to the stomach really. Glad I left Spain in short order. That country is a dangerous place to think too much.'

The two captains smiled warmly and Parmenio draped an arm around his friend's shoulders. 'I really thought we might have lost you for good when you disappeared off in that boat at Palos.'

'I was lucky to live through it. Damned pirates.' He paused and frowned. 'Though one of them also saved my life there, funnily enough...'

Nicolo tapped the side of his nose. '"Damned pirates" is a sentiment shared by many these days. The old Turk we met in Palos is the scourge of the seas now, though he's fairly careful in selecting his targets. Few Italian ships have fallen to him recently – Bayezid is in constant talks with Pope, you know – and those the pirate takes are generally ones with ties to the Spanish crown or the Kingdom of Napoli, but woe betide a Spaniard who comes within range of his guns.'

Skiouros nodded. 'So I'd heard. Kemal, they call him.'

'He's not so dangerous in Ligurian waters, though,' Parmenio added. 'He's careful to avoid entanglements with the Pope's allies – apart from Spain, of course. Anyway, are you here for a while? We've a few more chores to complete before the sun sets, but between us, Nicolo and I know every tavern worth a visit in the whole sorry place, and I for one want to hear every last detail of your voyage.'

'Such as where you got this,' added Nicolo, tapping the coloured design rising from Skiouros' doublet neckline and almost touching his chin.

Skiouros smiled. 'I'm certainly not rushing off. I have a lot of thinking and planning to do, and then sometime in the next month or two I will be heading south. I was hoping I could count on you for passage to Rome when the time comes? I'll try to fit in with your business of course.'

The older captain gave him a knowing smile. 'The false sultan's days are numbered, then?' he asked in a low voice.

Skiouros, surprised almost to the point of panic, glanced this way and that for anyone who might have overheard, but they were apparently alone. 'I don't know how you heard that, but it's not something to speak about in the open.'

'Agreed,' admonished Nicolo with a disapproving look at his former captain. 'Your mouth runneth over, Parmenio.'

'Ah calm, now. No one is listening, and anyone who might be within earshot's one of mine or one of yours. Still,' he added, 'it might be a subject better discussed with Cesare.'

'He's here then? In Genoa?'

'And has been this past half year, making a packet and a small name for himself as a mercenary captain with a small but effective group of professional soldiers. He ended a contract with the Sforzas a few weeks back and he and his men are back in the Palazzo counting their loot and recovering from their efforts.'

'It was Cesare who told you of Cem?'

Nicolo nodded. 'He's a perceptive one, young Orsini. He'd pieced together most of your story before your ship was even out of sight. When Parmenio and I filled in a few blanks in your past, it all fell into place. Cesare has been keeping tabs on the Turk prince through a few family members and contacts in Rome. He said you would want all the information we could provide when you resurfaced. He was always convinced you would turn up here on the way to your revenge.'

'*We* could provide?' Skiouros repeated.

'Yes. Parmenio and I do runs down the coast to Civitavecchia and Ostia quite regularly, and you learn a lot by keeping your ears open in a port.'

'So you have no objection to giving me passage to Rome? Even though you know my goal?'

Parmenio laughed. 'Hardly. Unless you want to go late in the year, of course. Then the currents change, and so does the wind. Sailing south after September is like trying to piss into a gale. Nothing much happens but you end up wet through and miserable. But rest assured, whatever you decide to do you won't have to do it alone, even if we have to ride rather than sail.'

Skiouros shook his head. 'This is *my* task, you two, and mine alone. It's a very personal thing, and so risky it'll almost certainly end in my death or my incarceration by the Vatican.'

'Bollocks,' grinned Parmenio. 'Cesare and Nicolo and I made the decision months ago. We survived Hassan's slave trade together and crossed half the Muslim world with nothing but our wits and the shirts on our backs.'

'And the odd case of the shits,' grinned Nicolo.

'We're not about to abandon you now. Anyway, Cesare will never let you go alone, and we owe him our livelihood now. With Orsini money behind us, we can afford to hold off the runs for a while. Nicolo? Can your chores wait? We should get up to the palace and let Cesare know he's reappeared.'

'Just got one or two urgent things to do first. Give me twenty minutes.' Nicolo slumped. 'But if we go there straight away we'll end up stuck in the Palazzo all night and we'll miss all the best taverns.'

'Who cares?' Parmenio laughed. 'The Palazzo's wine cellars are better stocked than any inn, and their larders packed with food. Come on, Skiouros. You and I will share a jar in Nicolo's cabin for half an hour while he finishes his work. Then we'll go and find Cesare. Stuff the rest of the jobs. They can wait on the morrow.'

Skiouros looked back and forth between his friends. Though he would never have asked them to join him in his murderous task, he could not help but feel relieved and grateful that they had offered their swords to his cause. It would make matters much easier.

The Palazzo Visconti had once been a grand affair – as its name suggested. It had clearly been one of the more imposing monuments of the city some years previously. Standing in a square, hemmed in on all sides by tall townhouses and mercantile establishments, it displayed all the grandeur of a royal residence, with delicate balconies hanging outside decorative windows, heavy walls which betrayed its original martial nature redesigned and painted pale yellow and with a heraldic shield above the door which drew the eye: a giant blue snake swallowing a man.

However, the paint was now peeling. Stonework was chipped and crumbling. Balconies missing struts on their railings. Scaffolding climbed up one quarter of the building with workmen repairing the more run-down parts. No guards stood by the door, and no flags, banners or drapes were in evidence.

'Looks like Cesare's family are feeling a pinch in the purse,' noted Skiouros.

Parmenio shook his head. 'Don't be deceived by appearances.'

Strolling across the open ground to the main doors, with Skiouros walking Sigma, Parmenio reached up to the rope that hung from the heavy bronze bell to one side and rang with four deep clangs. Townsfolk paused in their work to glance across at the visitors, but immediately went back to their business.

After perhaps half a minute the door creaked open and a cadaver in black with a thimble-shaped hat and a cold grey gaze stared out at them.

'Master Parmenio,' he nodded. 'Master Nicolo. Ser Orsini is in his study. Shall I show you up?'

Parmenio grasped the reins of Skiouros' horse and walked her forward a little, smiling. 'It's alright, Caruso, we know the way. Could you see to the stabling of this fine mare and then rustle us up some good wine and a plate of something pleasant?'

The pale, skeletal retainer arched an eyebrow but gingerly took the reins, looking with suspicious interest at Skiouros at the back of the line.

'He's with us, Caruso. An old friend of Cesare's.'

The servant nodded as though he couldn't care less and once they were inside, led the horse into the palazzo behind them, the hooves echoing hollowly on the marble floor. Leaving him to his work, Parmenio led the small group through the arched entrance vestibule and out into the courtyard at the centre of the palazzo.

'See what I mean?' Parmenio smiled as Skiouros took in the sheer beauty and delicacy of the courtyard with its triple-storeyed arcades on all sides, the hanging banners and the attractive willow in the centre. It reeked of old-fashioned and understated opulence.

'Why such a poor exterior then?' he asked.

A voice from above called down. 'Because the Visconti used to rule Genoa before the Sforza,' Cesare said from the next floor, leaning over the balcony. 'Now those of them who are left descend from bastards and offshoots who cling to a name not rightfully theirs. Given the hubris of the Sforza it suits the last scions of the Visconti to keep themselves as low-key as possible and not rile their successors.' He touched his forelock. 'Well met once more, Skiouros of Constantinople. Bring him up, you two. We have much to discuss.'

And without further ado he was gone. Skiouros blinked. Cesare had always been so sharp he could cut through silk, but he almost sounded as though he had expected them.

Again, the young Greek studied the rooms and stairways as they passed through the palazzo, noting the paintings, the tapestries and the exquisite marble statuary that looked so like the ancient Greek and Roman figures back home in Istanbul. Before he had sailed into the unknown, when they were still being hunted by Hassan the butcher, Orsini had told him that money was no concern. Now he understood – he'd never seen anywhere so richly appointed. This must be how *kings* lived. Until now he'd had no concept of the kind of wealth of which his friend talked – the three golden statues he had brought back from the Taino and he'd considered a king's ransom were probably worth less than one of the delicate vases lining the corridor. Truly, money *was* going to be no concern!

Up the stairs to the next floor his friend led him, along the balcony from which Cesare had spoken to them in the courtyard, and finally to a room, more austere than he had expected, given the rest of the building. Lit by one external window and an oil lamp, the room's frescos had faded somewhat and were mostly covered by hanging maps of Liguria, Italy entire, the Duchies of Milan, Florence and Modena and the Papal lands. A table was stacked with neat piles of maps and documents, and a single chair sat before it. As they entered the empty room, Cesare reappeared behind them, carrying two chairs, which he shuffled past them and dropped to the floor.

'Take a seat, my friends. You look well, Skiouros. Sea travel apparently sits well with you.'

'I heartily disagree,' smiled the Greek. 'But yes, I am well. Better than ever, in fact.'

'Good. As I said, we have much to discuss, but first I wish to clarify two things. We can speak plainly here. Only Caruso might drop by and the man is as loyal to our family as could be hoped for.'

Skiouros wandered over and fell into one of the chairs as Cesare gestured for them all to sit while he himself leaned against the table. 'You are somewhat more prepared than I expected,' the young Greek noted.

'I know you well, Skiouros, for all our brief acquaintance. I could not envisage a future that did not include you arriving at my door as part of your quest. But as I say, there are two questions of import before we go any further.'

'Go on.'

'The Skiouros I travelled with across Africa I do not think was capable of murder, whatever the cause. For do not be mistaken about this: no matter what your grand thoughts of revenge and justice, what you propose is basically murder. It is against the laws of man and God, and a man has to have a darkness in his heart to achieve such a goal – a darkness with which I am unfortunately rather familiar, given my family. Do you truly have that shadow in *your* soul, Skiouros? Can you kill a man in cold blood?'

Skiouros remained stony faced and silent.

'We will come with you,' Cesare said quietly. 'We will do everything we can to aid you – we have already agreed on this – but when you reach your goal, it will fall to you to complete it. This is not our vengeance to enact... it is yours. So before we embark on this great and dangerous task, I want you to be sure that this is what you wish and that you can actually do it.'

'I can do it.'

'Again. Revenge is a hollow achievement. It as oft destroys its perpetrator as its victim. Think about what you're saying and tell me again.'

'I can take the life of Cem Sultan, in cold blood, with malice and even if the man cowers naked and unarmed. Is that enough?'

'No,' replied Cesare flatly. '*Look me in the eye* while you say it.'

Skiouros fixed his friend with a direct look. 'I can kill the pretender sultan.'

Orsini paused, watching his friend's eyes. Finally he leaned back and folded his arms. 'I remain not entirely convinced. But *you* seem to believe it, so I accept it as the truth.' He rolled his head from side to side, his neck clicking. 'Secondly, this is not a quick jaunt. You are talking about assassinating a man in the custody of one of the world's most powerful rulers in a land that is almost constantly at war with itself. Getting to your target will be difficult and almost certainly a long, involved job. You were ever urgent and impetuous in Africa. A man with those traits going into this task is fated for failure and capture. Are you capable of the patience and attention to detail required?'

'I am, Cesare. I am not the boy you remember. I know the value of patience, and I am prepared for a long haul. I suspect it will take more than a year, perhaps nearer two. Are you satisfied?'

Cesare nodded. 'Fair enough. Now let me give you some information before we get down to the deepest business.'

He paused as Caruso appeared in the door with a wheeled trolley containing cups, glasses, drink containers and a variety of breads, cold meats, cheeses and platters of olives, vegetables and fruit. Once the servant had bowed and retreated, Cesare poured himself a glass of wine and took a sip.

'By now, unless you've been travelling with blinkers on and your ears muffled, you will have heard that we have a new Pope?'

Skiouros nodded and Cesare rubbed his temple as he talked. 'The Spanish cardinal, Rodrigo Borgia, became Pope Alexander the Sixth mere weeks after we last saw you. Since then he has been carefully weeding out his enemies in the Vatican and replacing them with supporters or 'bought men', even bringing in his own guards from home. If the rumours are true, and I see no reason to disbelieve them, Borgia basically bought, bribed and tricked his way to power and has brought his illegitimate children and his mistress into the circles of power with him, in flagrant disregard to Church law.'

'And yet your voice carries little disapproval,' Skiouros noted with a frown. 'I remember you telling me with distaste how much his predecessor sickened you with his immoral behaviour, yet you talk so matter-of-factly about a church man with a penchant for bastardy and bribes?'

Cesare smiled. 'You're not Italian. If you were, you'd realise that being a profligate usurer with a string of bastards doesn't even put a man in the top *half* of the list of deficient Popes! Anyway, while old Innocent was happy to leave the exiled sultan to languish in Vatican custody and claim the annual stipend from his brother, this Borgia Pope seems to actually like the prince and involve him in matters. He is often seen at social affairs and has his own apartments. It is said that the Pope treats with the Turk, despite the fact that Kemal Reis is sinking Spanish ships wherever he can find them and Bayezid's armies busy themselves rolling across the borders of Croatia at this very moment. I think that probably secretly pleases the Pope, since Venice holds a lot of the land that lies in the Sultan's path, and the Venetians are hardly Borgia's biggest supporters.'

Skiouros huffed and poured himself a drink. 'Italian politics is never simple, is it? So, will that make getting to Cem easier or more difficult, do you think?'

Cesare shrugged. 'That is yet to be determined. One thing is certain: our task will be a lot easier if the Vatican remains blissfully unaware of any threat, so we must be circumspect and subtle. Cem commonly resides in lavish apartments in the apostolic palace of the Vatican, under the Pope's own roof. However, a few months back there were rumours circulating concerning two plots – one to murder Cem, and one to free him. The moment the news reached the Pope's ears, our quarry was spirited away in the blink of an eye to the powerful Castel Sant'Angelo, where he was protected by high defences and a veritable army. Getting into the Vatican would take planning and subtlety. Getting into the Castel Sant'Angelo would take an army. You see my point?'

Skiouros nodded.

'What about guards?' he asked.

Parmenio cleared his throat. 'Interestingly, Cem is not in the custody of the Pope's own Vatican forces, or even his personal Catalan guard. You see, as a cardinal, Borgia was a great supporter and patron of the Knights Hospitaller of Malta, and so they are now Cem's guards. Ironic, really, since it was they who first took him captive after his failed coup, and who kept him hostage in France for so many years. Their involvement will make our task a little more difficult, I fear. Spanish mercenaries could probably be bought or bribed, and Vatican guards tricked or reassigned, but I know the Knights of Malta of old from my trading in the eastern islands, and they are unlikely to bend or be corrupted.'

Skiouros sighed. He could remember quite well the old priest in Tunis who had saved them from slavery and who had turned out to be just such a knight. Indeed, he could see that same knight's sword now hanging in its sheath from a peg in the study wall, brought all this way by, and still in the possession of, Cesare Orsini. If that old man was anything to go by, the sultan's guard would be troublesome indeed. Moreover, even if he had now decided he was capable of killing in cold blood, the idea that he might have to take a blade to one of those holy knights seemed very definitely wrong.

'There's his entourage, though,' Nicolo mused. 'If there is a way into his presence, it might be through them.'

Cesare nodded, noting Skiouros' questioning look. 'Cem is allowed many comforts. He corresponds with his mother, who resides in Cairo, and it is said he is even to bring one of his wives to the Vatican. He has an entourage of perhaps half a dozen of his countrymen who tend to him like the slaves of a sultan. They are the only people with continual access to Cem, apart from the knights and the Pope himself… and the Pope's eldest son, of course. My namesake. Cesare Borgia is a man to watch carefully. They say he will have a knife in your heart before you even know he's in the room. A dangerous and extremely intelligent man. And wearing the robes of a cardinal to boot, as he carves his own little empire out of the body of Italy.'

Skiouros took a swig of his wine, wiped his mouth with the back of his sleeve, and coughed. 'So far I hear very little that is encouraging.'

'There is *nothing* encouraging. Listen, my friend: this is not a simple task. Be prepared for setbacks and disappointments at every turn. But with the grace of God and the luck of the Devil, we will manage.'

'You have contacts in Rome, Parmenio tells me?' enquired Skiouros, trying to grasp for a sliver of hope in the face of all this negativity.

'Yes, but few we can rely on for more than a little gossip. And fewer all the time. The various branches of the Orsini family only avoid all-out war with one another because we hate – and are hated by – most of the other noble families, so there isn't time to fight among ourselves. That means that despite there being two noble Orsini landowners in the Rome area, neither would help us. More irritating still, I have a distant cousin who is a cardinal with feasible access to the prisoner, but he would rather help Cem Sultan assassinate me than the other way around. Add to that the fact that most of the Orsini branches are currently on poor terms with the Pope and you can see how fruitless the majority of my contacts will be.'

He took an olive from a plate and tossed it into the air, catching it in his open mouth.

'But…' he smiled as he chewed and swallowed, 'our luck might be in. My former confessor and theology tutor left our family pile after my own departure and now resides in Rome as a member of the Canons Regular of the Lateran. He and I are still in semi-regular contact and it is he who has provided much of what I know of the situation in the city and the Vatican. On him I feel we can rely. He is certainly no lover of the Turk, as he came to us as a refugee from Shkodra in Albania, where his family had died at the hands of the Sultan's army.'

'The Ottoman war machine is a thing to be feared,' said Skiouros darkly, remembering the Janissary Ortas he had met in his time in Istanbul, which in turn flashed an unwelcome image of his lost brother into his mind.

'So that is where we stand,' Cesare announced. 'We have one solid trustworthy contact in Rome. We have access to good sea transport, courtesy of our friends here. We have a small force of men we can rely upon, to whom I will come shortly. We have funds enough to do whatever we wish. Cem is well-kept as a distinguished guest in the Vatican unless there is word of danger, when he is shipped to the safety of the castle. He is guarded by the Hospitaller knights and has a private entourage.'

Cesare paused and narrowed his eyes.

'You any good with that stick of yours?'

'Fairly good. I was taught by the natives who use them, though I still carry a sword too.'

'Good. They could be useful. Now show me your tattoos.'

Skiouros blinked. 'What?'

'I can see the marks at your neck, but most of them are hidden. You can tell a lot about a man from the way he presents himself. Only sailors tattoo themselves without profound reasons, and for all your recent voyage, you are no sailor. That tells me that your marks carry meaning, and I would like to know what they are. Will you oblige?'

Skiouros thought for a moment and then with a shrug began to unlace his doublet and remove his shirt. The other three helped themselves to more food and drink as they waited and when the young Greek stood naked to the waist, his muscled torso sun-browned and decorated, they examined him with interest, Cesare raising the oil lamp to help illuminate the designs.

'Your shoulders have filled out,' Cesare noted, 'and your arms are more heavily muscled.'

'Sailor traits,' Parmenio nodded. 'That's the build of a man who's been hauling on lines and rowing boats for months.'

'Talk me through these,' Cesare said, gesturing at the colourful tattoos that began on Skiouros' right forearm and rose to his neck, extending even to part his right pectoral.

'Most of it is decorative,' Skiouros said, turning to show his upper arm and shoulder more clearly in the flickering light. 'These are the important parts.' He pointed with his free hand at two circular shapes surrounded by swirling patterns reminiscent of stylised knotted vines. One resembled a snarling face with hollowed eyes and bared teeth. 'This is the *guayza*. This is the living spirit of my brother, who is yet to rest.' The other circle was blank, but similar in shape. A hole in the tattoo. 'This is where the *opia* will go – the spirit of the dead. I will fill this in when I believe Lykaion is at peace, when Cem Sultan rots in hell. Until then it remains blank.'

He moved his finger up to his shoulder, to another stretched face reaching up to his neck, where the top of the head became dancing flames. 'This is dreadful Bayamanaco, eternally burning with the flame of wrath. I assume you can appreciate the significance of the ensemble.'

'You've been hobnobbing with too many savages,' snorted Nicolo. 'You look like a bad tapestry. Got bored on the ship did you?'

Parmenio however, bore a thoughtful expression. 'I don't know. I've seen a lot more gaudy and less meaningful tattoos on men who pulled ropes on my ship.' He turned to Nicolo. 'After all, there's a man I saw on your deck yesterday who appears to have a dead surprised turbot on his back. *And* it's the wrong colour.'

Orsini tapped his lip. 'It would appear that you take your goal extremely seriously. At least, I choose to believe so rather than that you have these permanent reminders purely to convince yourself and keep yourself on track. Good. Better get dressed. I'm going to take you somewhere in a minute.'

'Won't be able to go about pretending to be a priest now,' grinned Parmenio. 'Not with those inks up to your neck.'

'It would be of little use dressing as a Greek Orthodox priest in the heart of Rome anyway,' noted Nicolo scathingly. 'But Parmenio *is* correct about those marks. Time to start wearing a high collar or a scarf. All too interesting and memorable, those.'

'I disagree,' Cesare shrugged. 'For what I have in mind, something memorable and interesting might be just the thing. Perhaps you should unlace that sleeve and leave your decorated arm bare.'

'You want to infiltrate the upper circles of Rome and attempt an assassination with us as interesting and memorable as possible? With Skiouros looking like an ancient mosaic?' frowned Parmenio.

'Come.'

Cesare rose from his seat and left the room, replacing his wine on the table before he did so. Skiouros threw the rest of his own glass down his throat and followed suit. Parmenio and Nicolo exchanged quick glances and grabbed handfuls of beef and bread and a fresh glass of wine to take with them.

Back along the arcaded balcony and down the stairs they walked, back across the courtyard and into a corridor that was less decorative and more serviceable, flagged with stone rather than marble. The three visitors followed their host, occasionally looking at one another and shrugging in incomprehension. Once more they climbed, up a small spiral staircase that seemed to hearken back to the palazzo's days as a fortress. Finally, as they arrived at the top, they emerged onto a similar balcony, though much shorter and overlooking a smaller courtyard. There, Cesare stopped and rested his elbows on the rail.

The friends stopped next to him and looked down. In the courtyard, three men were busy sparring, stripped to the waist, their perspiring forms sun-bronzed and muscular. A huge titan of a man with braided blond hair was busy with a heavy sword hacking chunks from a wooden post. A thinner man with more traditional Italian colouring was stabbing and lunging with a pike at a wooden ring hanging from a rope, which swung in the breeze, while the third man – a stick-thin figure with jet black hair – wound a crossbow.

'Your mercenaries,' Parmenio shrugged. 'Nice to see they're keeping in shape between contracts. Didn't you have four?'

Cesare nodded. 'Adolfo lost an arm last month at Faenza. He chose to take a large payment and retire. With the money I gave him he can buy a good woman to replace that arm!' He laughed and then turned, his face taking a serious cast as he looked at Skiouros. 'Yes, these are my men. With them we form a unit of *condottieri* mercenaries – a 'Lance' is the technical term, though we are currently slightly depleted. I think that is about to change, though.'

Skiouros looked at his raised brow and frowned. As he glanced back down at the soldiers and the details of the missing man sank in, he shook his head. 'I'm no soldier, Cesare.'

'Oh but you are. Remember, I saw you fight more than once on our way across Africa, and you could hold your own in any ducal army. And if you're going to drive that pig-sticker of yours into the Turk's heart, it would serve you well to numb yourself to the taking of life first. You want to move in the higher circles of Roman society? You won't get there as a priest or a peasant, and you've not the name nor the blood to pass as a nobleman. You want access to the aristocracy of the Vatican? The only way I see that you can do that is to be hired by them. The Vatican army is often bolstered by large units of hired condottieri on long-term contracts. The Pope doesn't have the manpower to maintain a huge field army, but he's never short of mercenary captains willing to sign on. Think on it, Skiouros. We could sign on in Rome and you might be working directly for the Pope. How much closer can you get to the top? How else do you see us gaining access to the Vatican or the Castel Sant'Angelo?'

Skiouros was still shaking his head, though the vehemence had gone from the action. Below, the pikeman succeeded in hooking the wooden ring at the same moment the crossbowman put a bolt in the eye of the wooden figure standing across the courtyard. The two men laughed and jeered at one another in friendly competition as the giant continued to brutalise his practice stake.

'I'll save you the effort of thinking too hard about it,' Cesare sighed. 'I've been thinking on your problem for almost half a year now, and I've approached it mentally from every angle I can find. The result is, I'm afraid, there is no better hope for getting close to the pretender sultan than signing on as condottieri in the Vatican's service.'

Nicolo frowned. 'You never mentioned this to us.'

'That,' Cesare smiled, 'is because without Skiouros here, you would have said no.'

The two sailors shared their thoughts with their eyes alone and then turned back to him. 'Look,' replied Nicolo flatly, 'we can both handle a cleaver in an emergency, but we're sailors, not soldiers.'

'Every lance of condottieri needs a page and a squire,' their host grinned. 'Minimum action, maximum talk. Sounds like you two down to a tee.'

Skiouros sighed. 'So your plan is that we hop on board the *Isabella II*, head to Rome and sign ourselves on with the Vatican officers?'

'Ah, not quite.'

The three guests all concentrated on Orsini, who simply smiled impishly. 'Even with my recent successes, as condottieri we are largely unknown even here in Genoa. We are *total* unknowns in Rome, and with so many mercenary captains clamouring for the pay and the prestige of fighting for the Pope, we would be lucky if the Vatican even spat in our direction.'

'So what can we do, then?' Parmenio frowned, but Skiouros had already seen the plot forming in Cesare's head and narrowed his eyes.

'No use heading to Rome until we've made a name for ourselves, am I right? Until word of our deeds carries weight?'

Cesare laughed. 'Precisely. The best and most successful condottieri have a portfolio of their successes, and a name that travels ahead of them like a herald. We need that.'

Parmenio folded his arms defiantly. 'You're talking about vying with the best mercenary captains in Italy... noblemen who have fought in some of the greatest battles in living memory. Captains who command a thousand men, in some cases. We are...' he paused and glanced back down at the courtyard, 'seven, including three sailors! There's no way we can win the same kind of prestige as they.'

Orsini laughed again. 'You do think in such rigid lines, my friend. Of course there is. Instead of going out there with the intention of fighting a pitched battle in the open field and trying to distinguish ourselves, we need to pick our contracts carefully. Preferably very short contracts, even for just one action if we can manage it. But we need high profile targets and high profile employers. Then we have to make our actions memorable and laudable. If we work things right, in a few short months our names could carry the sort of weight we require. And being memorable,' he gestured at Skiouros' colourful neck, 'is part of that. Half of it is success. The other is being both highly visible and very memorable.'

Skiouros looked down at the courtyard once more.

Despite his words of reassurance earlier to Orsini, there had been a number of times in the past half year when he had questioned his ability to kill – whether he had the strength needed to carry out the task. When Bayamanaco burned on his arm, and his doubts assailed him. He had only ever killed in self-defence and in the most desperate of situations. Now might be a good time to test his ability to take a man's life in hot blood before he tried it cold... Numbing himself to the taking of life, as Orsini had said.

'You're right, Cesare. It's the best chance we have. And without you I wouldn't even have that chance, so I thank you from the deepest level of my heart.'

'Don't thank me too soon. You've got some hard training to do first.'

Skiouros nodded. 'But these two,' he gestured to Parmenio and Nicolo. 'Don't guilt them into coming with us. This is not their fight.' He turned to them and repeated himself. 'This isn't your fight.'

Nicolo threw an arm across Parmenio's shoulder. 'After you sacrificed yourself at Palos to save us? What kind of friends would we be? Besides, you heard what Orsini here said. Minimum action, maximum talk.'

CHAPTER THREE - Roccabruna, March 1494

'*M* *inimum action*, sayeth the Orsini,' grumbled Parmenio as his foot slipped on another section of what should have been loose scree had it not been welded together with ice. Recovering himself, he carefully planted his other foot against a jutting rock and began to scramble up the slope again. Behind him, Nicolo simply rolled his eyes, though whether in agreement with his comrade or in exasperation at Parmenio's perpetual mutterings this morning, none of the small unit could tell.

The captain of the *Isabella II*, now as far removed from his beloved sea as he felt it possible to be, muttered something else under his breath about his high level of visibility. Skiouros looked back from his position at the head of the climb and almost laughed. For all his friend's general tendency to complaint these days, the young Greek had to concede this point at least. While most of the small group were kitted for the fight, Parmenio and Nicolo – in their respective capacities as page and squire to Orsini – were decked out in the noble family's colours. A doublet divided down the centre, with the left breast and arm red and the others white and bearing a red rose, their top half was blinding enough. The hose of vertical red and white stripes were something else entirely. They certainly did not blend in with the glittering grey-brown slope of the hillside. The two sailors' clothing was partially enclosed in a steel breastplate, and each had a pair of gauntlets tied around their neck, padded with a scarf to stop them knocking around and clanging. Those, and their small, open helmets and the swords slung at their sides, chapes clacking off the frozen ground, labelled them more in truth than just page and squire.

Ahead of them, Skiouros looked more suited to the task at hand, his black hose dusty and marked, the mail shirt that hung to his thighs missing the right arm in order to display his colourful tattoos to the world. A tabard of striped white and red over the shirt confirmed his allegiance to the Orsini family and though he eschewed a helmet in favour of increased sensory capability, he also had gauntlets around his neck and both sword and macana club at his waist, as well as the *misericord* dagger that Orsini had given him.

As he paused to look back, he made sure to grip a protruding stone. Below, his friends climbed the steep slope and behind them, Helwyg, the Silesian giant, was making easy progress, his size and sheer arm strength making the climb a breeze for him. Despite the chill, he wore only breeks and hose and a linen shirt displaying the Orsini arms, his only concession to defence a pair of iron vambraces wrapped around his lower arms. His huge sword was strapped to his back, the great, burgundy leather-bound hilt jutting up over a shoulder. His blond braids swung as he climbed.

Behind him came Vicenzo, having regretfully left his lethal pike in camp and relying on his sword and a knife instead. Dressed in red doublet and hose with one white sleeve, his torso and arms were clad so heavily in steel plate that little of the colour could be seen. He already wore his gauntlets, which were of hardened leather and were no hazard to the climb. At his waist, a heavy coiled rope weighed him down.

Of their small party, Girolamo came almost last, struggling with the climb despite being burdened only by a breastplate and one mailed arm, his red and white colours in clear evidence, yet somehow easier on the eye than the stripes afflicting Parmenio and Nicolo. On his back swung the heavy crossbow with which he had achieved a level of impressive mastery, and a case of bolts at his waist occasionally got in the way of the climb, the leather bag on the far side swinging pendulously as he clambered up.

Orsini himself, the condottiere and captain of the force, brought up the rear. Despite being encased entirely in articulated plate mail, from the heavy visored helmet to the banded sabatons on his feet, he seemed to be nimbly picking his way up the slope in their wake. His armour gleamed evilly, all black with gold designs etched thereon, a cloak hanging from his shoulders displaying the Orsini colours.

Curse him for his ideas. Curse him doubly for being so self-assured about them.

Turning back to the climb, Skiouros spied their destination between the trees ahead. The heavy fortress of Roccabruna brooded on the tan ridge, unassailable and proud, its six towers and curtain wall almost insignificant when compared to some of the places Skiouros had visited, and yet powerful when placed on such a commanding crest. For all they did not live up to the walls of Istanbul or Genoa or Carthage, they might as well rise to touch the sky itself when the attacking force consisted of seven mismatched and generally grumpy mercenaries.

The Roccabruna seemed to mock him for a moment and then disappeared from sight among the trees. Skiouros turned once more and glanced back.

Past his friends, and down behind the gleaming black figure of Orsini, the army of Lord Alberici of Orvieto sat patiently, strewn across the valley below the fortress. Hundreds, even thousands, of footmen, archers and crossbowmen stood in ordered squares while knights on their destriers rode back and forth between them. The pavilion of Lord Orvieto shone in the cold sun across the valley, white and blue and topped with streamers and banners, surrounded by the tents of the other knights. Artillery – the very latest bombards and cannon – were lined up on the hill opposite, ready to fire in the hope that their range would be sufficient to pound the walls of Roccabruna to rubble when the order was given.

Not for the first time, Skiouros threw up a prayer to God almighty that the impetuous lord of Orvieto would give them the time they had agreed before he passed word to the artillerists to begin the assault. The very idea of being exposed on the slope below the walls when those bombards began to fire was heart-stopping. In the early winter, during the Veneto campaign, he had seen a man take a direct hit from a cannon ball and he still occasionally woke sweating in the night at the memory.

'I say again that we should have flatly refused to do this,' Parmenio snorted, scrambling at the slope and dragging Skiouros back from the remembered sight of that grisly death.

'I know. I'm tempted to agree,' muttered Skiouros, reaching up and pulling himself up the last stretch of open slope before the small knot of trees that hid their ascent from the walls. His early eagerness to throw himself into the martial life upon his return from the west was beginning to flag under the ennui of constant warfare. 'I'm so heartily sick of endless engagements and hovering among the crowd of men hoping I'll make it back this time. We've been so many months facing death down that we just have to seize an opportunity like this. He may be insane when it comes to planning, but Orsini's shrewd.'

And he was. After seven months of serving four different noblemen in the interminable internecine wars of Italy, they had been more than just fortunate to have managed to sign into the service of Lord Orvieto. Not because he was any better than the rest – he wasn't. In Skiouros' considered opinion, the man was a jumped up runt with a superiority complex who considered everyone but his direct family inferior and expendable. In fact, the young Greek had taken an instant dislike to the man on a level usually reserved for his enemies. But in the three times they had been in Orvieto's presence, there had never been less than three Vatican emissaries with him, including a cardinal, here as a Papal legate.

Orsini had been right in signing this contract. If ever they wanted an 'in' to service for the Vatican, this would be the way. Orvieto was here under Papal authority to take and hold Roccabruna – a small but strategically important fortress the master of which continually refused to acknowledge the overlordship of the Pope. Even then, with this final chance at recognition, the lord's army was so large that none of the four condottieri forces who served him would stand out above the common soldiery. And that had been where Cesare's plan had come in.

It still made Skiouros grind his teeth as he remembered that moment, the previous night, when Orsini had entered their tent and laid out the bones of his plan. It had taken all of his not-insignificant powers of persuasion to secure the agreement of his three friends, and even then Parmenio had only bowed to the pressure of his peers. When all had been agreed, Parmenio had nodded and suggested that Cesare approach the lord with his plan. Orsini had laughed and taken a swig of his wine before he informed them that he had put his proposal to the lord before he'd dropped by. Orvieto had agreed with some reservations, but the plan had already been approved.

When they had pulled Parmenio's angry hands back from Cesare's throat and calmed him down, the group had settled to come up with the finer detail for Orsini's plan.

And now, a mere twelve hours later, here they were scrambling up the slope on a mission to bring this troublesome castle and its recalcitrant lord back under Papal dominion.

Skiouros reached the line of vegetation and grasped a bare branch to help pull himself into the cover of the trees. Behind him, and with grumbles of relief, Parmenio and Nicolo skittered into the shade of the cold copse. While the others joined them, Skiouros pushed his way through the small stand and to the top edge, where he could finally see the castle of Roccabruna close up and all too well.

Cesare had been correct about the layout, at least. While the bulk of the castle spread out along the ridge, leading to a heavy gatehouse at the eastern point where the main road led up from the township below, this direction provided the only viable alternative entrance. Here, the walls had been extended to march a little way down the slope and protect a smaller postern gate which sat atop a small path winding its way down the hillside to a hamlet by the stream below, now swamped by the waiting besieging army.

The walls of the castle were not thronged with men as Skiouros would have expected when facing a siege, but Orsini had been certain that only lookouts would be posted up there. When bombards were lined up and pointed at the walls no defender in his right mind filled those parapets with his best men. Remembering that grisly cannon shot in Veneto, Skiouros could imagine why.

Two guards were close by, keeping watch over this sector. Others were just visible as shapes in the higher sections of the castle. Even if they saw what happened here, it would take them time to react. Speed was of the essence.

Skiouros glanced to his left. There, somewhere around a thousand yards away, was the edge of the forest of which this small copse was just an outlying fragment. He could almost imagine the four hundred men of Orvieto's most disposable unit seething up through those woods, unseen from above and ready to leap into action at the signal.

Again Skiouros prayed that Cesare had thought it through thoroughly enough and had been right in his estimates and guesses.

As the others appeared among the itchy, prickly pine-needle branches with Skiouros, Girolamo unslung his crossbow and unfastened his leather case, withdrawing two bolts of different sizes which he lay on the ground before fastening it again. While Orsini brought up the rear and the others peered between the branches at their target, Girolamo began to wind back the string until it met his satisfaction. Testing the tension, he nodded and proffered it to Skiouros, who frowned.

'Hold it for me.'

While the Greek gingerly took the weapon, being sure to keep his finger far away from the trigger, he watched with interest as the crossbowman opened up the swinging leather sack at the other side of his belt. From it, he removed what appeared to be a miniature version of the same weapon, some eighteen inches long. Swiftly, Girolamo hooked the string on this one back over the retainer and then cranked it with a small lever. Once it was so tight it creaked and hummed with torsion, he laid it carefully on the ground and slid the smaller of the two bolts into place.

'Rope,' he said, without looking around. As Vicenzo began to unhook the coiled rope from his waist, Girolamo picked up the larger crossbow bolt. Skiouros noted as the man held it up and turned it around that a narrow hole had been drilled through the shaft at the end, behind the flights. Taking a leather thong from his pouch, the archer threaded it through the hole and tied it off, pulling it tight. As Vicenzo passed him the looped end of the rope, Girolamo attached the leather thong to the hemp circle and tested it until it met his approval. Satisfied, he took his weapon from Skiouros once more and settled the bolt into place, making sure the leather thong was looped through the lath from the front to allow both arrow and rope free passage. Nodding his approval at the device, he cocked his head towards Skiouros.

'Pick the other one up.'

Skiouros did so, gingerly, and Girolamo hissed in irritation. 'Keep it level. Don't tip it, or the bolt will come loose. Make sure it's seated right. That's it. Now hold it still and level and pass it to me the moment my hands are free.'

He turned to Orsini. 'Are we ready?'

'Any moment. Wait until the two guards are looking in different directions. Other than that, everyone knows what to do.' His voice was made hollow and unearthly by the enclosing helmet and Skiouros wondered if Cesare was glad no one could see his face right now. If anything went wrong here, not only would they be in great danger, but they would look like fools to the Papal watchers and all would be for naught. It was almost fascinating watching Orsini's breath pluming through the rose-shaped air-holes in the helmet.

Skiouros frowned at the small crossbow in his hands.

'I've never seen one of these. Did you invent it?'

'Hardly,' muttered Girolamo, lifting his crossbow and peering between the pine needles at the walls and the two men atop them. 'It's a Venetian device, but I understand modelled after an eastern creation. Nowhere near as accurate or powerful as a proper crossbow, but quick and useful at short range. And it's often handy to have a spare loaded.'

'They've separated,' hissed the echoing tone of Cesare, and Girolamo nodded.

'San Sebastiano favour me now.' With a steadying breath, the Genovese mercenary levelled his crossbow in the steadiest hands Skiouros had ever seen and with the slightest of movements twitched the trigger.

With the twang and thud of the lath and string meeting once more, the bolt sailed out through the air in a surprisingly flat trajectory, the rope trailing after it like a line drawn artistically through the air. With a wince at the necessity of doing so, Girolamo dropped the weapon to the ground even as the rope continued to uncoil next to him, and grabbed the second bow held in Skiouros' outstretched hands.

Barely pausing to aim, he lifted the tip of the weapon and pulled the trigger, the smaller bolt rising into the air on a higher trajectory to account for the lighter weight and lower firing strength.

Skiouros turned to the walls between the branches and watched with fascination. The first bolt had already struck by the time he had turned, and he saw the guard stagger back, the bolt having passed through his chest, dragging the rope into his innards. The trailing line whipped through the air. Just as the man toppled back from sight with a squawk that was barely audible, the second, smaller bolt took the other guard in the neck, passing through his windpipe and dropping him silently and cleanly from sight.

Skiouros turned to the man, expecting a grin of satisfaction, but Girolamo was already packing away his small weapon and slinging his main crossbow over his back.

'Go!' barked Cesare in his hollow metallic voice, and Helwyg was first up, pushing his way through the branches and scrambling up the remaining distance of the slope towards the heavy, tan walls, heedless of the slippery iciness of the scree beneath him. Skiouros followed as the rest of the group hurtled out into the sunlight.

The rope that had trailed behind the deadly bolt hung down the wall from the parapet and trailed along the frozen ground below for a few yards, testament to just how well the archer had judged the height of the walls and the power of his shot.

No alarm was being raised in the castle. This was the most heart-stopping moment of all. At this point so much could go wrong with the plan. Skiouros made himself turn his attention to the rope ahead, deliberately forcing himself not to think about the possible hiccups facing them.

Helwyg reached the bottom of the wall with little trouble, while Skiouros and the two sailors slipped and skittered on the scree behind him. As the great Silesian reached the rope, he grabbed hold and began to give it a good heave. Skiouros felt his heart skip a beat as several feet of rope fell through the air, and he was convinced it had not anchored above. Then, as quickly as it had loosened, the rope tightened once more and stopped its descent. Helwyg gave it a hefty tug and it moved a little, but not too much. The big man turned to Skiouros, holding out the rope.

'Me?'

Helwyg nodded. 'I too big. You little man. Light for climb.'

Little man! But it was hard to deny the fact that he probably weighed half of the Silesian's huge, muscular bulk. If the rope had any give, it would certainly fail under *that* weight.

He turned to see Parmenio and Nicolo looking at him expectantly. Parmenio still looked less than impressed, but he was rubbing his hands together in anticipation of the action. Nicolo grinned. 'Think of it as climbing rigging and hurry up. We haven't long before his lordship decides we've failed and starts hitting us with bombards.'

With the added reminder of that possibility, Skiouros turned to the rope and gripped it with his sweaty hands – gauntlets would be hazardous now. He had to rely solely on his natural talents. At least he had always been a good climber, ever since he and Lykaion had scaled the church tower back home as children, not to mention the Nea Ekklasia…

Wrapping his lower legs around the rope, he began to climb, hauling himself up with his hands and then anchoring himself with his feet as he reached up once more. Again and again he performed the repetitive actions, ascending with ease and beginning to feel more confident as he rose.

Some seven or eight feet below the battlements, he felt his heart jump again as the rope suddenly slithered downwards and he found himself dangling ten feet back down, his legs unhooked. Wondering if any of his friends might be heroically stupid and stand underneath as he fell, he realised the rope had become taut again and he once more anchored his legs, forcing himself to repeat that part of the climb. As he reached the lower edge of the battlements, his hands encountered something wet and he paid closer attention to the rope than to the parapet a few feet above. The hemp glistened with dark liquid and he realised with intense horror that this section of the rope had passed through the guard's chest. His revulsion suddenly gave way to panic as he realised what that meant:

The rope was not well anchored and was coming loose from the body!

Desperately, knowing that the rope was no longer a viable climbing option with that unpleasant slimy coating, Skiouros reached in and grasped the machicolation of the wall – one of the gaps below the parapet through which stones and boiling liquids could be poured on attackers. In this particular case one of the most murderous methods of thwarting an attacker actually came to his defence. Letting go of the rope with his feet, he held onto the hole in the projecting battlements with both hands.

Trouble.

He was stuck.

The rope hung loose behind him and he could probably grasp it, but that would do him little good. He would get nowhere before his weight pulled the rope free of the body and he plummeted to his death among his friends. But equally he was now hanging directly beneath the projecting battlements with no hope of scaling the overhang and clambering up over the top.

His desperate eyes played across the defences from this angle taking in everything he could see in the panicked hope that there was an obvious solution he was missing. There wasn't. There was no helpful wider gap beyond the next jutting corbel. Nothing stuck out to help him. He felt his fingers becoming numb with the cold and the pressure of supporting all his weight.

Could he fit through this narrow gap?

Skiouros frowned into the hole above him. He was small and slight by build, but he had put on a lot of muscle this past half year aboard Colombo's ships, and with the added bulk of a mail shirt he was hardly sylph-like. He mentally measured the gap through which defenders dropped rocks and tried to picture his own frame from an objective viewpoint.

He didn't think so.

The fingers of his left hand slipped free and he found himself dangling over a long fall by four fingertips. It appeared that gravity and necessity were making the decision for him. Realising with regret that his weapon belt and gauntlets would not fit through the gap, he used his left hand to unfasten them, allowing them to drop to the slope below among his friends.

Unburdened, and with three deep breaths to prepare, he finally exhaled until his lungs were devoid of air and threw his free hand – the one that had slipped – up into the hole, reaching around until his fingers closed on the flagged floor of the wall-walk. He felt a moment of elation when they found it, and as soon as he was sure the new grip would hold, he let go with his right hand and reached up into the hole. Both hands were now gripping the floor above. He closed his eyes and threw up a brief prayer to the God of Christian, Jew and Turk alike to help him through this.

And he heaved.

His head suddenly burst through the darkness of the hole and gave him a floor-level view of the parapet walk. He almost laughed with the joy of victory…

… and then his chest wedged in the hole.

His eyes rolled in panic, his arms now laid out before him on the flagged floor, the cold sun gleaming directly in his face, the castle's interior displayed ahead, but his chest trapped and his legs dangling in empty air, kicking in futile panic in open space.

'Oh shit!'

It had meant to be whispered, but his panic had made the words too loud and he realised how easily he could attract attention right now. Desperately, he forced himself to calm down. He had to think this through.

The panic arose once more as he came to the conclusion that he had *no time to think*. His chest was wedged and he simply could not breathe in more than a mouthful of air. His ribs had no space to expand. Not only was he lying prone in an enemy fortress, trapped and dangling over a deadly drop, he was also remarkably close to suffocating.

So suddenly he nearly missed it, his foot found purchase against the tiny lip of a badly-fitted stone block in the wall's face. It was little more than the width of a fingernail, and his boots were lumbering leather things, but it was a beacon of hope in that panicked moment. Concentrating, he positioned his other foot on the same lip and pressed with his toes until he thought they might snap with the strain. At the same time, he hauled with all his might on his arms, scrabbling for better purchase with his fingertips. His left hand closed over the edge of a slightly larger flagstone and the combined pressure from pushing with his feet and pulling with his arms caused something to give. He shifted first an inch. Then two. He could feel the lack of oxygen beginning to affect him, tiny lights dancing in his vision and his wits filling with panicked fuzz. But another inch and then two and there was a horrible grating noise as the mail links of his shirt ground on the stone, and suddenly he was up, heaving in ragged breaths. With some difficulty – though nothing compared to what had gone before – he dragged his hips and legs up onto the wall walk.

He lay there for a moment, heaving in air and recovering, but it did not take him long to realise that every passing moment increased their peril.

Coming up to a crouch he looked around, taking in the situation. This section of the walls came down from the ridge in a U shape, enclosing the small postern gate. He could see the various timber structures of the castle's main bailey, along with the men and women moving among them. Other guards stood watch on the walls of the upper section. It seemed a miracle that no alarm had yet been raised, given the fact that many of the posted sentries were in view of each other, including the two Girolamo had shot. But then each man was watching the countryside beyond the walls intently, and those nearest the postern were concentrating on the huge army formed up in the valley and the array of cannon and bombards facing them on the hill opposite.

The guard with the bolt jammed in his neck had gone from view, presumably fallen from the wall inside the loop of the U. The man with the rope-bolt was wedged up against the battlements, having been dragged up against them when Helwyg yanked on the rope through his chest, anchoring it there. Skiouros could see the tip of the bolt projecting from the corpse's back between the shoulders and the flagstones around him were sprayed with crimson and strange coiled marks that resembled snake tracks but showed where the rope had trailed across the walk after having passed through his body. He had apparently done the right thing letting go of the rope. One more tug and it would have come free from the corpse and fallen away again.

Scurrying across to the fallen guard, he pushed the body back with distaste and began the grisly business of pulling the rope free. Ignoring the sticky slime on his hands, he grasped the rope and dragged it a few feet so that the wet section was above the parapet, looping it across a stone drain spout and tying it tight.

With a glance back at the castle's bailey and finding it hard to believe no one had seen him yet, he ran back across to the wall and gestured for the others to come up. Once Parmenio had begun the climb, Nicolo grasping the rope below him, Skiouros scurried over to the inner edge of the walk. The drop down to the area within the postern gate loop was perhaps twenty feet. He could theoretically survive the fall intact, but the chances were slim, given the rocky ground and the icy conditions. Instead, he crouched, keeping an eye on the other sentries so oblivious on the higher walls. His heart beat out the seconds as he waited and he was relieved beyond measure when Parmenio hooked his hand over the battlements and pulled himself across and onto the flags.

'This...' his friend heaved in a deep breath, 'is why I am a sailor and not an acrobat!'

As he lay on his back, his chest rising and falling, Nicolo's face appeared over the top and he pulled himself across to join them.

'You took your pissing time!' he said, slinging Skiouros' weapon belt and gauntlets over to him.

'I encountered a few problems!' snapped Skiouros in irritation as he caught the items and fastened the belt about his waist.

The three men continued to recover as Girolamo and Vicenzo arrived and joined them. As they crouched and looked around, Skiouros frowned. 'Where's Helwyg?'

'Too heavy to trust the rope,' muttered Vicenzo. 'He's waiting with Ser Orsini.'

Girolamo shook his head and tutted. 'The rope bolt was for speed. If we'd known you were going to take so long I'd just have shot him and we could have used a grapple.'

'Oh piss off,' barked Skiouros, eliciting a frown from the crossbowman.

'Come on,' Parmenio urged them, rising to a crouch. 'We'd better get moving. I can almost hear that artillery cranking up.'

As Skiouros peered down inside again, this time spotting the body of the second guard splayed out in a broken shape on the rocks, he heard a distant cry.

'We're discovered!' Nicolo hissed. Next to them, Vicenzo appeared, having hauled up the rope, and he dropped it instead down the inner face of the wall.

'Come on!'

The man gripped the rope in his hard leather gauntlets and slid with ease downwards, kicking out against the wall as he descended rapidly. Skiouros quickly pulled on his own gauntlets and followed suit, Parmenio, Nicolo and Girolamo coming on behind.

As soon as his feet hit the icy, slippery rock, Skiouros knew they were in trouble. Though there was no wall tower here, there was a doorway into the wall itself next to the gate, obviously a small guardhouse within the wall, and shouts of alarm were coming from within.

'Stay here,' commanded Vicenzo, 'and hold *them* off.' As he drew a needle-pointed poniard dagger from his belt, he pointed up the slope to the bailey. Skiouros' heart jumped as he saw perhaps a dozen men at arms running between the buildings, heading for this previously unnoticed incursion. Behind them, he could see many more guards arming themselves. With a quick touch of the wooden zemi figure on the thong around his neck for luck, he drew his sword and his macana, gripping the reassuring wooden handle. Behind him, Vicenzo disappeared into the doorway. There were shouts of alarm and the sounds of combat from inside the guard chamber.

As the others drew their own blades, there being no time for Girolamo to cock his crossbow, Parmenio dashed across to the postern gate. It consisted of an oak door some six inches thick, reinforced on the outside with iron plates and studs, and on the inside with three locking bars that slid at one side into the stonework and at the other dropped into an iron holder. He began to heave the bars free. 'There's a key required too,' he yelled, aiming his words at the guard room, and then ran for the doorway as the third locking bar hit the ground.

Skiouros, Nicolo and Girolamo braced themselves as the dozen men ran for them, many more assembling behind. With a crash and a yelp, the fight in the guard room was apparently done with, and as Skiouros glanced over his shoulder he saw Parmenio and Vicenzo reappear, rummaging through a leather satchel. Parmenio grabbed a heavy iron ring of keys and ran off to the door, while Vicenzo drew his sword to accompany his poniard and joined the other three defenders.

As Parmenio struggled with the iron ring, trying one key after another in the lock, desperately pulling on the portal each time, Skiouros prepared himself for the attack. The Roccabruna men-at-arms launched into the fray with gusto, each armed with long pikes or heavy, gleaming halberds.

Skiouros saw the first lunge coming and ducked his head to one side, the long pike swishing past his ear out of harm's way. Not allowing the man time to recover his weapon, Skiouros stepped forward and drove his sword into the soldier's belly, wrenching it back out only just in time to knock aside a halberd blade that swept across in an attempt to catch him at the junction of neck and shoulder, where his mail could not protect him.

Everything then devolved into a blur of battle, struggling for survival. After dodging or knocking aside a few more blows with his sword and rapping with his macana club on skulls and knuckles, dazing the enemy or loosening their grip on their weapons, Skiouros realised with a sinking feeling that he was retreating, being pushed back by the weight of the Roccabruna men. More and more men-at-arms were rushing to their aid and as he stepped back to avoid yet another blow, Skiouros saw the twitching form of Vicenzo being trampled by the enemy as they advanced. Nicolo gave a cry of pain and Skiouros glanced across to see him with his left arm folded across in front of him, blood evident among the glistening steel and the bright heraldic designs. They were holding up surprisingly well, but their numbers were dwindling while the enemy force continued to grow.

A razor edge he never even saw bounced against his ribs, ripping away links of mail and scoring a red hot line across his side. Once again he was grateful for the armour he had acquired at the Palazzo Visconti those months ago. That blow could have cut through rib and lung both had the steel links not turned the blow aside.

Suddenly his back struck stone and he realised they had reached the wall. Risking a momentary glance behind, he saw Parmenio struggling to open the door, but denied the space to do so as the fight had now pressed right back against him. Girolamo was fighting to give him room, but the enemy were too strong and too numerous.

'It's unlocked but I can't open the benighted thing!' fumed Parmenio, hauling at the door and trying to open it into the press of bodies.

A muted voice called something from beyond the door, then the unheard words were repeated louder with a German twang: '*Stand back*!'

There was as much chance of them standing back as of them leaping gracefully over the wall, but in response Girolamo and Nicolo joined him in attempting to heave the men at arms back. The Roccabruna men had taken on a sudden edge of desperation, realising that the postern gate was close to falling.

And then the door burst suddenly inwards, throwing Parmenio against the stonework and catapulting Nicolo forwards onto the bodies of the desperate enemy. Helwyg barrelled through the gate, freed of its resistance, like a bull in full charge, his sheer momentum shattering the defence of the men at arms, who were knocked aside like children's toys as the Silesian titan swung his huge blade, hacking off any protrusion in its way, be it weapon or limb. In the wake of this huge nightmare came the gleaming black and gold armoured figure of Cesare Orsini, sword in one hand, parrying dagger in the other. The steel-encased nobleman waded into the enemy like some sort of machine, cutting, jabbing, flensing and stepping between the fallen as though the heavy plate mail he wore were nothing more than a nightshirt. As always in the midst of combat, Skiouros was given cause to admire the sheer martial skill of his friend. A better swordsman he had never met.

The tide had momentarily turned. The arrival of the knight and the giant had collapsed the attack, but they were still horribly outnumbered and more and more men were hurrying towards them.

'Cesare?' he called.

The shining helm turned towards him. 'Hold for just a moment, Skiouros. Captain Cinozza is almost here with his men. We've done it, my friend. We've done it.'

Laughing gaily like a madman, Cesare waded off among the enemy, whirling blades and stamping down among the fallen. Skiouros paused for a moment and smiled. His ears picked out the sound of hundreds of men scrambling up that icy scree outside the gate. Cesare was right. Against all the odds, they had succeeded.

Captain Cinozza laughed with Parmenio at some joke the pair had shared, their arms draped across each other's shoulders and both spattered in the lifeblood of their enemy. Skiouros walked along behind as befitted a mercenary under his condottiere, Girolamo and Helwyg flanking him, Parmenio and Nicolo between them and the commanders as was suitable for Cesare's page and squire. Nicolo had taken a bad arm wound and a glancing blow to the hip when the big German had pushed him into the enemy line, but had announced that he would live, at least long enough to take Helwyg at cards for every coin he owned in recompense. Parmenio was undamaged. Girolamo had taken a blow to the head that had produced a sizeable blood flow but seemed to have left him with both life and wits intact.

Around them the camp of the lord of Orvieto was jubilant. Not a shot had been fired and the majority of the army had remained in position and watched the castle fall without a major engagement. A few people slapped them on the shoulders in appreciation as they passed, and Skiouros found it difficult not to feel smugly proud of their achievement. He tried – and failed – not to think of the figure of Vicenzo trampled into the mess by the enemy, his unseeing eyes failing to comprehend the thoroughness of their victory.

Ahead, the striped blue and white pavilion of Orvieto loomed ever closer, and as they passed the last of the military units, they moved between groups of officers and knights who were struggling with the effort of eyeing them with distaste while still smiling their congratulations.

Cinozza said something to the guard at the pavilion, and they were granted entrance, though a small group of serfs attended to collect their weapons before they entered the presence of the army's commander. Skiouros baulked for a moment at letting go of his macana, but a meaningful glance from Parmenio made him hand it over.

Inside, oddly, the light was dim but the air warmer, courtesy of the braziers burning at strategic positions. The huge tent was subdivided into rooms, but this – the audience chamber – was the largest, decorated with hanging banners displaying the arms of the lord of Orvieto, of Pope Alexander the Sixth, and of numerous other smaller nobles in command of sections of the army. A large table sat at the far end of the room, behind which Orvieto lounged on his wooden throne, padded with velvet cushions.

'Cinozza,' the lord greeted them with a condescending slow clap of the hands. 'Well done. Your men are to be congratulated. Such an easy victory. I shall see to it that appropriate reward is made when we settle in tonight and I discuss the nature of fealty with the dog of Roccabruna.'

The captain bowed his head.

In the brief silence that followed, Skiouros took the opportunity to look around the tent. Perhaps half a dozen noblemen, well-dressed for court life, stood watching them, as well as two men in cardinal's crimson and others bearing the arms of the Papal court. Two ladies in the finest gowns seated with a hound between them were watching the muscles leaping around in Helwyg's arm with something akin to naked lust.

Parmenio and Nicolo stepped back slightly, clearly feeling uncomfortable, and joined Skiouros and the others, leaving the two officers out front.

'And Orsini,' the lord of Orvieto smiled a lizard-like smile. Cesare had disarmed and removed his helmet, but was still in his near-priceless black and gold armour, liberally spattered with gore.

'My lord.'

'Orsini, you are to be commended. Such daring and brazen heroism, heedless of danger. Bravo, sir, bravo.'

Cesare nodded his head in acceptance of the praise. The lord briefly allowed his gaze to play across the rest of them but discarding them as unimportant he returned his attention to Cesare. 'I am beginning to regret agreeing to such a short contract. I was seeking men only for this brief campaign, but I have the feeling that you would do well permanently attached to my house.'

Cesare smiled. 'My thanks, my lord. But we are bound for more southern climes. I have a mind to visit the eternal city. It has been many years, and Rome was ever a place for a clever man to make a pretty packet.'

Orvieto laughed, but Skiouros noted the frowns of the cardinals at the idea of another Orsini in the city. 'Well I shall be sorry to see you go. And when you return to the mountains, seek me out if you wish for a lucrative contract.'

Again, Cesare bowed his head. 'Thank you, my lord. Might I risk a little impertinence?'

Orvieto furrowed his brows but motioned for Cesare to speak.

'Well, my lord, our pay is generous, of course, but we would be most grateful for a word of reference from a man of your standing. It would grease the wheels of the bureaucracy and might secure us a better contract in Rome.'

Orvieto's frown deepened as he fought with himself. These men were good, but could he be placing his own reputation on the line supporting them?

Though Cesare and Cinozza were apparently unaware of it, Skiouros noted a curious moment, as the lord of Orvieto glanced across at one of the cardinals – a man with a neatly trimmed black beard and flowing mane poking out from beneath his crimson hat – almost as if seeking approval. Skiouros' impression was proved right a heartbeat later as the cardinal gave Orvieto a nod of assent. His lordship turned back to the captains.

'Very well. Agreed. In return for your outstanding service today I shall give you a letter of recommendation that you may present to your prospective employers in Rome. And I shall grant you early release from your contract. I see no reason for you to spend your remaining week travelling with us when your destiny may lie elsewhere. Now come. I wish to hear more of your fight, gentlemen.'

Cinozza and Cesare stepped forward to where a serf brought them seats and set them up across the table from Orvieto. The rest stood in uncomfortable silence as the pavilion's other occupants watched them warily – with the exception of the Silesian giant. Helwyg was grinning at the two noblewomen and dropping into muscular poses, much to the disgust of a nearby nobleman. The ladies giggled and then retreated behind fans as they laughed.

Skiouros, aware the common soldiery were no longer truly involved and were simply waiting to be dismissed, leaned closer to Parmenio and whispered in Greek, 'Did you see him look to the cardinal for permission?'

Parmenio leaned in to reply but before he could, a voice from the side of the tent called out in a sing-song voice in perfect Greek. 'A fellow child of Achaea? Good Lord, how astounding?'

Skiouros glanced around in surprise to see a nobleman, immaculately attired in white and grey, step away from the small group with whom he had been standing. It hadn't struck Skiouros before as he'd initially dismissed the man as yet another nobleman, but his black curly hair, olive complexion and stubble gave him an unmistakably Greek appearance.

'And from the accent, a man of Thrace, yes? Perhaps of Byzantium?'

Skiouros felt a momentarily thrill of panic. His origins had remained unspoken, though for no good reason, really. He could hardly imagine the heritage of a mercenary soldier would raise even slight comment from the nobles of Italy. But this man was now stepping out towards him. The truth. Skipping certain facts, it was always easier to tell a version of the truth than to manufacture a lie.

'Born of Hadrianopolis, my lord.' He bowed as well as he could manage and was rewarded with a broad smile. As he straightened, Skiouros was aware that the rest of the pavilion had fallen silent and now every eye was on him. He felt that thrill of fear again.

'Will you do the honours, Orvieto?' enquired the Greek noble, with a lazy wave of his hand.

Orvieto, clearly irritated at the interruption, and with a look of almost murderous contempt at the new speaker, cleared his throat.

'Allow me to introduce his Imperial Majesty Andreas Palaeologos, true Emperor of Constantinople and Despot of the Morea.'

Skiouros blinked as he peered at the short, swarthy man with a pronounced nose and a gently-curved, almost feminine jaw.

'I know,' smiled Andreas, sketching a brief bow. 'A grand title for a small man. Emperor of a land and despot of a region both held by the Turk. I am a ruler *in absentia*. He gave a light, carefree giggle. 'Sadly, "in absentia" of money as well as lands. You are from Hadrianopolis? I feel I should be honoured. You are the first of my titular subjects I have ever met!'

Skiouros felt distinctly uncomfortable and smiled weakly.

'With the permission of the Lord Orvieto I will withdraw and enjoy the brief company of a countryman.' He nodded at Cesare. 'And with the permission of his commander, of course.'

Skiouros found himself hoping Cesare would object, but to his irritation his friend simply smiled and nodded. 'Be my guest, Your Majesty. If you would be so good as to return him by mealtime so that he can scrub the pots.'

Skiouros tried to aim a poisonous look at Cesare but his friend had already turned back to continue recounting his tale to the lord of Orvieto. Skiouros followed the beckoning finger of Andreas Palaeologos, trying not to think too hard on the fact that he was here in the man's presence when, had the walls of Byzantium held against the conqueror Mehmet four decades ago, this man would now be his emperor, living in the glorious palaces of Istanbul. The very fact that he could come so far from home by such curious routes and find himself face to face with this man was, to him, proof not only that God existed in some form, but also that He liked a good laugh as much as anyone.

As he considered the situation, stepping through into another room, he began to warm to the man. His initial panic had been the cause of his recalcitrance. But Andreas Palaeologos was to be pitied at the very least. He had been born to the last Imperial line of the Roman world. He was an echo of the power that had built Istanbul... the last echo of a fading call, admittedly, but he should be pitied... No, he should be *sympathised with* rather than pitied. He was every bit the exile and in no greater position in the world than Skiouros, for all his titles.

'Your Majesty?' he began as the tent flap fell back behind them, but Andreas motioned him to silence. 'I fear such a title is more burdensome than it is use. If you must stand on ceremony, then 'my lord' will do. But I am equally happy with Andreas. It is not as though the world is leaping to address me in *any* manner.'

Skiouros smiled uneasily.

'Thank you my lord... Andreas. If it is not a matter of extreme impertinence, could I ask what brings my emperor to the siege of Roccabruna? It is a coincidence I find difficult to wrap my wits around.'

Palaeologos chuckled. 'I can imagine. Not for me, though. My life has been a constant dance from one disaster to the next and coincidences are things to grab onto in the swirling eddies of fate.'

Skiouros couldn't help but laugh. It was as if the exiled emperor had described his own life.

'Anyway,' Andreas heaved in a breath, 'I have been residing at the court of the delightful Pope Alexander and his even more delightful daughter for some time. My sponsor – Bishop Lando of Crete – is attempting to persuade His Holiness to announce a great crusade to retake Constantinople, though His Holiness is reluctant to commit to such an action, and instead treats with the Turk. Lando is the Latin Patriarch of Constantinople, you see, and I believe it irks him intensely being the patriarch of a city that worships Mohammed.'

Skiouros shook his head. This was all earth-shaking news to him. A crusade? To remove the Ottoman Empire from Constantinople? It sounded too farfetched. It was surely impossible? The Turk now covered most of the Balkan region. No Pope had the strength to do such a thing. No wonder His Holiness was reluctant!

Somewhere deep inside Skiouros, a nugget of something hardened in his soul. His memory of Bayezid the Second. "The Just" they called him. For all Skiouros' Greek origin and the Sultan's Turkish nature, all the events that had turned Skiouros' life upside down these past years had been born of his belief in the justness of Bayezid. His father had called Bayezid the only good thing about the Ottoman world.

He remembered everything Cesare had said about the warring nobility of Italy, about the dreadful immoral behaviour of the Popes and the political games they played while paying scant regard to the religion they claimed to lead. Could such a thing be allowed? *Should* such a thing be allowed?

And yet sitting opposite him was the man whose right it was to rule where Bayezid now commanded. Never had Skiouros felt more conflicted. But regardless of Andreas' claim, if it came to a choice between the Papacy and Bayezid, Skiouros felt a strange pride that he knew heart-deep where his loyalty would lie.

And it was not with this Spanish Pope who had bastard children and had bribed and cheated his way to power.

Sorry, Andreas.

'So,' the exiled emperor grinned, dragging Skiouros from his troubled reverie, 'Lando and the Pope have decided that if the time might come when I sit on the throne of Byzantium once more, then I need to be a leader of the *crusading* type. A Richard of England, or a Godfrey of Bouillon. Lando feels that I need to be considerably more martially minded if I am to play the role he has in mind. I am, quite frankly, as martially minded as my horse, who has an uncommon affection for flowers and tends to fall asleep if he's not actually walking. But I am reliant upon Lando's patronage and the Pope's hospitality, and so I am here to observe an army sitting in idleness, scratching their backsides, while one of my own countrymen takes the castle for them. I am not sure precisely what lesson His Holiness is expecting me to learn from this outing, but it seems unlikely that it is the one that I am actually learning.'

Skiouros couldn't help but laugh again, and Andreas grinned an easy grin.

'What is the city like… I'm sorry, I don't know your name?'

'Skiouros, son of Nikos the farmer, my lord.'

'Well met, Skiouros, son of Nikos the farmer. I am Andreas, son of Thomas the despot.' He grinned. 'Tell me of my city?'

Skiouros sighed. 'To be honest, I do not know where to start, Majesty. It is the greatest city on earth. Nowhere compares. And for all you might have heard of the Turk, I would be lying if I said they had ruined the place. They have embellished its grace and beauty with their own stamp. It is heartbreaking in its glory.'

Andreas sighed sadly. 'I may never see it. Even if the crusade goes ahead and succeeds – which is unlikely, given the Pope's reluctance – the Morea may be my true destiny. But I would have liked to walk the lands of my father. God willing, I shall do so one day.'

The 'emperor' paused, his head cocking to one side. 'I hear Orvieto winding to a close. He is nothing if not predictable.' He chuckled. 'And dull, too. We should return to the meeting. But I wish we had had time to talk of my lands. Perhaps there will be another opportunity. Did your captain say he was bound for Rome?'

'Indeed, my lord.'

'Then when you are in Rome, seek me out if you can. I reside in the Vatican apartments.'

Skiouros' heart leapt momentarily.

'If His Holiness were not so strict on his security around his other *guest*, I would introduce you to another exiled countryman who resides in the complex. The exiled sultan and I have much in common, particularly given that neither of us has ever seen Constantinople!'

Andreas chuckled again and gestured to the tent flap.

'You are friends with the Ottoman pretender?' Skiouros had tried to hold the words in, but they tumbled from his lips as they moved back towards Orvieto's audience room.

'Oh I know we are enemies by heritage,' Andreas laughed, 'but we are brothers in exile. Necessity makes strange bedfellows eh, Skiouros, son of Nikos?'

63

Skiouros was about to enquire further, but Andreas swept aside the flap and ushered him back into the main room of the tent, where things were clearly finished with. Parmenio and Nicolo raised their eyebrows questioningly at him, and Cesare was bowing to the lord of Orvieto and turning to leave. 'Ah... Skiouros, good. I have a mind to veal for tonight's meal. I wonder whether you could run a few of your thoughts on recipes by me?'

Stepping ahead of the others, with a nod of respect to Andreas, Cesare made his way out of the tent. The officers gathered outside had dispersed and Cesare led his men by a roundabout route to their camp, waiting until they were out of earshot of all but the lowest soldiery before clearing his throat.

'I am interested to hear what transpired between you and your emperor?' He smiled at Skiouros. 'But first, I will update you on some urgent matters.' Looking around to be certain they were not overheard, Cesare stopped and placed both armoured hands on Skiouros' shoulders. 'My friend, the word is that Charles of France has a vast army massing on the northern borders, ready to move into Italy. Orvieto tells me that King Ferrante of Napoli has passed away, and that leaves us with the usual Neapolitan struggle for succession. The Spanish will be supporting their claim, hoping to bolster their ever-expanding empire. Ferrante's own line will claim their right, but will need Papal support, and whether a Spanish Pope will give it to them is yet to be seen. And Charles of France is ready to ravage Italy on his way to conquer the place.'

'The French have a claim?' frowned Skiouros.

Cesare nodded. 'Not a particularly outlandish one, either. As good as anyone else's. Orvieto tells me that His Holiness busies himself with communiques, trying to talk the French out of war, but if Charles has his mind set on conquest nothing short of the hand of God will stop him. The French ever love a fight.'

'This country is almost as dangerous as Spain,' Skiouros sighed.

'When you've been here a little longer,' Cesare grinned, 'you'll realise that it's *far* more dangerous than Spain!' He straightened. 'Anyway, Orvieto recommends we move to Napoli. Work will be abundant there, with the threat of invasion.'

Skiouros shook his head, but Orsini simply laughed. 'I know. Rome. Be content. We shall leave for Rome as soon as possible, though I would like to visit a few family holdings on the way. Given the letter of recommendation I will collect in the morning, we will be able to secure a good position in Vatican circles. All is progressing as we'd hoped, my friend.'

Skiouros stood, shaking his head – not in disagreement, but to clear it of the fluff of uncertainty. He took a deep breath.

'Now let me tell you what *I* learned…'

CHAPTER FOUR - Siena, April 1494

Skiouros dropped his saddle bags next to the table and slumped into one of the seats. Somehow, while he was busy finishing up with the groom and settling their mounts for the night, Cesare and Parmenio between them had managed to secure a table large enough to seat eight in a tavern room that was already packed to the gills with locals. Without prying, the Greek sighed and took the weight off his feet.

They were still only halfway to Rome, despite having already travelled for more than three weeks, due to the strange, zig-zagging tortuous route that Orsini had selected in order to pay a visit to numerous holdings of his family as they passed.

As he stretched, the zemi figure on its leather thong caught in an uncomfortable position and dug into his collarbone. Leaning forward again, Skiouros fished out the figurine and peered at it. Maquetaurie Guayaba – lord of the land of the dead. He who ruled over Lykaion's restless spirit and would continue to do so when he was finally laid to rest. Months had passed since last Lykaion's shade had come to him, with words like a silent breath from the otherworld. He shivered involuntarily and tucked the zemi back in a more secure position.

'You really ought to take that off,' Nicolo grimaced from the far side of the table.

'It is a reminder for me. And of personal value.'

'It's pagan idolatry, and while I don't give an Arab's fart-flap whether you get struck down for blasphemy, I don't like the idea of being around you when it happens.'

Orsini shrugged. 'I see no problems with it, but Nicolo is right to be cautious. We are bound for the bastion of God's church on Earth – and the home of the Inquisition – so it might be a good idea to keep it well covered.' He smiled with a twinkle in his eye. 'Oh and when you drop something or trip, try not to call up to Heaven in Arabic. That's not going to make you many friends where we're going!'

Skiouros frowned. 'I don't...'

'Yes you do. Under your breath, admittedly – but if I can hear it, then so can others.'

Skiouros nodded. If he ever managed to return to his homeland, it would be a curious relief. In Istanbul you could call upon Allah and his prophet, or beg the aid of Christ – or even of Jehovah – without fearing a session in a dark room with some men in black that would leave you a foot taller. What was it about the western church that made it so rabidly self-important and unforgiving?

Parmenio arrived at the table once more with Helwyg at his side, carrying a tray of glasses and mugs. Girolamo made a space for the drinks and everyone sat down with relief.

'I for one don't understand how you can have any time for the heathen faith, let alone such idolatry,' muttered Girolamo, gesturing at the thong around Skiouros' neck. 'The latter's clearly pagan witchcraft, and the former... well, you're talking about a people who *enslaved your own*.'

Skiouros pursed his lips. Girolamo was less fervent about his church than many Italians, but Skiouros' openness of faith clearly unsettled him. He was a man to play cautiously around on the subject of religion.

'No insult is intended to your own beliefs, Girolamo, but I have, on balanced reflection, found a lot more acceptance of the Church among the Turk than I have of Islam among the Christian. But I may be viewing the matter from a strange angle. After all, my faith is that of the Eastern Church, and not founded in Rome. Perhaps the Sultan and his people are less accepting of your church than of mine?'

'But we are all Christian,' Girolamo pressed, 'while the Turk are deniers of Christ's divinity. Surely you would call *us* brother before *them*?'

Skiouros glanced around at the table, well aware that this sort of discussion could very easily erupt into more violent disagreement. He had expected, even hoped, that the others would step in and defuse the matter, particularly Orsini who was ostensibly their commander now. Instead, all eyes were flashing back and forth between the two speakers with interest. Cesare in particular had a frown of concentration. Skiouros sighed and took a sip of the drink Helwyg had placed before him.

'My faith is no simple matter, Girolamo. I have met and spoken with Muslims, Jews, pagans, and Christians of both faiths, and for all their differences the one thing that they all have in common is that they are men. Good men and bad men. Pious men and evil men. Fallible and complex, they are just men. Whatever name they give to God, they are either good and have his ear, or bad and have the Devil's. In the heart of the Maghreb live tribes who have no difficulty melding their own beliefs with the teachings of Mohammed. If pagans can manage such a fusion, why cannot we who at least acknowledge the same God?'

Girolamo shifted uncomfortably. 'Hardly the *same* God,' he muttered.

'Pshhh,' hissed Nicolo and inclined his head toward the door. The others turned and glanced across to see another party enter the inn, travel-worn and bearing saddlebags. A small group of guards in drab travel clothes and bearing no noble's livery accompanied a man in a voluminous cloak with a deep cowl. Skiouros was about to question Nicolo's silencing of them when he spotted the red robe between the shifting folds of the cloak. The table's occupants turned back to one another, judiciously ignoring the new arrival and initiating small-talk, though their privacy seemed to be at an end since the cardinal's companions strode across to a table by the fire, which happened to be next to the one the friends occupied. As the cardinal's guards approached the table, the old local seated there and warming his bones rose and vacated, leaving his cup half full and making his way to the bar. It appeared that even this far from Rome, the crimson robe commanded plenty of respect and fear.

As the guards cleared off the table and repositioned it, dusting down the chair, the cardinal removed his travelling cloak, revealing a spotless robe of red and a pale, aquiline face that, from the lines upon it, had likely not seen a smile in a number of years.

Orsini nodded encouragingly at his friends as he rose and gave a small half-bow to the cardinal who looked up, apparently unimpressed.

'Good day, Your Eminence,' Cesare smiled. 'Allow me to introduce myself: I am Cesare of the house Orsini, condottiere and lord of Carloto. I hope the evening finds you well?'

'The evening finds me abhorrent, uncomfortable and more than a little put out, thank you.'

'Perhaps I could buy you a glass of wine and help temper your woes?'

'Thank you, no,' responded the cardinal, removing his scarlet gloves and rubbing his hands vigorously. 'Never trust the muck in a common inn. I will partake of water, and even then only that which we have carried with us from the aqueduct basins of Rome.' Skiouros tried to catch Cesare's eye, but the nobleman was paying close attention to the cardinal alone.

'It is a strange time for a member of the Sacred College to be travelling north? Mayhap you are bound for King Charles with letters from His Holiness?'

The cardinal narrowed his eyes suspiciously and Cesare gave an easy smile and shrugged. 'We have been in service to the Papal forces of the lord of Orvieto. Word abounds of the French army hovering at our northern borders like a bird of prey watching a hedgerow, and of the Pope's attempts to divert His Majesty from his current course.'

'Pah!' snapped the cardinal as he held out his hand and one of his lackeys placed a glass in it, uncorking an earthenware jar and filling the vessel with crystal clear water. 'His *Holiness*,' – Skiouros could hardly fail to notice the dripping contempt with which the cardinal infused the title – 'is bound on a course of self-destruction and is determined to topple the throne of Saint Peter. You are bound for Rome?'

Cesare nodded. 'We are seeking a contract with the Papal forces.'

'Then you are clearly mad. The Pope has agreed against all my urging to confer the crown of Napoli upon the young prince Alphonso, the fool.'

Skiouros frowned. 'Is he not the legitimate heir of the king, Your Eminence?'

Shock rang through his system as Cesare reached across the table and gave him a ringing slap across the cheek, causing him to bite into his lip.

'Forgive my insolent men, Eminence,' Orsini asked the cardinal quietly. 'This one is newly arrived from the east and has much to learn of good manners.'

The cardinal gave Skiouros a look that contained mostly scorn, sewn with a little superiority. 'He will probably go far in the Rome of Alexander the Sixth! Where was I? Ah yes. Well with that quasi-Spanish runt on the Neapolitan throne, there is no longer any doubt that the French will march on Napoli and, given the insult of being denied the crown, there is every likelihood that Charles of Valois will pause on his journey long enough to flatten Rome and everything in it. Had His Holiness gifted Charles with the Neapolitan throne, we would have an ally in France.'

'And an enemy in Spain,' noted Cesare with a frown.

'Spain is no concern,' dismissed the cardinal with a wave of his free hand. 'They are busy with their new lands and with rooting out heresy. They are too reliant on the Pope's continued goodwill to make trouble. But the French…'

He sighed. 'So in truth, the answer to your question is yes: I am bound for Genoa and then the French King, though not with letters of peace and conciliation. I go to try and keep the homicidal lunatic from destroying the throne of Saint Peter in his passing. To attempt to limit the damage the Borgia Pope has done to our standing.'

Cesare, giving a meaningful look to Skiouros, who was wiping the blood from his lip, leaned closer to the cardinal.

'Surely, Your Eminence, even the warlike French would not make a direct enemy of the Pope? To sack Rome is unthinkable for a Christian monarch, whatever His Holiness might do?'

'How little you seem to know the French, Orsini. And even less, the Pope. The French King could be the saviour of Christendom if matters were played correctly. His Majesty intends a crusade to recover the east. He marches on Napoli and will use it as his staging post when he takes sword and fire to the heathen. Had His Holiness given the crown and that Turkish sack of faeces to Charles, the French would settle for Vatican blessings, use the pretender prince as a pretext for war, and march on the Turk.'

Skiouros' eyes widened and Cesare flashed him a dangerous warning look.

'The exiled Ottoman prince?' the young nobleman asked of the cleric.

'Yes,' the cardinal spat. 'The French King would hold him up as a banner and march on Constantinople, waving him in the face of Bayezid the demon-Sultan. But His Holiness has a *liking* for this heathen. Indeed, for *all* heathens, it would seem. While he mutters of a potential Holy crusade, instead he treats with the Turk. The Sultan has had ambassadors in our court for months. In defiance of all that is legal and holy, the Borgia monster even invites the Turk to the Neapolitan coronation! Can you imagine?'

Skiouros was almost trembling now with the difficulty of keeping himself uninvolved in this debate. He chewed on his bloody lip as the cardinal resumed.

'So now Charles will march on Napoli and he will crush Rome on the way – if not for the Pope's insult, then to take the exiled prince for his own.' He turned a sickened face on the rest of the group. 'If you seek a contract, try Napoli. They will shortly be needing men desperately, I fear. Better still, come north and sign with the French if it is victory you seek. If you make for Rome, you march into the arena and wait for the lion of Valois to savage you.'

'Such a war would pay well, Your Eminence,' Cesare shrugged, 'and better to fight for the vicar of Rome than for the French.'

'Then I wish you all the gold, blood and death you could hope for, Orsini, and I am certain you will find it.' The cardinal turned to the man next to him who was trying to pour more water into the glass. 'Be still, you imbecile! I have warmed sufficiently and have no interest in staying in this nest of filth and rats any longer. I will retire to my chamber. Have my food cooked, tested, tasted and then sent up.'

As the cardinal rose from the table, acknowledging the mercenaries with a faint nod of his head, Orsini stood and bowed in return. The rest of the cardinal's entourage scattered like leaves in a strong wind, rushing to their tasks in an effort to keep the cantankerous cleric content. As soon as they were gone from earshot, Cesare leaned forward.

'Try not to be so outspoken, Skiouros. Remember that Italy is a place of complex manners and etiquette. Apologies for the blow, but courtesy demanded it.'

Skiouros nodded his understanding, but his eyes were angry and cold. 'Our task just became far more difficult, though, didn't it?'

'How so?' Cesare sat back.

Skiouros looked around to check they were not being observed too closely and leaned forward, talking in a low tone. 'Well it was a difficult enough proposition gaining access to a prisoner in the Vatican in the first place. Then I discover he is being guarded by the Knights Hospitaller, which complicates matters. Now we learn that Sultan Bayezid has emissaries in the Papal court and that, to top it all, the King of France is bound for Rome to snatch Prince Cem and remove him from my grasp, probably forever!'

'I will grant you that things seem more difficult in a surface appraisal,' smiled Cesare. 'But what appears to be a setback could instead be an opportunity. If the French intend to take Cem from the

Pope, then he will be drawn from the tight protection of the Vatican and may, consequently, actually be easier to reach.'

Skiouros frowned at the idea. 'I suppose that's possible. But whether the King takes Cem or not, I think we need to reach Rome quickly and secure our position.'

Orsini smiled. 'No more dawdling, you mean? No more dropping in on distant relatives? Straight for Rome?' He pulled an offended face and Skiouros rolled his eyes. 'You are correct, of course,' Cesare laughed. 'We must ride for Rome in the morning and seek out a good contract. I estimate a journey of five more days if we do not delay.'

Skiouros nodded, satisfied, wondering how long it would take a massive French army to travel half the length of Italy and knock at the Pope's door.

Patience, he reminded himself. Everything in its time.

CHAPTER FIVE - Rome, May 1494

'I have to admit,' Skiouros noted wearily as Sigma clumped heavily down the flagged road beside Cesare's horse and at the head of the group, 'despite the danger and responsibility of what we're here for, I am rather looking forward to seeing Rome.'

'It is a great city full of marvels and glories and hope and beauty,' replied Cesare, peering off into the distance ahead. 'But do not let that fool you. It is also a stinking cesspit of whoring, villains, corruption and decay.'

Skiouros tried not to be too disheartened by his friend's words. Brightly, he replied: 'I hail from the second greatest city of the ancient world. Constantinople was the capital of a great empire for centuries, and yet Rome was its predecessor. A man cannot help but be impressed by that!'

'Wait 'til you have the flux and the pox and are having to defecate in an alley while a local cutpurse takes everything you own. Rome is not a place for the innocent.'

'Then it's a good job I'm no innocent.'

Cesare gave him a look that suggested otherwise and gestured ahead. The Via Nomentana climbed a long low slope to the edge of the city, and Skiouros could just make out the blur of the urban sprawl, but this area was still extremely rural, all rolling fields and vineyards and small orchards and streams. It was hard to believe they were as close to the greatest city in the world as Cesare suggested. Then Skiouros' eyes picked out what his friend was indicating: not the city on the distant crest of the slope, but a complex of buildings just ahead of them, on a small rise of their own.

'Now, I know I'm a stranger here, but that's not the Vatican.'

'Correct, my friend. That is the church of Sant'Agnese with its monastery and lands, and *that* is our current destination.'

Skiouros threw a questioning look at Cesare. 'We're not going into the city?'

'Not yet. All in good time, my friend. First we have to prepare ourselves lest we walk into unexpected trouble. I said I had an acquaintance in Rome: my former teacher and confessor?'

'Yes, but we're not *in* Rome.'

'Figure of speech,' shrugged Cesare. 'For now we are at our safest outside the walls until we are certain of the situation in the city. Possibly even then it would better suit our purposes to continue to base ourselves on the city's extreme periphery. Come on.'

Skiouros tried to hide his irritation at having such an important decision made for him without any input on his part and focussed on the complex for which they were bound. Every step Sigma took brought it into better focus.

A heavy, rectangular church of modest size – with a brick exterior that was far plainer and more austere than its equivalents in Istanbul – stood on the near edge of the rise, the ground sloping away before it and to their right. A rocky cliff face torn from the fabric of the hill itself extended a little to the right down the slope, appearing bare of vegetation. Behind, slightly higher on the crest, stood a circular structure that dominated the ensemble, which was completed by a ruined wall of impressive size striding across the hill. As they closed on it, Skiouros could see a collection of other buildings on the far side of the main church, almost connecting it to the rotonda. He found himself thinking that if a man were to add some towers to the surrounding walls it would be as well equipped for defence as many smaller castles he had seen.

As they approached, Skiouros became aware of figures in black robes among the gardens and fields and orchards around the complex, stoop-backed in their work.

Ignoring the church itself, which failed to present a door facing them, Skiouros followed Cesare's lead to a wide archway that led beneath a squat tower some centuries old, riddled with reused ancient stonework. The door to the complex was open but Cesare reined in before it and slid from his horse, wandering across to the bell whose chain dangled by the arch's pier. Somewhat redundantly the nobleman yanked the pull, allowing the bell to clang half a dozen times, the visitors watched intently by black robed figures both inside the gate and out.

Finally, a particularly old specimen with a straggly beard and bushy grey brows that almost hid his eyes wandered over to the gate and acknowledged them with a look born of curiosity and suspicion, and a faint nod of the head.

'Can I help you, my son?'

Cesare sketched a perfect bow and smiled disarmingly. 'Greetings, venerable father. We are seeking Canon Bartolomeo of Nerola. Would you be so good as to have word sent to him that Cesare Orsini is at the gate?'

The old man's brows beetled and his lip did some sort of dance as he mouthed words to himself and finally nodded in answer to his own question.

'Come,' he grunted and turned, walking off across the courtyard beyond the gate, muttering inaudibly to himself. Cesare looked at Skiouros and shrugged. 'He probably doesn't mean for us to bring the horses.' With a smile, he gestured to the hitching rail by the gate and strode across, tying his own beast's reins to the wooden post and then hurrying to catch up with the old priest who was now waiting impatiently at the far side of the courtyard. Skiouros followed suit and rushed across, Parmenio and Nicolo tying up their horses and then jogging to catch up. Helwyg and Girolamo waved them on, staying with the mounts and keeping a watchful eye on the gathered priests as though they might suddenly throw aside their robes and steal the nags at sword point. Skiouros wondered what sort of place Rome was to elicit such caution.

The old priest led them across the courtyard and past fragments of ancient stone being reused as garden ornaments, the names of long gone senators and generals etched across planters filled with greenery and surmounted by delicate statuary. Beyond them, past a line of shrubs and cypresses, stood the ruined wall Skiouros had seen as they approached. Up close it was rather impressive, some hundred yards long to the far end, where it turned into an apse that stood proud at the top of the slope. The wall was easily the height of three men and enclosed an elongated garden formed of rows of shattered columns jabbing up to the blue sky and areas of coloured marble flooring all interspersed with flower beds, shrubbery arrangements, ancient trees and sections of low wall, dotted with classical statuary that had been placed in artistic positions. The great circular rotonda stood to one side, its doors firmly closed, exuding a powerful and ancient brooding presence.

The old man led them along a pleasant gravel path which ran beneath the ruined wall and paused at a statue of a naked hero thrusting a blade at a bull-headed demon.

'There!' grumbled the old man, pointing at the apsidal end, where a white marble bench stood amid the trees. Two figures in black sat upon the bench and Cesare nodded his thanks before leaving the old man and striding across the gravel towards the pair.

Skiouros, Parmenio and Nicolo wandered along just behind their friend, keeping respectably subdued. As they approached, it became clear that the two black-clad clerics were involved in a heated debate of some sort. Both wore the same midnight robes as the rest of the complex's occupants, and both had their heads bare, tonsures in evidence. The left-hand of the pair had pepper-flecked moustaches draped above his lip, his grey hair so wild and windblown that his tonsure was only sporadically visible, displaying skin in flashes as the wind whipped the locks about. The other figure, neatly arrayed with tidy hair and clean-shaven chin and yet giving off the same feel of borderline mania, was busy waving his arms like a flightless bird attempting to break the hold of gravity, speaking easily in Italian but with a strangely unidentifiable thick accent.

'I tell you that silk is no crime against God, Barty. And the gentle lull of swishing fabric makes the very day worthwhile. It is like sweet birdsong to the nethers.'

The grey-haired cleric shook his head in a manner that suggested a father admonishing his son. 'I am not denying the sensory value of good silk braies or their acceptability within the ordinances of the Lateran dogma, my deranged friend. I am simply questioning how a man who is so vocal about his vow of poverty managed to acquire not one, but *two* pairs of such silky blessedness.'

'I have… contacts. What more can I say? You *are* aware that if this conversation comes to the attention of Father Laurentinus we will be flagellating ourselves 'til our backs are salmon-hued, and said braies will be burned as unacceptable. Laurentinus is a savage in the matter of clothing. I swear the man wears apparel made from old sacks. His cassock is his most giving garment.'

'I also know,' said Grey-hair with an arched eyebrow almost lost beneath the flowing strands of hair, 'that you have some dubious contact within the wine trade and that there are at least three bottles of something of which Father Laurentinus would be most disapproving beneath your cot. A bottle of said beverage in return for my silence over your illicit braies should be an acceptable trade.'

Neat-hair glared at his companion and Cesare was forced to clear his throat to make their presence known.

'Eavesdropping is a wicked habit, young man,' Neat-hair garbled in his strange accent. 'And eavesdropping on blessed sons of the Church could land a man in a whole heap of trouble. The wrath of *God* could be unleashed!'

'Or the wrath of Alba, anyway,' grinned Grey-hair, settling his gaze on Cesare. 'Young Orsini, in the living flesh. You once told me that wild horses and a cart full of demons could not drag you to this city. Has the change in our Holy Father so readily eased your fears?'

Cesare smiled. 'It is a matter of priorities, Father Bartholomew. Without wishing to sound rude or impolitic, we have matters of a delicate nature to discuss. Perhaps we could find somewhere private?'

The neater-haired of the two canons looked at his companion, and Father Bartholomew simply shrugged. 'There is nowhere in the monastery more secluded than this garden during the heat of the day, and even given the nature of the business upon which I suspect you have come, you will find my friend Father Alexander here quite safe to speak in front of. He and I are partners in ecclesiastical crime, so to speak.' He rolled his eyes. '*Silk braies* indeed!'

The nobleman studied the other cleric for a long moment and then bowed at the waist.

'Cesare Orsini, once the student of this fine man of God. Might I ask as to your place of origin, Father? I cannot place your accent and it most assuredly is not Italian.'

Neat-hair slapped his hands on his knees in a business-like fashion. 'Young man, I am Father Alexander, formerly of clan Keith, from the holding of Dunottar in distant Scotland.'

'A pleasure to make your acquaintance, Father Alexander. If Bartholomew here trusts you then I would be advised to follow suit.' He turned to his old confessor. 'Father, I am here with my companions – a notable lance of condottieri – regarding matters upon which we have corresponded this past year.'

Skiouros watched the eyes of the two priests with interest, given the circumspect nature of Cesare's words. A guarded acknowledgement arose in Bartholomew's. Oddly, Father Alexander's eyes also betrayed neither surprise nor interest. Either he could not care less, or he was already party to the matter.

'The pretender sultan,' sighed Bartholomew. Skiouros watched the other priest intently. His gaze did not even flicker. *He knew, then.* Cesare seemed to have reached the same conclusion, simply raising his eyebrow questioningly at the second cleric. Father Alexander smiled. 'We are brothers of the soul, young man. We share everything.'

'Except wine and silk braies,' retorted Bartholomew with a meaningful look.

'It would be unseemly and perhaps physically difficult for us to share braies, brother. As for the wine, the coming evening will tell.' The second priest smiled at Cesare. 'I cannot pretend to understand your interest in the Turkish prisoner, but I am as guilty of making a discreet enquiry on your behalf as Barty is.'

Parmenio and Nicolo both wore expressions that revealed their own misgivings over the involvement of an unknown, but all four of them were aware that the deed had already been done and the matter shared. Whether they liked it or not, Father Alexander was party to the affair.

'Firstly, Fathers, we are newly arrived and I do not wish to become embroiled in the city until we are thoroughly prepared. I wondered whether you had any suggestions of a good place for the four of us and our two friends at the gate to reside until we are ready? As you know it has been many years since I was here, and my friends are all new to Rome.'

The two clerics looked at one another and shrugged. 'I will speak on your behalf with Father Laurentinus. We shall secure you a place in the guest house. With the way things are at the moment, pilgrimages here are at a low ebb, and there are rarely more than two or three visitors. There will be plenty of room for all six of you there for the foreseeable future.'

Skiouros glanced back uncomfortably at the church. Memories of the chanting monks on the docks in Spain and of heretics hanging in cages and on gibbets all across that land leapt into his head. 'Perhaps somewhere more secular might be advisable?' he nudged Orsini subtly.

'Nonsense,' grinned Father Bartholomew. 'We have the room, the comforts, the anonymity and the aid that you require. You need not fear for yourself, young man. I will offer my hand and my protection as far as it will reach. So putting aside the matter of accommodation, what else is on your mind, young Orsini? I cannot believe you sought me out for hostelry advice?'

'Naturally, Father. Could I enquire as to the latest on Prince Cem's situation? We have heard some interesting rumours regarding him and the intentions of the King of France.'

Father Bartholomew folded his arms and leaned back on the bench, crossing his legs. 'Little has changed in that regard, Cesare. For all the talk of King Charles marching on Rome to take the Turk into custody, His Holiness continues to hold Cem in the Vatican, allowing him the lifestyle of a courtier.' It struck Skiouros as he watched the cleric's face that Father Bartholomew was a man given to good nature and humour and was almost perilously open and accommodating, and yet something dark and dangerous flashed into his eyes at the mere mention of the Turk.

'Courtiers are not hard to get to,' Parmenio said quietly. 'Easier than prisoners, anyway.'

The Father shook his head. 'Merely gaining *access* to the Vatican is troublesome these days. Noblemen and mercenaries such as yourselves have more chance of rising through the air on a strong gust of wind than walking the hallowed corridors of the apostolic palace. With so many cardinals and churchmen setting themselves against His Holiness, only those of us in the cloth who have been approved are given free access.'

Father Keith nodded. 'I myself have only been accorded direct access once since the *Pascha crucifixionis*, and even then I was under the escort of a member of the apostolic camera and two of His Holiness' Catalan guards. And *I* am considered no threat to his papacy.'

Nicolo pursed his lips. 'So security is tight.'

'Always. And even at the occasional social events to which Cem Sultan is invited, he is inevitably surrounded by such a crowd of Hospitaller Knights that he looks like a gaudy bauble amid a congregation of magpies.'

'We *need* access to the pretender sultan, Father Bartholomew,' Cesare urged in low tones.

The priest sighed uncomfortably. 'I am in something of a quandary, my young friend. I wish to help you as much as I can and yet I am hampered by my lack of specific knowledge with regard to your aims.' As Cesare opened his mouth to reply, Bartholomew held up a silencing finger. 'However, I do not wish to know the details, and neither does Alexander here.'

Skiouros saw the momentary flash of disappointment on the other priest's face and almost smiled. Father Alexander clearly *did* wish to know, quite badly.

'Even in these days of bloodshed and chaos in the halls of the blessed, murder is a sin of the deepest foulness and so I choose to believe that you require access to the sultan in order to put a proposal to him. Do not rob me of that. I have no wish to hear your confessions after the darkest of deeds, either.'

Cesare nodded. 'We were planning to secure a contract with the Vatican forces. Though I understand the Pope hires only the stronger of the condottieri and we are but a single lance, we have a glowing letter of recommendation from the lord of Orvieto.'

Father Bartholomew shook his head. 'Forgetting for a moment the fact that the Vatican does not pay its mercenaries well, no matter what you have heard, but relies upon the piety of its hirelings and the prestige they win from the contract, there is one prime reason not to seek such a position.'

Cesare frowned. 'Because of the French?'

'Because of the French. With the impending threat of invasion, His Holiness is indeed increasing his army, and you would likely secure such a contract with ease, but it would send you to war with Charles of France.'

'Frankly,' Nicolo shrugged, 'I am no more afraid of fighting the French than any other man.'

'But,' sighed Cesare, placing his hand on his friend's shoulder, 'the Pope will not wish to fight the French in the halls of the apostolic palace. The Vatican army will deploy in Charles' path, along with every supporting city-state upon which the Pope can call. If we proceed with our plan, rather than achieving access to the Vatican, we will end up lurking in a ditch somewhere in deepest Umbria awaiting the sound of the French cannons. We would, in fact, be moving ever further from our goal rather than towards it.'

Skiouros closed his eyes and kicked angrily at a pebble on the path. 'Damn it!' He ignored the looks of disapproval at his curse from the two clerics. 'Months of planning undone!'

'In fact,' Father Bartholomew sighed, 'I would be happier if you were to leave Rome anyway until this crisis had passed, though perhaps east, away from the coming war. I do not relish the thought of having to write to your father with the bleakest of news.' His eyes flicked up to Skiouros. 'Remember that vengeance is a harsh taskmaster, which as oft destroys the perpetrator as the target.'

'I said something similar to my friend back in Genoa,' Cesare shrugged. 'I am afraid that we must stay and we must act soon. Our business with the sultan will be rather more troublesome if he is whisked away by the French and taken on a holy crusade. If service to the Vatican army will not gain us the access we require, we must needs find another way.'

Father Alexander tapped his lip thoughtfully. 'There might be another way, Barty.'

'Oh? How so?'

'His Holiness is not the only resident of the Vatican with a tendency to hire condottieri…'

Father Bartholomew smiled. 'One of the more martially-minded cardinals? Dubious, though. Many of them are at odds with the Holy Father, and loyalties change every few minutes. Sadly, in the modern church, allegiances may as well be written upon holy water.' He narrowed his eyes. 'You have someone in mind, though?'

'I do. And if he is amenable, it might gain your friends the access they require.'

'You would approach him?'

Father Alexander smiled. 'I have been of service to him in the past, as have you. He will at least listen to my words if not my advice.'

Skiouros shared a look of qualified hope with Cesare and the latter cleared his throat again. 'How would we go about signing on with this man? You would make the introductions?'

Father Bartholomew rose, rubbing his back. 'Leave that to Alexander. I will show you to the guest quarters and get you and your men settled in. You may have a while to wait, so get used to the place and have a bite to eat. We will send to you when there is progress.'

The knock at the door was light and Skiouros almost missed it. Roused from warm slumber, he knuckled his eyes wearily and slid his legs from the bed, preparing to cross the room and awaken Cesare, his roommate in the monastery guest house. His friend was already sitting upright and wincing at the cold of the flagged floor on his bare feet. Nodding to him, Skiouros stepped over to his small table and retrieved his macana stick, hefting it.

Cesare frowned at him and he shrugged. 'Always better to be prepared,' he mouthed in less than a whisper.

As the young nobleman hobbled on cold feet across to the door, Skiouros took up position to one side with his club raised. With a nod to the Greek, Cesare reached up and unlatched the door, swinging it open easily.

'Come with me,' whispered Father Alexander, standing in the corridor outside. Skiouros lowered the wooden weapon and stepped into view.

'Do we have time to put on our boots?'

The priest looked them up and down and nodded. 'Bring your cloaks, too. The nocturnal air has a bite to it tonight.'

Peering briefly past the priest to be sure they were otherwise alone, Skiouros padded across to his bed and hauled his cold boots onto his bare feet, forgoing the hose for speed. Cesare did the same, throwing his travelling cloak over his shoulder and motioning for Skiouros to do so. The nobleman paused for a moment, his hand reaching for his sheathed sword, but decided against it and crossed to the door unarmed. Skiouros retained his grip on the macana and followed the other two out into the corridor. Through the next door he could hear the tell-tale rhythm of Parmenio and Nicolo sleeping, one deep snore and one light and easy, working in perfect counterpoint to mimic the sawing of a log.

'The others?' he asked, gesturing at the door.

Father Alexander shook his head. 'His Eminence is expecting to meet only the condottiere in charge. He may be unhappy even that I brought *two* men.'

For a moment, Skiouros considered returning to the room. After almost a week of languishing in the depths of the Latin countryside among taciturn monks with no news, he was apprehensive about any factor that might upset the situation. Patience was one thing, but enforced inactivity was another entirely.

'Who is this man?' Cesare asked quietly.

'He is a cardinal. I will say no more at this time. Should he show interest in your services, he will tell you himself. If he decides against you, he would not wish his identity known. Truth be told, after speaking to others in the Vatican, I am surprised he agreed to a meeting at all. He must have an extra reason to meet with you, beyond my own recommendation.'

The Greek felt a chill run through him. Who else *knew* of them?

A moment later they were at the door which led out into the gardens and as the cleric opened it, a blast of chilly air slapped across them, making them all shiver, despite their cloaks. Across the cobbled yard he led them, through the garden with its ancient marble fragments and to the great archaic wall that traversed the hill. Finally, he paused in front of the doors to that impressive rotonda that dominated the skyline. Skiouros felt a slight thrill of discovery. So far, in the week they'd been here he had seen little but the monastery's guest house, the gardens and the general living and eating spaces. Throughout that time, he had eyed the looming circular building with interest. 'I trust I can leave you to find your own way back, gentlemen?' the priest asked.

Skiouros frowned. 'You are not coming with us?'

'His Eminence values his privacy and, besides, Barty awaits with a jug full of something illicit and rather intoxicating. I will see you at Prime, or to break your fast if you are not attending services… again,' he added meaningfully and with a touch of admonition.

As Father Alexander returned to the monastery buildings, the two friends stood before the great ancient building and shared a look. 'Shall we?' Cesare smiled.

Skiouros nodded and the pair strode across to the door, testing the handle gingerly and peering into the dim interior nervously as the portal creaked open. The inside was lit only by a single candelabrum at the centre, and the light was nowhere near enough to illuminate more than the basic shape of the place.

As they entered, the young Greek felt a chill that had nothing to do with the temperature this time, as he was struck by the atmosphere of this ancient, austere place in which he could imagine a parliament of ghosts debating his fate. The interior was spacious, an ambulatory corridor running around the edge, separated from the central circle by a ring of delicate twin columns. Though he could not see that high in the gloom, he almost *felt* the mosaics above him telling ancient tales of saints and emperors in the manner of the Byzantine churches back home. What *was* this place? A chapter house? A church?

A tomb?

'Close the door,' ordered a voice from somewhere in the gloom, its accent refined and soft, like silk to the ear. Cesare reached round and did so, removing roughly half the interior's illumination.

'This is a remarkably clandestine environment for discussing the terms of possible employment,' noted Cesare easily.

'I favour anonymity and discretion.'

'Might we have a little more light, lest I fall over a step?'

There was a moment's silence and then the whisper of silk as a man moved on the far side of the room. Skiouros tightened his grip on the macana stick at his side.

'You are one of the *Orsini*.'

Skiouros felt his heart sink at the inflection with which the speaker imbued the name. Perhaps it should have been him coming and Cesare who'd stayed behind.

'I am.'

'My experience with the Orsini has not been overly-favourable. Your family are at best a fractious collection, and Romano Orsini in particular has been something of an obstacle to me recently.'

Cesare smiled in the gloom. 'You are a supporter of the Borgia papacy, then? I know my cousin Romano's mouth is a little large and well-used – when his foot is not firmly wedged in it – and his mind occasionally unhinged, but as far as I am aware only His Holiness has been the target of the idiot's spite.'

'You are clever, Orsini. That does not necessarily endear you to me – a clever Orsini.'

'Why then arrange this meeting at all?' Cesare countered. 'If my name alone was enough to put you off.'

Skiouros licked his lips. A thought had just struck him. 'You were there, weren't you, Your Eminence?'

A moment's silence followed and Skiouros nodded to himself. 'There were at least two cardinals in Orvieto's army at the fall of Roccabruna. I noticed one of them looked rather bored. The other was watching our group rather more intently. I would be willing to place a coin on a wager that man was you, Your Eminence?'

'Another clever one. My my.'

'And that's why you only needed to see Orsini tonight. You've already seen us before. In court and in action.'

Cesare took up the conversation with an appreciative nod to his friend. 'And you are already half decided, but my family ties make you recalcitrant. Can you trust an Orsini, even if he fights for pay?'

'And can I?'

There was another sound of swishing movement and a flicking noise. Sparks danced and a taper began to glow. The friends' eyes fixed on the man's location as he moved around the circular columns, touching the taper to the candle holders between each set of columns, throwing the austere and ancient splendour of this place into glowing golden relief.

Skiouros found himself looking up at the ceiling as the mosaics he'd already known were there danced into view, flickering and dim.

'Beautiful, aren't they,' the cardinal said as he approached slowly around the ambulatory, lighting candles as he went. 'They betray the pagan origins of the building. Christ sits enthroned in each of the apsidal scenes but all the rest are of ancient origin. I like this place. It sits well with me. I feel it is a perfect metaphor for myself. The spiritual and the practical, harmoniously side by side. The pious and the wicked, which live in all men in varying degrees of balance. The harvesting of the wine grapes among the figures of ancient gods. The tearing of the vines. Reaping. Cutting. Severing.'

Skiouros felt that chill return in force at the tone the cardinal had slipped into.

'Why should I place my trust in an Orsini and consider employing him?' the man repeated.

Cesare stood still and calm as the cardinal came to a halt before him. Almost a head taller than the condottiere, the cardinal was dressed in rich black velvets and silks, embroidered with silver designs, a hat worn at a jaunty angle doing nothing to eradicate the impression of power and tension. Skiouros tightened his grip on the macana as he realised the cardinal was wearing good leather fighting gloves and bore a sword and parrying dagger at his waist.

Once more he began to wonder what this place was, where a man of the church would stoop to clandestine meetings with mercenaries and eschew his official scarlet for the dour colours of a sword-fighting nobleman.

'You wish some sort of guarantee, Your Eminence? And I imagined you a man more familiar with Rome and its transient ways.'

The cardinal gave a humorous snort of laughter, swishing the taper he held until the flame died away, and Cesare shrugged in the flickering candlelight as a zig-zag of light remained on their retinas. 'What guarantee can a man *give* in these times? I could give you my word, which I hold in high esteem, but to you it would simply seem to be yet more dissembling of the Orsini. I could sign a legal document, but then I would be doing that anyway should you contract us. Perhaps I can make some sort of vow over the altar here? Though I fear that a promise to God is also worth as little as a clipped penny in this city.'

Skiouros frowned at his friend, wondering what he was playing at. He was about to lose all chance of securing a position unless he started to show some deference, some loyalty.

'More than a grain of truth there,' the cardinal said.

'And in the interests of transparency, I feel that I ought to let you know that I am aware of who you are, despite all your secrecy.'

'Oh?'

Skiouros was shaking his head. *Don't do it. Don't push him too far, Cesare. We need him!*

'You are my namesake, of course. You are Cardinal Cesare Borgia, son of His Holiness and the lady Vannozza dei Cattanei.'

'Far too clever,' smiled Cardinal Borgia coldly. 'A clever Orsini. I cannot decide whether that makes you useful or more dangerous than any man in Rome right now.'

'Simple deduction, Your Eminence,' Cesare smiled. 'There are remarkably few pro-Borgia cardinals from what I hear, and to state the position of the anti-Borgia Orsini so early in negotiations, you had to be one of the most important. I have met half a dozen of the more senior cardinals, including Della Rovere, who we encountered in Siena fleeing to the arms of the French king with his tail between his legs. And one thing I do know about those men is that their position is *everything* to them. The power of their robes. The only time they are to be seen without their vestments is when they are naked as the day they were made and cavorting with the courtesans of Rome.'

Skiouros felt his blood run cold as his friend blithely insulted the entire college of cardinals in a single sweeping statement. Cesare relaxed into the silence and rubbed his hands together.

'But a cardinal, a nobleman and a sword-fighter with the security of the Pope as his prime concern? Who else could you be?'

'You have still not answered my question to any level of satisfaction,' replied Borgia calmly. 'Why should I trust you?'

'There is no solid answer I can give. Look me in the eye and decide, for the eyes are where our secrets hide, do they not?'

The cardinal leaned slightly closer, studying Cesare's face, and then he brushed the matter aside with a black-gloved hand. 'The Orsini were ever good at playing the game. Your Greek here is a different matter. He seemed almost boyishly innocent at Roccabruna for all his martial achievements, and all the time we have stood here he has been twitching at your flat statements and blatant insults, unable to hide his shock and disappointment in you. Your eyes, Orsini, hide their secrets well and tell me only that which you desire I know. This young man, however? Well, he seems an open mirror for your true intent.'

Skiouros tried not to sweat profusely as the cardinal stepped towards him, leaning down to gaze unblinking into his eyes. He suddenly felt like a child being questioned after some mischief that he knows was his fault. By the time those ice blue eyes moved back, he was almost ready to confess to anything the man cared to name. As Borgia stepped away towards Cesare, Skiouros was embarrassed to feel his nerves force a little bile into his mouth.

'Your Greek friend is uncommonly nervous, Orsini, but not – I think – through any deceit. He genuinely wishes for this contract and appears to fear that you are losing him his chances of securing it.'

Cesare stopped rubbing his hands and folded his arms in a casual manner, almost challenging. 'Your tone tells me that you have made a decision, Your Eminence. Might we know what it is, so that we can end this game and return to our beds? The night grows old.'

Borgia gave the first laugh that contained genuine humour since they had arrived.

'I like you, Orsini. Your Greek too. God help me, I really shouldn't, but I do.'

'Then you are inclined to take us on?'

Cardinal Borgia stepped back and leaned against the delicate pillars. 'I am *inclined* to do so, yet am not ready to agree altogether.' He gestured at the ceiling. 'As I said, the mosaics echo my soul. Light and dark together. In the service of the Lord a man can afford to be a shining beacon of church morals. In the service of the Papacy, one has to be prepared to move in darker circles. I employ only those of whose unswerving loyalty I am convinced, and those who accept my service must be willing also to accept the need to do my bidding, no matter how morally troublesome the task to which I set them.'

'Condottieri are soldiers, Your Eminence,' Skiouros interrupted, not liking the direction the conversation was heading.

'True indeed, but you showed such devious ingenuity back at Roccabruna, young Greek. And there is something about your manner and your stance that tells me you are no simple sell-sword. That you are accustomed to moving in those same dark circles.'

'Cut to the chase, Your Eminence,' Cesare said, straightening and unfolding his arms.

'Very well. If I am to trust an Orsini, I would have his contract signed in blood. You will solve a small problem for me, and when you have done that to my satisfaction, I will give you your contract. You will find my terms of employment hard to beat. I pay well and the benefits are unmatchable. But first you will prove your ability, your worth and your fidelity.'

'How?' Skiouros blurted.

'You will bring me something that I very much wish to have.'

'And you're really comfortable with this?' Skiouros muttered unhappily to Cesare.

'I wouldn't say that, given an infinite choice, this is how I would be filling my time, but when the devil drives and all that.'

'He's your *cousin*!'

'He's an idiot who fell foul of Rome's most powerful family because he is permanently unable to extricate his enormous foot from his immense mouth. In the Rome of the Borgias only a fool stands in opposition to the Pope.'

'It sounds like there are a surprising number of fools in the college of cardinals, then!'

Cesare scratched his chin. 'You met Borgia. Would you cross him?' He watched the expression change on Skiouros' face. 'No, I thought not. And he is only *one* of them. He has a sister, brothers, half-brothers, his *father*, of course, and even his mother is a force to be reckoned with by all accounts.'

'So you *are* happy with it?'

Cesare rounded on the Greek as he leaned back into the pitch dark shadows of the alley. '*Of course* I'm not happy about it! But I pledged my sword to your task, and I do not back out of such things with ease. To gain access to the Vatican and Prince Cem, we need that contract with Cardinal Borgia, and he is not going to accept an Orsini in his service without damn good reason. He set us a task and we have to see it through. I thought your peculiar aversion to any recognisable faith would allow you some ethical leeway? It's those of us who hold to our faith in the Lord God who have to panic about the repercussions of this night.'

Skiouros leaned back in the face of Orsini's anger. 'Just because I can see a truth between and beyond the liturgies does not mean I lack the morals of any of them, Cesare. I am confident in our goal and in my abilities, but I am uncomfortable with *this*. Are you sure there's no alternative?'

'Of course there is,' snapped Cesare. 'You can wait until Charles of France walks into Rome and then back out with Cem in an iron collar and then try and infiltrate the French army if you prefer?'

'And what of your men? What of Girolamo and Helwyg? I cannot imagine this is the sort of thing they signed on with you for. Are they happy with following you and me this close to Hell?'

Orsini gave him a hard look. 'I pay better than any other condottiere they might find. Besides, I am the lord of Carloto – where Girolamo's family live – and in serving me well, he secures a comfortable and pleasant life for them. As for Helwyg... well, he owes me of old, and has sought to pay me back for years out of some grand Germanic sense of propriety. We are set, so stop muttering.'

Skiouros sighed and ducked out of the deep shadow, peering across the dark market square to the brown, smooth façade of the palazzo opposite. A tall building, perhaps three floors high and purpose-built as a grand residence rather than formed from the bones of a centuries-old fortress in the manner of many of the city's palaces, this one presented ordered rows of windows, the lower floor's ones protected by heavy wooden shutters. They were closed as one would expect given the lateness of the hour. The *earliness* of the hour, Skiouros corrected himself, looking up at the dark sky, the moon having now passed from sight.

'Cover that damned tattoo, will you?' Parmenio growled at him from behind. 'I'd rather not have heavily armed men come knocking later because we were easy to identify.'

Skiouros quickly yanked down the sleeve of his poor workman's jerkin, purchased from a shop on the far side of Rome that morning, along with all the other ragged, nondescript clothing the six men wore. As suited the impoverished classes of Rome, they had also forsaken their swords, bringing only easily concealable clubs and daggers. Skiouros had fought against the command to leave his macana back at Sant'Agnese, but the others were adamant that the weapon was far too recognisable. The dark business they were about tonight had to be performed without the chance of repercussions if it was to be done at all.

'Do you think he will come to harm?'

Nicolo rolled his eyes. 'Give your mouth a rest, Skiouros.'

'I just need to be sure about what we're doing.'

'The cardinal is a man with a shadow on his heart, for certain,' Cesare said with a stony face, 'but he is also a bright one. He is hardly likely to damage such an asset, else he negates the value of everything we do tonight. Cling on to that fact.'

'Come on, then,' Skiouros grumbled. 'If we're going to do this, let's get it over with.'

'Wait,' Cesare held his hand up as Skiouros moved. 'The door.'

The others followed his pointed finger. At the end of the long façade, at the palazzo's corner, a tower stood at an angle, a later addition to the building and bearing the hallmarks of decorative modern Roman work. Next to the base of the tower, where the featureless plain wall of the palazzo marched off down a side street, stood a small door and as they watched, a crack of yellow at the door's edge widened. As the portal opened fully, a figure silhouetted in it stepped out and began to close it.

'Come on.'

Cesare led the way, with Skiouros, Parmenio and Nicolo close at heel, and Girolamo and Helwyg – the latter enclosed in a voluminous hooded cloak to disguise his foreign features – skirting around the periphery, watching for any interested onlookers. The streets were quiet and dark at this hour, but drunken revellers were not unknown, as well as cutpurses and desperate whores. As they closed on the street down which the figure had departed, Skiouros caught a better view of her. A woman of indeterminate age, she wore rough, cheap woollen garments and carried a heavy wooden bucket in each hand.

Skiouros bit his lip nervously as the six of them hurried along the street behind her, their boots scraping on the cobbles, all of them keeping to the edge of the street and staying back so that she would not be spooked by the noise of pursuit. Half a minute of following her passed before Cesare stopped at a corner and held up his hand. Skiouros came to a halt next to him and peered around the corner to see the woman standing in the centre of a wide piazza, filling her buckets from a large, white marble fountain with little decoration barring an ancient grinning bearded face whose mouth spouted the continual flow into the basin.

Finally, the woman picked up the full buckets, struggling with the weight, and turned back to the street where the six men lurked.

'Come on,' whispered Cesare. 'Back to the nearest alley.'

Comfortable now that the serving woman was returning to that same door, the party of mercenaries hurried back along their route until they saw the palazzo up ahead. As they neared its corner, Cesare gestured to a dark entrance on the far side of the street. 'You take Parmenio and Nicolo that way. I'll wait in this alley with Girolamo and Helwyg. If she's on this side of the street, we'll move first and then if there's trouble, you pen her in. If she's on your side, you go first and we'll play shepherd.'

Skiouros, still experiencing the most powerful of misgivings over the whole affair, nodded and scurried across the street and into the shadow with his friends. Parmenio displayed a similar look of uncertainty, but Nicolo, pragmatic as always, simply looked business-like and determined.

Skiouros started to count his heartbeats, keeping his nerves under control, and edged slightly closer to the alley mouth, making sure to keep his face to the shadow. He almost ducked back as he spotted the woman struggling with her buckets on the far side of the street, but realised that he was well concealed and the movement would be more likely to betray his presence than anything. Silently, he threw up thanks to God that the woman was on Cesare's side. At least he would be spared this unpleasantness. For all his self-assuredness and control – born of years of hardship and brutal, unsought, lessons – he was still uncomfortable with the concept of collateral damage and having to take misery to the innocent in order to bring justice to the wicked.

He watched with bated breath as the woman neared the alley mouth, unconcerned, more worried about spilling the precious water than any potential villains lurking in wait in the alleyways leading off.

It happened in the blink of an eye.

A brief muffled gasp was all she managed and suddenly the street was empty, two buckets clattering around on the cobbled ground, their contents gushing through the channels and into the nearest drain. With a deep preparatory breath, Skiouros beckoned to the two sailors in the shadows and the three men ran across and into Cesare's alley.

The woman was against the wall, her back ramrod straight as Helwyg's strong arms pinned her, a ball of cloth jammed in her mouth to prevent undue noise. Cesare was busy motioning for her to calm down. To add to Skiouros' growing moral distress, the woman was of advanced years and clearly terrified.

'We intend you no harm,' Cesare said quietly. 'If you do as we ask, you will be fine. However, I am about to take the gag from your mouth and if you scream, this large fellow next to me will have to silence you. Do you understand?'

The woman gave a panicked nod.

'Good. Now remember. Quiet if you want no trouble.' Pausing for only a second, Cesare reached out and plucked the rag from the woman's mouth, his other hand slapping across her lower face before the muffled scream began. He made a tutting sound. 'That's your free scream. Another one and we will have to stop you. Now be calm, and take a deep breath.'

Once he was happy that the woman was silent, Cesare removed his hand.

'Good. Now I want four pieces of information from you and that is all.'

As the woman remained silent, Cesare stepped back and nudged Skiouros aside to reveal a view of the palazzo across the street and little further down. 'Firstly, tell me which window is Romano Orsini's.'

The woman was still wordless and Cesare sighed. 'I know it is his palazzo and he is a man of ostentatious tastes. His apartment will be in the high, grand wing, with this majestic façade. Now which window is his?'

The woman cleared her throat and croaked, 'Top floor.'

'I had assumed so. Which window?'

'The nearest.'

'Good. Now my second question is: which window is the room of his son?'

The woman's eyes widened and she shook her head.

'Don't make me repeat my earlier threats,' Cesare sighed. 'I am not a bad man in truth, and I hate to make threats, but I am also a man of my word and will not back down from one.'

'Two windows down,' the woman said wretchedly. 'The room between is a solar.'

'You see? Easy, isn't it? Now we're almost there. The door you left by… is it locked? And if so do you have the key?'

The servant shook her head. 'Not locked.'

'Good. And last of all, how many guards?'

'Twelve,' the woman said with almost defiant confidence. 'You won't get past them.'

'I think you might find that an erroneous statement. Not all twelve will be on guard at this hour. How many will be about?'

'Two or three,' she replied, some of the wretchedness returning to her voice.

'Good. Now we are going to leave you in peace. Thank you for your assistance.' He turned to Girolamo. 'Bind her.'

The crossbowmen produced three wide strips of cloth. As Cesare pushed the fabric ball back into her mouth, Girolamo tied one around her lower face to secure the gag, then brought her ankles together and bound them tight with the second. At his gesture, Helwyg let go of her and the crossbowman shuffled her along the wall to where a heavy corroded metal downspout jutted, binding her wrists to it.

'Someone will find her at first light if not before,' Cesare said quietly, and leaned close to the frightened woman. 'You have my profound apologies that this was necessary, and I hope that all improves for you in the coming days.' With a sympathetic smile, he dipped into his belt purse and produced two gold ducats, which he reached down and pushed into her hand, closing the fingers.

'Romano Orsini is an idiot with a dangerous future, who spreads sedition and rumour about the powerful men of Rome. You would do well to enter the service of another family, especially after tonight. I heartily recommend that when you are freed in the morning you walk away from this place and find a new position. This money will tide you over until you are settled once more.'

Skiouros almost smiled at his friend as they left the alley and Parmenio and Nicolo were looking a little relieved, though Girolamo was all business and Helwyg's expression suggested that he was less than impressed with Cesare's show of compassion. Ahead, Cesare crossed the street to the base of the palazzo's grand façade and looked up at the two indicated windows, marking their position on a mental map of the complex. The crossbowman paused en route to collect the two buckets that would have marked the trouble spot for anyone who happened along the street.

Rounding the corner of the palazzo beneath the angled tower, Cesare came to a halt before the small servants' door and waited for the other five to join him.

'Remember: quick, quiet and subtle. We want no undue trouble. I will be extremely put out if there is any killing tonight. In fact, I will be grandly displeased if a single wound is caused. I will consider a bonus payment upon completion if we manage to leave tonight without drawing blood at all.'

Skiouros nodded his wholehearted agreement, and Nicolo and Parmenio smiled their consent. Helwyg and Girolamo were professional soldiers. Their faces betrayed no emotions on the matter, but they would do whatever was asked of them to the best of their ability, especially at the prospect of a bonus.

Pausing only to be sure they were all ready, Cesare reached up to the simple iron latch that was the door's only feature. Pulling a short wooden club, perhaps eighteen inches long, from his belt, he depressed the latch and swung the door inwards, moving inside with the grace of an acrobat and the speed of a racing hound. Skiouros was second in.

A low, basic hallway lay beyond the door, with arched openings to left and right and another plain door ahead. Skiouros was interested in passing to note ancient stonework and arches incorporated into the walls. This palace was built upon the skeleton of an antique building. Trying not to be distracted, concentrating on the job in hand, he watched Cesare duck through the right-hand arch and – in a calculated move – mirrored him, passing beneath the ancient arc to the left.

He found himself in a storeroom, with shelves lining the walls and freestanding timber racks that held various foodstuffs in between. Lamps guttered in twin positions at opposite ends of the room, and Skiouros heaved a sigh of relief. He was about to turn and leave when a voice from beyond the racks called out, 'Margarita? You took your time. Get that water on the boil, sharp now, woman!'

Skiouros felt a sudden burst of anxiety clawing at the edges of his mind and swallowing, forced it down into the pit of his stomach, where it continued to dance uncomfortably. Another civilian to deal with. Another innocent victim hanging on the crucifix of his vengeance. Realising he had only moments until the man questioned the lack of a reply, he padded lightly down the racks towards the voice, wishing he had his macana club, and drawing the basic, sharp dagger from his belt sheath.

Briefly, through the racks and between the small sacks of herbs and foodstuffs, he saw a bald head with its back to him. As swiftly as he dared, he rounded the wooden structure at the room's far end and leapt. The man, who had been taking inventory of the shelves, gave a muffled squawk and dropped his chalk and slate to the flagged floor as Skiouros' hand went around his mouth from behind. Hoping to God he'd judged it right, the Greek brought the pommel of his dagger down on the man's head with a thump.

The servant went instantly limp, slipping to the floor through Skiouros' arms, and the young man paused, leaning down to check his condition. The servant was still breathing, but flat out. With a sigh of relief, Skiouros ripped some cloth from bags on the shelves, bound the man's hands and gagged him, and then quickly ran through the storeroom, checking for any other occupants. As he reached the arch once more, he found Parmenio standing at the corner. The captain raised his eyebrows questioningly.

'Old man. He's dealt with – out cold.'

They turned to see Helwyg and Cesare heading back towards them from a large kitchen area through the other arch. Nicolo was standing by the next door and Girolamo disposing of the two buckets.

'Anything?' Skiouros asked breathlessly.

'Young serving lad. He was in the kitchen cellar. Just locked him in. Seemed easiest.'

Skiouros nodded. He couldn't hear the lad shouting, so nor would anyone else. 'What now?'

'Now,' said Cesare with purpose, 'we get what we came for.' He turned. 'Girolamo? You're scouting. I want you one corner ahead of us at all times. Helwyg, you bring up the rear.'

'Is that wise?' Skiouros frowned. 'We can lead.'

'Girolamo can put a man down quickly and quietly. Can you?'

Leaving the question unanswered in response, Skiouros sighed wearily. 'Come on, then. Let's get it over with.'

At a nod from Orsini, Nicolo depressed the latch on the second door and swung it open, stepping aside. Girolamo ducked into it glancing this way and that and, signalling for the others to follow, dipped to his left, out of sight. Skiouros followed on in the wake of Cesare and Nicolo and found himself emerging into a square courtyard with a paved floor, the high residential wing of the palazzo on his left, the servant's wing behind him, a low range ahead, and the blank rear walls of other structures forming the fourth side of the yard on their right, vines growing up decorative trellises to disguise the ugliness of the bare wall.

This was not a decorative grand palazzo courtyard in the style of the Visconti. This was more like the practice yard where Skiouros had first seen the other mercenaries in Cesare's lance. Bare and empty, the yard was quiet. Nicolo and Parmenio were hidden from the faint starlight in the shadow beneath the eaves of the kitchen wing. Girolamo was already across the courtyard and sidling up towards the main entrance. Timber rails flanked a slight ramp on either side, leading up to a heavy, well-polished wooden door in the corner of the tall wing. The windows on this side of the high structure were very similar to the external ones, and Skiouros wondered for a moment whether that wing was only one room thick, but quickly discarded the theory. There had to be corridor space at least.

As he watched, Girolamo gestured to one of the shuttered windows on the ground floor only three along from the door. Skiouros squinted at it and realised that he could see light in the cracks between the shutters. Carefully, he scanned the other windows, but it appeared to be the only room with light. It wasn't too much of a leap of assumption to mark that room as the guard quarters, given the lateness of the hour. Girolamo appeared to have reached the same conclusion. As he reached up to the door's handle, which would admit him to the main section of the palazzo, he drew a knife from his belt. His hand pushed the door gently, opening it only a crack. The resulting creak echoed out across the courtyard and everyone froze. Moments later, the crossbowman took a deep breath and thrust the door open wide – not the subtle way he'd planned his entrance, but the best way to minimise the creaking noise. As he paused, silhouetted in the light from the corridor within, everyone breathed shallowly. Ten heartbeats passed with no alarm raised, and with a wave of 'all clear', Girolamo slipped inside. Cesare, Skiouros, Nicolo and Parmenio hurried along the shadowed edge of the servants' wing and slipped in through the door in short order, leaving Helwyg to cross the courtyard at the rear, watching for trouble and then following them in and closing the door behind them.

Skiouros pushed through the stubby entrance hall and into the corridor which ran the length of the wing, a grand staircase rising directly ahead which would grant access to all floors. As his gaze flashed this way and that, taking in the situation, Skiouros was surprised to see Girolamo backing towards them along the marble corridor, dragging a body by the shoulders, the man's boots skidding on the floor with a faint leathery squeak. Cesare hissed at him quietly: 'Pick him up!'

Parmenio rushed over and grabbed the boots to silence the dragged body, and the two men carried the unconscious guard over to the rest of the group. A trickle of blood ran from the man's scalp, matting his hair and filling his ear. Girolamo repositioned his hand so that it caught the first drip and prevented it from dropping to the black and white marble floor tiles. He glanced up at Cesare on the way past with a raised brow.

'No, it doesn't count against a bonus,' whispered the nobleman with a shake of his head. As they waited, Nicolo watching the door of the suspected guard room, Parmenio and Girolamo carried the unconscious guard to the stairs and lowered him to the ground, pushing him into the shadowed space beneath the staircase.

'Right,' Cesare said, rubbing his head. 'Helwyg, I want you to stay here. Keep your eyes on that guard room. If there's any trouble, deal with it. If you can do it quietly and subtly, all the better. If the alarm goes up, shout to us so we have a chance to make it back.' As the big Silesian nodded, Cesare turned to Nicolo and Parmenio. 'One of you needs to stay, too. Keep the back door ajar and watch the other wings. You are our quick exit. The moment you see us coming back, get that door open, cross the courtyard and prepare the way through the kitchens again. Helwyg, you wait until we're down and play rear guard again on the way out.'

Parmenio and Nicolo looked at one another. The older captain shrugged. 'If we have to carry him, I've got the back for it. You stay.'

Nicolo snorted quietly. 'With your knees? Stay here and keep the doors ready. I'll go.'

Ignoring the irritation in Parmenio's glare, he crossed to the stairs. 'Come on, then.'

As they began the ascent, their eyes roving across the upper regions, Helwyg padded down the corridor towards the guard room and Parmenio moved to the exterior door and edged it open, wincing at the resulting creak.

With infinite care and light steps, the four remaining men climbed the staircase, Girolamo back out ahead and cresting the landing before the others. His dagger remained in his hand, reversed to deliver a pommel-bash rather than a deadly stab. As he reached the first floor, he paused and looked around. The other three moved up behind him, and the crossbowman turned to them with a warning glare, his index finger reaching up to his mouth to shush them. As the three came to a halt, their breath held, Girolamo listened out. There was a faint rhythmic tapping from above. He turned and used his hand to mime a walking figure and then pointed up.

Cesare nodded and the crossbowman reached to his belt, pulled two cloth pouches from it and slid one over each boot. Skiouros watched in fascination as Girolamo set off once more up towards the top floor, his passage so quiet that it sounded like the echo of a ghost's whisper.

The three mercenaries remained still at the top of the first flight and waited in silence. After a protracted pause, they heard the muffled sound of a surprised indrawn breath and then a soft thump, and five heartbeats later, Girolamo appeared once more at the stairs, beckoning.

Cesare heaved in a breath and turned to Skiouros. 'This is your post.'

'What?'

'Like Parmenio and Helwyg downstairs, you need to watch this corridor and keep the stairs clear for us.'

'But this whole undertaking is for me.'

'Who commands this lance? Who is the condottiere here?'

'Well you are, but…'

'Then do as you're told, soldier,' Cesare whispered. 'And knock off the talking. Too dangerous.'

Without waiting for Skiouros to argue, Cesare was already on his way up with Nicolo. As the pair reached the top, Girolamo was busy propping another unconscious guard behind a long drape, where he was not immediately visible, though he would soon be spotted with even a cursory search.

'Third-to-last door on the left side,' Cesare prompted the other two, though neither needed the reminder. Quietly, they padded along the corridor towards their goal. As they neared the other end, Girolamo danced ahead on light, silent feet, listening at doors. As he reached the target, he paused and then gestured at it, miming a sleeping man with palms pressed together beside his cheek. Cesare nodded and the crossbowman moved on to the last door, at which he listened and then repeated his mime. Girolamo took position outside, on guard with his dagger raised, the blood-and-hair-smeared pommel presented to the door.

Nicolo and Cesare moved to the third-to-last door and paused outside. Cesare tilted his head in silent question, and Nicolo nodded.

With a tense pause, Cesare gently turned the handle and pushed the door open a short way. The room's interior was pitch black. Swiftly, Cesare pushed the door wider and slipped inside, Nicolo following on. As soon as they were inside, the sailor closed the door behind them and there was a long, anxious moment as the pair held their breath and waited for their eyes to adjust, blinking a few times in an attempt to speed up the process.

The room was edged with fine furnishings. A wooden horse large enough for a child to ride sat by a side door and Nicolo for the first time considered the possible age of the boy. He'd not thought to ask, and had assumed a young man in his late teen years. This clearly was not the case, and he began to have serious doubts about their course of action.

Cesare crossed the room to the large, well-appointed bed beneath the shuttered window and loomed over the figure of the sleeping boy. He was perhaps eight years old. The nobleman felt the black morass of a pit of wickedness open beneath his feet and for a moment, he paused. He would make this right in due course if Borgia did not.

Reaching down, he placed one hand over the boy's mouth and held him down with the other. Nicolo, himself looking far from pleased, began to bind the boy's ankles. Suddenly the young Orsini was awake and panicked, thrashing around and trying to shout out. Nicolo forced his flailing hands together and tied them as Cesare removed his hand and gagged the boy.

Without delay, Nicolo lifted the boy and threw him over his shoulder, where he had to hold on tight as the prisoner fought to be free. As the sailor carried his captive to the door, Cesare completed their mission, opening the shutters enough to allow a narrow strip of moon- and starlight to shine in across the bed. Quickly he removed two things from his pouch. He placed the jet carving of a bull – the Borgia emblem – on the pillow where the depression from the boy's head remained. Next to it he laid the scrap of paper, carefully penned with an extract from the 141st Psalm:

Set a guard over my mouth, O Lord,
Keep watch over the door of my lips!

Sharing his friend's own personal hell over what necessity had driven them to do, Cesare turned and left the clear message to await Romano's eyes when he awoke and came looking for his son.

Skiouros stood shivering on the landing, listening to the faintest noises above and feeling the cold draft rising from the open door below. He shuddered particularly violently and closed his eyes.

That was not the shiver of a draft.

'Now is not the best time, Lykaion,' he whispered. Faint sounds murmured from around the house in reply. 'No. No I am not at all happy about doing any of this, and I loathe the fact that I've dragged the rest of them into it too.'

A faint whisper of air.

'Yes, you *are* worth all this. Of *course* you are. Soon, brother. Soon you will rest in peace back in Istanbul, where you should be, your death avenged and everything put to rights.'

The whispers of curtains, air and footsteps were louder.

'Fear not for my soul. I have spent years preparing for this. I can do it. I *am* doing it.'

Skiouros felt the atmosphere change and set his face into a resolute expression. 'While I miss you, brother, it is no threat to me that you stop these visits. Indeed, until this is done, I could really do without them!'

'Hey!'

Skiouros frowned. Somehow Lykaion's voice had changed.

It took him only a dreadful heartbeat to realise that this was no longer Lykaion. His brother's shade had evaporated into the cold air as it was wont to do on these strange occasions. By the time he was even thinking straight, Skiouros was already running. The man, only half-dressed and leaning out of a doorway, looking at him in anger and confusion, had only a moment to register the threat Skiouros presented before the Greek hit him at full speed, both men dropping to the ground. The man tried to shout but had been winded and his words came out as a single gasp. Desperate, Skiouros grabbed the man's hair and gave the back of his head a smart rap against the marble floor tile, hard enough to drive the wits from him. The guard – at least he presumed that's what he was – shook his head blearily, and Skiouros gave it another clonk on the floor, preparing for a third, but deciding it was unnecessary as the man's eyes rolled up into his head.

'You've been busy,' noted Nicolo, appearing on the stairwell where Skiouros had just been, the boy draped across his shoulder, struggling as they descended.

'All done?' asked Skiouros bleakly.

Cesare, appearing behind, nodded. Girolamo came down last, and Skiouros rose from the unconscious form of his victim and followed them down the stairs and out into the night, Parmenio and Helwyg joining them as they passed.

'This has been, I think, the low point of my life,' Skiouros grumbled as they emerged into the street once more.

Cesare levelled a humourless stare at him.

'None of us relish this, Skiouros. But we will do what we can to make it right. And remember what I said about Rome: it seethes with evil and corruption and it gets under your skin and infects you. Why do you think I avoid the place like the plague it so clearly is? My father was a good and honest and pious man when I was a boy. A few months in this hell hole and he was unrecognisably amoral. Why do you think there's never a worthy man in Saint Peter's chair? Now come on.'

Cardinal Borgia stepped into the candlelit glory of the mausoleum-church of Santa Costanza, once more in his black doublet, with the sword slung at his hip. From their position inside, the friends took note of the half dozen men awaiting him outside the door before he closed it.

'You encountered no problems?'

Cesare, stepping out from behind one of the sets of twin pillars, gave the cardinal a bitter look. 'I wouldn't say that exactly, Your Eminence, but not in the way you mean. There were no deaths or woundings. The message was left exactly as you asked.'

And the boy?'

Skiouros and Parmenio walked the young son of Romano Orsini out into the candlelight. The boy had been crying – every tear of which seemed to have tried to drown Skiouros' soul – but had settled now into a defiant, proud silence, his chin high. Skiouros found himself silently willing the boy into ever more boldness. Indeed, in the few moments he'd had with young Paolo he had attempted to console the boy and promised that things would be fine. It had felt like a blatant lie, but he had felt better to witness the same promises being made to the boy by Cesare, Parmenio and Nicolo en route.

'You have done a remarkable job, condottiere,' the cardinal murmured, clearly impressed. 'My men outside will take him from here and you may attend the guard offices just off the Piazza San Pietro two days hence to sign your contract. I believe you have earned it.'

'Not quite,' hissed Cesare, stepping into the centre of the domed room, between the cardinal and the boy. 'We have, I hope, proved our worth and loyalty, to support my given word. However, I find myself somewhat less than comfortable with such a task. We are soldiers, as my man told you last night. Set us against any fighting man and we will put him down for you. I am flexible enough even to deal with a few less straightforward problems for you, but we are not stealers of children.'

'Evidence suggests otherwise, condottiere.'

'This is the last mission of this nature I and my men will perform for you. You have my loyalty, but not my soul. And before I release this boy into your custody, I demand one promise and will deliver one in return.'

'Go on,' the cardinal replied coldly.

'Give me your word as a man of God and a nobleman of good family that the boy will not be harmed in your custody and will be returned to his father in due course when your issues with the man are at an end. The threat of simply having him should be enough to secure Romano's cooperation.'

Cardinal Borgia stood silent.

'And in return,' Cesare went on, 'I promise you this: we are your men to the hilt for any duty that does not transcend the scope of a God-fearing man. But if a hair on this boy's head is harmed, contract or no contract, I will hunt you down to the very gates of Hell. Are we clear?'

Borgia narrowed his eyes and a humourless smile touched his face.

'We are very clear. I feel that I should be put off – even insulted – by conditions being applied to this, and a very clear threat voiced. And yet somehow it is precisely the sort of thing I would expect from the man into whose eyes I looked last night. Very well. You have my word. Young Orsini will be treated as a guest in my palazzo and shall want for nothing as long as he remains there. And as soon as his father either gives me a Bible-touched oath of fealty or his word that he will leave Rome and retire to some rural retreat, they shall be reunited. I am a political animal, condottiere, not a monster.'

As Cesare stepped to one side, the cardinal beckoned to the defiant boy. 'Come, Paolo Orsini. Think of this as a short-lived adventure, after which you will return to your family, safe in the knowledge that your father's head will stay precisely where it belongs.'

The boy strode proudly from the room in front of Cardinal Borgia, and when the doors closed, Skiouros heaved out a deep breath. 'I feel as though I just sold my soul to a black-garbed demon.'

'Not a long leap from the truth,' muttered Cesare. 'Rome corrupts more than any devil.'

'Do you think he will keep his word?' Parmenio asked, a hint of worry in his voice.

'I believe so. He has nothing to gain from harming Paolo. And one of the reasons I was willing to deliver the boy to him in the first place is that my cousin Romano is a blabbermouth and a fool, but he is also a doting father. I am confident that he would now move the world a little to the left if Borgia asked him to. He will soon be reunited with his boy.'

He straightened and a dark look crossed his face. 'And if he is not, I will carry out my threat with every ounce of spirit I have.'

Skiouros leaned towards Parmenio.

'Despite my desire to see the place, I find that I am almost twitching to leave Rome now. This is a dreadful city, and as soon as I have dealt with Cem I shall seek passage for Crete once more.'

'God grant that we last that long,' mumbled Parmenio with feeling.

CHAPTER SIX - Rome, summer 1494

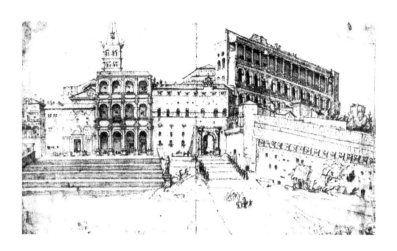

'It doesn't look like the churches back home,' muttered Skiouros, eyeing the grand façade before them. A massive monumental staircase led up from the grey dusty mess of the streets with their piles of horse muck and refuse, their beggars and cutpurses. At the top of the stairs, a piazza, surrounded by a delicate balustrade, overlooked Rome. The far side of that piazza was dominated by a row of structures tall and elegant, their walls painted with scenes and designs in bright colours. While each of the five visible buildings butting up against one another were clearly very different, their lower levels were all arcaded with fine marble columns supporting balconies, their doors surrounded by decorative stone scrollwork, their windows grander than any he had previously seen. It was breathtaking. It was stunning. It was rich and ostentatious. It was not clearly... holy.

Cesare smiled.

'That's not it. Those are just the buildings used by various authorities, groups and commanders in the Vatican. The Piazza San Pietro and the great basilica are behind it.'

Skiouros blinked. These were *offices*? No wonder the Church of Rome was ever expanding its reach and weeding out non-believers. If they had to support this sort of riches, they would never be able to rest. It was so far removed from the village church by his father's farm outside Hadrianopolis it might as well be in another world. This unconscionable display of worldly wealth and power by the man who was supposedly

God's vicar in the world of men was yet another side of Rome he was discovering – the city seemed to be multi-faceted like a cut diamond, albeit a dark and wicked stone – but it did little to improve his opinion of the place and, in fact, added a little impetus to the waves of homesickness he was beginning to feel for the great city of Constantine.

'If the Pope sold off just that one façade of buildings, he could eliminate the poverty we've seen in the streets,' Skiouros grumbled with a disgruntled expression as they began to climb the staircase.

Parmenio rolled his eyes. 'You're not wearing your priest's robe now, Skiouros. Try not to be too critically pious until we're back outside the city walls. This is not the best place to start condemning the Papacy for its riches.'

'Lead on.'

Cesare reached the top step and made for the largest of the five buildings, central in the row. Scenes of saintly piety painted in gold by Italian masters loomed jarringly above them. A painted man in ragged robes knelt in poverty at the feet of the gilt figure of a holy man. Sickening. A queue of people of all walks of life extended towards them from the door for which their leader was making, and two guards were checking every entrant before allowing them through the archway.

As the six men joined the back of the line, Skiouros ran over the coming meeting in his mind. They were about to sign on with the man who had kidnapped – or rather had had *them* kidnap – a young boy just to silence his father. Could such a man be worthy of any real level of trust? How could they agree to obey and serve such a man?

An image of Lykaion arguing with him beside the red wall of Istanbul's Bloody Church shot into his mind. Lykaion had done just that with the Janissaries and had taken pride in that service. Of course, it had turned out that his direct commander had been a traitor, a conspirator and a murderer, but that was not the point. His oath as a Janissary had been to the Sultan Bayezid, not to Hamza Bin Murad, and Lykaion had felt true pride in his service. Could Skiouros? After all, for all Cardinal Borgia was a slightly more worthy man than Hamza Bin Murad, the Pope could hardly measure up to the Sultan.

He was picking over the finer points of blind servitude when he realised that Cesare was speaking, and he dropped back into the real world in time to see the guards nod and gesture for them to pass. Either the queue had moved remarkably quickly or he'd been absorbed for quite some time by his moral quandary. Quickly, he took a last look at the façade above him. One of their prime goals today was to examine everything they could while they were here. Any inside knowledge of the Vatican and its buildings and occupants could be vital when the opportunity arose and the time finally came to hunt their quarry among these halls.

Shuffling his feet a little, he followed the others through the arch and into the hallway within. The grand room inside occupied the entire ground floor of the building, as was evident by the sunlight shining in through the doorway opposite. A grand staircase rose at one side of the room, guarded by another soldier in the red cloak of the Vatican, with the crossed keys and papal crown livery. The walls were gold and marble and displayed more wealth than many palaces, a row of columned niches marching around the room halfway up, each containing a statue, presumably of a saint. Most of them, Skiouros noted with a huff of disdain, bore a weapon of some kind. How could a cardinal or a pope be expected to be a man of peace when even their saints were armed?

And then they were passing through the second doorway and out into the brightness of the Piazza San Pietro. Skiouros felt the breath torn from his lungs as he beheld the grandeur of the Pope's worldly realm. The Piazza was huge, dominated by the great eastern face of the basilica of Saint Peter, with its twin rows of three large coloured windows and the rose one above, all rising over a claustral arcade that surrounded the piazza on all sides. That colonnaded veranda itself – and the square it surrounded – was fantastic, each column the height of six men and with a ceiling covered in painted images. At the centre of the piazza, which was continually crossed by men in fine clothes, in red cassocks, or in armour with crimson cloaks, was a great statue of Saint Peter himself beneath a gilded canopy, and behind that a wide, exquisitely carved fountain, jetting water up into the warm, hazy summer air.

'Perhaps we should take time to explore a little?' he prompted Cesare, but his friend shook his head. 'Do not mistake the apparent easiness and unconcern of the people you can see for what it seems. Be assured that we are being watched. We are expected by Cardinal Borgia and have been admitted on that basis and directed to the appropriate office. Should we deviate from our course, I have absolutely no doubt that a couple of men in armour will be at our side in moments. Search the Vatican with your eyes and commit the place to memory, but keep your feet pointed toward our destination.'

Skiouros frowned, his eyes now picking out more than mere architecture and occupancy, but also trying to spot anyone who might be watching them. For a moment a man in plain buff-coloured leathers standing by the fountain seemed to be looking directly at him, but as he was about to point the man out, a second figure joined him and the pair fell into easy conversation, laughing.

By the time the six mercenaries, with Girolamo and Helwyg bringing up the rear, had passed beneath the colonnade off to their right and made for a door that led into the next part of the complex, Skiouros had counted five people he thought might have been watching them, though he could be certain of none of them. If Cesare was right and they *were* being carefully observed, then it was likely the same would happen any time they came here, and that would add a further level of complexity to their main task.

Even these corridors and rooms into which they now passed, the directions given to Cesare by the guards at the steps, were decorative and rich. That the bureaucracy and the low officers who oiled the wheels of the Papal machine should go about their business bathed in such opulence seemed overly extravagant to Skiouros, and he found himself beginning to become jaded by the constant gilt and masterful imagery.

Finally, his eyes having picked out little he could imagine ever being of use, they arrived at their destination and Cesare rapped on the door. A small painted sign beside it proclaimed it to be the office of the clerks to the captain general of the Vatican forces. A voice bade them enter and Cesare pushed open the door and led them inside. Skiouros had half expected to see Cardinal Borgia himself seated at the desk but instead was treated to a view of a man in the guard's crimson uniform, unarmoured and seated at a desk with a stack of documents before him. He looked up, sharp eyes beneath a sheltering brow studying their faces and apparently finding them of passing interest at best.

'Yes?'

'We are here to sign our *condotta* contract for Cardinal Borgia.'

The officer, clearly uninterested in the extreme, waved them over to a second, longer desk at the side wall behind the opened door. At this second desk sat two men in less impressive garb, presumably lesser clerks. One of them, a man with a crooked nose and a pale, elongated face, sat back.

'Ser Cesare Orsini with one lance of men, consisting of a page, squire, crossbowman and two men-at-arms, yes?'

Cesare nodded. 'We have not yet been offered the condotta terms. The cardinal left the matter to you, I presume?'

The clerk withdrew a document from a stack of identical ones on a shelf behind him and smoothed it out with a pale, bony hand before turning it on the desk to face them.

'It is a standard contract but amended to allow for the somewhat generous terms of Cardinal Borgia's service. You will sign on for a one year contract, which can only be terminated early in the event that you or two of your men suffer a debilitating wound or if the Cardinal is dissatisfied with your service. Contract will be considered breached if you fail to deploy promptly when required by your employer, if when deployed there are fewer than six men, unless by prior agreement, if your men are not kept well equipped and at an appropriate level of fitness, or if it comes to our attention that you are also contracted to another individual. In any engagement, captives or captured estates and castles will become the property of your employer, but any portable goods taken from the enemy are yours to keep, unless by prior advice from His Eminence. Do you understand your part in these terms?'

Skiouros blinked at the speed and efficiency with which the bureaucrat had rattled off the details. Of course, only a small proportion of Papal forces were volunteer militia or paid guard. The vast bulk of the pope's might were condottieri, and these clerks must have dealt with the hiring procedure a thousand times before. Cesare simply nodded contentedly.

'Good,' replied the man, who reminded Skiouros curiously of a vulture. 'In return, Cardinal Borgia will pay you four hundred florins a month to divide in any manner you wish between yourself and your men. This figure is not open to negotiation and is already noted upon the condotta.' He gestured to a figure visible in the second paragraph. 'An initial payment upfront of six hundred florins will be made once your signature is committed to paper, in order to secure lodging and to make sure your men are appropriately equipped.'

Skiouros started at the words 'secure lodging', and he cleared his throat to interrupt, but Cesare flashed him a warning look and nodded to the clerk, who continued in his dead monotone.

'Pensions and lump sum options for various wound compensations are detailed in paragraph seven of the contract, though I will not list them verbally in full. You may examine the text before signing. Bonuses or extra rewards are not set in figures at this time, and will be paid by the Cardinal at his discretion. At the contract's conclusion, you may be given the option to extend for a further year but if not, you will receive a final payment of eight hundred florins in return for an agreement not to serve any of the Cardinal's enemies – who shall be detailed at that time – for a further year. Do you understand His Eminence's part in these terms?'

Again, Cesare nodded.

'Then take a moment and peruse the contract. Be sure that you are happy with the conditions and then sign or make your mark, and our business will be complete.'

Cesare began to pore over the neat text on the page as the others stood passive behind. Finally, apparently satisfied, Cesare nodded and marked his name at the bottom of the page. The clerk checked it, notarised it, applied a wax seal to it and then returned it to the shelf in a different pile of documents.

'I will have a copy of the contract prepared for you to collect on the morrow. Any further questions and details you can direct to your commander, who will be waiting for you in the corridor when you leave. He will take you to the fiscal clerks to arrange your initial payment.' Skiouros frowned. If someone waited outside for them with the clerk having sent no word, it lent a great deal of credence to Cesare's belief that they were being watched carefully whilst on Vatican grounds.

Cesare straightened and inclined his head politely. 'Thank you for your time.'

'God be with you,' the clerk replied with as little feeling as the rest of his monologue, returning to his work without paying them any further attention.

Cesare gestured to Girolamo, who stood close to the door and turned, making his way outside once more. As the small party emerged into the corridor, they were surprised to see that the 'commander' who waited for them was garbed in grey and black doublet and hose, but covered with a draped red cloak displaying the white cross of the Knights Hospitaller. He was not a young man, perhaps fifty summers old, and his hair and beard were as much grey as they were black. His eyes, though, were alive, alert and every bit as sharp as the blade in his hand along which he ran a whetstone while he waited. He looked up at them.

'Ser Orsini, I presume?'

Cesare bowed politely. 'I am he, sir. And you are Cardinal Borgia's man?'

'I am. Sir Antonio de Santo Martino of the Order of Saint John. You've signed on with His Eminence, then?'

'Yes. Can I enquire what comes next, commander? In my previous contracts we have regularly served with standing armies, usually on direct campaign. The Cardinal does not wish us quartered to hand, then?'

Sir Antonio shook his head as he sheathed his sword and stood straight, revealing his full height to be a good head taller than Cesare and rivalling the impressive size of Helwyg. 'Since you are clearly neither cardinal nor whore you have no place within the halls of the apostolic palace,' he smiled, 'and the main barracks and military wings of the Vatican are reserved for the standing Papal forces and His Holiness's Catalan guard. You are one of four small, unique condottieri units His Eminence now employs, and all are expected to quarter themselves independently using their pay. Need I point out that the inflated rates His Eminence pays should easily cover such expenses?'

Cesare smiled as he shook his head. 'Hardly. The cardinal's terms are more than generous. So where would you advise we look for quarters, and what else do we need to attend to? How will we know if the cardinal requires us?'

'Accommodation is entirely your own affair,' the Hospitaller replied easily, gesturing for them to make their way along the corridor and back towards the piazza. 'His Eminence's only stipulation is that you be able to attend his office within an hour of his call. As soon as you have set upon your quarters, inform the same clerk you met just now and the information will reach myself and His Eminence promptly. You will need to return tomorrow for your contract and I expect to have an address from you then. As for the next step, keep yourself busy and train your men as best you can and wait for our call. You will find service in the cardinal's employ sporadic and... shall we say interesting?'

'Oh?' Cesare smiled. 'How so?'

'His Eminence rarely requires the service of his condottieri but when he does, the tasks he will have for you will be unusual, often dangerous, and always vital. You may find that months will pass before he calls for you, but do not become complacent. When he calls, be ready.'

Skiouros felt his shoulders slump. *Months*? Months of sitting around impotently waiting for a call. And in that time they would languish somewhere with no more chance of meeting the usurper Cem than before. Somehow he felt as though their step forward had brought them nothing but responsibilities.

He sighed as they made their way back through the corridors of the Vatican towards that grand square. The idea of living in the rat-runs of Rome among the filth and crime appealed less the more he thought about it. As Sir Antonio stepped out ahead, Skiouros motioned to Cesare, who dropped back a little, and the young Greek whispered.

'Do you think brothers Bartholomew and Alexander could find it in their heart to extend our stay in their guest house?'

'Trying to save me money, Skiouros?' Cesare grinned, but his face quickly became serious again. 'No, I agree with you. Rome is not a good choice, and Sant'Agnese is well within an hour's walk. Moreover, His Eminence is familiar with it.'

'Looks like we've gained nothing from our signing, though,' sighed the Greek.

Nicolo nudged him, and Parmenio leaned closer. 'Time will tell. At least we can enter the Vatican now whenever we need to speak to the clerk. That's a sight closer than before, Skiouros.'

The young Greek nodded a weary acknowledgment and picked up the pace again with the others. He would have to keep his thoughts positive, and in the meantime, they would settle in like the good mercenaries they were, take the money and wait.

Weeks turned into months as Skiouros and his friends languished daily in the claustrophobic complex of the monastery. Within a week of signing the condotta, the young Greek was already convinced that they had made a tremendous mistake in joining Cardinal Borgia's force. His mantra – the one that had kept him in control and had seen him through seemingly endless days since his return from the western seas – was wearing thin. *Patience*. Patience was everything. But the interminable waiting eroded the edges of that patience more with every passing day.

The cardinal had called upon the six of them just three times since Cesare had signed the document. The first had been only a week later, and though it had been but a simple task of collecting a package from a minor Lord in the Romagna region, in an area infamous for banditry, Skiouros had felt a surge of hope that they were at least moving and active. Then, upon the completion of that task, they had spent a little over three weeks trying to keep themselves busy, wallowing in impotency. Skiouros had explored every brick and blade of grass of the monastery and its ancient ruins. He had walked the imposing walls of the city of Rome five times in various directions and explored the great sprawl for its monuments, trying to ignore the poverty, corruption, crime, impiety and evil so evident in its streets. He had even taken to sketching a few of the buildings after seeing some of the artists for which Italy was becoming renowned doing the same in the forum. Apparently art seemed not to be his forte, though, and most of his sketches were immediately discarded.

Then had come their second call, and they had hunted a spy belonging to the Colonna family throughout the city's darkest alleys, delivering him intact, spitting bile and issuing threats, to His Eminence. Skiouros had baulked a little at the mission, but the improprieties of the man were self-evident, and he had infiltrated the household of the cardinal's sister for nefarious purposes. What had later happened to the man in the cardinal's cellars they did not know, but Skiouros could hardly imagine his end being a happy one. The Colonnas' reputation was one of wickedness anyway.

Then finally, as the heat of the summer began to wane and the dusty dung-filled air that stifled the streets settled under a thin coverage of leaves, they had gone to war. It had been but a small engagement with that same Romagna lord from whom they had retrieved the parcel in the late spring, but the man was familiar enough with their employer that he had prepared thoroughly and the fight had been a hard one.

Girolamo had broken an arm – a potentially critical wound for a crossbowman – and had been offered the chance to pension out by both Cesare and the cardinal, but had chosen to take a lump sum in compensation and stay with them. His arm was on the mend now, but whether he would ever recover his excellent marksmanship remained to be seen. Parmenio had taken a sword wound to the shoulder, but it had been a glancing blow and he was fast recovering. In truth it seemed to have given him something to keep himself entertained, complaining bitterly about the lack of compensation he'd been offered for his pains.

Skiouros's self-assuredness and confidence had gradually waned over the months since his return, taking a knock with every innocent he had been forced to harm, and he was beginning to feel more than a little uncertain of his ability to carry out his task in full. Not that he would ever reveal such a thing to his companions, of course…

Now, as September began to clutch Rome in its russet grip, they had been inside the Vatican precisely five times, each time only to the offices with which they were already familiar – with the single exception of a quick visit to the great basilica once to attend a mass given by their employer himself.

Skiouros sighed and flipped through his surviving amateurish sketches of the ruins of the forum in the dim candlelight of the room he shared with Cesare. Nicolo and Parmenio sat at their table playing dice, the latter periodically grumbling and accusing his friend of selling his soul to the devil in return for luck at the game.

'Perhaps it's time to move on?' Skiouros said quietly.

Cesare looked up from where he was buffing a black enamelled shoulder plate with gilt edging and shook his head.

'We signed a year-long contract and we've served less than half of it. To break a condotta agreement would be to acquire infamy the length of Italy. We would become effectively unemployable. Also, we would have to break our word, and you know how I feel about that.'

Parmenio, rubbing the itchy healing wound under his bandaged shoulder, nodded his agreement as he reached for the dice again. 'More to the point you'd piss off His Eminence and Cardinal Borgia is not the kind of enemy to make lightly. You'd be setting us up for a huge fall.'

Skiouros settled unhappily back into silence, flicking through his folio of sketches, and was just opening his mouth after a brief pause to try another approach when he was interrupted by a knock at the door.

'Come in,' called Cesare, laying the gleaming pauldron and his polishing rag down on the table. The door clicked and creaked open, revealing the familiar shapes of fathers Bartholomew and Alexander – the friends who, to Skiouros at least, had helped make their time in this place that bit more bearable with their good natured banter and generous nature.

'Good evening gentlemen,' the smiling clerics greeted them in a friendly tone. 'I trust you are well?'

Father Alexander nudged his companion aside slightly. 'Come on Barty, make room.'

'No need to barge, old thing.'

Cesare smiled at the pair. 'What can we do for you?'

'There is a visitor for you in the gardens, but he is not one of His Eminence's men so we did not like to admit him to your quarters unannounced. He comes armed and informs us that he bears a message for 'the Greek'.'

Skiouros frowned, and Cesare turned to him and threw him a questioning look. 'Outside?'

'I think so.'

'Shall we accompany you?'

After a moment's thought, Skiouros nodded. 'Perhaps it's best, given our activities this summer. I was never short of enemies, but I suspect in His Eminence's service, that list has reached new lengths. A man with a sword might be nothing, but it could be trouble.'

Leaving Girolamo and Helwyg undisturbed in their room, the four men followed the priests out, along the corridor and into the garden. The indigo sky and evening air were pleasant, though the temperature was dropping rapidly as the hours passed. On one of the rustic benches in the garden sat a figure Skiouros did not recognise. Dressed in nondescript tan clothing, he was neatly shaven and barbered, with a sword slung at his side.

'Can I help you?' Skiouros enquired, stepping to the fore.

'You are the Greek?'

'I am.'

The man stood and inclined his head politely. 'I bear an invitation, sir.'

'From?'

The man cleared his throat and drew a long breath. 'His Imperial Majesty Andreas Palaeologos, Despot of the Morea, Basileus, Sebastos and Emperor of Byzantium, invites you to dine with him this evening. His Majesty apologises for the lack of forewarning, but he is recently returned to the city and only learned of your own presence quite by chance. Also he apologises for the method of delivery, but His Majesty's household is small. He hopes that you will be able to accept his invitation and, if so, I am to escort you to his apartments.'

Skiouros tried not to allow the sudden leap of hope in his heart to show on his face. The exiled Byzantine! That friendly, excitable man he had met in the aftermath of the siege of Roccabruna was back in Rome and actually seeking his company in the Imperial apartments... the very *heart* of the Vatican!

He turned to Cesare with a strange smile. The nobleman chuckled and looked past him at the messenger.

'My friend Skiouros of Hadrianopolis would be delighted to attend. Would you please wait here while he attires himself suitably?'

The man bowed and then returned to the bench and Skiouros found himself being propelled gently back towards the guest house. 'What's the matter?' he whispered.

Cesare rolled his eyes. 'You have been invited to dine by royalty. Royalty in *exile*, but royalty nonetheless. And in apartments within the Vatican, no less. This is no occasion for your usual rough scruffy attire. This is the time to raid my spare clothing and see what we can come up with.'

Skiouros followed the man-at-arms, whose name he had learned was Paregorio, through as-yet-unseen halls in the Vatican complex, all the time trying not to tug uncomfortably at the stiff formal collar of his black broadcloth doublet stitched with silver thread. Even his own comfortable linen shirt beneath, which he had insisted upon keeping next to his skin, could not ease the discomfort of Cesare's doublet, which *almost* fit right – at least to the naked eye. His hose of fine wool with one leg in grey and the other in black were itchy and new, and the less said about the boots the better, except that Cesare must have unusually narrow feet. Over the top of it all, he wore a pleated and scalloped cioppa robe in grey and black. In the face of Cesare's insistence, he had flatly refused the sable hat with the silver feather and had at least managed to win that one. He felt like a monochrome peacock. Or the board for a game of Queen's Chess.

Close on Paregorio's heels, Skiouros stepped out from a staircase and emerged onto a landing, looking down three storeys to the marble floor of the hall below. The walls here were painted with scenes of nymphs and satyrs cavorting through woodlands in a most unchristian manner for such a holy place, and Skiouros found himself actually blushing at a couple of the ensembles they passed.

Finally the man-at-arms stopped before a doorway and stepped to one side, motioning for him to enter. Skiouros halted beside him and turned to peer through the door. The room within was clearly a hall or vestibule of some kind, well-furnished and remarkably tasteful given everything else Skiouros had seen throughout the apostolic palace. Beyond, a set of double doors left open led to a large chamber which was brightly lit with numerous lamps, the centrepiece a huge oak table laden with platters and goblets and wine bottles. As he stepped in through the doorway at the prompting of the man-at-arms, a figure he'd not previously been able to see for the long table's clutter rose from the seat at the far end.

Andreas Palaeologos, exiled Emperor of Byzantium, appeared every inch the Italian nobleman from his neatly tended beard and carefully trimmed hair through to his fine attire and to the elegant bow he gave Skiouros.

'Good evening, my friend. I am so immensely pleased that you were free to accept my invitation.'

Skiouros returned the bow with a clumsy echo and strode through the double doors, smiling at the thought that he might have been too busy to come. Inexpertly, he unclasped his robe and shook it out, draping it across a stand by the door, next to a green one of similar design. He smiled.

114

'I had kept my ears open these past months, Majesty, but every time I heard tell of you, you were somewhere to the north accompanying this or that Papal force on endless punitive campaigns.'

Palaeologos made a face. 'Endless. *Absolutely* endless. Or so it felt, at least. I am fairly certain that Bishop Lando would still have me sat ahorse somewhere high in the Apennines had the danger not driven us south once more.'

Skiouros stopped at the table's foot, shuffling to adjust his uncomfortable doublet, his brow puckering. 'Danger, sire?'

It was Palaeologos' turn to frown as he gestured for Skiouros to take a seat in a chair not far from his own. 'The danger. Have you not heard? The French crossed the border weeks ago with a force the size of which has not trod Italian soil since the days of the Caesars' – a slight self-deprecating smile accompanying that last. 'They are marching south determinedly, though their vast swathes of earth-shaking artillery slow their pace and give His Holiness a little time to prepare.'

For some reason, despite the months passing so slowly, the threat of French invasion had slipped from the fore of Skiouros' mind and he had all but forgotten it in the convoluted politics and internecine fighting of the central Italian states. Now, with the news of Charles' approach, the fear that Cem Sultan's capture was on the cards arose anew. The months of wasted time inactive in the monastery of Sant'Agnese rankled all the more.

He bit down on his cheek. All the more reason then to concentrate on the task and make the most of this night, which offered the possibility of true progress. With a serious expression, he rounded the table's corner and walked along its length. 'I had heard that the Papal forces were moving out of the city in bulk, but the word is that it is some exercise or other in the Romagna.' It had not unduly excited any of their group. Papal forces marching into the Romagna seemed to be an almost-monthly occurrence.

'Word put about so as not to panic the population,' Palaeologos replied quietly. 'The entire Papal force has moved as far as Tuscany and now awaits defeat and probable obliteration at the hands of the French, who purportedly outnumber them twenty to one, even with the allied lords and numerous condottieri at the pope's call. I am relieved to find you here and not attached to that army. But enough of such dark thoughts. I have to confess that after all these months I had entirely forgotten your name, but that of the Orsini is too ever-present an appellation to forget. Upon my return I asked around among the remaining guards here after an Orsini condottiere with a single lance of men. Lo and behold you were located for me with remarkable simplicity. Come. Sit.'

Skiouros nodded easily. The more information he could gain tonight the better, but intimate details of the French invasion were of limited interest and so that subject could be let go. All being well he and his friends would be done and gone before Charles of Valois arrived in Rome demanding crowns and hostages and pointing his infamous cannon at the walls of Saint Peter's.

'Let us talk instead of my homeland and what you remember of it,' Palaeologos smiled. 'I want you to dredge up every memory you have. Every sound, sight, smell and taste of the east. And for the love of all that is simple, do stop weighing me down with titles and honorifics and use my name. No one – other perhaps than His Holiness and the bishop – believes I am anything more than a burden on the Vatican treasury.'

Skiouros smiled and allowed himself to relax slightly. It was hard to remain too formal in this man's presence. Pausing on a whim as he moved along the table, his hand reached out to a fruit bowl on the sideboard, and Palaeologos half-rose from the seat urgently.

'Not that one, my friend. Here… there is fruit on the table for us.'

The Greek paused for a moment and looked down at the bowl. The apples gleamed red, and there were grapes, pomegranates and cherries. They looked fresh and appetising. He frowned and turned his puzzled gaze upon his host.

Palaeologos was out of his seat now and strode a few paces across to the sideboard. Picking up his napkin, he used it to line his palm like a glove and selected a rosy apple from the bowl. Skiouros' furrowed brow only deepened until the exiled emperor jerked out his hand and held the apple beneath the Greek's nose. Skiouros stared as he noted after a moment the acrid aroma of the fruit.

'I don't understand,' he blurted, reaching up and rubbing his nose reflexively, his nostrils pulsing. Palaeologos gently lowered the apple back into place in the bowl.

'Highly poisonous,' he replied, carefully folding the napkin and tossing it into the fireplace nearby where it burst into flame. 'Treated with the 'poison nut', shipped in periodically from India. Awful stuff. Tortures the body for a long while before the end.'

As Palaeologos moved back towards his seat, Skiouros stared in incomprehension at the deadly fruit and skirted past it, making for the chair previously indicated while he peered suspiciously at the food upon the table. Palaeologos laughed lightly. 'Oh fear not, my friend.

This is perfectly healthy, but if you are nervous, I will sample anything for you. This is the same food that the cardinals eat, so you can be assured of its efficacy.'

'But why the poison?' questioned Skiouros, still shaken, as he took his seat.

'A man in my position makes enemies through his name alone, my friend. For all my exile and political impotence, a man who effectively holds the rights of two crowns must take care. In my time I have watched three would-be-assassins intent on doing me harm fall foul of just such a fruity trick.'

'And yet you trust the palace food?' asked Skiouros suspiciously, peering at the platters before him.

'A man who meant to poison me would likely poison the entire college of cardinals in the attempt. As I said: I eat the same food as they, and the only time it could be tampered with separately is when it is conveyed to my apartments, which is all done by the three men I can call loyal in my service. You see, I am *most* careful. I do not even trust a taster, for tasters can be bought, and have developed tricks of their own over the centuries.'

Skiouros nodded dubiously and watched as Palaeologos began to collect food from the various platters onto his own dish, pausing here and there to sample the goods first. The young Greek watched, still nervous, as the emperor began to tuck in to the meal and finally, with a shrug, started gathering the more tantalising dishes from the table onto his own plate. Satisfied that he had enough not to insult, he selected a chicken leg in some sticky sauce and nibbled it carefully. Half expecting to convulse and collapse in agony, he was pleasantly taken aback by the sweet, sharp taste, flavoured with wine and herbs. Clearly the Vatican lavished as much care and funding on its sustenance as it did on its décor.

'Tell me about Constantinople,' Palaeologos said quietly between bites.

Skiouros continued to chew, allowing his memory to furnish him with images.

'I have limited experience, Majesty, in truth. As a Greek in the Ottoman city it was safer to keep to Greek zones. The sultan is surprisingly accepting of his non-Turkish subjects, but even after four decades, the city is a long way from integrated and tensions can run high. By the Golden Horn, close to the city walls lie the areas known as Phanar and Balat. There most of the Greeks live, and many of the Jews in the latter.'

'But you *have* visited the rest of the city?'

117

'Upon occasion. Many of the churches are now mosques, and more are converted each year, but the sultan continues to allow some churches to serve the Christian communities. The old buildings of the ancient city are often crumbling hulks now, and those that become dangerous the Turks dismantle or convert. Our old bath houses thrive with little change, though.'

'And what of the Imperial residences?'

Skiouros shrugged, pausing to take a bite of bread soaked in olive oil. 'The sultan lives in the so-called New Palace built by his father on the headland above the Hagia Sophia. The Great Palace has been little more than a ruin for as long as anyone can remember. The Bucoleon is now used to house ambassadors and foreign dignitaries... or at least *half* of it is. The other half is in disrepair and occupied by homeless thieves and vagabonds. The only Imperial palace left in any liveable state would be the Blachernae, but even that was damaged when the Turks breached the walls and is now used more as a prison and barracks than anything else. The area around the Blachernae has become the domain of the Romani.'

Palaeologos sagged a little. 'My father had fond memories of the Bucoleon and the Blachernae. I have heard reports from ambassadors and merchants, of course, but nothing compares to a true insider's view. And what of the people, then?'

'Only the old men remember the days of the emperors, in reality, Majesty.' He tried not to let memories of his father fill his head, the old farmer complaining bitterly about this man's uncle – the last true emperor – eschewing the capital and being crowned in the provincial city of Mistra out in the Greek Morea. About the former emperor's plans to merge the true Orthodox Church with the Pope's own gilded artifice. Old Nikos the farmer had displayed more respect for the conquering sultan than he ever would for the man who would sell out his Byzantine world to Rome. He had not been alone in that, either. It would not be kind to bring up the uncle's failings in front of the nephew, though.

'And what of the man who rules there now?' Palaeologos prompted, reaching for his chicken. 'They call him 'the Just,' I understand. Is the cognomen deserved?'

Skiouros felt a moment of suspicion. There was a hunger suddenly in the exiled scion's voice and he wondered whether the man really wanted the truth or simple vindication? He took a breath.

'As with all overlords, Majesty, he has good points and bad. He is strong, and relatively accommodating of other faiths and peoples.

118

Those of us without Turkish blood are able to take roles in the Ottoman court and military, though not without converting.' He noticed a slight darkening of his host's expression, which confirmed his suspicions, and he sat back. 'Of course, no amount of minor freedoms he allows his non-Islamic subjects can make up for the fact that his armies roll like a cloud of black conquest across the Balkan lands, annexing kingdom after kingdom, and his pirates who ravage the western seas.' He was gratified to see these bold anti-Turkish statements pick up the man's mood a little and banish some of the darkness and for a moment, he saw an opportunity.

'And his half-brother lives here under the same roof as yourself, his own apartments a gilded Papal cage. It must bring back the injustice of your exile whenever you set eyes upon him?'

Palaeologos paused with a forkful of something hovering before his face. His eyes focussed on that for a moment as he replied. 'There are moments when the knowledge that he is here raises unhappy memories and dark thoughts.' He shrugged. 'But then it is not his doing. His father deposed my uncle by the sword and his brother rules my empire. Prince Cem, however, has done nothing to me. We have far more in common than we do keeping us apart.'

He bit and chewed the morsel and Skiouros peered at him in the silence that followed. The man had good reason to despise Bayezid, of course, and no real reason to hate Cem. But that had not been the point of his enquiry. He was about to prompt again when the emperor swallowed and answered his unspoken question anyway.

'In fact, the matter rarely arises. I see the exiled sultan but rarely and never in personal circumstances. He is valuable to the Pope and, with the added threat of the French bearing down upon us, the ever-present Hospitallers who surround him are all the more defensive and suspicious. For all his status as a glorified prisoner, he is better protected than His Holiness.'

Skiouros nodded his understanding, trying to hide his disappointment. If even this fellow exile who lived beneath the same roof could find no opportunity to gain access to Prince Cem, then what chance did an outsider stand? 'Of course, the captive sultan's future is somewhat uncertain, with the French marching on Rome and Napoli,' he prompted.

Palaeologos gave a strange knowing smile which caused the Greek to narrow his eyes. 'Not *that* uncertain,' the man said. 'In fact, if what Bishop Lando tells me is true, then Cem might actually be looking forward to his French liberation. I am led to believe that if Charles of France manages to secure Napoli and launch his crusade, then he will crush Bayezid the Second and place Cem on the throne of Constantinople as a French puppet sultan.'

Skiouros felt a chill run through him. That was almost exactly what the conspirators had been trying to achieve all those years ago when this whole mess had started! 'And you would watch this happen? To your empire?'

The exiled Palaeologos grinned. 'He would rule the city only in Charles' name, but to free Constantinople, the French will have to conquer the Balkans, Greece and the Morea. And then one of my titles becomes reinstated. Cem can have his pretend crown with a French sword at his back. I will have the Morea for my own, with the authority of the French King and with Papal investiture. Cem's lot would improve immeasurably, but after a life in exile I achieve more than I could ever hope for. You see? For all His Holiness has done for me and the terror of the Roman people at the thought of French invasions, I for one am anticipating King Charles' arrival with some eagerness. And I suspect my fellow exile feels the same.

Skiouros' blood ran cold through him and he placed his garlic sausage half-eaten back on his plate, his appetite entirely deserting him. When Charles and his French army reached Rome, they would take Andreas Palaeologos and Cem son of Mehmet and make them client kings, raining righteous holy wrath down upon Bayezid II and his empire. Three years had passed since Ottoman traitors and Mamluk assassins had threatened to destroy the peace that Bayezid nurtured in the city, and now that harmony was about to be threatened once more. Not this time by the plotting of a circle of power-crazed zealots, but by an invading army of Christians. *Catholic* Christians, no less. No one in the eastern world had yet forgiven Rome for sacking the great city and bringing rape, fire and destruction against their fellow Christians almost three centuries ago. Skiouros' own father could not speak of the Pope without spitting a curse and warding against evil.

No. This could not happen.

He felt his anger and determination burn like a fire in the belly after months of stagnation. Without Prince Cem as his pretext for war and crusade, Charles surely would not dare move against the Turks? Without Cem, he had no legitimate cause and his fellow monarchs would fail to back him. Would the Pope even lend his support then? No. It was critical: Cem had to die, not just to assure Lykaion of eternal rest, but also to prevent a religious apocalypse that could engulf the east and scorch the land black.

For the rest of the meal, which lasted perhaps fifteen more stifled minutes, Skiouros made small talk, changing the subject entirely and laughing as lightly as he could about the frivolities of court life. In the end, Palaeologos seemed to become aware of Skiouros' failed appetite and his lack of enthusiasm but if he was disappointed, he hid it well.

When the bells rang out for compline across the city, Skiouros finally leaned back and sighed with fake repleteness.

'I must take my leave now, I am afraid, Your Majesty. It has been pleasant to speak of the old country for a change, and I hope we have the chance again in the coming months, but for the moment I should return to my companions.'

Palaeologos rose slowly, dabbing his mouth with his napkin and stretching. 'It is a shame to leave such a feast barely touched, but I daresay my entourage will be more than pleased to help demolish it for me, and the various Hospitallers who wander the corridors from time to time look upon me kindly as a source of snacks to help guard duty pass more comfortably.'

He smiled and continued. 'My time here is somewhat rigidly measured by my host and the good bishop, but when the opportunity arises I will attempt to invite you to accompany me again, or perhaps I will visit you outside this glorious building. I would suggest we ride or hunt in the Caffarella valley to the south, but His Holiness has a standing order that Vatican residents should not leave the confines of the city walls without both permission and appropriate military support. After all, not only are the French marching south, but many of the notables and city governments of Italy are already wavering in their allegiances, preferring to support Charles' massive army than the endangered Papacy.'

Skiouros nodded. He could well imagine the nobles of Italy flying the Valois banner in a move of supreme self-preservation. 'Once again, Majesty, thank you for the meal and the company. I look forward to a time when we can hunt and ride as you say. Shall I find my own way out?'

Palaeologos shook his head. 'The palace is still carefully controlled by His Holiness' men. You would find yourself under guard in short order. Paregorio will escort you.' Walking across to Skiouros, he gestured to the door. The Greek wandered over to the stand upon which his black and grey cioppa robe hung and struggled into the heavy, unfamiliar, restrictive garment. The scion of Byzantium waited patiently and when Skiouros was once again suitably attired for the streets of the city, escorted him out through the double doors to where Paregorio lounged on a chair by the outer door, cleaning his fingernails with a poniard. The man-at-arms rose to his feet at his master's presence and bowed from the waist.

'Master Skiouros will be returning to his residence, Paregorio. Would you accompany him?'

The man nodded, and Skiouros added, 'As far as the outer piazza will be fine, thank you. I can find my way from there.' Palaeologos accompanied them to the landing outside the suite and as Skiouros gave a short bow and said his goodbyes, the exiled emperor suddenly smiled, looking over Skiouros' shoulder, and held up a hand in greeting. The young Greek turned and his spirit sang out with dreadful recognition.

The man standing on the matching landing at the far side of the three-storey drop was bedecked in Ottoman robes of the finest quality, with two clearly Turkish attendants. Three men in red robes with white crosses stood a few yards ahead of them, and a matching trio lurked behind.

Cem!

His mind immediately committed that face to memory: unmarked skin crossed with faint lines of wear, thin lips beneath the shadow of well-tended drooping moustaches, chiselled, even jutting chin, thin angular nose and tired, careworn eyes. He was a morose reflection of the great Bayezid the Just.

After three years, Skiouros was finally face-to-face with the last of the conspirators for whose crimes Lykaion had paid with his life, and yet there might as well have been a thousand leagues between them. He had a brief, mad moment where he estimated the distance of the gap between landings – not even a demigod of ancient legend would make that jump – or the speed he could achieve racing round the periphery. But he was unarmed and too far away. And the six Hospitaller knights accompanying Prince Cem were veterans of numerous wars and carried heavy, sharp blades at their hips.

He was impotent in the face of his enemy.

Oh for a crossbow... and the skill to use it!

Cem Sultan held up a hand, returning Palaeologos' greeting, and gave a smile beneath sad eyes and Skiouros resolved that the next time he saw that face, he would leave those eyes bereft of life.

CHAPTER SEVEN - Castel Sant'Angelo, late autumn 1494

Skiouros shuffled forwards in the queue behind Orsini and in front of Parmenio, the others tagging along at the rear. Their small party formed a line snaking in the wake of Sir Antonio de Santo Martino of the Order of Hospitallers – Cesare Borgia's man – along the bridge that crossed the raging Tiber.

Ahead, the great bulk of the Castel Sant'Angelo – the Pope's earthly fortress – loomed powerful and ancient. Once a Roman emperor's tomb, it had been successively strengthened and fortified over the centuries into a castle of impressive proportions. Indeed, work had been carried out at His Holiness' command these past few months to reconstruct the parapet and provide an extra defensive wall and tower between the bastions... hurried work in the face of French aggression.

And aggression it truly was, gaining the support of self-serving Italian nobles and councils the length of the peninsula. While the bulk of the French army marched slowly, inexorably south over the summer and autumn, meeting crumbling will and minimal resistance en route, the Colonna family had declared for King Charles, delivering their castle at Ostia – Rome's main connection with the sea – into the hands of a French advance garrison. The French king had issued bold statements that he would celebrate Christmas in Rome and the way things looked, the chances were high that he would.

The armies of the Papal States had been withdrawn from their defensive positions to the north and now garrisoned the Castel Sant'Angelo, the Vatican, and the *borgo* – the newly-walled suburb of Rome that connected the two. The populace of Rome lived in perpetual anxiety, fearing the coming storm, and all signs in the city pointed to a siege which nobody believed they could withstand.

'I don't understand why the Pope and his cronies are moving to the Castel now,' Nicolo mused. 'The French are still months away, apart from the small Ostia garrison. Seems a little previous. At this stage anything could still happen.'

Orsini shrugged. 'They say there's been word of plots against the Pope and Prince Cem – letters from Firenze. Probably fictions cooked up by the Colonna family to put the fear of God into His Holiness, but apparently they're being taken seriously enough that the focus is shifting from the church to the castle. Can't say I blame the Pope, given the state of affairs in Italy now. The bigger the battlements surrounding him, the safer he'll be... until the bombards arrive, anyway.'

Skiouros looked around to check how attentive the mass about them were being. No one was paying the small party of mercenaries the slightest notice. Between the line of supply wagons to their left, bringing provisions to the castle, and the ordered ranks of Papal soldiers to the right, shouting out orders and suggestions and complaining about their feet, no one cared to examine a few condottieri under a cardinal's escort fighting for space in the middle. He leaned closer.

'I for one am all for it. After all this time it puts us and *him* under the same roof. We come ever closer.'

'It's just a shame we have to be besieged by the most dangerous army in Europe just to achieve a little proximity to your friend,' Parmenio sighed. 'It's starting to look as though even if you do achieve your goal, we'll all end up spitted on a French pike.'

Skiouros ignored his friend's gloomy appraisal in favour of his own optimism. After months of waiting, their chances had looked to have improved immeasurably when Cardinal Borgia had sent his Hospitaller friend to tell them that they should pack up their gear for a move into the Castel Sant'Angelo.

Orsini had quizzed Sir Antonio in surprise. It transpired that the bulk of the Hospitaller order resident in Rome were the scions of French noble families and, given the approaching French threat, the Pope had judged it imprudent to maintain a guard within the Vatican or even the borgo that might be given to sympathy for the French king. Consequently the entire Hospitaller presence in the city had been dismissed and sent back to their fortresses on the eastern islands and the Anatolian coast, with the exception of Sir Antonio who claimed only Catalan leanings, distrusted the French himself, and enjoyed the personal patronage of the cardinal.

And so the various units of condottieri and a small Catalan guard had been assigned positions in the Castel, and some directly to the entourage of Prince Cem himself. Of course, the latter duty had gone to the Papal Catalans and the longer-standing of Borgia's men, but even the newest among them were now in the same building as the exiled Turk. Chances would never be better.

Suddenly Skiouros found himself staggering into the back of Orsini, who recovered his balance easily and turned a questioning look on the Greek. Skiouros had already spun to face the pikeman in the Papal uniform who had bumped into him, calling him a clumsy oaf and threatening to find a new place to sheathe the pike.

The soldier sneered and emptied the contents of his nose with one nostril thumbed shut, muttering something about mercenaries. Skiouros was about to launch into a fresh tirade when his angry gaze picked out something unusual behind the careless soldier's shoulder.

'Look there!' he hissed, nudging Orsini. They had all slowed as they neared the arch of the castle gate in the recently constructed river wall beside the heavy circular tower. The gate was acting as a chicane for the three lines of traffic filtering through it from the bridge, and giving the men guarding it more than a slight headache.

Orsini turned at the comment, peering around. Skiouros pointed to the figure just beyond the insolent pikeman, perhaps six bodies down the line towards the gate. Cesare frowned and finally settled on Skiouros' pointing finger, just as the figure slipped from sight among the crowd.

'Damn it.' Skiouros craned his neck, but his short stature did him no favours among the press of people. The figure was lost among the press of grumbling bodies.

'Come on,' urged the nobleman, stepping forward and closing the gap with their guide. But Skiouros was still trying to reacquire his target, craning and jumping to no avail.

'Damn. I swear that was one of the Hospitallers.'

Orsini shook his head. 'They've taken ship for the east.'

'Not this one.'

Parmenio, catching the conversation, leaned forward. 'It's possible there are other Hospitallers in the city that aren't French, I suppose. Not all of them could have been guarding the Turk.'

Skiouros shook his head, still trying to see. 'Not this one. I've a good memory for faces and the last time I saw this particular sallow face he was a few steps ahead of Cem with a hand on his sword hilt. He was one of the pretender sultan's guards, I tell you.'

'What would he be doing here?' Parmenio said disbelievingly.

'If it was him, then you can be sure he's here on Papal business,' Nicolo shrugged. 'Don't forget His Holiness is a patron of their order.'

As Skiouros continued to crane, Cesare tapped their escort on the shoulder. 'Sir Antonio? Might I enquire if there are others of your order in the city?'

The Catalan rubbed his chin as he shuffled slowly forward in the press. 'None that I am aware of. My brothers rode out for Brindisi yesterday to take ship for Rhodos.'

'And none of them were retained for service in Rome?'

Suspicion crossed the man's features. 'No. Had I not been in the service of the cardinal and a good son of Catalonia, I'd have been with them. Why?'

'Just satisfying the curiosity of one of my more imaginative men,' Cesare smiled and turned back to Skiouros as they neared the gate and the Hospitaller fished their documentation from his belt, ready to show the gate guard.

'I don't care what he says,' Skiouros whispered adamantly. 'I saw him. One of them is still here. And if he's not supposed to be, then something strange is afoot.'

'You'd recognise him again?'

Skiouros allowed his expression to answer the question, and looked around furtively. 'When we get inside, can you cover for me?'

'Are you mad?' Parmenio hissed from behind. 'With threats of assassination and an approaching French army this place will be shut up tighter than a fish's fart-hole.'

'Not in the grounds,' Skiouros countered. Look at this place. With all the supplies and so on it'll be chaos inside. The security is all here at the gate or inside the main keep.' He pointed at the huge drum shape that was formed from the ancient mausoleum itself, battlemented in new brick and surmounted by the squared tops of the Papal apartments.

Orsini shook his head. 'You step out of the line and our escort will have both your balls and mine. We only have a few minutes until we'll be led to our quarters.' He mused for a moment. 'Unless... give me a moment.'

He turned to their escort and waited patiently as Sir Antonio cleared their documents bearing the Borgia seal with the guard, who counted off the bodies to confirm that all were present to enter. As soon as the group shuffled through the gate arch and into the utter bedlam of the courtyard, the Hospitaller paused, rubbing his head as he contemplated their route through the madness, and Orsini cleared his throat.

'We're going to be on duty here, Sir Antonio?'

'Yes. In the courtyard and outer ambulatory and on the walls and the bastions. You will probably occasionally have duty inside on the lower levels too.'

'Then since we're all new to the castle, before you show us to our quarters, would you submit to a brief tour of the place, so that we're a little more familiar with our duty?'

The Hospitaller gave a sour look as he took in their surroundings, clearly weighing up the value of a grounding in the castle's layout against the difficulty of navigating the total chaos of the court. With perhaps twenty to twenty-five feet between the drum keep and the surrounding defences, the courtyard was packed with carts and men, soldiers going about their various duties and workers loading, unloading and ferrying supplies. Any kind of tour would be a little like trying to swim in tallow. And with the almost deafening cacophony of a thousand competing voices, the chances of Sir Antonio making himself heard would be minimal. Eventually, with a sign of resigned regret the monkish knight nodded his acquiescence. 'But let's get up onto the walls where we can move. I'll take you round the perimeter and point out everything important – shouldn't take more than ten minutes. Then we'll come back to the gate and I'll take you into the places assigned you in the Bastion of San Matteo.'

Parmenio thanked Sir Antonio with a smile and as soon as the Hospitaller stepped forward to demand a man shift his wagon full of grain so that they could get to the stairs, he leaned close to Skiouros. 'Make your move, but you've got less than ten minutes to be back here and fall in with us.'

The Greek nodded and, straightening as Sir Antonio flashed an exasperated look at them while they waited for the wagon to roll a couple of paces forward, he paused. As soon as the Hospitaller looked away again, he stepped back behind a trio of crossbowmen in some unknown livery arguing about their billets.

Left or right? It was an arbitrary choice. His quarry had been ahead of them in the queue and must be inside the walls by now, but where he had gone was an unguessable question. Left or right? Or even straight into the keep? Or up onto the walls?

He allowed his seething mind to calm and looked around. Another set of four men stood guard at the entrance to the great cylindrical keep, and they looked a little less flustered than their counterparts on the outer wall. Doubtless few men would be given access to the interior. Certainly it was unlikely that his prey would. And the tops of the walls were relatively clear of men, apart from the guards at their regular positions. So, yes: left or right.

The decision was made for him by simple expediency. To the right, Sir Antonio was pushing his way past the cart to lead them all up the wall stairs. Less chance of being noticed by their escort if he went the other way.

With a quick look at his friends, Parmenio and Nicolo both miming their vehement wish that he be careful and rejoin them as soon as possible, Skiouros disappeared past a cart full of barrels that gave off the sharp, acrid stink of pitch.

A last glance back as he made his way between the endless shouting hordes, and he spotted his friends climbing the staircase. They would circumnavigate the fortress and then return to the bottom of those stairs. He had minutes.

Pausing at a stack of barrels where a teamster was arguing with a guard about their destination, he clambered up onto the heavy oaken containers and slowly turned a circle, his hand above his eyes to dim the glare of the watery white sun. He blinked away moisture. There would be rain before nightfall, Parmenio the weather authority had stated this morning, and the air was already beginning to threaten with a misty blanket.

It was an impossible task. Even Skiouros' non-scientific mind could easily perform an estimated headcount and see that this undertaking was like trying to spot a florin in a room full of ducats. Again, on the verge of being overwhelmed with negativity, he forced himself to calm, to relax, to breathe slowly. With exaggerated sluggishness, he closed his eyes and conjured up a mental image of the man. He had seen him months ago in the Vatican apartments, dressed in the crimson robe and white cross of the Hospitallers, on the far side of the front row of escorting knights. He had not been wearing a hat then, and neither had he today. He was blond. So blond as to almost be white. He had not submitted to the fashion for beards currently sweeping the upper classes, but had been poorly shaven on both occasions, his facial hair a slightly darker shade than his crown, more of a gold colour. He'd had a hooked nose and thin lips. One shoulder at a slightly lower slope to the other – almost certainly from some long-healed wound – which had given him a slight stoop and an odd walk.

He opened his eyes and turned again, slowly.

The man was nowhere in evidence. Damn it.

Suddenly, he felt a thump against his calf and looked down to see the angry teamster glaring at him. 'Any time you'd like to step down would be good for me, dickhead,' the man snapped.

Skiouros flashed him a smile that was half thanks and half apology and dropped from the barrel. A little walk further round the encircling ambulatory and he paused again. He was now perhaps a third of the way, fighting against the current of humanity for every step. Here the carts had thinned out and the mass was almost entirely formed of men porting goods and stacking and unstacking things. Nothing obvious to use as a platform for a short man here. Frowning, his gaze fell upon a horse tethered to a post against the inner drum keep wall. The beast bore a good saddle and a somewhat anachronistic caparison bearing a white eagle splayed upon a blue background. Skiouros glanced this way and that for a long moment, but the horse appeared to be entirely unattended and, without delay, he crossed to it, lifted his leg until he felt his thigh muscles creak and slipped his toe into the stirrup, grasping the saddle pommel to pull himself up above the crowd. The horse was a destrier, bred for battle and the joust, and was quite the largest steed Skiouros had ever touched. Consequently, it gave him an excellent view.

As he scanned the crowd seething between the cylindrical keep and the outer defences, he turned the situation over in his mind. Was he on a fool's errand? So what if the man was here and he had been assigned to Prince Cem's guard at the Vatican? Even legitimately, there could be a hundred reasons for the man to be here now, and almost none of them would have any bearing on Skiouros' end goal. And yet there was just something that drew him to the matter. Something was wrong – it sent a prickle among the hairs on the back on his neck. His free hand went reflexively to the hilt of the macana club looped at his belt. He *knew* the man was engaged in some clandestine, underhand behaviour, and with his connection to the Hospitallers and to Prince Cem there was too little probability of coincidence for Skiouros to ignore it.

His eyes worked their way across the crowd and came back to his target after disregarding him once. The man had hoisted a hood over his white-blond hair and had been looking away on the last pass of Skiouros' gaze. But on a return journey, the man had turned and his golden face fuzz and hooked nose caught the Greek's attention. The man was wearing the nondescript tan doublet and hose of an ordinary mercenary with an equally ordinary cloak over the top, a plain blade with a finger ring and knuckle guard sheathed at his side. Nothing marked him out as one of the Order except Skiouros' memory.

The man was over by the curtain wall, close to the rear left bastion. Even as Skiouros focused on him, he turned back to the wall and worked feverishly at something unseen, hidden by the hooded cloak he wore over his doublet. Carefully, Skiouros noted the man's exact location, using the decorative sections of masonry above and counting the merlons in the battlements from the far bastion to be sure. After all, when he climbed down he would be too short to...

His world blurred as his foot was pulled from the stirrup, hauled back by force, tearing his fingers from the pommel. He hit the flagged floor hard and it took a moment for him to orient himself before looking up into the angry face of a man in a breastplate and articulated arm pieces, a steel gorget lifting his chin to a haughty angle, his torso covered with a surcoat of blue bearing a white eagle.

'My lord,' Skiouros said with urgent respect, inclining his head.

'Troublesome peasants who do not know their place and lay hand upon their betters' possessions are looking for an early opportunity to face God for their sins. What have you to say, dog?'

Skiouros took a steadying breath, aware that he was no longer watching the Hospitaller and that time was passing by.

'Answer the lord d'Este,' barked a man at his shoulder, presumably a squire or herald for the lord. Skiouros remembered the name from one of Orsini's many lessons on the interminable warring families of Italy. The Este. Currently one of the few great families still throwing their weight behind the Borgia Pope. Only, in Orsini's opinion, because they had calculated the favour they would win should Borgia survive this crisis and were willing to place a fat pile of coins upon a single roll of the dice – not from honour or loyalty.

'My lord, I meant no offence,' Skiouros said with respect and care. 'I found myself separated from my lord Orsini and my height denied me an opportunity to locate him.'

'So you thought to stand on Pegaso? It surprises me not that a double-faced, untrustworthy and impious animal like an Orsini would take such a creature into his service. It only worries me that you could be the best he has and that I might find myself standing close to you when Charles of Valois begins to pound our walls. When the time comes, boy, try not to piss on my boots or accidentally stick my page with your blade.'

Skiouros fought the almost irresistible urge to knock this pompous arrogant dunghead onto his backside and, teeth gritted, kept his head politely inclined.

'Be off with you, boy,' d'Este sneered. 'Find your master and tell him to keep his pets under better control.'

As Skiouros stood, bowed sharply and turned in the direction of his quarry at the wall, Lord d'Este made a quick move to cuff him around the ear but missed, the young Greek swift and agile, disappearing between two groups of teamsters.

A moment later, Skiouros reached the wall and his heart sank as he realised his prey had vanished. A quick look up confirmed he was at the correct position, and he shuffled two merlons along the wall to be in exactly the place the incognito Hospitaller had been. Nothing. Not a thing marked the man's position. With a quick jump, Skiouros tried to scan the crowd, but there was no sign and nothing for him to stand on.

He reached up to an iron bracket, newly placed to help a recent wall repair solidify, and used it to haul himself up long enough to quickly glance left and right. Still no sign. The man was gone. With a sigh of irritation, Skiouros caught sight of Orsini and Sir Antonio on the wall top by the bastion, rapidly approaching his position. He would have to head to the steps any moment if he was to return to the group seamlessly. He was out of time and he had lost the man.

One a final thought occurring to him, he turned to the part of the wall where the Hospitaller had been working and peered closely. Curiously, one section of the recently-strengthened wall – around four different bricks – had clean, white, new mortar, of which a small section had been chipped and scraped away, possibly with a small blade. Two bricks further along, the mortar had been wetted with something and appeared to have corroded and been eaten back into the bricks where it still frothed like a foamy wave. Skiouros was about to reach out to it when it struck him what a monumentally stupid move that could be. He stayed his hand.

The sound of Sir Antonio almost above him, exchanging conversational fragments with Orsini, made him leap back into action. With a last glimpse at the mortar, he began to push through the press of men, staying close to the wall to keep hidden from those walking along the top of it, and made for the stairs. Arriving at the ascent just as the voices reached the top, he ducked back into the shadow and watched as the Catalan knight led Orsini and his men back down to the ambulatory.

'Come, now, and I will lead you to your quarters,' Sir Antonio said, walking past the skulking figure of Skiouros. 'Once you are settled in and all this fuss has died away, one of the castle's clerks will drop by and give you a schedule of duties. I will call in from time to time as my own responsibilities require. Make the most of this lull. When the French get here in a few months, these will seem like balmy halcyon days past.'

Orsini nodded his agreement and gave Skiouros a curious look as the Greek fell in with the group easily. Dropping back only slightly, so as not to lose the knight in the press, Orsini leaned towards Skiouros. 'Well?'

'Found him. I don't know what he's up to but it's not good. What eats mortar?'

Orsini frowned in surprise. 'I'm not sure. Aqua Regia, perhaps? I've heard of it being used for similar purposes as well as melting precious metals. I don't think I like the sound of this.'

'Nor I,' Skiouros sighed. 'I lost the man again, thanks to a pompous idiot called Este. What the man's up to is beyond me, as is how it might be connected with Cem.'

'I think we had best keep our eyes wide open during our sojourn in this place,' Orsini murmured as they passed through a doorway and into the bustling corridors of the structure. '*Very* wide open.'

Despite the change of venue, little changed in Skiouros' life over the following weeks, a routine of guard duties, exercise and training, patrols and the like falling into place as they came to learn the ways of the castle and its officers. Perhaps once a week, some task took them into the lower levels of the castle's main keep, but brought him no closer to the hidden Turkish hostage than that. The main ancient section of the huge cylinder with the weathered stone face was a solid mass containing a wide entry hall now used as a guard room, and a sloping passage that curved up the outer edge and then passed into a last guard chamber before emerging out onto the modern, upper section with the papal apartments, courtyards and halls. No one but the Catalan guards and the officials serving His Holiness or the Castle's seneschal passed that higher guard room.

Sagging in the knowledge that he was nearer to Cem than ever, but looked like getting no closer than this, Skiouros had instead set himself the task of investigating the elusive and secretive Hospitaller. But rather than relieving the frustration of his main task, his continued failure to locate the clandestine warrior drove him ever further into vexation. Not once in the ensuing nine weeks did he even lay eyes upon the man. He eventually came to the inescapable conclusion that the Hospitaller had left the castle the same day that

Skiouros had spotted him. Surely he had not penetrated the upper layers of the castle keep, given how his Order were under Papal command to absent themselves from Rome? And Skiouros had scoured the rest of the castle time and again to no avail. The man had vanished. Every few days, the Greek checked that portion of wall too, but nothing had changed there. He had even scanned all the other visible wall sections of the complex and found nothing.

Nothing. That was the theme of his time in the castle.

Or at least, it had been until December came calling with its cold winds, the intermittent bone-chilling rain lashing the battlements, and ever-deepening troubles.

The continued blockade of Papal sea transport, with Ostia in French hands, combined with the unwillingness of local lords to supply Rome with food while they were themselves faced with potential sieges, had led to a rapid diminishing of the city's stores. Food had become rationed on the first of the month, a number of units of regular soldiers and condottieri alike taking rotations in the unenviable task of controlling the distribution of rations to the people. Skiouros had noted on the only time he had been seconded to such a duty how few of the city's population seemed to be classed as 'people' where supplies were concerned. The poor and the homeless had to make do somehow with eating fresh air and drinking rainwater. Those who owed fealty to a patron relied upon their master to provide. It was a hellish situation, further enforcing Skiouros' extremely negative opinion of Italy in general and Rome in particular. Though no such siege had yet struck Istanbul since the Turk had taken control there, when the day came for the French crusade, Skiouros simply could not imagine Sultan Bayezid the Second unfairly restricting rations by class. Every day in this accursed place heightened his urge to return home and had it not been for his vow and the knowledge that he had to lay the spectre of his brother to rest, he would have been there some time ago.

There would be no leaving Rome now, though.

The gates in the walls of the borgo had been blocked and sealed tight, the walls garrisoned along their length and every weak point strengthened, the few cannon at the Vatican's command run out to face the surrounding countryside to the north.

Disaffection within the city had begun to become rather vocal. Even those under Papal protection in the strong borgo were hungry and starting to feel trapped. Those in the main bulk of the city across the river were virtually undefended, with just a few militia to hand and a couple of roving patrols from the Papal armies, their walls all but offered to the enemy in order to strengthen the defences of the borgo.

The last supply wagon reached the city on the third of the month, having raced there from the only accessible local port at Civitavecchia just as the French army had swarmed in and secured it against the Pope. Things were beginning to look more desperate by the day.

Then the news came that the Orsini family had thrown in their lot with King Charles. That particular unwelcome morsel had made Skiouros' friend unapproachable for a day or two as he ranted and raged about his family's lack of honour and foresight. He only began to subside after he had been drawn into the Pope's presence, along with Cardinal Borgia, and questioned somewhat strong-handedly, being forced to swear a new, hard oath in light of his family's betrayal. In addition to Cesare's continued service, one pleasant piece of news emerged from the questioning. Apparently the only other Orsini in Lazio who had remained loyal to the Papacy was the erstwhile troublemaker Romano, and in response Cardinal Borgia had released young Paolo from his captivity and returned him to his father. Small consolation, but consolation nonetheless.

And then one morning, as the icy rain lashed the battlements of the castle, a shout had gone up when a lookout spied movement. Within half a day the horizon to the north and west, hemmed in to the east by the river, had become black with the swarming figures of men, horses, cannon and wagons.

The French had arrived.

By the evening of the twenty-third day of December in the year of our Lord fourteen hundred and ninety-four, the world of Pope Alexander the Sixth had shrunk to encompass the borgo and the city of Rome – all his seaports in French hands, and all the local lords either siding with the French or overwhelmed by them. It seemed as though Charles' boast that he would pass Christmas in Rome was destined to come to pass.

Then, the previous day, things had come to a head in the city across the river to the south. Despite the fact that the French forces presented little threat there, the bulk of their enormous army lying to the north of the Pope's private domain, the starvation and panic had built to untenable levels and when one of the Papal patrols had been forced to push a starving man back from their number, a small riot had broken out, which had led to the death and mutilation of six Vatican soldiers and to the four survivors fleeing back across the river under a hail of makeshift missiles. It was said that the Pope spent most of his time now in solitary seclusion in the chapel atop the castle, praying to a somewhat indifferent God for their deliverance.

His cardinals had urged him to come to terms; that was common knowledge. Even his own son, Cesare Borgia, had agreed that there was now no alternative; that if a day or two more passed as things were, the people of Rome would rise up against their Pope and assault the borgo from the city itself. The army might hold for days or even weeks against the French, but not with the people of Rome ravaging their rear.

The Pope had lost. It was that simple. Plain truth that all could now see.

Skiouros leaned on the battlements, peering into the array of cannons lined up facing the castle, ready to thunder death and destruction at a word. And yet Charles had held off. It was tempting to think that perhaps he still held enough respect for the Pope for this to end well, or that he had no wish to pulverise the glory that was Rome, filled with innocents. But, as Orsini had clarified in his matter of fact manner, Charles would not flatten the castle with his cannon, since he knew Cem was held within, and his war against the Turk relied heavily upon his securing the usurper Sultan as his living banner.

'We should be ready,' he said quietly.

'Oh?' queried Orsini next to him. 'How so?'

'Something is about to happen. It has to. And whatever it is, it likely means that Prince Cem will be moved. The moment he leaves that great doorway to the keep may well be the only reasonable chance I will ever get. If he is to be given over to the French, it will most certainly be the last.'

Parmenio, at his other side, snorted. 'Revenge or no revenge, you'll find it near impossible to get close enough to do anything. And if you do manage, by some miracle, to kill the little bugger, you will follow him to the grave, after a short sojourn in a cellar in the company of some very professional men and their collection of sharp and glowing pokers.'

'And we'd be right behind you there, too,' added Nicolo with feeling.

'Then what has this all been for?' Skiouros sighed. 'I cannot believe that God has brought me this close to my goal, that wrathful Bayamanaco would allow me to lay eyes on the man that will complete my work but not permit me to do anything about it.'

'Your strange perceptions of God and your fealty to weird foreign heresies aside,' Orsini smiled with a little stiff discomfort, 'I think you will find that it was your *companions* who brought you this close. God does not approve of vengeful men, though he might oft be so himself.'

'Happy bloody Christmas,' grunted Parmenio, rubbing his cold elbows and resting them on the battlements once more.

A little further along the wall, Helwyg the Silesian giant hefted the polearm he had taken to carrying, and turned to them.

'This no weather for Christ Mass,' he rumbled. 'Where I from, even summer worse than this. Christ Mass in snow deeper than I. Forests buried white.' The big man sighed, apparently missing his homeland more than ever. Skiouros could empathise well with him, though not in respect of the cold.

Girolamo patted the Silesian on the shoulder comfortingly.

Orsini smiled. 'His Holiness seems to have managed to keep the French wolf from his door for the day, though, despite all Charles' boasts. He must be praying hard to God that Rome does not pay the price for his vanity in denying the king that small victory.'

A voice from behind – smooth as molten gold and quiet as a feather's passing – replied, 'His Holiness has made his point.'

The six men turned to see Cardinal Borgia standing at the rear of the wall, wrapped for once in his red robes of office. Skiouros was interested to see the black-clad forms of the canons Lateran – fathers Bartholomew and Alexander – behind him, as well as the ever-present solid form of Sir Antonio.

'Respectfully, Your Eminence,' Orsini smiled humourlessly, 'His Holiness' point might be the trigger that causes the death of a lot of Rome's people. And not a few cardinals.'

Borgia's lip curled in a manner that put Skiouros in mind of a hunting dog facing a difficult prey. 'The few cardinals still walking these halls are men who will make any incursion a matter for extreme regret. Many of them work a sword better than you, Orsini. Those whose entire goal in the house of the Lord is the acquisition of wealth and the avoidance of work have fled to safety among the Frank-lovers.'

Skiouros caught sight of the two canons behind the cardinal and the look the pair shared spoke volumes about their opinions of taking up the sword in defence of their Pope. He tried not to smile as one of them made hand signals to the other of a somewhat suggestive nature, clearly revolving around the phrase *work a sword*.

'What brings Your Eminence out onto the battlements in this cold?' Orsini asked casually.

Borgia placed his hands on his hips and straightened. 'His Holiness has decided that the time has come to agree terms with the king of France, on the condition that they are not too unfavourable to the chair of Saint Peter.'

'His Holiness intends to try for a beneficial arrangement while he sits here with his head inside the lion of France's mouth and tickles its balls with a feather?'

The cardinal laughed. 'Such might easily be my father's motto. The Borgia have faced insurmountable problems more than once in our time, and yet we are still here and at the apex of this pile of robes and bones and gold that is the Church. As I say, my father is to send a deputation out to the king.'

Skiouros felt his blood chill as he saw the blocks of his near future falling into place.

'His Holiness will send his Vice Chancellor out as his ambassador. Despite the man's family's utter disregard for the Pope's position and their continued opposition and enmity, Ascanio Sforza remains a loyal member of His Holiness' higher court. However, when I was asked to supply the escort, it pleased me to think that the one member of the Sforza plague who still stands by my father might be accompanied by the one Orsini who holds a commission here. It is a curious symmetry.'

'I can imagine,' Orsini smiled. 'Do I presume that the deputation will be departing presently?'

'The Vice Chancellor and his retinue are already forming up at the gate. You will need to obtain horses from the stables and prepare. You have fifteen minutes.'

'Respectfully, Your Eminence, what happens to us if Cardinal Sforza simply decides to follow his family's lead and kiss the French king's arse?'

'Then, Orsini, I will be extremely interested to see how you handle the situation, given the parallels with your own circumstances.'

Orsini bowed his head with a sly grin.

Skiouros settled into the saddle with all the ease of a deranged camel riding a clothes horse. He had not ridden since his arrival in Rome, and even before that had hardly been what could be termed a natural horseman. His faithful steed Sigma was still stabled at the monastery of Sant'Agnese, as safe as anywhere in Rome, and this animal seemed to be at best a wild creature with no love of bearing a man's weight.

'Would you try not to look so out of place?' Parmenio grumbled, sitting comfortably atop a steed that was little more than a placid mobile hairball that needed a good kicking even to get it to step forward.

'If this thing would stop trying to drop me I would.'

'Note, if you will,' Father Bartholomew smiled, 'how the young man with his easy hose and doublet sits astride his beast with all the grace of a nervous cat on a hot platter, while the Cardinal Sforza, who I am given to understand has not ridden a horse since before he took his vows, and wears an unaccommodating robe of ankle length, seems to be perfectly at home and in control. Curious, is it not, brother?'

Beside him, Father Alexander of Clan Keith chuckled. 'Be kind, my brother. A dancer in a tin suit is still a dancer, while an ape in breeches is still an ape.'

Skiouros flashed an angry look at the pair, but the smiles they bore were full only of friendly humour and no true mockery.

'Perhaps one of you would like to take my place?'

'Ah now,' Alexander laughed in his thick, strange northern accent, 'we would be as much use defending the Vice Chancellor in a sudden melee as you would be in taking the lurid, shocking, wicked – and thoroughly invigorating – confessions of the castle soldiers.'

'In seriousness,' Bartholomew said quietly, leaning closer, 'be very careful and more than a little diplomatic. Ascanio Sforza is both clever and tactful, and you should encounter no problems. But His Holiness sends out the Vice Chancellor partially as a test of loyalty, and his cardinal son does the same for you. It may be that you are about to see a higher step on the Borgia ladder if you perform appropriately.'

'Oh?' Skiouros leaned forward eagerly and almost toppled from the horse as the irritating beast actually managed somehow to roll its back with the movement.

'One of His Eminence's more important and long-standing units of condottieri has been dismissed from service and expelled from the borgo. It is not common knowledge, though, so keep it to yourself. One of the men in that lance was a Frenchman by birth and in an unfortunate argument he put a pike point through one of the Catalan guard's feet. Terrible business. His Eminence has thus far kept you at arm's length, treating you as something of an unknown, but now he is shorthanded and I believe he seeks to shuffle you up a place.'

Skiouros felt a rush at the thought. To be high in his service would certainly take him closer to the opportunity he sought. 'We are loyal to His Eminence and the Pope,' Orsini shrugged, 'but I thank you for that. We will endeavour to make our fidelity ever more clear.'

The two canons smiled like favourite uncles and stepped back as the huge gate opened and the column of mounted men moved out. The short journey through the castle's postern and out through the borgo was quiet and suffused with an air of grateful dejection. No one, even the starving populace of the city, truly wished to offer their necks to the mercy of the king of France with his reputation as a warmonger, and yet every living soul in Rome knew that the alternative was death, either by hunger or by the blade's edge, and the very idea of survival outweighed the potential agonies of life under French control. The gate in the borgo wall opened with a quiet creak that cut through the silent city like the waking groan of a titan as the populace held its breath.

Skiouros felt his bones chill as the small ambassadorial party crunched across the cold wet gravel of the road and out into the countryside that lay beyond the borgo's northern wall.

The French army, confident enough in their given victory that the nearest units were arrayed within easy cannon-shot of the walls, covered the countryside like a forest of glinting steel. The bores of the artillery threatened all and any who approached like tunnels into the heart of Hell. The cavalry units were at rest, the horses corralled and grazing. A unit of arquebusiers half the size of the entire Papal infantry stood at rest, their heavy wooden guns mounted carefully on racks beneath wicker roofs to keep them safe from both rain and dew. It quite simply boggled the mind how any force could hope to withstand the might of King Charles. Skiouros doubted that His Holiness would have stood against them even had the combined nobility of Italy thrown in their lot with him. Terms would be agreed today, but Charles would probably decide them.

On a somewhat dejected whim, the Greek turned to peer back at the powerful bulk of the Castel Sant'Angelo, which suddenly looked rather small and feeble against the forces arrayed before it. Skiouros was about to turn back and concentrate on the matter at hand when his roving eye picked out two things that stopped his breath. His eyes struggled to maintain focus on both but, straining, he dropped his gaze from the tiny form of the Turkish hostage in the window high above the battlements to the lurking figure of the hooded man standing almost directly below.

It was impossible to identify the figure's features at this distance, and no man would claim to be certain of another's identity with the evidence of their eyes alone, yet Skiouros knew, beyond the shadow of a doubt, that it was the Hospitaller he had sought for so many weeks.

How cruel were the powers above and below that after months of seeking the two men, he should finally lay eyes on both on one of the few occasions that he was outside the fortress walls and entirely unable to reach either. Reflexively he reached up, risking his marginal control of his steed, to touch the zemi figure of Maquetaurie Guayaba at his neck.

'Keep your eyes forward,' Orsini hissed.

'I see Prince Cem.'

'Can you stick a knife in him?' the nobleman growled.

'Of course not.'

'Then pay attention to the matter in hand. If you want to get closer to him you need to rise to the top of the cardinal's service, and that means excelling in this duty.'

'But I saw the rogue Hospitaller too.'

'And you can stick your knife in him, yes?'

'Well, no,' muttered the Greek.

'Then use your head instead, Skiouros.'

With the greatest of difficulty, the young man tore his gaze from the walls and the two men looking out from them, and turned to face the breathtaking might of France.

Charles de Valois, by the grace of God his most Christian Majesty King of France, Duke of Brittany and self-styled King of Napoli and of Jerusalem, sat with his retinue in the semi-circular space defined by the arc of nobles' tents, with the royal pavilion at the centre – a canvas palace of blue and white peppered with golden fleur-de-lys.

The great and good of France, along with a number of cardinals, both French and allied Italian, stood in their finery and robes of state, the man who had brought terror to Rome seated on a dais at the centre. Skiouros took a moment to size up the opposition as they approached.

For all his power, Charles was a pasty-faced man in his mid-twenties, with an impressive beak of a nose, a jowly jawline and an entirely unimpressive short and heavy frame. His hat sat at what was probably intended to be a jaunty angle, but in fact looked slovenly and ill-fitting. Had the situation not been quite so grave, Skiouros would have laughed at this almost comical figure who commanded so much fear across Europe.

The impression was heightened as the party came to a halt and the king of France smiled in a strangely disarming manner, crossed his legs and leaned on the arm of his chair, addressing the visitors in Italian, with a thick French accent.

'Cardinal Sforza, if I am not mistaken. Greetings of the Yuletide. I bring a gift for His Holiness and do deeply hope the vicar of Rome intends to reciprocate.'

His casual manner and easy smile were so charming that Skiouros was forced to remind himself of how much rode upon this grand meeting. Cardinal Ascanio Sforza, a severe looking man with fishy lips and hard eyes, raised an eyebrow and shifted his weight on the horse to bow slightly.

'I fear His Holiness may consider Your Majesty's gift a little *too* grand, though I am sure he will see how many he can fit in his barracks. Would you not like to retain at least a few *chevaliers* to escort you back to France, Your Majesty?'

A curious silence fell across the crowd and Skiouros saw noblemen and cardinals alike bristling, their fingers playing with the pommels of their swords, until suddenly Charles of Valois threw back his head and roared with laughter.

'Cardinal Sforza, if His Holiness is graced with even a fraction of your wit and balls half your size, he will prove a formidable opponent.' In the blink of an eye, the humour passed from his voice and suddenly he was sitting straight without having appeared to lift from his slouch.

'And now, to business, Vice Chancellor.'

Sforza bowed his head. 'Of course, Majesty.'

'My men have had a long journey from France, Cardinal, and precious little opportunity to show their mettle or slake their thirst for war. I fear that unless we can come to very favourable terms, my generals will have a great deal of difficulty restraining their men and preventing the looting and rapine of the Holy City. Consequently... impress me.'

Sforza simply nodded again and cleared his throat.

'His Holiness wishes to avoid bloodshed, not through his fear of Your Majesty's forces, but for the sake of your eternal soul. No man, be he bandit or king, may contemplate bringing war against God's chosen in the heart of the Church without imperilling his immortal self. His Holiness would save you and your men from excommunication and certain Hell.'

'His Holiness is most generous,' drawled Charles.

'Indeed he is, Your Majesty. His Holiness requires time to prepare to receive such an august visitor in adequate style, but would like to formally issue an invitation to Your Majesty and your court to enter Rome on the eve of the new year and dine with His Holiness at the palazzo of the turncoat cardinal Della Rovere.'

Skiouros was suddenly supplied with a flash of memory and scanned the faces of the gathered men in crimson, settling upon the face of the Cardinal whom they had last seen at an inn in Siena, and whose face was dark as thunder. Flashing a quick, cruel smile at the furious cardinal, Sforza continued his words to the king.

'The gates of the city of Rome will be opened to the men of France on the understanding that they will act with all the appropriate decorum of visiting guests, though the soldiers of France are not to be admitted to the Papal borgo, the Vatican, or the Castel Sant'Angelo.'

King Charles leaned one elbow on the arm of his chair, cradling his heavy chin in the 'L' of his thumb and forefinger, a curious smile playing across his lips. 'Has His Holiness any word for me on my investiture as King of Napoli or my request that he pass back the hostage Cem to his rightful host? After all, the Sultan resided on French soil before the knights Hospitaller decided to move him to Papal lands.'

Sforza leaned back in his saddle. 'The soil of a Hospitaller fortress, Your Majesty, is no more French than it is Italian, since it is land given to God. But surely Your Majesty will concede that these are not matters to be discussed between ambassadors in the cold air and in view of the rank and file of both our nations? His Holiness suggests that such delicate matters be discussed in person in the New Year.'

There was a pause as a number of the more belligerent looking French nobles glanced at their king, clearly half expecting him to leap from his seat and skewer the troublesome Sforza. In fact, Charles leaned back again with an easy smile.

'I have waited many months to discuss such matters with the Pope. What is one more week? I agree to His Holiness' terms. I would request that the Papal cannons are run back in from the battlements as a sign of our peaceable circumstances, and in return our own artillery will be turned from the walls.'

'Agreed, Your Majesty. I am also instructed by His Holiness to offer you my ear in the matter of confessional.'

King Charles furrowed his brow, his comical face twisting in suspicious surprise. Orsini flashed a quick warning look at Skiouros and the rest and returned his gaze to the Papal legate, calmly.

'I am not sure I understand,' King Charles frowned.

'It is no secret that Your Majesty and your forces have travelled the length of Italy, seizing a few cities that denied you and dealing with some of the more devious noblemen of the peninsula. Such a journey cannot have passed without sin, and His Holiness is sadly aware that the most senior cleric who travels with you and could take your confession is among the worst of the sin-wagers.' His eyes fell on the seething form of Cardinal Della Rovere, and Charles let out a loud guffaw as his own gaze passed over the red-clad churchman.

'I am not without sin, it is true. In fact, Your Eminence, I may very well be the most sinful man alive, but I have no need of your services at this time.'

Skiouros found himself turning over every word and examining it as it passed through his ears. To the innocent, the entire exchange sounded so banal and simple it would easily be glossed over. To the extraordinarily suspicious, it could easily be replayed as a request by the Pope's Vice Chancellor for a secret one-on-one meeting with the Vatican's enemy, which had subsequently been denied. Equally, it could have been His Holiness' machinations to try and place Sforza in a position to probe His Majesty about various Papal enemies. In fact, the more Skiouros took apart the words and rebuilt them, the more possibilities leapt to mind until his brain started to hurt with the effort. What was it with these Italians that they seemed entirely unable to conduct a simple conversation without there being a dozen layers of intrigue coating each phrase?

Something had passed between Sforza and the king. It was unspoken and momentary and had Skiouros been looking away he would have missed it, but he wasn't. And he didn't. What it was, he couldn't say, but he had the unswerving feeling that some decision had just been made in silence.

The cardinal gave a bow from the waist and straightened once more.

'Then, Your Majesty, I look forward to hosting you on the eve of the new year. May the days in between pass in peace and comfort.'

Skiouros listened to the standard exchanges and farewells, his eyes leaping back and forth between the king, the Papal ambassador and Cardinal Della Rovere and trying to discern whether every flicker was an admission of guilt on some part. Soon, however, the meeting was at an end, and Sforza turned his horse and began the slow, stately journey back to the gate.

Skiouros endured the trip in tense silence, his gaze scouring the walls of the castle in an effort to locate either Prince Cem or the Hospitaller and failing to find either. He was still feeling somewhat cheated by the whole affair when the column pulled up in the castle courtyard and pages and stablehands rushed across to take their reins and lead the beasts away. As Skiouros slipped from the saddle with all the grace of a sack of turnips, he was unsurprised to see Cardinal Borgia awaiting them, arms folded and with an expectant look. Orsini took his time, allowing Cardinal Sforza and his retinue a few minutes to move off and enter the keep before approaching their patron.

'Tell me,' Borgia demanded quietly.

Orsini removed his gauntlets and stretched his neck muscles.

'I do believe Cardinal Sforza was entirely within His Holiness' remit at all times. He offered the king the opportunity to ply him for information in private but the king refused, I suspect at the behest of Della Rovere. Likely Della Rovere is attempting to keep the king as far as possible from Sforza's influence, and the king does not wish to be unduly influenced either way until he speaks to His Holiness. I am assuming that his offer of 'confessional' was planned by the Pope?'

Borgia nodded, clearly surprised.

'You are sharper than I suspected, Orsini. Very observant. And what of your own kin?'

Skiouros frowned. He'd not thought about such a thing, but clearly his friend had.

'Three of my cousins and uncles were present, including a lesser condottiere and a cardinal. The other is no matter, commanding little respect and even less might. I assume you are already aware of the nobleman and the priest?'

'Indeed,' Borgia smiled. 'And what of your cousin Virginio?'

Orsini's face darkened, leading Skiouros to wonder what lay between the two family members, but his voice was calm and steady when he replied. 'As you are almost certainly aware, my Hell-bound cousin shares with me the distinction of being the only Orsini not clamouring for King Charles' attention. He languishes at Capua as a garrison commander in the pay of King Alphonso of Napoli.'

'And if I choose to send you to Capua? Will there be trouble there?'

Orsini tucked his gauntlets into his belt and rubbed his hands vigorously. 'Not on my part. While Virginio and I see far from eye to eye, I serve you, not Lady Vengeance.'

Borgia nodded, apparently satisfied. 'Stay alert these next few weeks. I may have interesting duties for you and your men.'

CHAPTER EIGHT - January 1495

As the last of the most recent chilled cloudburst fell in fat droplets to the paving, sending up crowns of water, Skiouros, Parmenio and Nicolo strolled along the ambulatory that skirted around the inside of the castle's walls. All three shivered in the cold despite the layers of warm wool that each wore. Since the weather had turned cold, Skiouros had taken to keeping his arms fully encased in warm fleece, despite Orsini's original directive that he bare his Taino tattoos in an effort to stand out. Of course, being memorable was now irrelevant, since they had achieved the highest level of service in the Vatican for which a lance of condottieri could hope. And it seemed appropriate to keep the fiery vengeance of Bayamanaco fully covered in the presence of so many churchmen. The tattoo still burned occasionally, reminding him of his unfinished task.

A distant scream broke the strange silence, its anguished sharpness rebounding off the low, heavy grey blanket of the sky from somewhere deep in the city across the river. It was followed by a dull roar that could be the usual impotent civic reprisals or the sound of the French soldiers celebrating whatever obscenity they had just perpetrated.

'How long before they're in the halls of the Vatican with their hairy, uncultured arses, raping priests, defacing paintings and prising gemstones from works of art?' Nicolo huffed.

'Such is always the way with armies, I have noticed,' Parmenio shrugged. 'You can lay down the law as much as you like and as often as you like, but soldiers are a rough bunch and unpleasantness will happen. Not that sailors are necessarily much better,' he added as an afterthought, remembering a few choice incidents in years gone by.

'If King Charles and his generals cannot keep a tighter rein on them they should have been kept outside in the camp and never been admitted to the city,' Nicolo spat.

Skiouros rubbed the back of his neck, where heavy trickles of water were settling from his hair into his thick wool scarf. 'Don't kid yourself. Charles never had any intention of keeping his men under control. He seems a reasonable man, against all odds, I'll grant you, but the Pope insulted him by making him break his vow to be here by Christmas, and now Charles is repaying His Holiness for his pride. This will go on either until the French have what they want and leave the city or until Rome is broken, dead and deserted.'

The three men fell into a gloomy silence, each contemplating the truth of Skiouros's words. There was nothing the Papal authorities could do, and everyone knew it. And the heavy grey pall that hung over the whole region, periodically dumping what felt like a million gallons of freezing water on them, did little to raise anyone's spirits. As if to add to their woes, the sky gave a faint groan and threatened a fresh deluge.

'Well met, my Greek friend.'

They looked up in surprise at the mention of Skiouros' nationality, and the latter rested his gaze on the figure of Andreas Palaeologos, strolling down the staircase from the walls with a curiously inappropriate spring in his step, his hat at a jaunty angle and a smile plastered across his swarthy features. Skiouros frowned. He'd heard the exiled Byzantine was in the castle, and had assumed him to be – like the rest of the great and the good – locked away in the Papal apartments in the keep's upper reaches. The Pope himself now divided his time between residence in the castle and duties in the Vatican, using the covered, raised walkway that ran between the two to keep himself secure from any potential threat. Well, the walkway, and two dozen scarred and deadly Catalan soldiers, anyway.

The three friends paused as Palaeologos dropped the last few steps to the flags, almost lost his balance on the wet stone, but regained it with a dancer's poise and then grinned broadly. Skiouros sketched a brief bow, which was not echoed by his friends, wondering why the exiled scion was wandering alone, without his entourage, or even the usual threatening presence of Paregorio.

'You appear extraordinarily chipper, Your Imperial Majesty?'

Palaeologos took off his hat, shook the rain from it and ran it through his fingers.

'I am having a good day, Skiouros of Hadrianopolis. An *extremely* good day.'

'I am sure that the population of Rome wish they could say the same,' rumbled Parmenio in his customary dark tone.

Palaeologos, without a crack in his smile, wagged a mock admonitory finger at the Genoese captain. 'Now now. You will not break my mood today.'

'What has lifted your spirits so high?' Skiouros asked, his voice still as gloomy as the grey sky that sat so low above them.

'I, dear Skiouros, am the recipient of a piece of good fortune in the form of a deal with the French.'

'You need to watch that. Deals with the French seem to have a way of turning sour,' Parmenio grunted, his words perfectly punctuated by another shriek from the city across the river.

'Not this one. I have just returned from a meeting with his glorious Majesty, King Charles – Duke of Brittany, King of France, Napoli and Jerusalem...'

He spread his arms wide in an elaborate gesture.

'... and Emperor of Byzantium.'

Skiouros found that he had taken an involuntary step backwards, the colour draining from his face.

'What?' The word was delivered with an edge as sharp as any sword and lacking any of the courtesy or deference Skiouros habitually delivered to the exiled emperor.

Palaeologos laughed easily. 'A most profitable deal with Charles. In return for my signing over all rights to the Byzantine crown, his most gilded, wealthy majesty has agreed to pay me a sum that would have a Jewish usurer sweating uncomfortably, and the promise to honour my position as despot of the Morea.'

'The King of France?' Skiouros almost whispered. 'Emperor of Byzantium?'

'Indeed. I will end my days rich and powerful, ruling a solid, cultured region. In return, I have given Charles all the pretext he needs for his crusade and he gets to deal with the troublesome city. He will have his war and his conquest and I just have to sit in Rome and wait until the Fleur-de-Lys of the Valois flies over Constantinople and then walk into

Greece and claim my inheritance. Really, things could not have worked out any better for me.'

Skiouros shook his head in shock. 'You would hand over the centre of the world to the French? They will bring the Church of his Holiness to the east!'

Palaeologos shrugged. 'What do we care about that?'

It was a good question really. What *did* Skiouros really care about that? He was rather surprised to find that he only had to delve into the upper layer of his thoughts to discover that he felt somewhat strongly on the subject. He had long held that God was a central truth around which men built their own churches to their own needs. Time spent with the Tuareg had brought him to that impression. He had come to terms with the knowledge that his heretical beliefs could have him burned or staked in any nation of Europe or the east. But while he could appreciate the Church of his fathers in which he had been raised, which considered piety and goodness to be paramount, and he could appreciate the world of Islam and the prophet with their focus and strong value system, and he could appreciate the ancient patience of the Jews, and he could even appreciate the strange faces the Taino put on God... he had little time for this church of Rome that would gild every cross and shower a sinful priest in coin while letting a poor friar starve. No. The Church of the Borgia Pope should never be given a toehold in the east. Their golden corruption already spread too far.

He could remember when he first met Orsini, back on the ship leaving Crete, when the young nobleman had explained how sickened he was by the corruption of it all. Skiouros, it seemed, had had to see it to truly appreciate it.

There was another low groan from the sky, intensifying Skiouros' burgeoning bad mood, and he looked up at the roiling dark grey, even the location of the pale, watery sun unfathomable beyond the cloud.

'Sounds like a big storm coming. Never liked thunder since that one in Istanbul.'

Parmenio nodded, remembering the dreadful storm that had presaged Skiouros' departure from the city aboard his ship a few short years ago.

'Err... you two.'

Skiouros turned to see Nicolo with a furrowed, worried brow.

'What?'

'That's not thunder.'

'What do you mean?' Parmenio asked quietly.

'Last I checked, thunder came from above. From the clouds.'

'What?'

'That came from over there somewhere…'

The three other men turned to look in the direction that Nicolo was pointing. In the inclement weather, few of the castle's staff, guards and denizens braved the outdoors, and the only figures the three friends had seen apart from the Byzantine exile had been the guards stationed along the walls above at regular intervals. But now, not far away, a nobleman in an expensive grey hooded robe emblazoned with red lions strode in their direction, a small party of courtiers close behind, each huddled tight in their plainer cloaks against the chill and the wet.

Another groan issued around the cold, damp air of the castle, and Skiouros felt the hair rise on the back of his neck. Nicolo had been absolutely correct: that noise had not come from the clouds. Indeed, it had come from the ambulatory, close to those figures.

Skiouros was running even as the pieces fell into place in his head. Behind him, Parmenio and Nicolo scrambled to follow, confused but trusting their friend's instincts. Palaeologos stood on the bottom step of the staircase watching in surprise.

Skiouros knew he was shouting something even as he closed the distance between himself and the nobleman and his courtiers, but the exact words were lost on him. His mind was too busy running through everything. The wall. The Hospitaller. The Aqua Regia. The creaking noise.

The next groan was something else entirely, louder than those before and encompassing the sounds of cracking and splintering. The small party of noblemen were almost underneath the place, and had paused, brought to a halt in surprise at this mercenary running at them and yelling incomprehensibly. A few of the figures turned slowly from the closing figure of Skiouros and looked at the castle wall, their eyes slowly rising up its height to the top, which was even now beginning to lean precariously inwards.

Skiouros hit the nobleman in the midriff, the man's guards distracted by the sight of the wall as bricks and stones tore from their neighbours in a shower of mortar, a section of the defences some fifteen feet long seeming to pause in mid-air as though gravity were of only the slightest concern. And then the noise began. Such a noise as Skiouros could only remember hearing once before as the Nea Ekklasia in Istanbul had exploded and disappeared from the world of men. Some of the party would not make it out of the way, he realised, but he could only concentrate on the one man, and he had automatically gone for the noble in the grey, red-lion cloak.

Skiouros and the nobleman hit the floor and rolled just as the first stone block smashed against the flagstones, leaving a crack across the ground and tearing cobbles free with the force of its fall, other stones smashing into the ancient Roman brickwork of the central cylinder keep. There were several screams as courtiers and guards were caught in the collapse, others leaping out of the way just in time. Parmenio and Nicolo were suddenly there in his wake, pulling people out of the way of the last falling bricks even as the men stood stupefied, rooted to the spot and watching the last pieces of wall fall towards them.

Despite the damp air, the world was then engulfed in a cloud of mortar dust which billowed out from the fallen masonry and filled the ambulatory passage, turning the air choking white and obscuring every figure. Unable to see anyone else and confident that the wall had collapsed as far as was likely, Skiouros rose and reached down to the figure somewhat trussed in the entangled red lion robe, grasping his wrist and shoulder and helping the dazed nobleman to his feet.

The figure rose and as he came upright, the hood fell back, revealing a swarthy face, marked with care-lines down to his well-defined chin. The tired, yet glittering eyes. The thin lips framed by the droop of moustaches. It was a face he had never forgotten. Would never forget. *Could* never forget.

Cem Sultan!

His world spun. He had finally, after all this time, found himself face to face with his blood-enemy. Close enough to touch. And had he exacted his brother's vengeance?

No. He had saved the man's life!

Oh how the God of Moses and of Ibrahim was laughing at him now. He could feel wrathful Bayamanaco burning into his arm, where the vengeful image twisted at the irony of it all.

His hand had suddenly, instinctively, dropped from Cem's shoulder down to his own belt, where it ignored the macana stick and reached behind for the needle-pointed misericord dagger he had taken to sheathing back there where a cloak usually covered it. His hand closed on the hilt and it slid free with barely a hiss.

Cem's eyes were still unfocussed, perhaps senseless still from the noise, the dust and the shock, in much the same manner as Skiouros. The usurper Sultan had clearly barely registered the figure that had helped him up, let alone seen any detail.

Skiouros' blade came up as the man struggled to extricate his trapped arms from the cloak that had somehow become fast around him.

Something happened.

The young Greek could not possibly say what it was at the time, but as he brought the point of the blade up to almost rest on Cem's throat-apple, shapes of other figures started to coalesce in the cloud as the dust began to settle. Whether it was the sudden fear of discovery or some other strange sense that drove his arm, the blade angled at the last moment and cut through the loop that held the robe shut at the throat. The Sultan's cloak fell away to the ground, revealing his fine Turkish garb beneath.

The man's eyes suddenly seemed to focus and he gave a weak smile as he reached up and clasped Skiouros' shoulders. The Greek stared into the eyes of his enemy, surprised to see none of the disdain or wrath in them that he had expected. Even so, he easily calculated that the man's hands being so raised left his armpit wide open to the deadly point of Skiouros' dagger. He could quite possibly kill him and wipe the blade before anyone saw what happened.

The strange slow silence that had followed the collapse exploded into a blur of noise and motion.

Parmenio and Nicolo were there with mouths open in surprise. Behind them a third figure approached. One of the courtiers in the group had lowered his hood, and Skiouros was somehow not surprised to see the intelligent, dangerous features of Cardinal Cesare Borgia, nodding his gratitude. And there now, with Palaeologos watching fascinated from the step, Paregorio watched the events unfold. It seemed that all the world had witnessed Skiouros save the man's life!

All was noise and confusion, and there was still a whining in Skiouros' ears from the crash of the wall's collapse. As the cardinal spoke, he had to force himself to concentrate even just a little over the rush of blood, noise and dust and the mind-destroying enormity of what he had just done. Something about good reactions, Borgia announced. Something about quick thinking. Something about good men. Skiouros lowered his head respectfully, his misericord returning to his belt. Something about hostages and the king. Something about missions.

His head was still whining and spinning a little.

But once again, his mind was focusing through the mess. The wall had collapsed just as Prince Cem walked past. The wall that had been weakened a little several months ago by a rogue Hospitaller who had previously served as one of that same prince's guards. It was no coincidence – couldn't be. But how had the man timed it to collapse on that specific moment?

Simply: he couldn't. So how had he managed it? He had to have been there to trigger the collapse at the right time.

As the cloud finally settled completely, Skiouros' eyes slowly slid upwards. The remnants of the wall were lying in heavy chunks of masonry across the ambulatory amid the dust and rubble. Sections remained up to more than the height of a man, but the parapet was missing for some ten feet. Skiouros was no engineer, but he could see how perhaps the wall could have been weakened over time and then given a final, hefty nudge at the right time.

One of the wall guards had been at the collapsed section and had had the foresight to jump as the walkway fell away. He was now leaning, wide-eyed, against the nearest intact merlon with his neighbour holding his spear as they stared down into the ruins.

Then Skiouros noticed the other figure. It shouldn't have stood out – just another cloaked figure on the walls along with all the others. But it didn't take a thoroughly academic mind to work out the spacing between the guard posts and see that there was one too many figures on the wall.

He was running again quickly, his feet pounding up the steps to the wall top, where he doubled back and made for the collapsed section and the extra cloaked figure crouched by the parapet. His heart sped up for a moment as he realised who it had to be, but then his spirits sank. He could just see the white-blond hair poking out from the base of the helmet, revealing it to be the renegade Hospitaller. But the figure was motionless. And that fact was equally eloquent.

As he reached the man, he slowed and moved into a crouch. The Hospitaller was dead – of that there could be no doubt. The glass jar he had been carrying was shattered and what remained of its corrosive, deadly contents had spilled out across the wall walk, eating into the gaps between the stones. But it had also eaten into the man who carried it. As Skiouros grasped the man's shoulder gingerly, being careful where he placed his feet to avoid the dissolved sections and the danger of the Aqua Regia on his own boots, he closed his eyes in shock and held his breath until he could pull his scarf up over his nose.

Had it not been for the hair, he'd not have recognised the man. More than half his face had collapsed in on itself as had most of the chest cavity, as well as the arm that had been wrapped around the jar.

The smell was appalling, and the sight even worse. Behind Skiouros, the duty officer, who had scurried along to find out what had drawn his attention, suddenly took a sharp breath and then vomited copiously onto the wall walk.

Skiouros turned, his face stony, and made for the stairs once more, where Orsini had appeared from somewhere and was now standing with Cardinal Borgia, Parmenio and Nicolo, being brought up to date on events.

It was a simple enough explanation. The man had been waiting for his prey to pass and had poured the corrosive liquid into some weak spot. Likely he'd spent the past few months using a small vial at a time, burning a hole down from the wall walk between the paving slabs until he had a weakened area that was almost hollowed out inside. And just as the party passed below, the renegade had poured his Aqua Regia into that hole in bulk and stepped back from the dangerous spot. But in the confusion as the wall collapsed, he had accidentally fumbled with the bottle and ended up reaping the sick harvest of that mistake.

But while any guard or officer passing might believe that, even without the evidence of the weakened spot, Skiouros didn't. The sort of man who planned this, went against his own honour and holy orders and the commands of his Pope, and who had been so careful over so many months, was not the sort of man to fumble at the last minute and melt himself to death. How he had managed to do all this without being questioned by the other wall guards was another deep question, but the whole thing added up to there being a second man. One who helped distract the guards, possibly? One who disposed of the Hospitaller when he was no longer of use, almost certainly.

But there was no evidence. There were no leads, even. And Prince Cem would hardly be a man short of enemies. After all, had he known about the thing from the first, Skiouros may well have helped the rogue knight in his quest to kill the Turk and thereby avoided accidentally saving the man's life! And the Hospitallers had more cause to hate the sultan than most – a heretic follower of a heathen God, a man who had been captive of their own order but whom they had lost to the pope, a Muslim they may be made to support in a bid to recapture Constantinople. And now that the order had effectively been branded untrustworthy and dismissed from Papal service and sent to the east again? It would hardly be surprising to find one or more of them holding a grudge.

But then, who was the second man…?

As Skiouros, his ears finally returning to normal, closed on his friends and their employer, Orsini nodding to him without breaking his conversation.

'But was the collapse aimed at Prince Cem or at you?' Orsini asked quietly. 'Who knew that either of you would be passing, let alone together?'

Borgia took a deep breath. 'Enough people to make investigation extremely difficult. I and Sir Antonio were escorting the Turk to His Holiness and the French king. Cem is not yet aware of his fate, but he is to be passed over by my father to the king for a period of six months to aid Charles in his crusade. After that, he will be returned to Rome and to Papal custody. Charles will not need him now that he has the deeds to the Byzantine crown, while His Holiness holds the Turk in rather high regard.'

'Someone who does not want the French to have him?' Parmenio mused.

'Or just someone with a reason to hate Cem specifically, or the Turks in general,' Skiouros added. 'And that opens up your suspects to most of the world's population west of the Morea.'

Cardinal Borgia nodded irritably. 'Well done on your efforts, Skiouros the Greek. You and your men, Orsini, continue to prove yourselves of the highest value to me. And I believe that I have at least one more mission for you in the coming weeks – the most important of all. It seems that one of the conditions of this deal between His Holiness and His Majesty is that I accompany the French army as a Papal legate. A notable position, of course, and one that in other times cardinals would tear each other's eyes out to secure. But in this particular case, I think we can all see the role for what it is: hostage to the French. I will be restricted in my retinue, of course, and certainly in the manner of military escort. However, I will be able to push through one or two lances of condottieri in my entourage. Pack your gear ready and stand by. I have no set date for our departure yet, but I cannot see it being more than a week away. And whatever agreements have been made, I have no intention whatsoever of playing humble hostage and accompanying the French army to Napoli and then to Istanbul.'

Orsini bowed his head in acceptance and Borgia paused only long enough to look Skiouros up and down and smile his gratitude before taking the wall stairs two at a time and returning to the small gathering below where Cem Sultan – half-brother of Bayezid the Just

– and his courtiers, along with a few Catalan soldiers, stood staring into the rubble.

Peering down, Skiouros was disheartened to see what had to be the body of Sir Antonio, the Cardinal's own Catalan Hospitaller, among the dead. One of the few men here he felt he could almost trust.

As soon as they were safely alone, out of earshot of all others, Nicolo shook his head in wonder. 'How maddening is that? You were close enough to put a knife into the man, but instead you saved his life!'

Skiouros nodded, a bitter expression on his face. And yet, as he went back over that moment of dust and noise and confusion, he was not entirely convinced it was the danger of being seen by the others in the thinning dust that had stayed his murderous blade and moved it to free the man from his entangled robe instead. In the darkness of his own soul, late at night, he would wrestle with the worry that he had not actually been able to deliver that blow after all.

On his arm, the etched image of dreadful Bayamanaco burned with both anger and shame.

And now Cem Sultan would head south along with King Charles and his army. And Cardinal Borgia. And him. It seemed that this might not be his last chance to test his will, after all…

CHAPTER NINE - Velletri, January 1495

Skiouros crouched in the ditch, swiping irritably at the fronds and leaves and other plant life that seemed insistent on imposing itself upon his evening.

'Stop wafting your hands around like a fish salesman with a deficit and get dressed,' hissed Parmenio. 'I've never seen anything with less than four arms do such a perfect impression of a windmill!'

'*You're* alright,' Skiouros snapped irritably. '*You* got given the right size. A miracle, I'd say, given that you seem to have grown a size every month since summer, at least in the belly. I got given a child's one, I assume. Do they give you a toy sword as well, since I've had to leave my macana with the gear?'

Parmenio, glowering darkly as he tested his waistline in the face of such criticism, straightened the white tunic with the triple-towered castle livery of Velletri over his doublet. The tunic seemed voluminous and had had to be cinched up at the waist with Parmenio's belt. He ripped the sword from its sheath, spun it in the light of the torch burning on a pole rammed into the turf and then slid it back.

'No. *My* sword seems all grown up.'

Nicolo stepped up next to him in an identical tunic, this one a mite too long so that it had to be doubled at the waist. Orsini, moving from where the horses grazed on the roadside grass, adjusted his own tunic. 'Everyone received one that was as appropriate to their size as possible. If you think you have trouble, my Greek friend, you should see Helwyg trying to squeeze into his! And he has the rope round his waist too.'

Without further comment, but sporting a face like thunder, Skiouros finally appeared from the ditch, trying to shuffle his tunic into place. Clearly whoever had given the 'procurer' – as Borgia's man had called him – the required dimensions, had assumed Skiouros to be the size of a twelve-year-old. The tunic fit him like a sausage skin, his own doublet squeezing out of all the gaps despite his leanness and narrowness of torso.

'The moment I try to do anything other than walk as though I just shat myself, this thing is going to rip in ten different places. Are you sure I didn't get someone else's?'

'Perhaps you'd like to exchange with Helwyg?' Nicolo grinned.

'This thing wouldn't cover Helwyg's buttock! It barely covers mine!'

Orsini chuckled in the shadows. 'It only has to pass at first glance. Do not panic about the grander scheme of things. Bear in mind that so many things could easily trip us up that costumery is really at the lower end of the scale.

Girolamo suddenly appeared from behind a tree with his tunic in place and his crossbow slung across his back, looking so entirely natural in the uniform that he could easily have *been* a town guard in the service of the *podesta* of Velletri. His healed arm was strong again now, and regular practice with the weapon was helping him recover his impressive aim. 'Nice to see that this one only has one small slash and a pink stain in the armpit.' The archer shrugged. 'I think that adequately answers my question as to how these were acquired.'

Behind him, Helwyg appeared, looking like a giant wearing a child's clothes, the wool tunic stretched so tight around his chest that the triple castle looked more like a massive mountaintop fortress, each arrow-slit wide enough to drive a cart through.

'This not work.'

'Yes it will,' smiled Orsini. The six men, each dressed in a tunic of the Velletri guard, stepped out onto the narrow cart-track, the only light in the damp night air the single torch burning on the verge. The sky sat heavy and thick with cloud the colour of a moneylender's heart, threatening a fresh cloudburst at any moment. No one had seen the moon or a single star for almost a week now and the sun was missing, presumed drowned.

'If we're to risk our lives against the French army to get to a man, why are we here and making for the cardinal in Velletri instead of a little further north and going for Cem Sultan in Marino?' grumbled Skiouros, the stitching at his shoulders already giving way. In truth, the diversion in the service of their master was a welcome one. In the past week, Skiouros had entirely failed to come to terms with his apparent inability to carry out the one act that had become his heart's desire, and he was none too sure that he wanted another opportunity to test his resolve quite so soon.

'Because we need to honour our contract with the cardinal,' Orsini replied calmly, almost as if reading his innermost thoughts, 'and because here we have help from the cardinal's contacts that we wouldn't have in Marino, and because while Borgia is all but a prisoner in Velletri, he is accorded certain freedoms and is under the watchful eye of a couple dozen French soldiers at most, while Prince Cem is secured tighter than a nun's underthings in Marino with half the French army surrounding him in a circle. If you're going to complain, Skiouros, at least think through your arguments first. We had plenty of time to discuss things last night in Albano and we all agreed to this course.'

'Let's get it over with,' Parmenio sighed. 'The sooner we get going, the sooner we can all rest comfortably in our nice silk-lined coffins back in Albano.'

'If they can find one to fit you these days,' grinned Nicolo, pinching his friend's ribs painfully.

'I am *not* fat!'

'You're not *thin*!'

'Come on,' Orsini said with an almost paternal patience, and gestured to the torch, which Helwyg crossed over to and extinguished with the jug of water resting nearby. As soon as the six were gathered on the path, Girolamo untied the sheaf of pikes that leaned against an overhanging branch and passed them one at a time to the others. Skiouros handled his rather inexpertly, but then so did everyone except the powerful Helwyg, who seemed perfectly natural with the weighty, top-heavy weapon. They watched as the big Silesian settled the shaft comfortably against the hollow of his shoulder and hooked his arm over it to balance the weight, and gradually achieved the same with varying degrees of success. Helwyg wandered among them, adjusting their grip and the pikes' angles and once he was satisfied he nodded to Orsini.

'Come on,' the nobleman smiled, jamming his cheap 'kettle' helmet on his head, the others following suit so that their features were shadowed by the iron brims.

With Orsini in the lead, they fell into their assigned places, Skiouros and Girolamo side by side behind him, Parmenio and Nicolo following after them and Helwyg bringing up the rear. They had not had time to watch the patrols sent out by the podesta – the *justice* – of Velletri to see if they matched the standard format of such a unit, but had had instead to trust Orsini's knowledge of such matters, in which he was confident.

They were lucky, really. Velletri had high, strong walls and a lot of men, and under normal circumstances it would be extremely difficult to gain access. But with the entire French army in the locale, the podesta had not taken a great deal of convincing by Borgia's contact to send out regular patrols into the lands beyond the walls.

The party, to a casual glance one of the numerous patrols in the area, rounded the corner from their hiding place and beheld the strength of Velletri.

The city, once a rival to Rome – in the days before the Caesars – sat on a hill among the numerous ridges and craters of this unstable region, its golden walls and red roofs a jumble and muddle, though all rather hard to make out in the gloomy darkness. Even the heavy many-towered walls that ringed the city and separated the civic area from the vineyards and orchards that covered the land were hard to make out with any clarity. Their position and size were mostly gleaned from the flickering light of the torches that stood along them and atop each turret at regular intervals, almost inviting an attack, as though to proclaim their confidence in their own strength.

Their destination, the Porta del Portone, stood powerful and impressive, two heavy drum towers with a solid gatehouse between, the only aperture the gate itself, which stood closed like all the others, the towers not even decorated with arrow slits. It was an imposing concern, and Skiouros was glad that he wouldn't be able to see it with any clarity until he was too close to back out.

The track soon joined a more major road which connected the city to the great Appian Way that ran south from Rome into the Kingdom of Napoli. Still they saw no other sign of life, barring the odd rural hut that had a narrow stream of black smoke issuing from a chimney to ward off the bone-chilling cold of an Italian January. Trying to keep to a military step, the six men tramped down the road to the shallow defile that ran below the looming bulk of the city.

Skiouros tipped his head back so that he could see the walls, the wide brim of his kettle hat cutting off his upper peripheral vision. He wished he hadn't. Not only did the walls look daunting and impenetrable from this low angle, but it so happened that the heavy black clouds chose that moment to issue a white flash somewhere in the distance that lit the defences for a split second in all their martial glory. A deep brontide rumble followed somewhere off to the north perhaps three quarters of a minute later. Skiouros made a quick mental calculation that put the storm around ten miles north. More or less over Cem Sultan's prison at Marino, in fact.

'That had better be going the other way,' Parmenio grunted. 'If I'm going to die horribly tonight I'd at least like to do it in the dry.'

Nicolo shook his head. 'I heard it faintly before and I reckon it's hardly moving at all. I'd wager we'll be heading back into it at the end of all this.'

'Be quiet, the pair of you,' hissed Orsini as they began the ascent to the gate.

'That's close enough,' came a voice from the wall top, and the party of men stumped to a halt, Helwyg scratching his neck casually with his free hand.

'State your business,' the watch officer called.

'Unless you're *blind*,' Orsini snapped, 'you can see exactly what our business is. Now let us inside before it starts to throw it down.'

There was a brief exchange above the gate, including a little childish sniggering.

'You're back early,' a second voice called. 'Frightened of a little water are we?'

'Open the damn gate.'

'Give the password.'

'Octavianus,' Orsini shouted up and Skiouros held his breath, aware that they had only the word of the cardinal's turncoat friend that the password would be accepted.

'Did you say *octopus*?'

'You know damn well what I said. Now let me in so I can report to my commander. There's a party of French scouts huddled in a farmhouse a mile away. I think he'll want to know about that, don't you?'

There was a brief, muted debate once more, then finally a deep clunk and some scraping, followed by a click, and the small man-sized door set into one leaf of the main gate swung inwards. Orsini gestured to the others and they moved forward, stepping across the threshold and into the city of Velletri with the feigned confidence of long-time residents. Skiouros held his breath once more as Orsini turned to his left and headed for a street that would lead towards the walled compound to the north where they understood the French to be quartered, carefully restricted to one area by the city authorities.

'Where do you think you're going?' the guard at the gate barked suspiciously.

Skiouros felt his heart skip a beat. Such a simple mistake. They had no idea where they would be expected to report, and Orsini had turned towards their true destination. The guard was pointing down the street from the gate, presumably in their expected direction of travel.

Orsini yanked his iron hat from his brow and spun to the guard with an angry look on his face.

'I have been on patrol for hours carrying this damned pike and sweating my bollocks off. If it's alright with you, I'm just going to dip my face in the fountain to cool down. Happy, pisspot?'

The guard looked at Orsini, whose finger was now wagging at a large stone trough with a trickle of water pouring into it at the corner of the street. With a sheepish grin, the guard held up his hand. 'Just stand out here for another half hour and you'll get all the fresh water you could want, I'm thinking.'

'I'll be inside eating lamb stew by then,' Orsini replied irritably, crossing to the trough and propping his pike against the wall behind before leaning forward, plunging his head in and then straightening, sending a spray of cold droplets up into the air in a rainbow, shimmering in the light of the torches.

'Right. *Now*, I'll head off and report in,' he snapped again prissily at the guard, who stepped back and returned to his companion who had closed the door behind them all.

The six friends traipsed off along the main street towards the heart of Velletri, not even trying now to keep to a military step, Orsini flashing one last irritated glance at the guards. The city streets were all but deserted, and Skiouros started twice as they moved towards the centre, the first time at a flash and following peal of thunder – which together confirmed that the storm *had* barely moved – and the second time as the bells of the city began to clang, announcing midnight.

Passing one of the rare locals out at this time of night who wore the furtive guilty look of the secret lover or the addicted drinker, they made their way around the street's gentle curve and as they lost sight of the gate and its men, Skiouros exhaled deeply. 'I thought we were in the shit, then. Quick thinking, Cesare.'

Orsini flashed him a surprised frown. 'I was not aware I had made an error, Skiouros?'

'You *were* going for the fountain?'

'Of course. A mile in this kit is warm work.'

Skiouros shook his head in humorous wonder at his friend as Orsini led them into a side street with the carefree ease of a man who clearly knew his course. Two or three more turns, and Skiouros had lost track of their route, coming to rely entirely on their leader's innate sense of direction. Thankfully, Orsini seemed to be confident and as they neared the end of an alley that narrowed as it progressed he held up his hand to halt them.

'This is far enough for the men of the podesta,' he smiled as he lay his unwieldy pike in the gutter as quietly as he could, placed his helmet with it, and then started to remove his tunic, returning to his usual nondescript, if high-quality, hose and doublet. Taking their cue from him, the other five men discarded their pikes – Helwyg with some regret – and their helmets. 'We leave the gear here and pick it up once we have the cardinal. I wish we had a spare for him.' As the others removed their tunics and Skiouros struggled, eventually giving in and using his knife to slit two of the seams for easy removal, Orsini leaned close to the alley's entrance. Opposite them stood a large building, a heavy construction made of local stone. Its civic nature was clear from the coat of arms above the door, which was reached by three wide, balustraded steps. Clearly the place had a number of outbuildings and the whole complex was connected and encircled by a high precinct wall, just as their contact, Francesco del Sacco of the Velletri guard, had described. Skiouros, as he joined his friends, wondered just how packed the place was with men, given the number of French soldiers that must be quartered somewhere within.

'What now?' he whispered.

'We look for a way in. Capitano Francesco said the cardinal would be in one of the outbuildings. They would want him kept in isolation, he thinks, and that would put him somewhere on the other side. I am very much hoping our local contact was right, since infiltrating the main house would be troublesome, given its level of garrisoning.'

'Troublesome is right,' Nicolo breathed. 'Suicidal is another good word. So we need a way into the compound, without using the house's front door.'

'Yes.'

'Then look around the side there,' he said, pointing.

Orsini frowned a question at him.

'Horse dung in the street,' Nicolo replied, gesturing. 'Mostly concentrated at that end. That means there must be a stable block nearby. And no one wants horses clomping up stairs and through their entrance hall, so there must be a gate round there.'

'Quick thinking,' Orsini smiled. 'And good eyes, too.'

'Can't see anyone watching,' Skiouros noted, his eyes raking the façade of the house and the top of the boundary wall.

'It's not designed for defence,' Orsini agreed. 'There'll be eyes at the windows close to the front door. Whether or not they've put someone on duty at the stable remains to be seen. I'd suggest going over the wall but for the uncertainty of what might be waiting on the other side. The stables it is, then. Come on.'

Without further pause, Orsini sauntered out into the main street as though he had every right to be there, crossing the wider thoroughfare and picking his way between the mounds of dung, making his way towards the alley opposite, which ran alongside the precinct wall. The others hurried along behind, trying not to look too suspicious just in case, and failing dismally.

In the event, there was no sign of trouble or interest, and the party of six reached the shade of the far alley easily, where Orsini gestured towards Nicolo's stable door with a grin. The access consisted of a large heavy double gate in a single archway, with a smaller door inset in a similar fashion to the city gate through which they had entered earlier.

'Any thoughts from here?' Parmenio shrugged as they halted before the large wooden portal in the darkness, eyes picking out tiny flickers of golden light around the edge, confirming that the interior was well lit.

'All this time,' Orsini smiled, 'and you still think me unprepared?' As he stepped back, Girolamo moved towards the door, drawing an arcane instrument from his purse, selecting a straight implement with a shaped end and peering closely at the join between door leaves. Skiouros smiled. He would have gone with a different tool, himself, but each to their own.

'Oh how quaint,' the crossbowman said with dripping contempt. 'A single locking bar.' As he put away his implement, he drew a solid, inflexible hunting knife and slid it with professional ease into the crack between the gates before jerking it upwards and dislodging the bar. Careful not to lift it so far that it fell noisily away, he held it up as he eased the door open and then caught the bar with his free hand, lowering it again inside. The gate swung wide, revealing a large stable with stalls for more than a dozen horses – four of which appeared to be occupied, a couple of subdivided storage areas and a mezzanine hayloft reached by a ladder.

In the blink of an eye, Girolamo was inside, Orsini immediately behind him. With the practiced ease of men who had served together in a dozen campaigns now, the six men spread out into the stables, which seemed to be miraculously unoccupied, barring the steeds. Within a minute they had checked each stall and the separate rooms and moved towards the centre, gathering to discuss their next move.

'There are guards in the yard,' Girolamo announced quietly. 'I saw them through the window over there. I counted six in sight: two by the main house's rear door and a pair by each of two outbuildings.'

'Shame. That gives us *two* possible locations for the cardinal.'

'Shhhh!' Parmenio hissed, holding a hand cupped to his ear. The others listened carefully and quickly picked out heavy footsteps in the yard, approaching fast. Helwyg gestured for them to scatter with a stretch of his fingers and without pausing to ask questions, the other five disappeared into whatever hiding places they could find as the Silesian giant stepped behind the door that led into the yard.

Moments later, there was a click as the latch went up and the door swung inwards. A groom in shabby working leathers and a tabard bearing the insignia of Velletri over the top stepped inside and turned to close the door behind him. As the big wooden portal closed with a click, he turned back again, his eyes widening in panic, his cry of shock stifled as a great, pale, hairy hand closed on his mouth.

The rest moved in from their hiding places and Helwyg lifted the groom from the ground with ease, carrying him, still gagged and held tight, across to one of the stalls, where he lowered him to the straw.

'In a moment,' Orsini smiled reassuringly, 'my large friend here is going to remove his hand. If you make a single sound, he will then hit you hard enough to flatten your head to a disc. If you doubt my words, just look at him and make your own mind up.'

As Orsini paused for a second, Helwyg allowed the groom to turn his head enough to look upon the giant that held him. The man's eyes rolled in panic, but he nodded emphatically.

'Good. I have a question for you and if you answer it without giving us any trouble, you will live through this night with little more than a slight headache. Are you happy to cooperate?'

Again the man nodded wildly.

'Let him go.'

As Helwyg released the groom, he lifted his huge, meaty paw in a threatening manner, ready to bring it down hard and knock the brains from the man.

'We need to know which outbuilding holds Cardinal Cesare Borgia, the Papal legate, and who else might be inside the building in addition to those guarding the door. Now speak.'

The groom tried to answer, but his voice came out as a nervous croak. Swallowing, he tried again. 'The second building from this side, next to the pine tree, Master. There are two guards on the door, but no one else inside. His Eminence has irritated the French marshal, and in response they have given him solitary confinement. His entourage are kept in the Gilded Goose on the other side of the city, far away from him. Ground floor is unoccupied and used for storage, but upstairs was the head groom's quarters.'

'Good man,' Orsini smiled.

'What do we do about the entourage?' Nicolo asked quietly.

'Nothing. Our orders were clear: the Cardinal is our goal. His lackeys will have to survive on their own wits, I'm afraid. We have to hope that the French will not wish to start a war now that they've got what they really want, and will not execute them all. With the Kingdom of Napoli awaiting Charles, causing a war with Rome to their rear could be disastrous even for an army this size, so he will likely be restrained, even when furious.'

Skiouros nodded. Leaving the other Italians to their fate seemed harsh, but there would be simply no way for the six of them to free Borgia and his entire retinue. Getting back through the gate would be dangerous enough with just one extra body.

'I'm getting a strange feeling that we've done all this before, you know?' he muttered. 'Last time it was a kitchen wench. This time, a groom. We seem to be bending a lot of effort to breaking into places that have nothing to do with Cem.'

'Look on it as practice,' Orsini said quietly, and then to the marksman: 'Girolamo? Go to the window again. Check out that building and report back.'

As the crossbowman nodded and scurried off, Parmenio gave a low chuckle. 'Something amusing – and potentially useful – occurs to me.'

'What?'

'Does this groom remind you of anyone?' Parmenio grinned.

The rest of them peered closely at the nervous man and smiles slowly broke out among them. 'He could almost be the cardinal in poor light,' Nicolo whistled.

'Yes. And grooms get everywhere without being looked at twice. They tend horses and walk them, gather supplies and often even run errands. I could not possibly think of a better disguise for the cardinal in these streets. Helwyg? Lay him out.'

The look of fresh panic that raced into the groom's eyes was instantly replaced by a vacant one as the pupils rolled up into his skull in response to the heavy blow the giant delivered to his temple. As the unconscious man slumped to the straw, Nicolo and Parmenio began to strip him of his gear and then bind him with a set of reins from the stall's side, gagging him for good measure, but checking his nose to make sure he still breathed well.

By the time they had finished, Girolamo had returned and settled into a squat beside them. 'The building has two floors, but the upper one is low, built into the roof with dormer windows. The lower one is clearly some sort of store, just as the groom said. There are no windows I can see there, but a few small slits for ventilation. It stands some ten or twelve feet from the perimeter wall, which is almost of a height with the windows. There's no obvious way in apart from the guarded door, but a nimble man could get across from the wall.'

'There are few more nimble than our Greek friend,' Orsini smiled, and Skiouros let out a resigned sigh.

'Is there no better way?'

'Essentially: no,' Girolamo murmured. 'If we leave this building through the main door, we will be in view of the guards, and this whole night will be over very quickly. If one or two of us move along the wall-top from the stables, we will be out of open view unless the guards happen to look in the right direction at the right time. A rope from there could be secured to the upper floor window, and then we can cross, enter, prepare the cardinal and then bring him out the same way, back into the stables, where we dress him.'

Orsini shook his head. 'Despite the potential difficulties, I think we had best *all* go along the wall. Once we've got His Eminence, we can then drop straight over the wall and melt back into the city without coming back through the stables at all. We'll take the groom's clothes with us and get him ready before we leave.'

Two minutes later the six men were moving through the stables and climbing into the small hayloft that would grant them access to the wall. Skiouros was not surprised when the rest held back and waited for him to move out first, and he examined the wall as it sloped away from the low gap beneath the tiled roof. It would be a gymnastic move to get from here onto the wall without falling into the yard. He very much doubted Parmenio and Nicolo would make it, let alone Helwyg, but they were urging him on. The 'window' of the hayloft that opened close to the wall was protected by a heavy wooden shutter hinged at the top and when he pushed it, with a heart-stopping creak, it only went up to just less than horizontal before a hinged wooden strut went taut at the side and held it open. Taking a deep breath, he yanked the strut from the window frame with a crack that he was sure must have been audible as far as Rome. Amazingly, the guards at the yard doors never looked up as he swung the shutter high and climbed up onto the narrow wooden sill, poised like an acrobat.

'Shit,' he whispered with feeling, and then tensed.

A bunching of muscles and he sprang, landing atop the narrow wall and almost tipping straight down the other side. As his breath calmed, he secured his equilibrium and rose to his toes, balancing carefully. It was perhaps thirty yards to the point where they would be hidden from view by the building for which they were aiming. Carefully he took half a dozen steps along until he was in the open. As he turned back to the others, the first heavy drip of rain blatted against his forehead.

Wonderful!

In a few minutes, a high, narrow wall would become a high, narrow, *slippery* wall...

As he opened his mouth to whisper for the next man to join him, Girolamo leapt. His landing was not particularly graceful, but he made it safely enough and rose to his feet, shuffling along to Skiouros and urging him on. As the Greek moved out of his way, he watched Helwyg cast the rope across, which was caught by the crossbowman and anchored on a protruding brick. Not wonderfully safe, but it would make the others' crossing much easier.

Skiouros watched with held breath as the Silesian crossed the gap with little grace and had to be grabbed by Girolamo so as not to fall again. As soon as Helwyg was secure, Skiouros turned his attention to the next stage, happy that if the big man could cross then so could the others.

Carefully, and as quietly as he could, he made his way along the wall, listening to the muted conversation of the guards in the yard, which was becoming slowly less audible beneath the rising din of the rain, which was now starting to come down with force. Skiouros had become used to Roman rain these recent months, and knew that they had minutes at most until this spatter of fat droplets became a torrential downpour.

Finally, gratefully, he slid out of sight behind the bulk of the building, his eyes locked on the window from which golden light issued. Glancing back, he could see that all his companions were safely on the wall, and were now removing the rope – shaking the coiled loop free – to bring with them. With a nod to Girolamo at the front, Skiouros turned and took a deep breath. Wishing he had his old soft leather boots rather than these clumping military things he'd picked up in the autumn, he failed to curl his toes over the wall's edge and instead threw up a prayer to the Lord and leapt out into the open air.

It was only ten or twelve feet down to the yard, but that would be enough to make a return to the wall top extremely troublesome and time-consuming. And potentially painful, too, of course.

His fingers closed on the sill of the open window and he gripped tight as he slammed hard against the wall, the wind driven from his chest for a moment. Then carefully, yet with speed, he hauled himself up to the window and dropped inside, hurriedly rising to his feet in case of unforeseen enemy presence.

Cardinal Borgia stood in the centre of the room, a travelling cloak already about his shoulders.

'What kept you?'

Skiouros heaved out a breath. 'We need to go now, Eminence. The rain is getting worse and that will make the wall more dangerous.' He paused. 'But I'm afraid you'll need to change first.'

Borgia raised one eyebrow, but began to remove his travelling cloak and doublet without question.

'We have a groom's clothes for you, Eminence. A man who bore a passing resemblance to yourself.'

'I would say lucky him,' Borgia smiled as he unlaced his doublet. 'But I suspect he is not feeling very lucky at the moment.'

'He will live, Eminence.' Turning his back, Skiouros peered out of the window. Girolamo was waiting on the wall with a bundle. As Skiouros gestured, the crossbowman threw the wad of clothing to him. Skiouros rolled his eyes as the grey hose and rough leather doublet fell to the paving below, but he caught the tabard by some stroke of luck. With an irritated shake of the head to Girolamo, he turned to the cardinal. 'You might as well leave the doublet on, Eminence. Just throw this tabard over the top and muss up your hair and beard like a commoner.'

Borgia did as he was bid and Skiouros turned back with another gesture to the wall top. This time, Girolamo tossed over the rope. Skiouros glared at the man as the rope fell into the wide gap between buildings. Though he couldn't shout, and a whisper would go unheard in the increasing rain, Skiouros tried to convey his feelings in a glance: *How could such an accomplished marksman not hit a wide, bright window with a bundle of clothes or a rope?*

Clearly the crossbowman's broken arm some half-year back was still not quite right. Quickly, Girolamo wound back in the rope and coiled it for another try. This time, Skiouros caught the end and secured it to the solid leg of a huge, heavy oak table in the room.

'You first, Eminence.'

As the cardinal climbed up to the window, Skiouros saw Helwyg cast the rest of the rope down the outside of the perimeter wall and, gripping it tight, slide down it and out of view. With the giant's weight on the other end, it went taut and at a nod from Girolamo, Skiouros urged the cardinal out onto the rope, where he gripped the line with both hands and looped his legs over it, crossing his ankles and then quickly – and rather lithely for a cardinal – shuffled along it to the wall.

Skiouros waited until the cardinal had been helped up onto the wall at the other end and then began the crossing himself, illuminated by another flash of light, blanketed in the clouds. By the time he reached the wall top, the only other person still there was Orsini, who gestured for him to go next. Skiouros nodded, and almost slipped from the wet wall as there was a fresh crack of thunder and the rain suddenly increased in intensity tenfold, coming down with such force that it was hard to see anything, his vision akin to a view through a waterfall.

'Good thinking,' Borgia was saying as they landed in the alley. 'The tabard, I mean. No one we bump into in town will look twice at a groom.'

Orsini nodded. 'We have our uniforms in the alley opposite. In less than ten minutes we can be at the walls, hopefully without raising an alarm. My only worry is what happens at the gate. I can argue most cases, and there are a thousand reasons for a groom to be leaving the city, even in the company of guards, but not in the middle of the night and in a rainstorm.'

The Cardinal nodded. 'Fear not, Orsini. Close to the church whose belfry you can just see over there is a postern gate. It is guarded, but only by one man. A good condottiere should be able to open the way for us easily enough. The only difficulty would be not being heard from the walls, but I suspect the rain will deal with that for us.'

Orsini nodded his clear relief. 'And then we find Francesco del Sacco, retrieve the horses and ride for Rome, yes?'

'After a fashion,' the cardinal laughed lightly. 'I have urgent business in Rome and beyond – far away from the French – but I think you will have one last task to perform for me, I'm afraid.'

Leaving Velletri proved to be a far easier prospect than entering it had been. Overcoming the one guard at the small, generally-unused postern gate was a simple enough matter, and Helwyg hit the man hard enough that he probably wouldn't wake until there was a new pope.

Twenty minutes later they were back at the cart track where their own kit waited, along with their horses. They abandoned the tunics, pikes and helmets of the town guard in a small copse and walked their beasts the five minutes to the unused barn where Captain Francesco del Sacco waited with Borgia's horse and important baggage. Back in their own clothes, the eight men began the ride north along the Via Appia towards Rome at speed, for fear of the French giving chase.

Some twenty minutes later, having moved alternately at a canter and a gallop in order to eat up the miles without breaking the horses, they slowed at Cardinal Borgia's gesture as they made their way up the steep slope from the stream bank towards the vertiginous streets of Albano.

The rain was coming down in a continual sheet of water now, punctuated by the blinding flashes of light and crashes of thunder, though the latter had clearly just passed over Albano and was now working its way south, leaving torrential rain in its wake.

The riders slowed to a trot, drenched and cold, water running from their extremities and dripping down to the street, which ran like a shallow river, carrying dirt and refuse with it. Finally, as they reached the crest of the slope that carried the Appian Way up into town, Borgia signalled for a stop.

'This, my friends, is where we part ways,' he called loudly enough to be heard above the rain. 'And, sadly, for now, I think we shall part services as well.'

Orsini leaned back in his saddle, giving the cardinal a questioning look.

'I will be required to disappear for a while,' Borgia shouted. 'Else His Holiness could find himself in an embarrassing position. He can currently tell King Charles with all honesty that he has no idea where I am, and I intend for things to remain that way. You have served well in my household and when this affair is over, should you find yourself in Rome, you can be sure of a new contract.'

Orsini shook his head. 'Eminence, you of all people must know that to break the terms of the condotta would…'

The cardinal smiled and slapped a reassuring hand on Orsini's shoulder with a squelch. 'I have no intention of breaking our agreement. You will continue to receive your pay, which will be placed in the account with the Medici house, as well as your final payment and a substantial bonus for your recent work. Moreover, I will waive the usual restrictions on change of service and make sure that the authorities in Rome are aware of your loyalty and aptitude. If you do wish to re-employ with me, I would ask that you avoid any contact until after the French have left the peninsula and have embarked upon their crusade, and then seek me out through the Vatican offices. I trust that these conditions meet with your approval?'

Orsini nodded his agreement, and Skiouros felt a horrible conflict coursing through him as fast as the rainfall upon him. Leaving the cardinal's service effectively severed any links with the Papal household and negated all their efforts in attempting to get close to Cem. But then the pretender Sultan was no longer in Papal custody anyway, and there seemed little likelihood that continued service to the Borgias would bring them any closer.

'Our last task?' Orsini prompted.

The cardinal rolled his shoulders. 'The French will be well aware of my departure by now. The guards had taken it upon themselves to check in on me once every hour or so. As we crossed the countryside and made for the horses, we heard bells pealing in the city, but it was not to mark the hour. Rest assured that French horsemen are even now on our trail. They will not need to track us – everyone will assume we are heading for Rome.'

'But you are not, Eminence?'

'My destination is now none of your concern, Orsini, but I do require a little more certainty that I will reach it unmolested. Consequently, we will part ways here. Del Sacco and I will ride north and make for a safe house. You and your men will remain in Albano and waylay the French pursuit.'

'Now I understand why you had us spend last night here,' Orsini smiled his understanding. 'Familiarising ourselves with the city.'

'Indeed. I care not whether the French dogs live or die, but I require at least an extra hour lead on them. Can you do that for me?'

Orsini laughed. 'Of course, Your Eminence. God go with you.'

'And with you, condottiere. *Benedicat vos omnipotens Deus, et Filius, et Spiritus Sanctus.*'

With a twin-fingered signing of the cross, Borgia inclined his head in respect and then wheeled his horse, his turncoat friend joining him as they broke into a canter, clattering along the ancient paving of the Via Appia north through the city in the direction of Rome.

As soon as they were out of sight and the sound of their hooves was masked by the hammering of the rain, Orsini cleared his throat and raised his voice over the din once more.

'I think we need to settle upon a new plan in due course, but in the meantime we must deal with the French pursuit. Thoughts?'

Girolamo shrugged. 'There were only four horses in the compound stables. That means that the French soldiers with the cardinal were infantry with a few officers, and not cavalry. Even if they commandeer steeds from the city guard, there will be few competent riders among them. I cannot see any likelihood of more than a dozen men in pursuit.'

'Agreed,' Orsini nodded. 'And they will not be looking for anything other than the cardinal himself and an accomplice. They will most certainly send a rider or two to Marino to warn the larger French force of what has happened, and then on to Rome, where the bulk of Charles' army is still preparing to leave. But any rider will have to come through Albano unless he feels like riding through the thick forest around the lake. Borgia chose his spot well. We are almost guaranteed they will all pass through here.'

'A thought occurs,' Parmenio coughed and everyone turned to him. 'I assume that everyone else has made the natural leap in assumption that our next move is going to have to be siding with the French?'

'Possibly, though nothing is certain yet.'

'Then we either have to imprison these men without them seeing us clearly and being able to report on us, or we have to kill them all and leave no witnesses. Otherwise there is every chance that we will be actively targeted by the French and will never get close to Cem again.'

Skiouros nodded. Deep in his heart he was still troubled by his faltering blade that day in the castle, but unless he wanted to spend his life knowing that Lykaion lay unavenged and with the face of Bayamanaco burning on his arm, he would have to grit his teeth and finish the job.

'Did these Frenchmen do anything to us?' he asked, more concerned than usual over the idea of killing men with whom he had no issue.

'If you need to focus on anything to drive your sword arm,' Nicolo rumbled, 'just remember all those screams of women and children you heard across the river in Rome, where the occupying Frenchmen – men just like these ones – raped, murdered and looted with gay abandon. I for one will lose no sleep in the knowledge that half a dozen of them are sliding down the slope to Hell.'

There was a moment's silence as the roar of the rain insisted itself upon them, and they all nodded solemnly. Nicolo had made the point that would drive each of their blades this night.

'Very well,' Parmenio said quietly. 'How do we do this?'

'We split up,' Orsini replied. 'The French will be looking for Borgia and for a man who aided him. I am well-dressed and with a similar hair colour. If I hunch in the saddle, there is a good chance they will mistake me for the cardinal and the man with me for my accomplice. That man will be Parmenio, I think. We will sit in the open until they spot us and will then turn and bolt up the hill, leading them with us.'

'And the rest of us?'

'Helwyg will wait at the northern end of the city with his rope. String it across the road to drop any riders and then deal with them. They will surely send one or more men on to Marino and Rome, so it is your job to stop them and prevent word of our actions reaching the French.'

Helwyg nodded his understanding.

'On his own?' Skiouros frowned but Helwyg grinned.

'Unfair, no? I outnumber French, maybe one to three?'

'I think we can rely upon Helwyg's abilities. Similarly, Girolamo will return to the southern end and take up position to watch for any further pursuit and prevent any survivors making a break for Velletri. However many come, we want to contain them and not risk their sending for friends.'

The crossbowman nodded professionally.

'This will come down to blades and to cunning,' Orsini announced. 'There will be no use for arquebuses or bows, as the powder and strings would become too damp to use in moments. I am of a mind to lead them up to the amphitheatre at the top of the hill. Yesterday I spent an hour strolling about up there, and it would be a good place to deal with them without drawing too much attention from the residents. Skiouros and Nicolo, you lie in wait up there and we shall spring an ambush there. Many of the arches are already blocked with rubble or earth and with four of us we should be able to pen them up in the arena and deal with them.'

Skiouros and Nicolo looked at one another and nodded.

'Alright. We may have only minutes, so let's go.'

Skiouros crouched low on the wet, slippery stonework high among the crumbling arches of the ancient amphitheatre which rose like the bones of a long-dead empire from the hillside above the city. The rain continued to pound down at a pace that astonished the Greek and would surely soon empty the sky and evaporate the clouds to reveal the panoply of stars beyond. Almost slipping for the hundredth time, he reached out and grasped the thick stem of the bush that grew from the crack in the wall, its roots eating away at the mortar.

His eyes once more raked the slope below with as little result as the past dozen times. The rickety arches provided the best viewpoint of the city, which lay in an extended trapezium below, the two angled main streets converging on the high amphitheatre and then fanning out to intersect with the Appian way at the far end some two or three hundred feet below. However, with the continual curtain of vertical water, visibility was as poor as could be and despite his location, Skiouros could hardly see a few streets past the nearby church into the city, let alone way down to the main road or the hillside that continued to slope away beyond to the valley some three hundred feet lower again.

Once more, he adjusted the hood of his sodden wool cloak, doing nothing to alleviate the cold or damp, but granting him a momentary relief from the feel of the cold, drenched fabric sticking to his body. A fresh trickle of freezing water ran from the disturbed hood into his eyes and down his cheeks.

Behind him, he could feel Nicolo's gaze boring into his back. His friend had remained, sensibly, it seemed, on the lower parts of the amphitheatre, sheltering in one of the huge tunnels, most of which were blocked and filled with rubble, plant life and thick mud.

A quick survey had revealed that the amphitheatre had until recently been in use as a cemetery, two Christian chapels having been carved out of the corpse of the Roman arena. Much of the stonework had been robbed over the centuries, but what remained was still a good oval amphitheatre with arcades along the downward slope towards the city, while the other side had been shaped from the solid rock of the hillside. With the stolen marble missing from the seats and the centuries of weather-wear on the carved side, it was difficult to clamber up the sloping sides, especially with the rain having turned them into cataracts of water tumbling into the oval centre as continual torrents.

Of the thirty or so arches on the downhill side, only the grand one facing the west was large enough and clear enough to admit a man on horseback, and only two of the smaller ones were unobstructed enough to grant pedestrian access without a struggle. Orsini had clearly taken careful note of the place's defensive qualities during his wanderings up here yesterday as they waited for nightfall to move on Velletri and free their employer – typical of the man.

Skiouros held his breath and cupped his hand to his ear. All he could hear through the din was the muted sound of their own horses which were tethered in one of the blocked tunnels on the far side of the arena, and the only hint of life were the three twinkling lights he could make out in the streets below.

'Any sign yet?' called Nicolo from below, his voice curiously hollow and echoey from inside the tunnel.

'No. Not...' Skiouros fell silent as his eyes caught just a flicker of movement near the church of San Paolo atop its grand staircase. For a moment he held his breath, uncertain as to whether the movement was a trick of the rain. At least the lightning and thunder had moved on and were now rumbling over the hills to the south like a man losing an argument. But then, just as he was about to turn back to his friend and proclaim the area silent, the movement caught his eye again and within a heartbeat, two riders burst from the cover of the trees in the small square. Through the arch by the church they rode, and into the open ground beyond the walls. Skiouros squinted in an effort to identify the men, but the conditions revealed only two dark, cloaked shapes that could be anyone.

Confirmation came only a moment later as a small party of half a dozen riders emerged into the square at pace behind the pair, racing on for the gate.

'They're coming, and the enemy are right behind them. Six, I reckon.'

'Odds of two to three, then,' Nicolo said quietly, drawing his sword and parrying dagger in the Stygian darkness of the tunnel as Skiouros dropped from the upper curves, concentrating on keeping his footing as he clambered down to the lower levels of the structure.

'You ready?' Skiouros called as his friend emerged from one of the dark tunnels and into the deluge once more.

'No. Are you?'

'No,' the Greek smiled. Neither of them were warriors – just a sailor and a thief cast into the wrong roles. 'Come on, then,' he sighed.

The two men moved across to the wide archway that led in from the west, the sailor moving to the far side, clambering up the steps and crouching ready, blade in each hand. Skiouros moved into position opposite, drawing his own sword and reaching for his macana club – then pausing. Instead, he crouched and grasped a heavy chunk of fallen masonry just smaller than his fist.

By the time he was straightening and preparing himself, he could hear the hoof-beats of his friends' horses pounding across the compacted turf just outside. As Orsini and Parmenio pushed their way into the arena, the former looked up to both sides, clearly expecting to find his friends exactly as they were.

'Block the exit after them,' he shouted. 'Horses?'

'In there!' Skiouros called, pointing with his sword to the recess at the far end where they had stabled their own beasts. Orsini nodded and kicked his animal into a fresh burst of speed, cantering across the deep grass of the makeshift oval graveyard and slowing into the darkness with Parmenio at his shoulder.

Even as Skiouros silently urged them on, he heard the next set of hoof-beats outside, betraying the arrival of the Frenchmen. The Greek tensed, his teeth chewing on his lip in apprehension. The way Orsini had laid it all out, it had sounded so sensible and easy. Now, as the thunder of six trained killers pounded through the arched tunnel into their oval killing zone, everything seemed so much more stupid and he wondered bleakly whether he might shortly occupy one of the unmarked graves in this ancient theatre of death.

Then, as was always the case, the adrenaline and the necessity for urgent action took over and the world exploded in a flurry of activity. The six Frenchmen, uniformed in blue and gold and all looking far more expert and at home in the saddle than Skiouros, despite their earlier belief that few of the enemy would be trained horsemen, roared into the arena. They were armoured in breastplates only, with heavy leather riding boots, long gauntlets and metal caps to protect their heads. None bore a shield, but each man had his sword out and poised while they chased down their prey.

As the last of the six thundered past, Skiouros brought the odds a little back into their favour with a cast of his jagged chunk of masonry. The throw was far from expert – a good throw from a professional would probably have stoved in the man's head. But it was enough. The glancing blow smacked into the rider's head at the base of his skull and the shock and the force of the blow combined to throw him from the horse, where he hit the ground hard and lay, twitching but otherwise immobile. His horse went merrily on without him into the oval arena.

Through the sheerest luck the French rider closest to him was looking a different way and the din of the storm concealed the noise of the attack, so the remaining five horsemen rode on into the arena with their extra empty horse, looking this way and that to try and locate their prey. Not one of them looked back at where they had entered.

The French soldiers moved quickly and professionally, the man who seemed to be their leader despite a lack of insignia gesturing this way and that. Two of the men dismounted and ran off towards the various tunnels and chapels that led off the arena, swords held tight. Then, even before Parmenio and Orsini appeared from the small stable passage, the Frenchmen finally realised they were a man down and pointing fingers and raised voices singled out the prone form in the entry tunnel, the horse having wandered off to the side of the arena where it had decided that the soaking grass looked appetising.

Skiouros and Nicolo took a look at one another. Nicolo glanced questioningly down at the passageway between them and Skiouros nodded. They could not afford to let a man go. With acrobatic ease, the two men dropped down to the ground, Skiouros coming up and drawing his macana in his off-hand, Nicolo pausing only to drive the point of his blade into the prone French body to be certain he was out of the fight.

Parmenio and Orsini appeared at that moment from the darkness of the tunnel where they had tied their horses, roaring eagerly as they charged, weapons raised. The two French soldiers who were making for the other tunnels veered off to intercept and the officer clearly discounted any further danger from there since he turned his horse to watch instead as his two men who were still mounted raced towards the arch and the new figures who blocked it on foot.

Skiouros felt his heart rise into his throat as he watched the riders coming. He was no soldier or tactician, but he had seen enough action in the service of Orsini this past year to know that the only way for infantry to stand against cavalry was with a good long spear, not a sword and a club. Sure enough, the two riders aimed for the pair in the tunnel, one apiece, picking up pace for a full charge. The only positive thing Skiouros could think of in those panicked moments was that the Frenchmen both lifted their swords up and away from a sweep, realising that there would not be room in the passage and relying on the sheer force of a running horse to deal with the pair standing against them.

Skiouros risked a momentary glance at Nicolo and saw his friend cast the parrying dagger aside and grasp his sword in both hands, bracing his feet to meet the charge point-first. What the hell was he doing? Skiouros realised the answer at the last moment, but could do nothing about it as time had run out. Turning back to the horse bearing down on him, he cast up a prayer half a heartbeat long that Nicolo would survive his brave and stupid attempt to stop the man.

The young Greek was not such a straight-forward thinker – never had been. A boy does not survive for the best part of a decade in the streets of the world's greatest city living off his wits alone without coming to realise that there are always a thousand other ways to do things than the obvious, and most of them are less troublesome.

As the rider hunched down behind his steed's neck, bracing himself to flatten the insane man standing before him, Skiouros threw himself sideways, flat against the wall, but he did not stay there. Instead, as he hit the ancient stone he rolled along the wall with the momentum, past the charging horse but so close that he could feel the sweat spraying from the shining flanks even among the raindrops as hot water amid the cold.

The rider had not even realised that Skiouros had moved. As he reined in and his head came up and round to look for the corpse of the man he assumed he had ridden flat, Skiouros swung from behind with his macana, smashing the heavy wooden staff across the man's rein-holding arm hard enough that he felt the crack of the bone, even though he could not hear it over the deluge. Before the man could react, even as the hand fell away from the reins, the Greek thrust out with his sword. Not an elegant blow, but with the rider in shock and facing away, it was an easy enough attack. The point slid into the man's side above the hip and just below the cuirass, grating up past a rib and into the organs.

A hiss of effort escaping, Skiouros yanked the sword back out along with a spurt of blood and took half a dozen steps away from the panicked horse as the rider slid, agonised, from the saddle to land in the mud. Quickly, he was round the rear of the horse, giving its back end a wide berth. No one who's seen a horse kick out wants to be too close as those chestnut eyes roll over white with terror.

His heart fell as he rounded the beast with the intention of coming up behind the other rider. The Frenchman was already extricating himself from the saddle with difficulty as his horse, collapsed in agony from the sword wound to its chest, thrashed and screamed, every movement further pulverising the lifeless mess beneath it that had so recently been Nicolo di Siginella. Fury coursed through Skiouros as he set his hard eyes on the French soldier. Here and there, between flailing hooves and sheeting rain, he caught a glimpse of Nicolo out of the corner of his eye, and in every flash his friend looked less and less like a human being.

The rider must have seen in the Greek's eyes something of what was coursing through his veins for, as he stood, finally extricated from the horse and bringing his weapon to bear, he apparently changed his mind and, turning on his heel, fled for the open ground beyond the amphitheatre.

Somehow, through the blur of anguish and hatred that was suffusing Skiouros, he managed to retain enough reason to pause and turn, checking the situation in the arena. Parmenio had not seen what was happening, busy as he was fighting the French officer in the middle of the grassy oval, his back to Skiouros. Orsini, fighting two men at once and apparently still managing to maintain the upper hand, looked past his opponents and laid eyes momentarily on the Greek.

'Get him.'

Needing no further encouragement, Skiouros turned and jogged through the tunnel, casting a quick look at Nicolo as he went to further fuel his ire. As he stepped out into the open once more, the battering rain slammed into him like a slap from a weather God and he had to blink away the excess water to locate his prey. He had been late to respond, checking on Parmenio and Orsini first, and had moved slowly through the passage, but the rider had apparently twisted his leg when his horse had gone down to Nicolo's blade, and he was moving slowly enough that the vengeful Greek would have no trouble keeping up. Indeed, as Skiouros watched the Frenchman move through the tufa arch and back into the city proper, the man slipped on the wet stonework and went down painfully into the torrent of water rushing down the street.

Skiouros stomped at an inexorable pace after him, and as he passed through the arch, he saw the man only halfway across the square in front of the heavy, squat church. His ankle was truly slowing him down. The French soldier looked over his shoulder, spotted Skiouros across the square through the vertical rods of water, and a flash of panic crossed his face. He had clearly come to the same conclusion about their relative paces, because he suddenly put on an extra turn of speed, but the extra effort caused him to slip once more on a wet cobble, bringing him down with a shriek. Skiouros continued to close the distance like some avenging demon, blade in one hand, macana in the other, his face a mask of violent intent.

The Frenchman was whimpering, Skiouros could tell. He could hear snatches of it through the roar of the weather, for he was little more than twenty paces behind, now. He would catch up soon enough, and could be on the man in moments if he chose to run. But no. Nicolo's killer had to feel this one coming with every step.

In panicked desperation, the soldier turned away to his left, preferring the chance of losing this pursuing monster in side-alleys to the risk of the precipitous street with the slippery cobbles and the rush of ankle-deep water.

Skiouros smiled to himself. *No way out down there.* This was one of the few places Skiouros had visited on their sojourn here yesterday, and he had done so with eagerness. His home city had been full of underground cisterns, their roofs propped up by ancient columns. After all, he'd almost died in one a few years back. Some people said there were so many in Istanbul that the city was built over a hollow world, like an eggshell after the contents have been sucked out.

And Albano had such a place, too. Oh, it was nothing compared to the great edifices of that eastern capital, but still impressive in its own way, providing enough stored – and continually replenished – water to supply a legion. This narrow, stretched yard with its rough grass and half-grown trees granted access to that place, but to there alone, with the far end being fenced off. A man in the peak of fitness would have no trouble with that fence, of course. Skiouros would manage it well enough. But a man with a twisted ankle? In a downpour?

Skiouros rounded the corner at that same, measured, inexorable pace, his face unchanged. The Frenchman was already close to the far end of the alley, and even as the Greek hunter picked him out in the gloom, he saw the man realise he was trapped, peering hopelessly at the enclosing fence. With another whimper, the man turned and made for the only other possibility the narrow yard offered.

Skiouros closed on the side door, built into the wall next to all the bricked-up arches, as the Frenchman wrenched at the handle desperately. Even over the rush of the heavy rain, Skiouros could hear the roar of the water in the subterranean tank behind that door, falling from the aqueduct channel down through the cold, damp darkness and into the reservoir below.

Skiouros slowed his pace slightly with an unpleasant smile.

Nicolo was gone. He knew that on some small level the blame could be thrown at Cardinal Borgia for assigning them this dangerous task simply in order to buy him a little more time to run and hide. On the grandest level, the blame had to stick to Skiouros himself for dragging his friends into this pitiless crusade for vengeance, and he would crucify himself for that particular fact in due course. But the immediate blame could be plainly and simply pinned to this French soldier who had ridden down his friend and crushed him beneath a hundred stone of horse and rider.

Vengeance was nothing new to Skiouros, of course, but until this moment it had always been a vague, distant, almost ethereal thing.

Now it was immediate and right in front of him and while he had faltered at the Castel Sant'Angelo, he had never felt more focussed and determined than this. It was proof that he *could* do it. He had lied so many times to Orsini and had lived with this deep, shadowed fear that he would not be capable of taking revenge when the chance finally arose, but with the heaviness of his heart in this dreadful night came a strange freedom as he finally knew beyond all doubt that he could do it – he could take a life in cold blood. *Would* do it. He sheathed his sword.

The Frenchman finally succeeded in ripping the door open and flung himself inside. Skiouros waited for the inevitable, and almost laughed as he heard the panicked scrabbling of the man. Having visited the place yesterday, Skiouros had almost come to grief when he had entered, expecting more of a platform or tunnel inside that he'd actually found. Instead, there was only a staircase with a narrow landing, surrounded by a low stone wall, and beyond that the plunge into deep cold darkness.

Skiouros reached the door and flung it open as the soldier tottered, trying not to plunge into the hellish, pitch-black cavern, punctuated with columned arches and echoing with the sound of thousands of gallons of water falling into water. Skiouros reached out and grabbed the wrist of the man's sword arm, arresting his momentum and keeping him here on the landing. A puzzled look of gratitude flitted momentarily across the man's face but vanished again as the man realised that his salvation was far from assured, after all. Before the man could do anything, Skiouros brought his knee up as he wrenched the arm down. The Frenchman's wrist shattered with a noise that echoed around the subterranean chamber and his sword fell useless to the floor. As the man screamed, Skiouros lashed out with his macana, an expert blow that mirrored his last move, smashing the rider's left wrist and leaving him helpless. As the man began to shout something in his nasal French, Skiouros calmly shifted his weight, grasping the man's broken sword arm and bringing down his boot heavily on the man's foot, breaking most of the bones in it. Another shift, to the soundtrack of the man's agony, and he did the same to the other foot.

'It is a proven fact,' Skiouros said in a leaden voice, 'that a man can float on the surface of the water and does not truly need to swim.' He looked past the Frenchman into the darkness. 'You might live a while yet if you just lie on your back and try not to struggle.'

The Frenchman stared at him in incomprehension and replied in some French babble that was equally unintelligible to the Greek. With a shrug, Skiouros gave a sharp push and the Frenchman disappeared backwards over the low wall with a shriek that ended only with the splash below.

181

Stepping forward, Skiouros peered over the side, but all below was shrouded in black.

With another shrug, Skiouros stepped back out of the cistern into the rain, which was finally beginning to ease off, and closed the door. As an afterthought, he reached down into his belt pouch. A man with a background like his always carried his lock-picks, but a sensible man carried all sorts of small items that might come in useful. Selecting a small padlock from the pouch, he slid the bar through the door's lock and clicked it shut. Removing the key from it, he cast it across the open ground, somewhere into the deeper grass.

'Rest, Nicolo,' he said sadly.

The rain had finally subsided and the night air carried that fresh metallic tang that follows a heavy storm. A blanket of glimmering stars was being slowly unveiled as the cloud gusted off to the south, and four men sat in the small square outside an ancient church, heedless of the wet stone upon which they rested, for they were already sodden beyond hope.

'We will have to bury him.'

'Them,' corrected Orsini, and Skiouros nodded quietly.

'Did... did Nicolo have family?'

Parmenio, his face drawn and cold, shook his head. 'In truth, Nico was a bastard son. Left home young with a purse of bright coins, fond wishes of his mother, and a demand to stay away from his father.'

'We could bury him in the amphitheatre, close to where he fell?'

Parmenio shook his head, and Skiouros lowered his eyes. No one wanted to think of their friend resting in that arena of bloodshed for eternity.

'And what of Girolamo? What do we do with him?'

Orsini sat back heavily, casting a questioning glance at Helwyg, who was nursing a fresh cut on his arm in preparation for binding it in linen. Helwyg had killed two with only the one scratch to show, preventing their scouts carrying news to the army. Afterwards, he had gone to find Girolamo and discovered him bleeding his last from a chest wound amid the bodies of his own two victims. No survivors. And only two of their own men lost...

The giant nodded his unspoken agreement, and Parmenio gave his big friend a strange smile. 'I thought the old debt would be paid today, but it seems God has no use for you yet.'

Helwyg gave Orsini a strange look which slid into a sad chuckle and Orsini turned back to Skiouros. 'Provisions for the dead are included in our condotta and, since we are still being paid by the cardinal, those provisions still stand. We find a cart and we load them up and ferry them back to Rome. The officer at the Vatican will take care of the details, but one of my own addenda was provisions for interment in the cemetery of Sant'Agnese. Normally, the place is the sole reserve of the Lateran canons, but the good brothers Bartholomew and Alexander have made kind arrangements for us. Girolamo and Nicolo will rest in good company, safe from grave looters and body-snatchers, and when we return to visit them, they will have memorials to help us find them. Any objections, gentlemen?'

A miserable silence greeted the statement. It was as good a place to rest as any could hope, but little would lift their spirits this night.

'So we return to Rome?' Parmenio muttered.

'No,' Skiouros said with flat finality.

'Oh? How so?' Orsini asked quietly.

'Prince Cem goes south with the French. Nicolo and Girolamo died in service to my cause, for which I will pay in time, but I will not waste their deaths by turning round and scurrying back to Rome. If we return, we will stay there for the funerals. We will bury our dead and mourn at their graves. The brothers will do their best for us and in that time the French will spirit away Prince Cem beyond our reach forever. If we are to stand a chance of ever getting near him again, we must either join the French army or stay close enough to them to seize any opportunity that might come our way. If we wait 'til dawn, we can deliver the bodies to the Church of San Paolo up near the amphitheatre. A little donation to their coffers and I'm sure they'll deliver the pair to Sant'Agnese for us. Brothers Bartholomew and Alexander will take care of the rest.'

Orsini nodded slowly. 'Dawn is still perhaps four or five hours away. We should find a barn or something. Somewhere to dry out and perhaps catch a few hours of sleep.'

'One thing, though,' Parmenio said in a dark voice. They turned to look at him. 'We are not joining up with the bastards that rode down Nicolo. We shadow them. We follow them, and when the time is right, we make our move, even if we have to cut our way through the king himself. But we do not lend our swords to the men who killed Nicolo.'

A chorus of silent, grim nods. The dark night would soon end, and when the light came, each man would bend to their task with renewed vigour.

CHAPTER TEN - Napoli, February 1495

'Here they come,' grunted a local as he threw cheap, acidic wine down his gullet in an attempt to numb himself, his words a quiet echo of a call that was going up on the city wall and all around the piazza.

Skiouros took a swig of his own, rather finer, wine and caught the tense looks on Orsini, Parmenio and Helwyg's faces as they prepared themselves once more.

For a little over a month the four men had trailed the French army as it moved south through Italy. At first there had been something of a pause as King Charles had argued furiously with His Holiness over the vanishing act perpetrated by his cardinal son. The Pope had quite categorically stated that he had given Borgia no such orders and that he had absolutely no idea where the man was, except that he most certainly was not in the Vatican or in any other papal holding. According to credible rumour, the king had been apoplectic, spluttering and purple faced when the pope had smiled sweetly and informed him that everything unexplainable unfolded by the will of

God and that if the divine meant Cardinal Borgia to be free, who were mere mortals to defy him, even if they be popes or kings?

The situation had eventually diffused, the Pope offering a replacement legate, but the king waving away such a pointless gesture. The value of having the pope's son among his retinue could not be met by any other cardinal. Besides, two ambassadors from the court of the Spanish crown had arrived in Rome, demanding that King Charles abandon his campaign against Napoli or risk war with Spain. Charles would no more give up his campaign than give up a leg, but it all prompted him into urgent movement.

And so the French army had marched south, a vanguard always ranging ahead and the bulk of the army following on a day or so behind, including the king, his court and officers, and the tightly-controlled entourage of Cem Sultan. Despite the strained relations between the French and His Holiness, the army held itself in check throughout the march, bypassing towns and cities with an allegiance to the pope and camping in the wilderness for the most part.

Despite the fact that the desperate king of Napoli – Alphonso the second – had conceded the inevitability of defeat and abdicated the crown in late January, his nobles and generals had confirmed their decision to stand and fight, raising the king's young son to the throne as Ferrante the Second.

At the northern border of Neapolitan lands stood the great fortress of Monte San Giovanni Campano and on the thirteenth day of February the four friends had watched from a nearby hill as this most stalwart of Neapolitan defences stood defiant and proud in King Charles' path. The reputedly impregnable fortress had not fallen in four centuries of warfare, withstanding sieges by everyone from Arabs to Hungarians, and was a strong symbol of Neapolitan strength and defiance.

The friends had watched in awe as the French army brought its huge array of bombards and cannon to bear on the unassailable fortress and in a mere eight hours flattened the great walls and towers to jagged remnants. The garrison had little option but to surrender, though the French troops had their blood up, having been leashed since Rome, and what they did to the survivors of the siege, Skiouros could hardly imagine. Certainly no one had lived to speak of it.

In the aftermath of the siege, the Neapolitan army that had been moving north to help San Giovanni Campano, disheartened and panicked, turned around and made for Capua, the kingdom's second city after Napoli. The despondent Ferrante the Second had retreated with his court to Napoli in the hopes of raising new forces.

The four friends had moved quickly and easily on the periphery of the war. They had made it to Capua before the French and had watched events unfold there with no surprise. The three leaders of the Neapolitan forces there argued and, when it became clear that the garrison commander, Trivulzio, intended to open the city gates to the French and throw his people's fate upon Charles' mercy, the other two had taken their own forces and retreated south to Nola. One of those, they had been interested to hear, was Cesare's cousin, the powerful condottiere Virginio Orsini, and Cesare had snorted at the news and scoffed and told the locals in the bar that they should watch Virginio, for he would only stand his ground as long as it seemed profitable and would soon turn his coat.

As the French army had streamed into the twin towns of Old and New Capua to the adulation of the people, the four friends had sat in a roadside tavern, unarmed and dressed as miscellaneous locals, and watched their arrival. Prince Cem's entourage had passed them, the false sultan hidden and encased in a wooden carriage with no open windows, surrounded by his own people and a sizeable French unit of grizzled veterans. They had watched impotently as their target trundled past and into the heavily-fortified so.called Castle of Stones in New Capua, where he might as well have been on the moon as a few hundred yards away.

Sure enough, the French had hardly had time to plump their pillows in the second greatest city in the south when the condottiere Orsini and his companion sent messengers from Nola with overtures of peace and surrender. Cesare had snorted and toasted his cousin's cowardice. Then, while Charles and his army were still barracked in Capua and planning their next move, the messengers had arrived from Napoli, offering the city, the kingdom and the crown to Charles in return for his clemency. The young king Ferrante the Second, shocked and dismayed at the ease with which his capital collapsed, had fled to the island of Ischia, hoping for a miracle.

The four friends had stayed in Capua only long enough to be sure that Cem was truly out of their reach and to be certain of Charles' next move. When it became common knowledge that Charles and his entourage – along with the entire army – would leave for Napoli the next day to enter the city in triumph, the four saddled up, retrieved their kit and rode for the capital, keeping a step ahead.

Last night they had stayed in an inn – ironically named 'The Sword and Dagger' – on the north side of the large square immediately inside the Porta Capuana, through which the victorious king and his army would have to ride. They had stabled their horses and carried their huge, heavy kit up to their room in two trips, making sure to keep their weapons and armour well hidden among the heavy bags. To the casual viewer they were no different to any of the other foreigners that came in daily from the docks or moving ahead of the dreadful French army. With no swords or helms in evidence there was nothing to make them stand out.

Orsini glanced around the square, lifting his wine cup to his lips and using casual gestures to mask his true intent – checking the people at the neighbouring tables outside the tavern. None were paying them any attention. Still, he would be quiet and circumspect as always. Taking out a small coin and spinning it on the timber surface with his thumb and forefinger, he cleared his throat.

'This will be our last chance. You know that?'

Skiouros nodded. He was well aware of the fact. Charles had already won his war. He had invaded the kingdom of Napoli with the largest army the region had ever seen and met barely an ounce of resistance. One swift and brutal siege had undermined the pride and strength of the Neapolitan army, and only small pockets of resistance held out. Two of the city's four castles were still held by garrisons loyal to Ferrante, and their continued defiance could cost the people of Napoli dearly. But despite such small issues, the fact remained that the French were in control, and there was no denying it. Charles and his army would stay in Napoli only long enough to ensure its complete capitulation, and then they and the Ottoman pretender would depart with the French fleet for the east and their planned crusade. The 'war' Charles had initiated in Italy would look like a child's game compared to what would happen when he met Bayezid and the Ottoman army. No, once Cem had left Napoli, they would be highly unlikely ever to get close to him again. Napoli was their last chance.

Every time Skiouros thought about the moment he was finally face to face with the man because of whom Lykaion had died, he felt that familiar quaver of doubt. He pictured that moment in the Castel Sant'Angelo when he had held a blade to the man's throat and had yet stayed his hand. But each time that image arose, he crushed it with an image of the French rider, his limbs smashed, falling back into the darkness of the cisternone in Albano. If he was capable of such vengeance for Nicolo – a friend of four years now – how could he not be capable of a similar revenge for his brother? He would harden his heart when the time came and think of the cisternone, not Sant'Angelo.

The pressure was upon them now. And the level of danger would hardly decrease here. If Cem had been so tightly contained in Capua with its two fortified complexes, what would Charles order for him in a city with four powerful castles?

Skiouros' eyes strayed across the piazza from the east, where the city gate stood open and waiting, to the *Castel Capuano* opposite. One of the city's four, the castle stood as a squat, heavy square bastion, a wide space open around it and separating it from the crowded buildings of the city. The castle was the most modern of the city's fortresses, its plain walls having been recently punctuated with wide windows, crippling its defensive capabilities and transforming it in function to more of a palace than a stronghold. Still, the lower level of the walls was all heavy stone buttressing and iron grilles, supporting the more friendly upper part.

His attention was diverted once more by a change in the general atmosphere. The hubbub of the piazza, crowded with onlookers in the same situation as the four of them, died away into a tense silence, which was gradually filled with the sound of an armoured, mounted column approaching beyond the wall.

This was it: the fall of Napoli, heralding their last chance.

'Keep your eyes open and pay attention to every detail,' Orsini reminded them, somewhat unnecessarily. All of them had become old hands at this over the last month since leaving Rome.

The King's vanguard entered the city purposefully. Somehow, Skiouros had expected the King to lead, a triumphant victor in the manner of the ancient Emperors. But Charles was no fool. Better to forego the glory of revelling in his achievement and avoid the possibility of a trap or random assassins. Indeed, the man was clearly taking no chances with the Neapolitans. The lead unit of some two hundred cavalry filed into the square and fanned out, including perhaps forty knights in their colourful liveries and shining plate armour, light lancers in blue and white with the fleur-de-lys in evidence, and a small unit of arquebusiers, their guns apparently primed and levelled despite the lack of resistance.

Behind them came a swathe of footmen with pikes and swords and spears, wearing the blue and white of France. They spread out to line the main route through the piazza in a protective cordon, large numbers of men pouring up the stairs beside the gate to line the walls, removing the Neapolitan guards from their positions and supplanting them. Archers and crossbowmen followed, climbing the stairs and loading their weapons, searching roofs and balconies for any lurking local with murderous intent.

And so it went on for more than a quarter of an hour: streams of French troops moving into the city and taking control of every aspect of it, removing any hope of influence from the Neapolitans.

As the four watched, the smaller rear door of the Castel Capuano was thrown wide and the small garrison issued from it into the piazza, unarmed, lining up outside the wall facing the square and kneeling in subjugation to their new king. A unit of French swordsmen, led by a knight with a white swan crest upon his helm and shield, moved into the building, ignoring the hopeful chattering of the castle's former commander and searching the place. Another ten minutes passed, the French forces filing ever deeper into the city, lining the streets on Charles' route to the city's heart, and just as the Swan Knight and some of his men re-emerged from the castle, the royal party appeared through the Porta Capuana.

Charles and his court rode easily, the king with a glinting sword in his hand and resting casually upon his shoulder – a reminder that though he might have been invited in by the city, he still came as a conqueror. The cheering began as a small, half-hearted, nervous thing, probably at the instigation of a French officer somewhere on the periphery, but soon it rose to a tumultuous roar that filled the piazza, echoing back from the heavy walls of the castle. Charles waved his free hand casually at his subjects, guiding his steed with his knees for a moment before retaking his reins.

The four friends watched with a sinking feeling.

'I'd assumed he would encamp the bulk of his army outside the walls,' Parmenio said, raising his voice to be heard over the noise.

'I think we all had,' Orsini sighed. 'But it appears that the French army will occupy the city. By first light tomorrow, they will be outside the resisting castles, putting their artillery in place. And do you know what will happen then?'

Helwyg nodded soberly. Charles' army had a reputation for looting, murdering and rape in the aftermath of a siege. They were being remarkably restrained right now, given the opulence of the city, but if the small pockets of resistance continued to defy him, he would threaten them with an order to release his army upon the city. When that happened, what had caused all the screams across the river in Rome would pale into insignificance beside the fate of Napoli.

'If he sets his army on the populace, we will have to make damn sure we're away from here or very well hidden,' Parmenio muttered.

Helwyg nodded. 'I fight here before. I know place. Old Roman place under church. Good hiding.' The other three nodded their gratitude. Such a place might become necessary to save themselves in the next few days.

'Look!' Skiouros hissed at his friends, and they returned their attention to the gate.

Sultan Cem's carriage, still shut up tight and with the drapes closed, followed on behind the royal party, eight Turks accompanying the carriage on horseback, the usual French soldiers surrounding them.

'Why does he insist on being shut up in that carriage?' Parmenio grumbled. 'Before San Giovanni Campano he was riding a horse, while his whore rode in the carriage, but down here he's all tightly sealed up with her.'

'Wife,' Skiouros corrected.

'What?'

'She's not a whore. She's one of his wives, sent from Cairo with his other attendants.'

Parmenio rounded on Skiouros. 'Really? Everything that's going on and you pick me up on something as negligible as his marital status?'

'Perhaps he has no interest in the wars of the Italians?' Orsini mused before the argument could begin in earnest. 'Or perhaps he has irritated the king? Perhaps Charles fears he will become a clear target for Neapolitan marksmen? Whatever the case, I want to see him. We've only assumed him to be in the carriage since Teano; we've had no proof. What if we've been watching the wrong group?'

'Surely not, with his Turk attendants here?' Skiouros frowned.

'Probably not. He's almost certainly in there, but there has to be a reason for the change, and I wouldn't put it past his Majesty to pull a trick like that. Charles is a devious one.'

'Says an *Orsini*,' grunted Parmenio.

Falling silent and watching carefully, the four men kept their eyes on the carriage as it moved into the square. 'Be ready to move,' Orsini said, downing the last of his wine. 'We can't afford to lose sight of it.'

The others followed suit, throwing the smooth local vintage down their necks and gathering their cloaks and purses, but Parmenio suddenly reached out a restraining arm and stopped Skiouros as he rose from the seat.

'Wait,' he hissed and then pointed at the coach. As they watched, the vehicle slowed on the far side of the piazza, outside the Castel Capuano's door. The four relaxed back into their seats, watching tensely as the Turks dismounted and handed their reins to French serfs who ran over to help. Orsini grunted his irritation as the four realised that from this angle, the carriage's occupants would enter the castle without once moving into view. The Turkish entourage and half a dozen French guards filed around the carriage and disappeared from sight. Orsini was actually growling with a sound akin to a cranky bear by the time the carriage jerked into life and rumbled off across the piazza, revealing only the last few of the French guards entering the building. To further irritate the observers, the Swan Knight who had been standing nearby gestured to his men and the unit moved into the castle once more, leaving half a dozen soldiers outside, who moved to positions at the castle's corners and doors to watch for trouble.

'I think we have to assume that he was in the carriage,' Skiouros shrugged.

Parmenio nodded. 'And he's well-protected.'

'You have no idea, my friend,' Orsini said darkly. 'The swan crest was Louis de Valois, Duc d'Orleans and cousin of the king. He's a veteran of the tourney, it's said, and you can be sure that if he's in there, then the soldiers protecting the place are among the best the French have to offer.'

'Why after all this time assign someone so important as his jailor?'

'I don't know. Could be because the place is well-appointed. It used to be a royal residence, after all, so perhaps Louis chose it himself. Perhaps Charles only trusts his cousin with the Turk's safety. Either way it all adds up to a more difficult proposition now. Come on.'

Without waiting for the others, Orsini rose and pushed his way between the busy tables back into the tavern building. Entering the dingy interior, filled with hanging smoked meats, the smell of garlic, wine and sweat and the noise of the few people taking advantage of the fact that the crowd had concentrated outside to grab a place at a good table, Orsini made for the stairs to the upper floor.

By the time Skiouros and the others had caught up with him, he was approaching their shared room that provided a reasonable view of the piazza and the castle and gate on opposite sides of it. Unlocking the door, he moved inside and to the window. The others followed, and the door clicked shut behind them.

'Anything else we had to discuss, we needed a little privacy for,' Orsini said, watching the building opposite and ignoring the cavalcade of

Frenchmen passing beneath them and the endless serried ranks of foot soldiers pouring into the city.

'We're in trouble,' Skiouros sighed. 'Our last chance before he disappears into the heart of a holy war overseas, and they slam him up in a castle with a strong guard and the king's own cousin. What the hell do we do now?'

Orsini shrugged. 'We do what we can, what we're good at. We watch. We wait. We practice the patience that you once told me was second nature to you now. Charles will be occupied for a day or two. He'll have to establish control and a rapport with the remaining authorities in the city. Then he'll have to send emissaries to Ferrante the Second in Ischia. And there are two castles to lay siege to. Even if he manages to rush things, his army will not be ready to leave on crusade for weeks.'

'And if he decides to give Napoli to his men to loot and rape?'

'Then we put Helwyg's hiding place to the test and continue to practice patience.'

'Do you really honestly believe we can do it?' Skiouros asked, tentatively.

'We stole into a palazzo in Rome and took a man's son out from under his sleeping nose. We took the fortress of Roccabruna from an army with only a handful of men. We rescued Cardinal Borgia from a sealed town and a hostile French force and then dealt with their pursuit. And don't forget that we escaped a Turkish slaver and survived a flight across a thousand miles of mountain and desert. Never underestimate our ability to achieve our goals, my friend. And bear in mind that while this is a castle, and with three score guards or more it's a nicely modernised one with many wide windows and few external defences. Whatever the cost, we will do it, I pledge you that.'

Skiouros glanced around at the four of them. *Whatever the cost...* They had been seven when they left Genoa over a year earlier. His quest for vengeance had cost them Vicenzo, and Girolamo, and Nicolo. How many more would have to die before the usurper Sultan stood before God to answer for his crimes?

A mournful clanging across the chilled, darkened city announced the hour as two in the morning. Skiouros looked across at Parmenio, who had a thin layer of white frost forming on his beard and eyebrows – the weather had taken a cold turn yesterday. His friend, while not strictly speaking asleep, was close enough to dreamland that his eyes flickered constantly with the effort of keeping them open.

Skiouros had been irritated at first, but they had had a long and tedious day, and he was having some trouble staying awake himself. Parmenio was almost two decades older than he, and had had an erratic sleep pattern since the death of his oldest friend. That he was wearier than Skiouros was hardly a surprise.

He glanced down at their chart, formed over the past two and a half days of watching from their window – it had to be from the window, with the ever-increasing presence of French patrols in the streets and the growing number of daily 'incidents' involving the deaths of Neapolitans. With two men always on the lookout in six-hour shifts – Orsini had been immovable on the number, claiming that one man could too easily fall asleep, as was now being evidenced – they had watched each coming and going of guards and other folk from the castle and every tiny detail had been logged on the paper. A clear pattern had quickly emerged, just as Orsini had expected, given the military nature of the guard and jailors.

On cue, the door of the castle creaked open, a wide swathe of golden light spreading across the rime-coated paving of the empty piazza, and six rested and refreshed guards emerged, moving around the building, their breath pluming in the night air. Each soldier nodded to the man he replaced before they went off duty, entering the building and closing the door once more.

'Two of the clock and another guard change.'

'Mmph? Eh?' Parmenio queried, roused briefly from his semi-stupor and shivering awake again.

'Two of the clock,' Skiouros repeated. 'They've changed the guard again, and I checked. They're the same ones as earlier. I figure they must be being punished for something, what with the shifts they're being given.'

Parmenio hauled himself a little more upright and peered through the window. He squinted for a moment and shrugged. 'I can't tell the difference, so I'll take your word for that.'

'The two men who stand at the east door and the southeast corner are fairly distinctive. The latter has a leg injury, so he lurches as he moves, and the other one has the thickest beard I've ever seen on a human being and seems to disappear into the shadows to drain his bladder every ten minutes. They were both on duty this afternoon and now again tonight, so I can only assume this whole unit has rotated on the same times. And the same thing happened yesterday. The men who do the ten in the evening 'til two in the morning shift are the same ones as do the noon 'til five shift.'

That's still only nine hours,' Parmenio sighed. 'Whatever their pattern, there's no reason to assume they'll be tired. They still have two 'til twelve to catch up on their sleep.'

'I don't think so,' Skiouros disagreed. 'I remember when Lykaion was on a similar rotation with the Janissaries and missed our meet-ups at the Bloody Church. Just because he was on duty during the night didn't excuse him from being up at dawn with the others. The military is like that: they don't bend to accommodate such things.' He thought back with a sad smile. 'Those particular days, Lykaion was more troublesome and disagreeable than ever, but he was also tired and much easier to outwit.'

'I hope you're right.' Parmenio rubbed his freezing arms.

'I am. I'll speak to Cesare when we change over. I think tomorrow night is the time to go, about one in the morning, when they're at their most exhausted. And this corner is the obvious place to go for, since the bearded one at the door's so often out of sight, away from his post.'

'Has that lurker been back?'

Skiouros frowned for a moment, but shook his head. Two nights running, they had seen the shape of a man in a shabby brown cloak sitting in the freezing gutter over by the city gate. Almost certainly a beggar, since no one in their right mind was out in the streets these nights, and certainly not right beneath the French army's nose like that. Let alone sitting in a frosty gutter. 'No. Looks like he's been moved on.'

'Good. Then all that remains is to decide how we do it.'

Speculatively, Parmenio leaned to the window again, brushing furry white frost from the sill with his elbows as he peered down.

'Hello, what's this?'

Skiouros leaned forward to join him. Across the square, a small group of horsemen were making their way into the piazza. This was new. Foot soldiers were becoming common on every street corner, threatening the locals and taking advantage of the situation to rob and rape, but cavalry were a rare sight. The Greek squinted, trying to identify them. They were clearly French. Their blue, white and gold livery was visible even in the poor light. There were perhaps a score of them. What were they doing at this time of...

Skiouros shrank back from the window. '*Shit!*'

'What is it?' Parmenio frowned, trying to see what had perturbed his friend. Then he too recognised the king of France in his saddle at the centre of the group, his eyes widening.

'What the fuck is Charles doing here in the middle of the night?'

'Perhaps he's come to see his cousin?' Skiouros whispered. 'The duke of Orleans rarely leaves the place, after all.'

'Perhaps. But in the middle of a freezing night? It's to be hoped he doesn't decide to drop in for a chat when *we* happen to be over there!'

The two men watched tensely as the party tied up their horses outside the door under the watchful eye of the bearded guard with the bladder problem and entered the castle. 'Shall we wake the others?' Skiouros whispered.

'Let them sleep. If anything else happens we'll go and rouse them.'

The pair peered from the window in a state of near unbearable tension for perhaps fifteen minutes until the door opened again and the king and his soldiers emerged once more into the misty, freezing piazza, their boots skittering on the frosty flagstones, untying their horses, clambering into the saddle and riding off for the city centre.

'I'm starting to think that our time's running out faster than we anticipated,' Skiouros breathed, and Parmenio nodded. 'Tomorrow night, then. I'm with you. Let's get it over with.'

Henri Baillet stood at the south-eastern corner of the Castel Capuano, nodding faintly. The only thing that was really keeping him awake was the ache in his leg – even the numbing cold was faintly soporific. Never a good horseman, Henri had been crestfallen to have been thrust into the saddle of some local's disagreeable animal back in Velletri a month ago, and had barely made it out of the city gate before he'd been unhorsed and fallen painfully among the rocks by the road. Their task – to recapture the fleeing pope-son cardinal – had been urgent enough that his companions had ridden on at breakneck pace and left their fallen man behind, ignoring his absence.

It had been both a curse and a boon, his incompetence. He had returned to his commander, hobbling and leaning on a stick he found by the road. His commander had had him beaten for his failure and he had been assigned the worst shifts available for over a month now, with no relief in sight. But really... well, everyone else who had ridden on had been killed at Albano by some force presumably lying in wait at the cardinal's order. So really, he'd been a lucky man.

Of course, it would have been nice to be one of those men out in the streets, fleecing the local flock of their gold and ale. But his leg wouldn't really have coped with a four hour patrol around the sloping streets of Napoli, anyway. Better to stand here, perhaps, after all.

Occasionally he wondered how badly wounded he would have to be before he would be assigned to the medical section, currently quartered in a nice, cosy commandeered convent in the quieter part of the city? Sadly, for all the aches and discomfort, his leg was definitely on the mend. That meant that once everything was settled in Napoli and the local scum had accepted French dominion, he would be accompanying the army overseas to the east, into the desert to fight the Turk for control of Byzantium. He sighed, remembering the tales – mostly horror stories – of those great crusades centuries back when men in steel pots and chain shirts had sweated out their lifeblood in the sands of Syria while Saracens carved pieces out of them for the greater glory of their deviant God.

His thoughts turned back to Marguerite at home in Laon. How old would their child be now? He was too tired to calculate the months he'd been away. He wondered whether it had been a boy or a girl? Hell, the way things were going, the child would be married and he'd be a grandfather before he climbed the hill toward the glorious, grand abbaye de Saint Martin and their home that nestled in the shadow of its great church.

Curse Italy. Curse the Turk. Curse Charles de Valois for his thirst for conquest. Curse the *lot* of them!

His eyes had drifted closed again, and he only realised because a thrill of pain shot up his leg from his ankle and jerked him back to his senses. He straightened, shivering and trying not to slump, and wiped the frost from his pike handle before reassuming his stance. He was periodically in view of that miserable hairy bastard Jehan de Courcy by the east door. Every time the sour old pisspot came back into view around the projecting entrance tower, he glared this way. Henri had no doubt in his mind that if Jehan once saw him asleep he would report him to the officers, and then night-guard duty would be something to dream of by comparison to his next assignment.

He glanced, but de Courcy was out of sight – probably taking a leak behind the tower yet again. One more hour 'til shift-change. Then he could get a few hours' sleep before the miserable bastards in charge had him up and clearing the kitchens for breakfast. At least he wouldn't have to deliver food to the Turk, anyway. He'd had to do that the first day, but then young Nicolas had turned up for morning inspection with unpolished boots and had been given that unpleasant, onerous task as a reward.

Where *was* de Courcy, for the love of God? Was he busy curling one out in the shadows? Or had he dragged one of the street-walking girls aside to entertain himself in the privacy of his dark, urine-soaked corner?

He realised his eyelids had drooped again as he came alert with a start, a strong arm around his throat, cutting off his air. His eyes bulged and he panicked as he realised that hands had also closed around both his wrists. He felt his pike plucked from his helpless grasp. More than one person held him, then. His rolling eyes caught strange, colourful tattoos on the arm around his neck, just on the periphery of his vision. He was going to suffocate soon, but blessedly at least he would pass out first. And the ache in his leg would stop hurting then, too.

A creature of nightmare suddenly stepped into view in front of him. His eyes boggled at the troll, the Nordic giant before him, his wild hair and scruffy blond beard twinkling with hoarfrost. Dressed in dark doublet and hose and with a black wool cloak, the enormous, bearded blond monster had a face that displayed the clear and present threat of agonising violence. A voice behind Henri – the man with the tattooed arm, obviously – rattled something off in unintelligible Italian, and a second voice that belonged to the grip on his weapon arm replied in soft, well-spoken Italian. A third voice joined in from his other side. He had not a word of this liquid language, and the conversation was beyond his wits. He couldn't even discern the tone they were using, but that might have been less due to his incomprehension than to a combination of exhaustion and suffocation.

Finally, as he was starting to look forward to the oblivion of unconsciousness and very probable death, the grip on his windpipe loosened slightly and the huge thing in front of him bent low to address him face to face. The big man had quite passable French, astonishingly, with a faint Germanic accent.

'Tell us the direct route to the bedchamber of the false sultan Cem, or my friend's arm will tighten and will crush your throat-apple, leading to an excruciatingly slow and painful death. Nod if you understand.'

Henri lost no time in nodding as expansively as the tattooed man's grip would allow.

'Good. Talk. Quietly and very quickly.'

Henri swallowed with some difficulty. A good soldier of France would refuse to talk. He would die for his king and for his duty. But then a good soldier would not have fallen off his horse and been assigned all the shit duties his commander could find. A good soldier might not baulk at the idea of gasping out his last moments with a flat throat, clawing at his face as his tongue swelled purple and his eyes bulged pink. But Henri had seen a man choke to death back near Torino, and no amount of national pride was going to persuade him to submit to a similar fate. Settled on his course of less-than-heroic action, Henri pictured the interior and the corridors he had trod so often over the last three days. 'From the door over there…'

The arm around his neck tightened slightly and a brief Italian exchange occurred. The big French-speaker in front of Henri shook his head. 'Not from the door. From the window above you.'

Henri tried to look up in confusion, but the grip prevented it. 'Which floor?'

'Which floor is Cem Sultan on?' the giant breathed.

'The top, but it's very difficult,' Henri replied in a whisper. You will be caught. Better to give up now…'

'Just tell us. And anything else you think we might want to know, too.'

Henri sighed inwardly. Might as well be hanged for a wolf as a sheep. 'There's less men on the top floor than below, but they are the best the Duc has to offer,' he whispered. 'This end of the chateau is more complex than the other end, with quite a few side corridors, yards, light-wells and staircases, but its rooms are not occupied, so it's less often patrolled. The other end is a square built around one courtyard, with the best royal suites. The Turk is being held in a room deep in the castle's centre that overlooks that courtyard.'

'How will we know which room?'

Henri shrugged with difficulty. 'It has guards at the door. No other room does – apart from that of the Duc d'Orleans, and his apartments are over the main gate on the opposite side of the courtyard. But you would be better not doing whatever it is you plan. There are too many of us inside. You will all die.'

The big monster smiled. 'I do not think so.'

Henri felt a blow to the head and pleasant, welcome, foggy darkness enfolded his mind, driving away the ache and the constant cold.

Orsini rubbed his hands together. 'Remember, all of you, that we need to be as fast and as stealthy as it is possible for a human to be.' He ignored their long-suffering expressions and gave them a hard-eyed glare. 'I am *aware* that you all know this, but it's important enough to hammer into your brains once more. The force of Frenchmen in there alone could kill us without batting an eyelid, let alone the army out in the city. The moment we are discovered, we are done for. Every one of us would die. So it is vital that we deal with every last threat before the alarm can be raised. Only then do we stand a chance of both success *and* survival, and I for one am intent on both.'

The others nodded their weary understanding, and Parmenio cleared his throat, addressing the young Greek. 'You're confident you can get up there?'

Skiouros turned to him. 'How long have you known me again?'

'But with the frost...'

'Give me the rope.'

As his friend passed the coil of rope across, Skiouros threw it over his neck and shoulder and leaned into the slope of the buttressed wall-base. For the first ten feet or so the wall splayed outwards, formed from large, centuries-old blocks with easy handholds where the mortar had crumbled. For all the slippery, chilling frost, grip would not be difficult. Taking a deep breath, he began to climb, pausing every four steps up to blow warm life back into his fingertips.

The ascent held no fears for him. He had climbed much worse places than this in his life, including that castle parapet at Roccabruna. But the worry that nagged him as he rose, the one that had his face turning this way and that nervously, was that he might be seen. They had chosen this corner carefully, though. It had taken a well-aimed half-brick from the shadow across the street to knock the bearded door guard flat – Skiouros had been sceptical that Helwyg had such good aim, but had been thankfully proved wrong, the Silesian's hefted missile striking the back of the man's head as he stood pissing in the corner. After that, they had managed to approach the sleepy guard with the bad leg with relative ease.

At this time of the night, there would be few locals abroad in the city, and few shutters open. It was a rare street indeed that did not see a French patrol pass in search of easy pickings every quarter hour, but they tended to keep away from the piazza, the castle and the Capua Gate, as there was still a ban on looting and raping, and this area was a little too visible to the higher authorities, what with the king's cousin being based here. The two castles that resisted Charles' control in the city continued to hold out, and the whole of Napoli feared that ban being lifted and the horrendous reprisals that would follow – that the French army would be let loose to kill and rape with impunity. Only the bravest or most stupid Neapolitans made themselves visible just now.

Which were the four of them? Skiouros felt certain he knew that answer.

As long as they were quick, got in and had the job done before the guard change came, there was little chance of them being noticed outside the castle, and they would be back to the inn without passing into the dangerous streets beyond. Still, his nerves jumped and he peered around as he reached the top of the slope and found a reasonable handhold in the brick of the next stage: a short length of jutting wall with an arched base forming small buttresses. Taking a deep breath he soon slipped up the side of this with the assured ease of a spider in its twinkling white web. Now already halfway to his goal, he glanced right to the nearest windows, their shutters closed tight like all the others in the castle's outer-facing walls. The faintest of glows from behind the shutters suggested that the guard below had been correct, and that these rooms were unoccupied, the dim light coming from the corridor beyond. If the rooms had been occupied by a wakeful figure, the light would be much brighter, while a sleeping inhabitant would have the door closed, making it dark. Still, just in case, Skiouros moved that little bit slower to keep his ascent as quiet as possible.

A few heartbeats later he was above the first windows and approaching the shutters of the top storey, some sixty feet above the silvered paving where two of his three friends waited, Helwyg just returning from an alleyway nearby where he had dumped the insensible bodies of the French guards. With a quick glance at them, Skiouros pulled himself up to the shutters and peered in through the crack. The interior was gloomy, though he could see the faint glow of light from the door beyond. Trying to still his racing heart, he clung on tightly with his left hand and slipped a small narrow work-knife from his belt with his right, reaching up and sliding the point between the shutters. He felt a moment of resistance and when the latch came up and gave way, it freed so quickly that he had to grip all the more tightly to stop himself falling. With difficulty he swung the shutters back, causing a creak that sounded deafening to him, and ducked his head to avoid clouting it.

Pausing only for a cursory glance inside, Skiouros hauled himself up and over the sill into the blessed relative warmth of the Castel Capuano. As he rose from an automatic crouch, he spun. The room was gloomy and dim, but he could still see that it was some sort of bedroom that was clearly not in use. No bedclothes covered the wide, stale bed, and the furniture appeared untouched and uncluttered. Most likely only Cem and the Duc had rooms on this floor, which would be where the well-appointed ones were to be found. If anyone else lived up here, they would also be officers or noble guests. That meant that the bulk of the French military would be down below, and only patrolling guards would likely be encountered up here. It seemed their friend outside had been straight with them.

Satisfied that the room was entirely clear, he sheathed his knife, turned and removed the rope from around his neck, unravelling it and tying one end tightly to the window's mullion, treble-knotting it for sureness. Testing his weight on it and satisfied with the result, he leaned forward and threw it from the window, watching the falling rope uncoil as it tumbled to his friends below.

His fingers closed on something on the table below the window and he looked down in interest to see a thick, heavy book, fastened shut with a metal clasp, its leather cover marked with intricate designs.

'Halt!'

The voice sounded uncertain. Its owner had spotted movement – a shape before the window, but had not quite confirmed the definite presence of an interloper yet in the gloom. Skiouros turned, his fingers still gripping the book, and let fly. A French guard stood in the doorway, silhouetted against the lamplight of the corridor. Miraculously, given the spontaneous throw and Skiouros' lack of preparation, the heavy book hit him full in the face, knocking him from his feet. The guard hit the floor heavily, the wind driven from him. The Greek intruder wasted no time. Ignoring the window and his friends, he leapt across the room, grabbing the guard by the ankles and dragging him fully into the chamber, against the likelihood of anyone else appearing in the corridor and seeing the prone man.

The Frenchman was already recovering from his daze even as he slid into the dark room with a faint squeak of leather baldric on waxed floor. Skiouros reached down for his knife once more, ripping it from its sheath just as the soldier reached up and grabbed his wrist. Skiouros felt a moment of panic. As the Frenchman opened his mouth, his wits returning rapidly, preparing to shout the alarm, Skiouros' hand closed over the man's maw, muffling his shout to a stifled murmur.

The guard's other hand came up and reached for Skiouros' throat. He tried to rise out of reach, but couldn't do so while keeping his hand over the man's mouth. For a moment, they were locked there in a motionless stalemate, both straining for the upper hand, neither able to back down. Then, in a move that surprised Skiouros, the Frenchman bit deep into his palm. Skiouros instinctively drew his hand back a fraction, but the snapping teeth clamped onto his little finger and while Skiouros stared on in agonised panic, he gasped in horror as the Frenchman bit through the bone and removed his finger.

As Skiouros reeled from this unexpected and horrific reaction, the Frenchman attempted to bellow out a warning, but was halted by ill luck as the spray of blood from Skiouros' finger stump flooded into his mouth and he choked on the warm ferrous taste.

The struggle swung the other way instantly, as the guard coughed and gagged on the blood, his attention momentarily distracted. His grip on both Skiouros' neck and wrist relaxed involuntarily, and the Greek automatically took advantage, the knife forced down past the impotent hand and plunging into the Frenchman's neck. More blood sprayed up, and Skiouros leaned to one side to avoid being drenched in the torrent.

The Frenchman had all but forgotten him now, still coughing out the blood, much of it now his own, and reaching for the dagger buried in his windpipe, around which pink, bubbly froth was leaking.

Skiouros rose, a shocking pain throbbing in his left hand and repeatedly lancing up his arm. His eyes still upon the stricken, dying guard, he reached for the scarf around his own neck and yanked it free, tying it around his left hand and knotting it tightly. The dark blue wool immediately turned glistening black as his blood soaked it.

A thump behind him announced the arrival of Helwyg, and the big Silesian appeared next to him a moment later, looking down at the guard and then across at his wounded companion.

'You messy fight.'

Skiouros glared at the big blond warrior who merely grinned and grabbed the shaking body of the Frenchman, dragging him further inside the room. A moment later Parmenio and then Orsini dropped into the chamber, the latter turning and hauling up the rope, coiling it and leaving it on the table.

'If we're lucky we have half an hour or perhaps forty minutes before the man below's absence is noted. Possibly a lot less, though.' The nobleman left the rope attached to the mullion, but closed the shutters without, deepening the gloom of the chamber.

'Helwyg is right,' he smiled. 'You *do* make a mess.'

Ignoring Skiouros' face, he stepped past and peered out into the corridor. 'Clear.'

A moment later, the four friends moved out into the passage and Parmenio closed the door behind them. Skiouros was gripping his crippled hand tight, tears welling in his eyes. His finger was somewhere in the darkened room with the dead Frenchman. Orsini had whispered his fine sword and parrying dagger from their scabbards, and Helwyg had unsheathed from his back the long sword he favoured, despite its difficulty of use in such confines. Parmenio drew his own sword now, though Skiouros refrained, his left hand throbbing too much to be of great use and preferring to keep one able hand available. He would rely upon the others to deal with any sudden threats as they moved through the corridors.

Once more, as he fell into line with Orsini leading and Helwyg bringing up the rear, Skiouros found his mind wandering back to the Castel Sant'Angelo on a cold winter morning, and to the cisternone of Albano in the torrential rain. His revenge was almost upon him. After so long, and coming close so many times, they had finally committed to the act. It was ridiculously foolhardy, this. He knew that they all thought it. They realised their true chances of success for all their bravado. No one said anything, but he could see in Orsini's face that he didn't expect to succeed, or at least not to live through it.

Lykaion's rest and the vengeance it required had cost so much already: Girolamo, Nicolo and Vicenzo gone. It was hard to believe the rest of them would make it out of here intact, and for what? After all, he had heard less and less from the shade of his brother over the last year, and now nothing since their early days in Rome. His ghostly companion had fallen silent.

Skiouros gritted his teeth. Albano, not Sant'Angelo. Vengeful fury for the wronged, not hesitation through moral dilemma. Vengeance needed to be visited upon Cem. Bayamanaco satisfied, his fiery wrath subdued. The opia of his brother's resting spirit added to the ensemble on his arm, completing the tattoo.

He barely realised what was happening in front of him until it was over. A side door had opened by chance as they passed and a Frenchman emerged, only to find himself spitted from two angles as Parmenio's sword sank into his ribcage and Orsini's slid into the base of his throat, preventing him from crying out an alarm. The figure fell back into the dark room and Orsini smoothly closed the door on it, hiding the evidence.

They moved on through yards of corridor with doors and paintings, mirrors and expensive furnishings, occasionally catching a glimpse of the courtyards below. Two guards stood chatting in one of the smaller ones, oblivious to what was going on above them.

He almost walked into Parmenio's back before he realised the others ahead of him had stopped. They were at a junction: a corridor led off to their right as well as ahead. Before them, rooms continued on the left side but opposite, windows looked out, presumably over the large courtyard. Orsini was gesturing. Skiouros stepped forward and glanced around the corner for a heartbeat.

Halfway along the next corridor, two guards stood armoured and at attention by a door. Skiouros ducked back instantly in case they spotted the motion.

'What now?' he whispered, his voice little more than a breath. He used his good hand to wipe away a tear of pain from his eye and realised he had instead left a smear of blood across it from where he had been clutching his four-fingered hand.

Orsini looked up at them and shrugged. 'Leave this one to me.' With surprising deftness, he pulled the big wool cloak that he had kept pushed back for the climb around him, his arms now buried deep in the folds. He took a deep breath and then stepped out into the corridor, striding along it with a purposeful gait. He was moving with such assured speed that he had closed half the distance before the guards turned to him.

'*Qui est là?*' The Frenchmen changed their grips temporarily on their spears, being careful not to scrape the painted ceiling with the points.

'*Bonsoir,*' Orsini said casually as he approached. '*Avez-vous entendu le Duc d'Orléans...*'

He never finished his sentence since, as soon as he was close enough, he threw his cloak back with a flick of the shoulders and his sword and parrying dagger came up together, each buried to the hilt in a French breast within the blink of an eye. The two guards gasped simultaneously and, despite their mortal wounds, tried to bring the cumbersome spears to bear against their attacker in the confined space. Skiouros realised now why Orsini had been so brazen – he had known that it would take time for the guards to get their long, heavy weapons angled at him, and that time would be enough for him to strike, so long as he took them by surprise.

A moment later the other three had rounded the corner and were bearing down on the door, even as Orsini delivered two more blows to each man to make sure they were out of the fight and unable to raise the alarm. Gathering there, they paused, Helwyg piling the two men to one side and moving their spears to lie along the edge of the floor.

'Alright, Skiouros,' Orsini said in little more than a whisper. 'This is it. Move quickly and decisively. If you have to deliver some cutting line as you do it, then be quick. Time is now of the essence and you've not the freedom to gloat and delay. We are incredibly lucky not to have had the alarm raised yet, and every passing minute makes it more likely. We will deal with anything else in the room. You concentrate on Cem.'

Skiouros nodded, drawing his sword and hefting it in his good hand, wincing at another throb in his left. Helwyg tensed his fingers, his knuckles white on the grip of his great German sword. Orsini and Parmenio both prepared their blades, the former with his dripping, crimson parrying dagger in his off-hand, the latter reaching his free hand down to the door handle. Parmenio glanced around at his friends and at Orsini's nod turned the handle and swung the door inwards.

The four men burst into the room at speed, Parmenio at the rear closing the door behind them to dampen any sound for the rest of the castle. Skiouros had not realised until this moment that he had been half-prepared for this to be the wrong room – to find some French captain asleep within. He had also not realised that he'd been partially hoping for that to be true, so that he did not have to confront his greatest dread: actually completing his task.

But his fears – his hopes? – had been unfounded. Even had the occupants been absent, the room was clearly the apartment of the Turkish exile. Strangely, even the momentary glance as they entered was enough to send a huge pang of homesickness through Skiouros. It looked like the chamber of any opulent Ottoman. Delicate wall-hangings showed scenes of turbaned pashas hunting rabbits with hounds. Silk and velvet cushions lined the floor and the couches around the periphery of the room, and the polished wood floor was covered with thick, warm, exotic rugs. Somehow it even *smelled* like Istanbul. The whole effect combined to startle Skiouros and he paused as he took everything in.

Cem's small group of loyal countrymen were in the room, some seated on the couches, others on the floor, all of them staring in silent, numb shock at this sudden intrusion, any thought to cry out extinguished by the points of so many swords waving at them. One attendant sat at a desk near a window down to the courtyard, busy with a letter of some sort. Near him, a fruit bowl and a platter of bread were kept company by a bottle of wine and four crystal glasses. Clearly Cem's western captivity had led to him breaking his religious abstinence, then.

In the centre of the room stood a large bed, its elegant wooden corner posts almost touching the ceiling and holding up a canopy from which swathes of fabric fell, forming a curtain of privacy all around it.

Parmenio hovered by the door that he had closed. Helwyg moved into the centre among the companions, his huge threatening bulk enough to cow the seemingly gentle courtiers into continued silence. Parmenio moved for the man at the table, making threatening gestures with his sword as he drew the curtains on the two windows of the room for added privacy.

And through this strange tableau stepped Skiouros, son of Nikos the farmer, child of Hadrianopolis and of Istanbul that had been Constantinople, former thief, saddened brother, false priest, intrepid explorer of the western lands, reluctant sailor, condottiere and now, by a twist of fate, assassin.

His heart beating so hard he could feel every thump in the roof of his mouth, his pulse racing like the horses of the ancient Hippodrome, he stepped up to the bed and used his bad hand to brush the curtains aside, climbing onto the bed with his sword raised and poised to strike.

Albano, not Sant'Angelo...

Inside all was gloomy, the thick drapes blocking out the light of the room.

Skiouros paused for a moment, his eyes adjusting to the dimness. His heart was cold and fiery all at once. His mind rolled in a sea of turmoil. Castel Sant'Angelo. Cisternone. Lykaion. Nicolo. Vengeance. Goodness. Hope. Fate. Just what *was* Skiouros, son of Nikos capable of?

The gloom resolved into shapes. The figure of Cem Sultan, half-brother of Bayezid the Just and claimant to the Imperial Ottoman throne, resolved among the sheets, as did the shape of a well-dressed Turkish woman who had to be his wife, kneeling at one corner of the bed within the drapes.

Skiouros' arm came up, the sword point dipping towards the figure of Cem, his elbow bending, muscles tensing. He could feel the sweat on his brow like liquid fire, nothing at all to do with the temperature. He faltered, and then pushed down his uncertainty, preparing his arm for the blow.

And then he saw Cem, son of Mehmet the Second, *El-Fatih* – the conqueror.

Cem was an unhealthy grey colour, dappled with plum-tinted patches. His eyes were pink with burst blood vessels. His lips were purple and he sweated heavily, drenching the sheets from his cold, rubbery skin. Skiouros stared at this thing and his heart lurched. Only now did he realise that the strange, peripheral noise he'd been trying to block out was that of weeping. The woman in the corner was in tears. Even as Skiouros stared at the would-be sultan, he saw the man's chest suddenly rise and fall with a shudder, dragging in a troubled breath. He waited far too long for comfort for the next one.

'What happened?' Skiouros whispered in a shaky voice, his sword still raised in the killing position, despite its apparent redundancy. The tip wavered for a moment. He turned his head with difficulty from the sight of his mortal enemy and fixed the shivering woman with his gaze.

'*What happened?*' he repeated in a forceful hiss, realising suddenly that the woman probably spoke no Italian. He switched into Turkish with remarkable ease after so long.

'What happened to him?'

The woman recoiled, startled at the unexpected use of her own tongue from this foreign killer. She simply stared at him in horror, and Skiouros felt himself flinch as though she had struck him. Carefully and slowly, he lowered the sword and slid it into the sheath at his waist. Nursing his wounded hand as drips of blood from the saturated scarf wrapped around it fell to the bed clothes, he nodded at the woman in what he hoped was an encouraging and comforting manner. He could feel very little through the whirlwind of emotions whipping up his insides.

'*What happened?*'

After a long moment, the woman tried to talk, her voice cloyed with sobs and grief. She paused, taking a breath, and tried again. 'My prince has been ill for too long, beyefendi. We hoped he would recover, but it is clear now that this will not happen.'

'Illness?' Skiouros felt cheated and saved at the same time, and the combination did little to calm him.

'He fell ill on our journey south, Lord, after we left Rome. By the time we reached a place near Capua... Thino, I think...'

'Teano,' Skiouros corrected, numbly.

'Teano, yes. By the time we reached Teano, the sultan could no longer walk or ride. He was given a carriage by the king, to allow him time to recover. But he will not recover, I am thinking. Allah is about to claim him. His light will fade and leave my life in darkness in hours now, or perhaps days.'

Skiouros shook his head in shock. What should he do now? He could almost feel Lykaion looking over his shoulder. He could feel the ghostly forms of Nicolo and Vincenzo and Girolamo wisping on the very edge of his senses, perhaps demanding he complete the task for which they had given their lives, perhaps simply observing as the scene played itself out.

'His Majesty says that when my husband recovers he will be freed,' the lady whispered. 'I think he makes this generous promise because he knows he will not be required to honour it.'

Skiouros was still reeling, unable to think straight. The figure of Bayamanaco on his arm burned with rage at this turn of events. His hand trembled.

Illness!

After everything they had fought through and overcome… all the sacrifices and hardships. All the effort they had put into this almost *sacred* task. And nature had done the deed for them. In fact, if they had all sat still in Genoa for a year and a half drinking Orsini's wine, it seemed likely that they would have heard news of the Sultan's death in the coming days anyway.

Skiouros found that he was chuckling with a borderline hysterical tone. The woman stared at him. He straightened his face with some difficulty as his friends from the room beyond the drapes shouted for him to hurry up, asking what was going on.

'No,' Skiouros said to the woman. 'His condition is not funny, *Sultana*,' – it felt strange to use the honorific for her after denying Cem's own Sultanhood for so long – 'but the path God sets out for me is a darkly humorous one, I fear.'

One thing was clear: his revenge was pointless. Indeed, if he killed Cem now, he was certain it would be a kindness.

Taking a strange, sad, elated, panicked, hollow breath, he bowed his head to the lady. 'You have my sympathy, *Sultana*.'

Turning, he slid from the bed, wafting the curtains aside and returning, blinking, to the brightness of the room.

'Is it done?' Parmenio asked, his eyes sparkling as he kept his sword levelled at the courtiers in the corner of the room.

Skiouros could not find the strength to answer him. Instead, his eyes wandered, lost, around the room. They took in Orsini, poring over the letter the man had been reading. They took in Helwyg, polishing the apple he had taken from the fruit bowl on his doublet. Reaching up with it.

Skiouros felt the blood drain from his face as he whipped out his blade and leapt from the bedside.

Helwyg stepped back in shock as Skiouros' sword tip sliced deep into the apple, nicking the big man's finger. Skiouros raised the sword, lifting the apple away from the big Silesian. As the giant stared in surprise, blood dripping from the cut on his finger and splattering onto the priceless carpet below, Skiouros brought the offending fruit close and sniffed at it, recoiling at the bitter aroma he had entirely expected.

'What?' Helwyg frowned.

Skiouros, things falling into place in his beleaguered mind, turned his blade again, presenting the apple beneath Helwyg's nose. The Silesian took a sniff and lurched back, giving a sharp sneeze.

'Treated with oil from the poison nut tree,' Skiouros explained, 'all the way from India.' He moved the deadly orb away from Helwyg and tipped it from his blade next to a half-eaten one on the table. 'It is a rare and expensive poison, little known in Europe. Yet I have smelled it once before, in the Vatican itself no less, in a similar fruit bowl in the apartment of Andreas Palaeologos. It was how he dealt with those who threatened him.' Skiouros shook his head. 'I should have seen it coming.'

Orsini rose from the letter, a look of understanding crossing his face. 'You mean...?' He pointed his sword at the bed.

'Yes. He has hours to go. Days at most. Palaeologos had me fooled! I truly believed he sympathised with Cem. But now... when the wall fell on Prince Cem, Andreas was there on the stairs. He had been acquainted with Cem's Hospitaller guards, and I presume found it easy to persuade one to help after they had been summarily dismissed. Paregorio wasn't with the emperor on the stairs, because he was busy killing the Hospitaller, tying up loose ends! And when that failed, he ran out of time. He sent his favourite poisoned fruit away with Cem when he left the Vatican.'

Parmenio's face took on an unreadable expression.

'No. It can't be that,' contributed Orsini, shaking his head.

'What?' Skiouros felt a tiny moment of hope thrill through him.

'This fruit would never have lasted. It's been over a month since Rome. Any fruit the Greek emperor managed to get into Cem's presence would be rotten by now.'

He and Skiouros made the same connection at the same moment and turned to Parmenio in time to see the fact dawn on him too. His blade steadied, still pointing at the Turks.

'So he had an accomplice. Someone who's travelled with Cem from Rome. Couldn't have been a Frenchman, as he had to have been in the Vatican to begin with. And it can't be a Roman, as they never left the city. So it's one of his own.'

'Come,' called the female voice from the bed, its tone almost dulled to inaudibility by the drapes. Skiouros looked at Parmenio and Orsini, and they nodded. Helwyg retrieved his big sword as Skiouros sheathed his, parted the drapes once more and climbed onto the bed. His eyes fell upon the Sultan's wife and she gestured instead to the still form of Prince Cem on the bed. The prince's eyes had focused – apparently with great effort – and his head had turned slightly to face Skiouros.

'You,' the Turk breathed with a crackle. Skiouros frowned.

'You... saved me... in Rome.'

Skiouros shook his head in wonder. It was true. Astounding, as was everything about this situation. 'It was a matter of blind luck.'

'Then the Prophet... guided your hand.' He suddenly exploded in a burst of coughing, which seemed to drain him to the edge, blood infusing the spittle that it produced.

'It may... it may not look that way... but this is a blessing.'

Skiouros' frown returned.

'I... I have prayed that... if the king of France... wished to use me...' Another pause for a coughing fit. 'If Charles wanted... to use me as an excuse... to exterminate my people...' his head slumped back. 'Then Allah take my soul... before that can happen.'

Skiouros stared.

He waited for more, but Cem appeared utterly drained, barely able to breathe now, let alone speak. The Greek's confusion was clearing. The whirlwind had slowed to a drift. His mind was focusing. He had learned time and again these past few years never to take things at face value. He had refused to be tricked into blind acceptance of any man's creed since his travels began. And yet he had been blinkered by his revenge. He had seen Cem as a hateful usurper and a monstrous conspirator. Of course, quite possibly the man *had* been just that years ago when this all began, but clearly he was not that now. And if Skiouros could step back and look at himself and see the changes that five years had wrung in him, why should Cem not have experienced the same?

And through all the strange emotions and revelations, two things came to the surface:

The pure nobility of what Cem had just said.

And how much that reminded him of Lykaion.

An unbidden tear welled up in his eye and trickled down his cheek and he leaned over the pain-wracked body of the dying Turk.

'Allahu Akbar,' he whispered. Despite living among Muslims for much of his life, and travelling with the Tuareg across Africa, he had never experienced one of their funerals and knew nothing of the requirements and customs beyond those a passer-by might discover by observing from the outside. Understanding that all he could do was provide as much comfort as possible, he smiled weakly. 'May Allah and the Prophet grant you rest, Cem, son of Mehmet.'

Somehow all the force of his vengeance had drained in the face of this poor, broken creature and his dignity in death, placing his people above himself. Skiouros sighed. 'Know that I wish you only peace.'

Skiouros looked up at Cem's wife. He wanted to ask her something, but had absolutely no idea how to go about it. Possibly she understood, or perhaps misunderstood, but whatever the case, she nodded gently.

Skiouros reached to the top of the bed and picked up a bulky, down-filled pillow, lifting it in both hands. Cem muttered something inaudible, but Skiouros took a deep breath and gently lowered the pillow over the pretender sultan's face. He had expected a struggle, even with the man's weakness, but Cem simply lay limp and immobile as Skiouros gently, compassionately suffocated the last dregs of agonising life from his bitter enemy. His eyes drifted up to the man's wife, but she was simply watching, tears dripping from her cheeks. If a year ago in Roccabruna someone had told him that his last act against Cem Sultan would be one of mercy and respect, he would have laughed in their face.

Skiouros closed his eyes as he held the pillow there to be certain.

'*I bear witness that there is no god but Allah...*' Possibly the whispered voice was in his head. Possibly it was muffled out from beneath the pillow, or did the girl say it? Whatever the source, it sounded a great deal like Lykaion's voice to him.

After what seemed an eternity, he lifted the pillow once more and threw it back to the top of the bed, his eyes on the dead pretender. For confirmation, he held his hand to the man's nose and mouth and sensed not the slightest draft of breath.

Skiouros felt empty.

'Rest, Cem. And rest, Lykaion. It is done.'

Slipping to the edge of the bed, he reached up and threw open the drapes, dropping to the floor and staring at his hands as if they belonged to another man.

'Murder!'

Skiouros blinked at the shout and his drifting thoughts pulled back in as he focused on the source. The call had been in Turkish and one of the sultan's companions towards the back of the room was standing, pointing at the bed.

'Murder! The Borgia's men have killed the Sultan!'

Skiouros blinked again. And again. And suddenly the room exploded into activity. The prince's entourage started to shout and wail, shock and horror evident on their faces, pointing at the bed and at Skiouros, calling him a killer. One of the men even started to shout in Italian.

Somehow, through the numbness of his senses, he noticed the man who had first shouted, along with two others, making for the door to the corridor, taking advantage of the grief and shock of their companions to attempt an escape. They did not look shocked.

Skiouros narrowed his eyes.

'You!' he pointed at them. 'You are Andreas' men! You killed your own prince!'

The three men reached the door just as Orsini stepped in to block it, both blades held forth, threateningly. Parmenio and Helwyg were moving on them now, too, ignoring the wails and shouts of the other Turks, pushing them aside. Skiouros drew his sword. Whether or not these men presented a threat, their shouts must have roused the French by now.

'We have to leave!' he barked out, wondering whether he could still wield his macana club with his missing finger. With a last, regretful glance at the dead sultan and his wife, the Greek assassin ran across the room towards the others. One of the three Turks near the door reached out and pulled a tall candelabrum from beside the wall, the burning tallow candles falling to the floor as he wielded the huge, iron furnishing as a weapon, threatening Orsini with it. Unwieldy it might be, but it was also large and complex and might well break a sword if handled well. As Orsini shifted his feet to make ready, the second Turk pushed the third towards Parmenio and Helwyg, using his human shield to escape the closing ring of death. He reached the smaller of the two windows and slammed his hand into it, pushing it wide open, leaning through the curtains. He began to bellow out in Italian with a heavy Turkish accent, warning of a Papal assassin in the sultan's chamber.

Skiouros skirted round the edge of the clamouring mourners and drove his blade into the shouting man's chest. He was too late, of course. If there was a Frenchman in the castle who did not know there were interlopers now, then he was a deaf one. The Turk fell away from the window and Skiouros yanked his blade back, allowing the shaking man to collapse to the rich rug and pour out his life onto it. In half a heartbeat he was over with Helwyg and Parmenio, who had already dealt with the human shield. Only the man with the candelabrum remained. Even as Skiouros approached the scene, Orsini feinted with his sword and, as the Turk was distracted, Parmenio drove his parrying dagger into the man's back between the shoulder blades. The Turk went stiff, his fingers releasing the candelabrum, which fell to the floor.

'Run!' suggested the sailor helpfully, and Orsini turned and flung open the door. Immediately outside, a French soldier who was reaching for the door handle went wide-eyed and tried to bring his sword to bear. Without pause, Orsini slammed his own hilt into the man's face, which issued cracking noises as he fell away spraying blood and teeth. Orsini halted only long enough to look left and right along the corridor. Strangely, they were alone.

'Come on.'

Easily, speedily, Orsini charged to the right, the way they had come. The other three followed at his heel, Helwyg taking up his usual place at the rear, his eyes occasionally flitting over his shoulder as they ran. As he reached the junction to the next corridor, Orsini looked this way and that again, his face falling as he peered to the right.

'Damn it.'

He turned the corner and ran left and as Skiouros and Parmenio reached the junction behind him, they looked to the right only to see a dozen French soldiers running at them, the man behind them dressed in a night-robe of deep blue with a white swan upon it, his sword out at the side as he bellowed orders in French.

They would never make it. They might reach the room through which they had entered, but they would never have time to deal with the shutters and the rope before they were overrun.

Hearts heavy, they turned and ran anyway – what else could they do? The long corridor that led towards the rope room was empty ahead, at least as far as the room's door where it turned. Clearly the soldiers on this floor were concentrated at the end where the Duc d'Orleans resided, as one might expect. If only the soldiers weren't so close behind, the four friends might stand a chance. In an attempt to gauge their relative speeds and their lead, Skiouros glanced over his shoulder as he ran, and his heart fluttered at the sight that opened up behind them.

Helwyg had not followed them from the junction and was instead standing proud and enormous in the corridor, swinging his huge blade in ponderous arcs, daring the first Frenchman to approach him.

No... not *another one*! Skiouros wanted to shout out, to tell Helwyg to run. But nothing would help the big Silesian now. He was a dead man already. It was just a matter of how long he could hold them off – how many minutes he could buy his friends. Skiouros had a flash of memory back to that look the mercenary had exchanged with Orsini back in Albano. Debt paid...

With a heartfelt wish that his big Germanic friend die well, Skiouros turned his gaze to the front once more. As they reached the door to the room, the sounds of ringing steel on steel and cries of pain were echoing along the corridor. At the corner where the door stood, as the friends rammed their blades back into their sheaths, they glanced left only to see more Frenchmen coming.

Orsini wrenched the room's door open and the three men fell inside. Parmenio ran over to the window and threw the shutters open as Orsini removed the key from outside, slamming the door shut and locking it, and then helped Skiouros drag a heavy armoire over and lean it against the door.

With a nod to one another, the two ran to the window, where the shutters were now wide and Parmenio had thrown the rope out, watching it uncoil as it fell.

Thuds and thumps began to sound beyond the door and the armoire moved a couple of inches. Orsini reached up and wrenched the scarf from his neck. Quickly, he wrapped it around the rope near where it was tied to the mullion and then gripped it tight.

'See you soon.'

With a deep breath, the nobleman stepped up onto the table and threw himself from the window, sliding down the rope, using the scarf to prevent burn as he descended at lightning speed. With a last look at the door, which was thumping and shaking, Parmenio pulled on the gloves that had been tied at his belt and threw himself out, zipping down the rope at a frightening pace. Skiouros was alone in the room for a moment. He glanced back at the bulging, shaking door, listening to the racket on the other side and the various shouts in French, leading him again to wish he spoke the language.

Somewhere beyond that door lay the cleaved body of Helwyg, the latest victim of Skiouros' vengeance. Three left, now: just him, Orsini and Parmenio. Adrift and friendless in a city heaving with French soldiers, every one of whom would shortly be looking for them. Their chances of escape were slim, to say the least.

Clambering up onto the table, Skiouros looked down to where his friends waited at the bottom. Shouting could be heard around the other side of the castle now, and a bell was tolling a warning somewhere nearby. Unwrapping some of the blood-soaked scarf from his wounded finger, Skiouros held it in both hands and wrapped it around the rope. With a silent, instant prayer for deliverance for them all, he threw himself out of the window and slid down the rope at speed, the building going past in a blur. The descent was so fast that he barely had time to clamp his hands painfully together and bend his knees for the impact before he touched the paving. From the way

Parmenio was rubbing his own knee, it seemed he had also underestimated his speed and had landed hard.

'Where now?' Skiouros asked breathlessly.

'The port,' Orsini replied, the words forming a frost cloud before his face.

'And our horses? Our gear? I've got Sigma stabled in the inn!'

'If you live through the night perhaps you can come back,' the nobleman spat acidly, 'but this area is going to be swarming with the Duc D'Orleans' men shortly and our inn is no longer safe.'

'Nor are the streets, with all the French patrols.'

'But they're not looking specifically for us. Now come on.'

As if they needed any further incentive to move, the door to the Castel Capuano suddenly burst open and golden light spilled out into the dark again. Soldiers began to issue from it, fanning out, scanning the empty square and the streets leading off for their prey. In half a heartbeat they were shouting and pointing at the three friends. Skiouros turned and Orsini was already running, heading for a dark alleyway, slipping and skidding on the frosty stones.

More bells took up the warning and as the three friends disappeared into the relative obscurity of the dark passage, they could hear French voices raised in anger and alarm. They had lost their only fluent French speaker with Helwyg, though Orsini clearly had a smattering of the tongue, and really it didn't take any level of fluency to guess what the voices were saying.

Skiouros blinked in the unaccustomed shadow and almost fell over something that he suspected was the body of a stray dog, his feet spattering in ordure as he raced to catch up with Orsini and Parmenio, who was putting on a faster turn of speed than was his norm. The nobleman reached a fork, where a crumbling building barred their direct path south, and turned to his right. Skiouros frowned. He could hear French voices from that direction.

'The other way!' he shouted, pointing to his left.

'Goes uphill to the city wall,' Orsini yelled back without stopping. Feeling the strains of panic tugging at the edge of his senses, Skiouros followed his friends. 'Last time I checked,' Orsini shouted back at him, 'the sea was downhill from everywhere!'

Yes, thought Skiouros irritably as he ran, *but so, apparently, are the French!*

A horrible flashback assailed Skiouros as he pictured the three of them, along with Nicolo, racing down the narrow spaces between market stalls back in Palos a year and a half ago, fleeing Turkish pirates in an effort to reach the docks. His mind furnished him with a picture of the *Pinta* sailing for the western horizon with its sister ships, and he dearly hoped history was not about to repeat itself!

Continuing down the gentle gradient towards the sea, Skiouros saw Orsini burst out into a wider street from their narrow alley. Opposite, a squat and brooding – if impressively wide – church blocked their path. Two French soldiers were huddled outside the church's front door playing dice, and both looked up at the running footsteps. One of them shouted something challenging as they rose and retrieved their pikes from the door. Skiouros could do nothing about them, however, for suddenly a figure appeared out of a side alley and barged into him.

The Greek fell painfully to the cobbles and the muck, his assailant on top of him, and gasped as the man's knife plunged from nowhere. He felt the numbing punch of the impact and it took him critical moments to realise that he had not been wounded. The knife point had struck his leather belt and dug into it, bruising him badly, but preventing the blade from slicing deep into flesh and organs.

He tried to rise, but his assailant – no French soldier, probably just a mugger – held him down as he withdrew his knife for a second blow. Skiouros stared, wild eyed, and in a moment of clarity, bucked and then bent his head, clamping his teeth on the mugger's restraining hand. *Let's see how someone else likes it!*

The thug screamed and the pressure was lifted. Skiouros kept his teeth clenched and stripped flesh from the finger as the hand pulled back. He spat out the skin and blood as the mugger lurched to his feet, and then rose to face him. In a deft move, given that it was on the wrong hip for this, he drew his macana with his good hand and spun it twice before swatting the man around the cheek with it and then, as the thug leaned back from the blow, jabbed the end with impressive force into the man's gut. The thug folded up and fell to the ground, his knife clattering off along the cobbles.

Skiouros was about to lean down and finish him when he heard French shouts and remembered that time was the most pressing matter right now. As he emerged from the alley, he saw Orsini drive his blade through a Frenchman and rip it back out, clearing their way as Parmenio clutched his shoulder with his sword still in hand, blood seeping down his arm and darkening his sleeve.

'Where were you?' the sailor grimaced.

'I got a little held up. Where now?'

'Downhill,' Orsini reminded him and turned right, running from the church.

'What do we do when we get to the port?' Skiouros panted as they pounded down the frosty flagged street, skittering here and there and having to watch their balance on the slippery stone.

'We get onto the first ship we find that's not bearing the French flag, we pray that they're no lovers of the Valois regime, we pool every ducat we have and ask them how far away from Napoli it will get us.'

'Not much of a plan.'

'Do you have a better one?' Orsini snapped archly as they ran.

Skiouros thought better than to reply and they followed the slope of the hill, curving gradually to their left until they came to the rear end of another church, this time a tall and decorative one, with a tower that stood high above the city's towering residential blocks. As they ran past it, he became aware of French voices shouting from the streets to their left. If he had his geography of the city right, that way lay the walls. Had word reached there and men been mobilised? Or was it just another random patrol out ravaging the innocent populace?

As they turned again, always following the slope, Orsini pulled up short, and the other two almost stumbled into him. A patrol of French soldiers was making their way up the street. So far they were marching in tight formation and hadn't made a move for the three running men.

'They don't seem to be looking for us,' Skiouros whispered.

'That won't matter when they see us – three Italians, armed, covered in blood and out in the streets at night. What do you think they'll do?'

Sure enough, as the patrol spotted the three men, they shouted a challenge and broke into a jog, weapons levelled. Skiouros glanced wild-eyed at his companions. There were perhaps a dozen of the enemy – far too many for the three of them to take on, especially with Parmenio wounded. And they were blocking the slope downhill towards the port, too. Orsini skidded to a halt, slipping a little and going down to a knee to prevent his momentum carrying him rolling down the street and into the path of the patrol. Parmenio almost went over him.

'Back,' Orsini shouted in Italian as he staggered to his feet again. 'Round the church and lose them in the alleys on the other side. Then downhill again.'

The three men turned and began to scramble back up the slope towards the church with the tall tower, struggling with the sudden change of gradient and the slippery sheen of rime on the stony ground. It would not be too hard to lose a patrol in the narrower alleys, but there was always the dreadful possibility that they might meet another patrol coming the other way.

A loud *crack* rang out in the night air. A gun shot?

With a sinking feeling, Skiouros looked down. History continuing to repeat itself. After all, the bullet had apparently missed him in Palos through pure chance. Perhaps God had not saved him after all, but merely granted him a period of grace to save Cem. The divine did have a curious sense of humour at times, after all. His eyes played down across his chest and belly as he ran, expecting to see the tell-tale blossom of dark liquid on his doublet as his lifeblood flooded out to soak the material.

Nothing.

His sinking heart hit rock bottom and he skidded to a halt as he turned, dread pinching his every nerve ending.

Orsini was staring at him with a look of utter surprise as the nobleman staggered, his leg misshapen by the wound that had carved out so much flesh and come so close to shattering the bone. Skiouros' horrified eyes rose above Orsini to the Frenchmen who were advancing at pace, apart from the one arquebusier who was still on his knee with his firearm levelled from the shot.

Reaching out, Skiouros grasped Orsini to prevent him falling as his ruined leg buckled.

'Can you hop?'

Orsini shook his head. 'Only into the grave, my friend,' he winced.

Panic filling him, Skiouros glanced across to Parmenio and thrust his macana at the captain. Parmenio took it and the Greek turned, reaching for Orsini's waist to pick him up bodily.

'Don't be stupid, Skiouros. Run, or you'll both die with me.'

Pushing away Skiouros' grasping hands, Orsini spun his sword once in his grip and drew his parrying dagger, staggering again as the blood gushed from his leg, sapping his strength with every beat of his heart.

'No. No more deaths.' Skiouros' face was hard, pale and furious.

'I'm dead already. Go. To the port. To a ship. Go home.'

'You're not dead. A good doctor can save you.'

The Frenchmen were closing and Parmenio turned, levelling his sword and Skiouros' club ready to fend them off if he had to, but the macana drooped with the pain of his wounded arm.

'*Skiouros*,' Orsini leaned forward, almost falling as his leg trembled again. 'Helwyg was not the only one who took an apple.

Three bites was probably enough to kill me three times over. I am *already dead*. Let me go to the sword and not sweating out my life in bed.'

Skiouros stared, remembering the half-eaten apple on the table, next to which he had placed the untouched one.

No!

But Parmenio was grabbing him and turning him. His mind whirled. Not Orsini. Not *another*! Vengeance was lost now; done, futile. *Stop taking my friends*!

He hardly struggled as Parmenio began to push him back up the hill. The captain was shouting something at Orsini, but what it was escaped Skiouros entirely. All he could hear was his own thundering pulse and the sounds of bodies hitting the floor as fate, or God, or blind chance took his friends one after the other.

But he was running. Somehow, regardless of his unwillingness to move, Parmenio had triggered some primal instinct and he was fleeing once more. Despite the peril of the slippery flagstones and cobbles, he looked over his shoulder in time to see Orsini drive his sword into a Frenchman, recover, parry a blade with his dagger and remove the hand of a second. But then a soldier kicked him in the knee of his bad leg, and Orsini cried out and collapsed. Skiouros saw the three French blades raised for a downhill stroke and turned to face uphill once more, salty tears freezing into the corners of his eyes.

He ran, trying not to hear the scream that was cut short so fast.

Orsini's sacrifice had bought them precious seconds, but he knew they were not going to make it as soon as he looked up again. Another French patrol had rounded the corner at the top of the street, next to the church, and had spotted them, launching into action.

No! *Not Parmenio as well.*

Grunting through bared teeth, he began to recover his wits and ripped the macana from Parmenio's grip. 'Your turn. Say hello to Genoa for me.' As he stood still, hefting his macana and drawing his sword, Parmenio shook his head. Skiouros was about to push his friend away when over the running feet and the shouting French voices, he heard something he would never have expected in a thousand lifetimes:

A Turkish voice!

He was so surprised that he only realised too late that he'd not actually heard what it said. For a moment he wondered whether Lykaion's shade had chosen the most inopportune time imaginable to plague him. But Parmenio had clearly heard it too, for the sailor's head was spinning this way and that, trying to identify the source.

Before Skiouros actually saw it, Parmenio was once more moving, propelling him with a purpose towards a narrow alley mouth between two tall buildings: a butcher's shop and a shoemaker, he noted with ironic interest. His eyes picked out the shape of a man in the darkness of the alley. Blinking, Skiouros found his feet and his drive once more and ran into the darkness just as a second *crack* split both the night and the wooden post of the butcher's shop on the corner.

As his eyes adjusted to the darkness and Parmenio and he skidded to a halt before the figure, Skiouros once more started in surprise. It had been a shock to discover that one of the Turks had made it out of the castle and had called to them. It was a greater shock to realise that this was actually no lackey from Cem's entourage. The swarthy figure in the shadows was dressed in a black and silver jacket and baggy trousers tucked into knee high red boots, as well as the turban of an officer. A sailor! God knows, he had seen enough of them in that epic journey from Crete to Spain to recognise one even in the dark.

'Come with me,' the man said and turned on his heel.

Something about the man was familiar.

'I know you,' Skiouros said in a breathless whisper, but the man was already moving off down into the gloomy alley with the sureness of a native, leading them into the dark, away from the French.

EPILOGOS - A departure

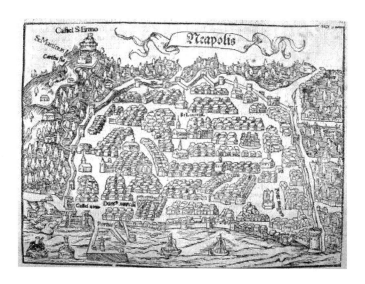

February, the year of our Lord fourteen hundred and ninety five.

Skiouros estimated the distance they had travelled, evading the countless dangers of Napoli only through what seemed to be the preternatural instincts of the Turkish sailor. Skiouros had tried to speak to the man several times over the… what, two miles? of their journey but their guide had refused to pause or divert his concentration, all his wits locked onto the complex, winding route that had led them down close enough to the port to smell the brine and the seagull shit, and back up, through the dark heart of the beleaguered city and then out to the north and west, ever further from the French threat.

Now, far from the clamour and the danger of the centre, they skirted the edge of a high ridge upon which sat a heavy fortress, surrounded by the ranks and lines of the French army, still holding out in the name of the Neapolitan King despite the clear fact that his kingdom was gone, delivered into the hands of the French with barely a fist raised. The neighbourhood around the slope was little more than carbonised timber and wreckage, an entire quarter of Napoli burned out to give the army a clear run at the castle. But it was equally clear from the encamped force that despite the fact that they had lost, the Neapolitan garrison were unwilling to admit it, and were giving the French something to think about.

Indeed, as they picked their way through ruined streets and between dangerously unstable timber skeletons, here and there they could see the remnants of a French artillery position smashed to pieces by their opposite numbers on the hill above.

If ever he had had a thought to stay, the sight of what was now befalling Napoli was enough to convince Skiouros that it was time to leave the city – to leave Italy entire, really, though hopefully via Parmenio's vessels that still sat anchored in Genoa's port, unless the French had taken the place and its ships on their march south.

The three men's journey became considerably easier as they moved from the patrolled streets of the city into this carbonised wasteland where grasping burned timber fingers pointed towards heaven, as if accusing God for what had been done to them.

Skiouros shook his head sadly as they passed. Strangely, despite the horror of what had been done here, it would not be his worst memory of Italy when – if – they escaped the place. Even putting aside the deaths of so many good friends, he would evermore remember the lavish, gilded corruption that painted every surface and every face in this dreadful peninsula. The stranglehold the papacy and the nobles had upon their people. The dreadful conditions. The murder and mayhem, condoned by the rich and by men of God – *perpetrated* by the rich and by men of God! The thin veneer of civilisation with which the Vatican and the Princes and Dukes covered the evil and base greed that ruled every 'noble' heart of Italy.

He blinked as their guide came to a stop.

Somehow, without him even noticing the change, they were out of Napoli itself. He hadn't even seen the walls as they passed. Had there been a sally-port that stood open? Ahead, a swathe of green fields meandered up the slopes to the right, and down to the left, towards the extended outskirts of the city, where fishing villages nestled in the lee of the metropolis, the bay's clear water lapping at them, a sizeable French fleet anchored within the breakwaters.

'Wait,' the Turk said quietly, and strolled off the side of the road to a farm shed that had seen much better days. Without a pause, the man threw open the door and stood back and to the side as there was a snorting and a creaking within and then finally a donkey and cart trundled out of the shadows, a wizened, ancient local on the driver's board seat.

'Get in,' their guide gestured, clambering up into the back and shuffling into a comfortable position among the sacks. His senses battered beyond argument or too much deep thought, Skiouros clambered up after him and dropped over the side, followed by Parmenio, who winced at the pain in his arm as he landed.

At a nod from the Turk, the driver shrugged and urged the beast into life, drawing them slowly away from the city. Skiouros shivered and pulled his cloak tight around him, and the Turk produced a thick, cheap wool blanket and threw it across the three of them to ward off the worst of the night's chill.

'Where are we going?' Skiouros asked in Turkish, aware that while Parmenio would recognise the language from his years trading there, he spoke only a few stilted words of it. His captain friend was clearly too tired to care, and simply lay under the blanket, shivering, probing the wound on his arm, wincing and thinking.

The Turk smiled curiously. 'For now, a tiny hamlet without a name on the far side of the hill from Posilipo perhaps three miles west of here.'

'Which means little to me.'

The man smiled knowingly, and Skiouros pursed his lips. They had passed the worst danger, and the man no longer had to concentrate on his route, just sitting in the cart and waiting for three miles to pass, bouncing with every rut of the farm road. Time to address his question at last.

'I know you.'

'Yes.' The Turk gave him an enigmatic smile from his wind-weathered, lined face.

'From Palos.'

Parmenio suddenly pulled himself upright. He may not speak Turkish, but that name was a name that would haunt them all for a long time to come.

'What are you saying?' the captain demanded of Skiouros in Greek. It struck the young man as interesting that a Greek had been speaking Turkish on Italian soil, and now an Italian was speaking Greek.

'Do you not remember this man? I last saw him in Palos. I know we were separated, but I think you might remember him too. He was with the old pirate on the hill when we ran. And I was nearly spitted by one of Hassan's men down by the waterfront, but this one came out of nowhere and saved me. He seems to be making a habit of it.'

To his surprise, the Turk smiled broadly and knowingly. 'There is more to learn yet, Skiouros, son of Nikos,' he replied in flawless Greek.

Skiouros and Parmenio both stared as the man reached up and began to unwind his turban. The moon chose that portentous moment to make an appearance from behind the clouds, as the last coil of the turban came clear and the man lifted from the centre the conical hat that formed the core of the headgear. Silence descended on the cart as Skiouros and his friend stared at the black locks that fell clear now, the fragments of white bone in them clattering as they moved and shining bleached white in the silver moonlight.

'You?' Parmenio frowned.

'But we lost you on board the Isabella when she was taken by Hassan!' Skiouros breathed.

'It would seem otherwise.'

Skiouros blinked. 'I heard someone – the old captain I think – shout a name when we were in Palos. I was too busy fleeing for my life to think about it at the time. *Cingeneler!*' He turned to Parmenio. 'It's a Turkish name for the Romani!' Back once more to the Turk… to the *Romani*. 'You went on to serve on one of the kadirga somehow? I did not recognise you in Palos.'

The man smiled and leaned back comfortably. 'I now serve under the greatest sailor and one of the best *men* in the Empire: Kemal Reis.' He tapped his forehead. 'Kemal Reis is not your enemy, Skiouros of Istanbul. Your enemies have never truly been known to you thus far. Your enemies are insidious and secretive.'

Skiouros shook his head.

'I *have* no enemies now,' he chuckled darkly, 'barring a few hundred Italians and the entire French nation, though it seems that soon they will bring their cannon and their vulgar papist conquest to my homeland too. When we reach this hamlet by the coast, will you let us go? Somehow, I suspect we will manage to make our way back to Genoa.'

The Romani shook his head, still smiling. 'Three kadirga lie moored off the coast, hidden from the French by the headland of Posilipo. Kemal Reis awaits my return, and you will come with me.'

'No. Not to ships. Not to the Ottoman pirates.'

'Again, Kemal Reis is not your enemy. But come with me and I will tell you of those who are.'

Skiouros glanced across to Parmenio, and to his surprise, the captain shrugged. 'Who am I to gainsay a guardian angel? The time has come to depart Italy, Skiouros, and Orsini's next of kin now owns my ship, so there is little point in racing back there. The sea is calling still, though, thank God.'

Skiouros sagged. He had never thought beyond the object of his revenge. Perhaps he had never truly believed that he would survive Cem's end. Certainly if he did, he had assumed that the way onwards would become obvious, but it seemed that God was not done complicating his life quite yet.

A strange, whispered chuckle floated on the night breeze, almost inaudible above the cart and the donkey – but Skiouros would recognise his brother's voice anywhere. *Lykaion's head*, he thought sharply. It remained in Heraklion in a casket, not resting where it should in the city of Constantine. And somewhere nearby, Don Diego de Teba would be eking out a living training some other poor fool in the art of the noble blade. He sighed and raised one eyebrow as he regarded the Romani who had changed – had *saved* – his life more than once.

'We're bound for Crete, aren't we?'

The night air whispered around the three kadirga as they lay at anchor off a small island in the middle of the sea far out of the sight of the Italian mainland. Kemal Reis had sent most of his men ashore for the night, and only a small group remained on watch. Skiouros and Parmenio waited on the Romani sailor to continue his tale...

Dragi sparked one end of a short length of hemp rope and blew on it until it glowed orange, offending the night vision of his audience. Once the rope was burning slowly and a continuous tendril of blue-grey smoke arose from it, he placed it in the bronze bowl before him and, cupping his hands around his face, leaned forward and took a deep lungful of the sweet, heady smoke, allowing it to trail out slowly between his teeth once more as he concluded his second story.

'And so the priest, when finally confronted with the object of his vengeance, discovered that only by becoming the man he so despised could he bring himself to kill him.'

Skiouros had the grace to look a little uncomfortable at the phrasing, but Parmenio was nodding his understanding. 'Revenge,' *the captain said,* 'is a hollow achievement. Orsini tried to tell us that in Genoa when this nightmare began.'

Dragi smiled with surprising sympathy. 'The priest could not kill the king, no matter how much he had desired it, for to do so he would *lose himself, and his own soul was more important to him than a blood price.'*

Skiouros cleared his throat. *'If this was supposed to be another of your prophetic tales, it fails on two counts: firstly, the deed was concluded before I heard it, and secondly, that is not how the deed ended.'*

'But you didn't kill him,' Parmenio said, nudging him.

'Yes I did. I snuffed out his flame with a pillow.'

'That didn't kill him,' the Genoese captain hissed. *'That released him. Palaeologos killed him.'* He waited until Skiouros looked at him and peered into the Greek's eyes. *'And you wouldn't have done it anyway. I don't think you ever could.'*

Dragi paused to take another lungful of blue smoke and grin as it wisped between his clenched teeth.

'It is a cautionary tale among some of my people, telling of the dreadful cost that vengeance demands of its perpetrator. It is a matter of some satisfaction for me that you did not succumb to the darkness of the wilful murderer. I had hoped to be able to tell you the tale before you embarked upon your quest, but this is the first time I have managed to find you since Palos.'

'And you've never quite explained that...' Parmenio frowned.

Dragi ignored him and smiled. *'So the vengeful priest remained a man of God and a good man, and that is how the story ends.'*

'The night is still young, Dragi, and there will be many more of them before Crete. If you really do only sing at funerals, you'd best have a lot of stories lined up. Better ones, for preference.'

Dragi smiled at Skiouros.

'Very well. Let me tell you the tale of the king-maker and the king-breaker...'

Author's Note

The Ottoman Cycle is closing the loop now. Even before Book One had ended, I knew that somewhere in the future, Skiouros would have to confront Cem Sultan. Clearly he was not ready for it in 1491. And so I took him west, delving into the world of the earliest Barbary pirates and bound for Palos de Frontera in 1492, because it had to be fate that Columbus would be setting off from there just in time for Skiouros to fall aboard. But when I came to write this third volume, it was clear that Skiouros had to have changed, to have grown a little, while retaining what made him quintessentially him.

He had been a thief. He *started* as a thief, and then, when I took him on one of the most fascinating journeys I could imagine, he became – for a time – a priest. I made a conscious decision to gloss over the six months or so of Columbus' first voyage. I wanted to have his time there something mysterious – a catalyst that has changed him, and I hope that came over. It was clear long before I came to write this book what its title would be. Skiouros has been a thief and a priest, and as he closed in his revenge upon Cem, he would have to become an assassin.

But would Skiouros really kill in cold blood? The character I had created was not a character who could have done what needed to be done easily, and the unanswered questions of history melded together to give me a neat solution. More of that shortly.

In the first two books, I had explored religion a little from Skiouros' rather unique perspective, growing up as a boy in the Orthodox church, beset with tales of the horrendous deeds of the papists during their brief, violent rule there, and now living in a Muslim empire. I had given him a fresh view in the form of the Tuareg, who happily combined Islam with their own early tribal beliefs. Now I had the opportunity to show him facing the Roman church at a time when it was a dangerous, powerful, corrupt body – the antithesis of what it should have been. I have not been kind to Italy, I fear, but at this particular juncture in history, it is much harder to find positive aspects than negative ones.

I hope I have kept Skiouros in line with his original character, despite the changes wrought in him, during this latest instalment, which has seen him travel the length of Italy in pursuit of a goal he could probably have never achieved.

All the locations in the book are real places, most of which I have visited and studied, with the notable exception of the castle of Roccabruna, which is entirely fictional and yet based heavily on a number of Italian hilltop fortresses I *have* visited. I needed a place with a specific setup and a conflict that does not appear in the history books, and this could only be achieved using the powers of imagination and fiction. This is one of two places where the book differs majorly from historical record, for those of you seeking inaccuracies. The other is in Napoli. In truth, King Charles was also quartered in the Castel Capuano during his stay, though I could see no real way I could have brought the plot to an end that way, and so... guilty as charged, m'lud. I tweaked history and had Charles elsewhere. It made sense. Well... it's 'historical *fiction*', after all! My descriptions of the Castel Capuano are largely fictitious, also; given that it has changed its appearance utterly since those days, few visual records survive of the earlier palace, and I have been unable to visit the building as it is now occupied by municipal offices and is not open to the public.

It is a matter of supreme irony that the exiled would-be sultan Cem was quartered in the same place at the same time as the exiled Emperor of Byzantium. This is true, if astounding, and while there is no evidence that Andreas was behind Cem's death, motivationally it fits very well, does it not?

A number of events I have used, as usual, were true ones, twisted to the plot of the book. During that winter when the French were camped outside the Castel Sant'Angelo, a section of wall did collapse. There is no truth to how I had it happen, and it was almost certainly due to recent shoddy work the Pope had had done, but I enjoyed playing with it.

The expulsion of the Hospitallers from Cem's guard and the Vatican is true, as is the fact that the one of them – the Catalan – remained. You might be gnawing a little on the fact that such an interesting plot thread as that vanishes with the death of the renegade Hospitaller – clearly in Andreas' pay. All I would say is: bear in mind where the Hospitallers were sent, and where Skiouros is now bound. Patience, my friends.

Cesare Borgia's flight from Velletri is well documented. Our friends' involvement in it is not, and nor is the fight in the thunderstorm in Albano, but after Skiouros' realisation that he might not be able to actually kill Cem, it was important to have him recover, to prove his strength of will to himself. And after a research trip to Albano last year, in which the rain was so torrential that I damn near drowned (!) I felt the urge to make a big show of the scene rather than the somewhat subdued action that was originally chalked in for that place.

And so onto the death of the Sultan. Cem (or Jem, if you're looking him up, or sometimes, Djem, or Dzem, even) is neither a hero nor a villain, though I pushed him towards the latter to begin with. Cem is something of a folk hero to some in Turkey, and probably had a better claim to the throne than his half-brother Bayezid. Certainly if you read documented sources, Cem comes over towards the end of his life as a rather sad but noble figure. The words I put in his mouth are paraphrased from words documented as his, and go a long way to explaining him.

Cem's death is a matter that will probably never be adequately explained. He suffered symptoms I describe, and declined in the timeframe I gave. Whether it was a natural death – a good many very intelligent folk have propounded various possible fatal illnesses – or a murder is still a matter of debate. I have not here mentioned Cem's food taster, whose survival is sometimes cited as proof that he was not poisoned, or indeed that he was involved in a poisoning himself. But, given that I have implicated members of his entourage, that is all something of a moot point.

So I tied Andreas and Cem together with a poisoning that neatly solved it all, and gave Skiouros his way out of a horrendous dilemma. Do you think he would have pushed that sword point down on the bed? I am still not sure! Certainly it would have been a difficult scene to write from his perspective.

In relation to Cem, I would just like to thank the master of Istanbul research, John Freely, whose excellent book *Jem Sultan* formed a chunk of my research, following on from two other of his books I have used before, and also Mandell Creighton's informative *History of the Papacy during the Period of the Reformation, Vol 3*. Along, of course, with the usual slew of excellent research texts, such as Osprey's informative works on *Condottiere* and *Italian Medieval Armies*, Brandenburg's *Early Churches of Rome*, D'Onofrio's *Castel Sant'Angelo*, Sabatini's *Life of Cesare Borgia*, and many others.

So now Cem is dead, and Skiouros' vengeance is played out, however he might not have expected. And so, why did I not end the tale here?

For three main reasons.

Firstly, this is the Ottoman *Cycle*. The first three books have taken Skiouros around three quarters of the Mediterranean (admittedly via America), but this cycle ends where it begins, and for proper closure, I think we all know that Skiouros has to go home.

Secondly, there are so many threads left untied. Lykaion's head still rests in a church in Crete and his spirit (or the figment of Skiouros' imagination that has become him, if you prefer) does not yet rest. Don Diego de Teba is an interesting character I am not done with, and there has been an undercurrent throughout the series involving the Romani that needs to be explained, from the old witch at the beginning, to a beggar/sailor who has steered Skiouros for years now. I was asked after *The Priest's Tale* what had happened to the Gypsy, and I tipped a wink in the direction that Cingeneler – the name Kemal had used for his new second in command – was a Turkish name for the Romani. He was always fated to return, and his future is tied in with the remaining plot of the cycle.

And thirdly, as with these books so far, a deal of the plot is driven by the interesting events of the time, and there are more to come yet.

As a last note, I will apologise to a few of you out there who will be riled by the deaths of Nicolo and Orsini. There were reasons for both – as well as the rest of my rather high body-count this time – but I will not go into detail until the story ends. But in addition, this tale, so much more so than the two that came before it, was a really dangerous one. The perils and odds faced by the friends have been intense. That they might breeze into the palaces of popes and kings and murder a very high-profile hostage without any losses, and then bound away like the heroes of Boy's Own Adventure was just too utterly unrealistic to contemplate.

Yet Skiouros goes on, with Parmenio at his side, and other figures loom in the wings, waiting to join them.

So, Skiouros has been a thief and prevented disaster in Istanbul.

He has been a priest and travelled the length of the world.

And now he has been an assassin, walking in the courts of the mighty.

Skiouros will return once more in *The Pasha's Tale*, concluding the Ottoman Cycle.

Thank you for reading, and I hope you enjoyed this journey as much as I did.

Simon Turney. May 2014.

If you liked this book, why not try other titles by S.J.A. Turney

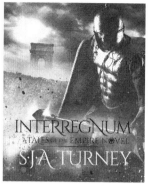

Interregnum (Tales of the Empire 1)

(2009) *

For twenty years civil war has torn the empire apart; the imperial line extinguished as the mad Emperor Quintus burned in his palace, betrayed by his greatest general. Against a background of war, decay, poverty and violence, men who once served in the proud imperial army now fight as mercenaries, hiring themselves to the greediest lords. On a hopeless battlefield that same general, now a mercenary captain tortured by the events of his past, stumbles across hope in the form of a young man begging for help. Kiva is forced to face more than his dark past as he struggles to put his life and the very empire back together. The last scion of the imperial line will change Kiva forever.

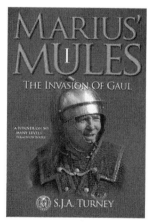

Marius' Mules I: The Invasion of Gaul

(2009) *

It is 58 BC and the mighty Tenth Legion, camped in Northern Italy, prepares for the arrival of the most notorious general in Roman history: Julius Caesar. Marcus Falerius Fronto, commander of the Tenth is a career soldier and long-time companion of Caesar's. Despite his desire for the simplicity of the military life, he cannot help but be drawn into intrigue and politics as Caesar engineers a motive to invade the lands of Gaul. Fronto is about to discover that politics can be as dangerous as battle, that old enemies can be trusted more than new friends, and that standing close to such a shining figure as Caesar, the most ethical of men risk being burned.

* Sequels in both series also available now.

Other recommended works set in the Byzantine & Medieval worlds:

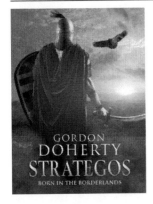

Strategos - Born in the Borderlands

by Gordon Doherty (2011)

When the falcon has flown, the mountain lion will charge from the east, and all Byzantium will quake. Only one man can save the empire . . . the Haga! 1046 AD. The Byzantine Empire teeters on full-blown war with the Seljuk Sultanate. In the borderlands of Eastern Anatolia, a land riven with bloodshed and doubt, young Apion's life is shattered in one swift and brutal Seljuk night raid. Only the benevolence of Mansur, a Seljuk farmer, offers him a second chance of happiness. Yet a hunger for revenge burns in Apion's soul, and he is drawn down a dark path that leads him right into the heart of a conflict that will echo through the ages.

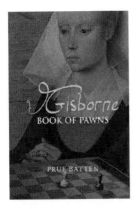

Gisborne: Book of Pawns

by Prue Batten (2014)

In a world where status means power and survival depends on how the game is played, two people, one a squire wronged in life and one a noblewoman, are drawn together by lust and a lost inheritance in twelfth century England. Guy of Gisborne is a man with secrets, Ysabel of Moncrieff, a naïve and opinionated noblewoman whose world comes tumbling down like the stones of a mighty cathedral on the death of her mother. Gisborne is ordered to Aquitaine to escort the young woman home to attend to her grieving father and whilst travelling, she discovers Gisborne's secrets are not just connected with his family but with the throne of England. And with revenge.

Suddenly Ysabel is confronted with the fact that history can be shaped unconscionably by those in power and that she and Gisborne could lose their lives.

* Sequels in both series also available

Made in the USA
Monee, IL
02 November 2019